For Nicole Settle

Follow the ink, the blackness that engulfs the world
Follow your name as if it was all you had
Pick up a pen
Dance across the paper
And you shall find something more

The World Beneath

Published by Philip A. Troy
Lakewood, WA 98498

ISBN: 978-0-6151-5509-8

Library of Congress Control Number: 2007906687

This book can be purchased at:
http://www.lulu.com/content/936605

The author can be contacted at:
Kopakageni@aol.com

First Mass Market Edition
Edited by Nicole Settle

Prologue: Martin Spire

Freak, monster, nerd... titles swirled around Martin Spire like a tempest, warning all who saw him to steer clear. Everything from how he carried himself to his gait seemed to be designed to ward off those around him. His build was angular, but carried an air of strength to it. His thin, pale face was rimmed by equally thin black hair that was the exact color of coal. His gait was elegant, but carried an air of authority to it as he strode wherever he went. Hanging around him like a shroud was an aura of mistrust and solemnity, and his iron gray eyes peeked from within his personal cloud like twin beacons of dull light, glaring accusingly at anyone who crossed his vision. His high, delicate cheekbones offset his powerful chin, giving him a glare that always made him look annoyed about something.

Some people joked that he was a vampire, or something equally as dangerous, because of his attire. Martin ignored the rumors. He dressed the way he did because he liked it. His usual attire included an expensive, Navy blue Loden coat over a white dress shirt and black pants. A pair of black leather shoes completed his ensemble, giving a studious impression. The coat served multiple purposes – its thick material making him seem larger than he actually was.

Bitter and angry, Martin always seemed to carry an impossible weight as he walked from location to location.

Quiet and reserved, the aura of mistrust he carried seemed to limit his speech to ten sentences per week, if people were lucky. However, his limited speech gave him one advantage – whenever he spoke, everyone around him instantly became quiet. Whatever the reason for his speech, people listened because it was rare to hear his voice. Instead of his voice being rough from disuse, however, Martin's voice was low and baritone. It had an air of firmness to it, but it never rose above conversational tones.

This was Martin Spire.

Chapter 1: Confrontation at Breakfast

Martin shifted his black briefcase from hand to hand, watching the other students at his current High School mill aimlessly around, waiting for their classes to be handed out. Some of them stopped to look at him, eying the briefcase cautiously. Everyone else carried a book bag of some color, shape or size, but Martin preferred a briefcase.

"Spire, Martin," said the teacher who was handing out schedules for the year. He was a short, balding man in his late sixties, his white hair thinning to wisps along the sides of his head. His thin nose and wide, watery eyes made him look very much like an anthropomorphic rat, as did his hunched stature and large ears. Martin said nothing to acknowledge he had heard his name being called, but strode up to the teacher nonetheless. The teacher blinked once, noticing Martin's eyes watching him.

"Here," said the teacher, extending a small white envelope out to Martin. A thin hand reached out from within the folds of his blue coat and took it, vanishing back into the navy blue depths. Martin nodded and walked back down to where he had been standing in the first place.

A few people cast nervous glances at him as he deftly slid a finger along the envelope, tearing it open with practiced ease. Martin drew out the paper, unfolding it with his thin fingers, and allowed his lead-gray eyes to scan over the writing on it. Without a word, he folded it back up, reinserted it into the envelope, and squirreled it in one of the pockets of his expensive Loden coat. He turned and walked off, leaving all students "T – Z" to receive their schedules.

Martin sat down on one of the black metal benches that littered the campus like pieces of a forgotten puzzle. Whoever had built them had given little or no thought to their placement. They were haphazardly placed in random corners or practically in the middle of the campus pathways. He closed his eyes, tilting his head back to look at the graying sky. It would rain soon.

No classes for the first half of the day. He allowed himself a small frown. What was he supposed to do for three hours? Twiddle his thumbs? He hefted his briefcase into his lap and slid his thumb along the three golden dials in the center, just below the handle. The dials were each aligned with a number, finally releasing the clasp and opening the briefcase with a dull *click.*

Inside was a laptop, along with various other school-related paraphernalia. A few pencils were parked neatly in small tube-shaped holders, as were an assortment of pens. Some neat, college ruled paper was standing at attention in some pockets, and his collection of calculators, digital dictionaries and thesauruses, and his internet cable were stored in a small divided box off on one side. Nothing was out of place – just the way he liked it.

Martin popped his laptop open, pressing his long finger against the green power button. He focused on the screen as it ran through the various checks of his virus protection, firewalls, and so on. Eventually, his fingers danced over the keys, inputting his password digit by digit until the computer acquiesced and allowed him access to his files.

Martin's plugged his computer's internet cable into the wall socket near the bench, attaching the other end to the laptop itself. A small connection icon flashed once or twice before recognizing the internet signature and opening the door to the so-called information superhighway.

Martin's usually dull eyes flickered with something akin to amusement as he methodically scanned his emails. Plenty of spam to feed his spam folder with, a few email alerts about new updates for his computer, an email from his uncle in Turkey, and an email from an old acquaintance back in Virginia littered his inbox, looking out of the screen and begging to be opened.

Martin hastily dumped the spam and alerts into their respective folders, and proceeded to read the emails from his uncle and his acquaintance. His uncle seemed to be doing alright with the archaeology gig he was working, and his so-called friend was going to be moving to Wisconsin in a month. Nothing worth his time...

Sighing with boredom, Martin glanced at the clock in the corner of his computer. 8:17. That was plenty of time to sneak into the cafeteria and buy some breakfast before going to the library to perform his favorite action in the world: reading.

He powered down his laptop, making sure everything was in its usual place in his briefcase before closing and locking it, scrambling the small golden dials on the case before standing up and wincing inwardly as his back let out a small pop. He massaged the base of his spine with one hand, making certain that the action was concealed beneath his coat.

His stomach let out a low moan, evidence to the fact that breakfast was something he normally failed to notice. He lifted his briefcase and began to walk down the pathway in the middle of the campus that led to the cafeteria. Several of the new students; freshman and transfer students mostly, were already choking the campus with their presence, and Martin made an extra effort to avoid them.

He lifted a hand out from beneath the folds of his coat, placing it against the smooth blue material that made up the cafeteria door. With a light push, the door swung inward and he stepped inside, the leather of his shoes barely registering on the tile floor of the cafeteria. Without a word, he strode across the small empty space between the door and the line and stood at attention, waiting to receive his morning meal.

He allowed his mind a moment to touch on different conversations in the lunch hall. It was something he did out of force of habit. Different students had different opinions, and Martin got some kind of thrill knowing how they felt about various things. Not to mention it could prove useful should he ever wind up in a confrontation with any of them.

One group was busy talking about the first dance of the year, and debating which girl or guy they should ask. Martin blanched inwardly. Dancing was not something he enjoyed. The old, classical style of dance was more suited to his grace, not the wild, gyrating nightclub style of dance that had evolved in recent years. He turned his attention to a different group.

Ah, here was something interesting. A small group of boys from the Freshman Football Team had noticed him, and they were busy making comments about him. He eavesdropped on them for a moment before realizing that there was little a small group of freshman could do to faze him and turned his attentions elsewhere.

Four people stood between him and the counter now, and Martin allowed himself a small smirk. It wouldn't be long before he could take some of their barely edible hash-browns and wash them down with a small carton of milk – the pair making up his morning meal before lunch.

"At least I'm not some kind of crazy bitch!" screamed someone in the cafeteria. Martin's lead gray eyes shifted lazily over to the confrontation that was unfolding barely ten feet from where he stood. Three girls had blocked the progress of a fourth. He mentally rolled his eyes – it was a classic feud. The three girls were cheerleaders, and the fourth girl was a classic 'nerd'. Thick red sweater, books under one arm, thick glasses perched on the bridge of a nose spattered with freckles, dark hair pulled back in a ponytail... it pretty much fit the description of any nerd he had ever seen.

The so-called nerd shrugged and said something, but her soft voice was lost to Martin in the reaction of the evident leader of the three cheerleaders; which happened to be an outraged shout followed by a swift slap to the face. The bespectacled girl crashed to the floor, her books and papers spilling from her arms. The pair of wire framed glasses skidded to a halt at the toe of Martin's leather shoe. He arched an eyebrow in mild interest.

Several of the boys in the area were whooping and whistling, making comments about wet t-shirts and catfights as the three girls began kicking at the downed girl. Martin's conscience gave a twinge, and he mentally threw his hands up in silent surrender. *Damn conscience...*

"Enough."

His voice carried enough volume and authority to echo through the commons area, silencing most of the activity. Several students gave a glance towards him, while others looked at each other. He stepped out of the line he was standing in, bending and picking up the glasses as he did, and began to walk over to the four girls.

The first girl looked up from kicking the pile of flesh on the ground that had once been the bespectacled girl. "What do you want?" she hissed, her green eyes glaring at him.

Martin bent down slightly, offering the glasses to the girl on the ground. She peered shyly out from beneath her sepia-toned hair, accepting them with a small smile. Martin then righted himself and turned to the three cheerleaders.

"You to stop," he said, finishing the first girl's question.

The two other girls looked at him with apprehension. Obviously they had been exposed to the rumors around the school. The third girl, however, looked annoyed with his interruption.

"And what business is it of yours, freak?" she spat, and Martin raised a black eyebrow at her.

"You can drop the venom," he said, "You're not impressing anyone."

She gave him a look of outright incredulity. "Do you know who I am?" she asked, her emerald eyes wide.

Martin allowed her to glimpse the ghost of a smile as it tugged at the corners of his mouth. "You must not be very memorable if even YOU cannot remember who you are," he said, folding his arms across his chest. "I am going to request you leave right now."

The girl drew her hand back and slapped Martin in the face hard enough to make him stagger back a step or two. He looked over at her with a flicker of annoyance in his iron eyes.

"That wasn't nice," he said casually. "Please, leave." He noticed with some interest that the bespectacled girl had managed to escape the scene. *Good...*

Another slap, this one harder than the first, met Martin's already stinging cheek. The result was to cause him to take a step backward and catch the edge of a table for support.

"Stop."

It wasn't any form of beggary. It didn't even sound like a request. It sounded more like he was telling her to stop, rather than asking. Just as she was about to slap him for a third time, another voice entered the scene.

"Alright, break it up."

Martin's eyes flashed between the figure that was striding toward him and the door. His hand tightened around the briefcase handle he was still clutching. Perhaps he could walk off.

"Martin Spire," said the form as it walked closer. Martin inwardly let out an expletive. Of all people, it just had to be the security guard, Travis Lancombe. Large and muscular, Travis seemed to inspire just as much fear as Martin, but that could be attributed to the handgun he wore at his hip. Travis was a large figure, standing probably somewhere above six feet in height, with iron gray hair and a wide face. If Martin had to choose one animal to represent him, it would have been a morbidly obese frog. Travis stopped just off to the side of the two warring parties and shook his head sadly, "Care to tell me what is going on here?"

The girl spoke first. "He butted in on our business," she said, glaring at him, "It was his fault." He made a noise in his throat, "Business that involves knocking down one of the transfer students?" he asked, watching color seep into her face.

"Stacy, Martin," Travis held up his hands, preventing any kind of 'physical interaction' between the two parties, "Let's stop this. Forget this happened, alright? I saw nothing, so I make no judgments – fair?"

Martin wanted to point out that it was Travis' job as security guard to *investigate* the incident further, but kept his mouth shut lest he wind up in deeper trouble. As far as the staff went, he was fortunate Travis took the easy way out – many teachers were itching for a chance to make him do In-School Suspension for menial things. Without so much as a nod, he turned on his heel and walked off, his appetite depleted from the encounter.

Chapter 2: Lunch

"Spire, please remove your feet from the desk!" trilled Martin's Math Teacher, a fiery-tempered redhead by the name of Abigail Morris. Martin never looked at her, but merely dropped his feet from the desktop to the floor with a muffled thud. He continued to stare out the window as though it was the last drop of salvation on the planet.

"And pay attention for once, you might learn something!" added Abigail after a moment. Martin's smoke-colored eyes glared daggers at her, but he shifted in his chair and folded his arms across his chest, his eyes fixing on the blackboard. The teacher shook her head, looking at him with something akin to pity.

"This would be easier if you didn't always pretend to be mute, Spire," she said, folding her arms in an imitation of him and giving him her version of his dirty scowl. A few students snickered, but knew better than to say anything. Martin shrugged, pulling a book from his bag and flicking through it. He could feel the palpable waves of contempt radiating from Abigail as if they were tangible.

"I don't recall our textbook being titled "A Tale of Two Cities," she said, conversationally. "Why don't you join us in the real world for a change? As a matter of fact, come do this problem on the board."

She quickly scrawled an algebraic problem on the board and held the chalk out in his direction, waiting for him to take it. Martin peered over the top of his book at the problem, and then returned to his book with little or no interest.

"You see," Abigail said to the rest of the class, "He didn't pay attention, and now he can't do the problem."

"Twenty-four," said Martin, without looking up from the book.

Abigail looked at him as though seeing him clearly for the first time. She looked back at the board, shrugged, and wrote another one. "Try this one."

Martin looked over the book again, took note of the problem, and turned his gaze to her. "Four."

Abigail decided to try another approach. "Alright, if you can answer all of the questions, why do people call you retarded?"

Martin carefully noted his place in the book and closed it, laying it gingerly on top of his desk. "Is that what *people* say about me," he asked, "Or *you* say about me?" He knew the answer, of course, was the former. Abigail, however, was dancing on his last nerve.

Abigail's face purpled, and Martin could see a vein standing out on her forehead like a gnarled tree root. "Out!" she shrieked, pointing toward the door, "Out!"

Martin nodded, and scooped up his belongings and made his way through the sea of students in his classroom to the door. He nodded at Abigail on the way out, and pushed open the door.

"And don't come back until you're ready to apologize!" she called after him, but Martin gave no indication that he had heard. He sat down outside the door, his Loden coat pooling around him on the carpet. He drew his book out of his coat, flipped to where he had been before, and began to read.

A page later, he heard a voice he didn't like that much. "In trouble again, Spire?"

He looked up silently at Travis, who was smiling down at him with his usual wide-lipped smirk. Martin returned to his book, turning the page with a slight rustle of paper. Travis' grin vanished. "What'd you do?"

Martin ignored him. Perhaps if he pretended the obese frog in front of him didn't exist, he would cease to do so. Travis, however, didn't seem to like the idea of vanishing into thin air, and glared down at the obstinate student in front of him.

"Do I confiscate the book?" he asked, leering down at the boy in front of him. Martin carefully inserted a bookmark into his book, closed it, and put it in his briefcase. Without a word, he stood up and walked off, ignoring the protesting shouts from Travis. Martin wanted to massage his temples, but that wasn't something he indulged in. Perhaps he would find some peace and quiet before lunch.

He walked down the concrete stairs, his mind playing over the possible locations where he could relax and finish reading his book. He snorted to himself. A book the likes of "*A Tale of Two Cities*" usually only took him a day or two to read. He had started it this morning, and still was not even halfway done with it.

So engrossed was he in his thoughts, he did not realize where he was going until he had run directly into a student who was walking across the hallway in the opposite direction. His gray eyes snapped up as the other student collapsed backward onto the floor. One of Martin's eyebrows arced gracefully as he recognized who it was – it was the girl he had 'rescued' during the breakfast rush.

She seemed to recognize him at the same exact moment as he recognized her. She scrambled hastily to her feet, brushing dust off of her jeans, and looked up at him.

"Er... hi?"

Martin's eyebrow receded as he inclined his head slightly toward her. "My apologies."

He made as if to walk around her, but she called after him. He looked back over his shoulder, watching her with the intensity of a laser.

"Um... thanks for helping me back in the cafeteria...what is your name?" she muttered, folding her hands behind her back and looking at him. Martin nodded, turning to leave again.

"Martin Spire."

Before she had a chance to ask anything else, Martin was already striding down the hallway and out of sight. He rounded the corner at the end of the hall, descending another flight of stairs to reach the main floor. After locating his usual dilapidated table (having only three legs qualified it as being shunned in a corner) he plopped down in an equally decrepit chair and propped his feet up on the table. He pulled the book from his bag and began to read once more. Perhaps this time, he hoped, there would be no interruptions.

Of course, all good things come to an end. The bell rang out shrilly, causing Martin to sigh – this time audibly. He hated lunch with a passion. He quickly hid the book in his briefcase and rose from his usual seat. While he was here, he might as well try to get ahead of the usual stampede for food and acquire some sustenance. He deftly inserted himself into the line, noting that today was slow because only four people were ahead of him.

Martin's lunch consisted of whatever the special was that day. He was flexible in his dietary choices. Today, he noticed, the cafeteria was carrying Teriyaki Chicken. He allowed himself a small grimace. He would eat it, of course, but Teriyaki was one thing he despised.

"Having a nice lunch?" drawled a voice from somewhere behind him. Martin did not turn around, but continued to ladle the sauce-drowned pieces of meat onto his plate. Behind him by one or two people was one person out of thousands who needed to get a life. (Or die, Martin was flexible with that too.)

"Pity the retard can't talk," continued the voice. Martin decided it wasn't worth his time, and slid his Student I.D. Card along the scanner, marking his lunch as paid for. He marched out of the cafeteria into the commons area, seating himself back at the table in the corner where he had been sitting in the first place. He impaled one of the pieces of meat with his fork, placing it in his mouth and chewing thoughtfully. Not as bad as the *last* time they had served Teriyaki. He had been inches from lodging a formal complaint.

He heard footsteps approach him, and looked up from his lunch as a familiar figure walked over to him. Martin wanted to scream. Of all the luck, he was being joined by the girl he had knocked down less than fifteen minutes ago. She paused, noticing the expression on his face, but then ignored it and sat down.

Martin took a deep breath, refocusing his attention on the Teriyaki. He wanted to die. He always ate lunch by himself – what right did this person have to come join him?

...Alright, so that may have been biased. People were allowed to sit wherever they wanted, but most knew better than to sit by the brooding student with the glare that could frighten most dogs. Apparently this young lady had not learned this fact of life... yet.

"Why did you run off?" she asked, picking listlessly at a small dish of rice. Martin decided it was not worth responding to verbally, so he merely shrugged. His cold demeanor, however, didn't seem to deter her. She folded her arms across her chest and leaned back.

"Why don't you talk?"

Again, Martin paid her no mind. He shrugged absently, popping another piece of meat into his mouth and utterly ignoring the girl seated at 'his' table. This gesture seemed to irritate her somewhat, and she leaned forward across the table, watching him closely.

"You're not very social."

Martin could not resist responding to this. His eyes snapped up, focusing on her face, and he allowed a small smile to form on his face. "Of course I'm not."

The girl leaned back again, re-crossing her arms. "Aha! We're making progress," she said triumphantly, smiling across the table at him. Martin turned his gaze to some of the students behind her, making certain they weren't going to try anything. The girl spoke again.

"Now, let's try for two. Why aren't you sociable?" she adjusted her glasses with a fingertip, watching him intently.

22

Martin shrugged, downing the last piece of meat and rising to leave. He deposited his small paper plate in the garbage can, but heard the girl call after him.

"Are you going to come to Game Night tonight?" she asked, dumping her now-empty dish of rice in the same can. Martin amusedly realized that she would have had to eat a small rice ball in the span of time from his rising and her joining him at the garbage can.

Martin nodded. Game Night was a special event – it happened only six times a year. Once at the beginning of the year, once near Halloween, once near Christmas, once near Valentines Day, once near Senior Graduation, and once at the end of the year. It was one of the few social gatherings Martin dared attend.

"Great!" she said, making Martin debate changing his mind for once, "I'll see you there." Without another word, she walked off; her books tucked neatly under one arm. Martin shook his head, clearing it.

Martin turned to walk out of the cafeteria, but found himself confronted by the owner of the voice he had heard earlier. He sighed. Christopher Arnott, head of the football team, and conceited rich boy. He made to walk around him, but Chris put a hand the size of a dinner plate on his shoulder.

"Going somewhere?"

Martin shrugged off the hand, glaring up at Chris with his slate-colored eyes. Chris laughed down at him. Martin inwardly sneered at whatever force of nature had made Chris a full head taller than him. Martin was tall for a Sophomore, standing at five feet and eleven inches, but Chris was a giant.

Martin skirted around Chris as the enormous boy made a grab for his shoulder, ending with Chris' unprotected back in front of him. He smiled inwardly.

"Don't ever show your back to the enemy."

With that, Martin strode off, his briefcase clutched in his pale fingers. It would be a pleasure to crush Chris at Game Night tonight. He had already discovered what the planned activity was – putting himself at an advantage.

It was a good thing he was good at Dart Tag.

Chapter 3: Dart Tag

Martin checked his trio of dart guns one final time, making sure they were in order. He raised the first, a three-shot pistol, to his face and examined it carefully. Nothing was out of place — a fact he was glad of. He quickly holstered it in one of the inner pockets of his coat.

The second gun was more complex: a two-shot shotgun that operated off of shell-fed darts. He quickly slid a pair of armed shells into the firing chamber and primed it, sliding a pair of extra shell casings into his pocket.

Finally, he turned to his third and favorite gun. A large twenty-shot machine gun with enough ammunition to drown anyone he encountered in the maze that had been set up in the gymnasium. He smoothly hid the shotgun beneath his coat and shouldered the machine gun. He filled the two easily accessible pockets of his coat with spare darts and allowed himself a small smirk.

Time to move out...

He walked into the gym, his eyes immediately seeking the entrance to the labyrinth. He spotted it a few yards away and walked over to it, flicking the safety of his gun off as he entered.

Dead silence surrounded him as he melded effortlessly with the shadows. The back end of his gun lit up, displaying his current score and avatar name. He had chosen to simply stick with his own name – it made the kills more interesting when people realized *exactly* who had targeted them.

With a low whine, the chamber of his machine gun filled with power, beginning to turn the firing drum in slow circles. It would speed up once he pulled the trigger. His hand tensed around the grip of the gun as he firmly planted the butt in the crook of his arm. *Twenty shots; that's all I get.*

He plunged deep into the maze, his eyes roving hungrily through the darkness as he sought his first target. He stumbled across a Freshman who was looking extremely lost. He quickly drew his pistol and fired one of the three shots into his quarry's back. The student's gun deactivated for the allotted twenty seconds, and he heard the boy curse and dive for cover. Martin picked up the dropped dart and reloaded his pistol before holstering it again.

He ignored the large shoot-out going on in one of the main chambers of the maze. Martin despised those. It was all confusion and flying darts. Martin preferred to seek out his prey rather than allow it to be felled by "spray-and-pray" tactics. He rounded a corner and immediately ducked to avoid the dart that came whistling his way.

It was a larger dart – closer in size and shape to a small missile, and Martin looked angrily at the person who had shot it. It didn't surprise him. Daniel Livan was Chris' best friend, and had a love of explosions. It didn't take a genius to figure out he would have grabbed the largest gun he could find.

Martin sneered as he dodged a second missile. It whistled past him with enough speed to ruffle the folds of his coat. Without hesitation, he drew the shotgun and unloaded the first shell into Daniel's stomach. The large arm-cannon he was wielding deactivated, and Daniel swore loudly. Without another word, Martin was back in his element; hiding in the shadows of the maze.

He quickly checked his stock of ammunition, knowing the sparseness and importance of the quiet lulls between large firefights. He still had plenty of rounds left, so he hastily reloaded the shotgun.

Martin stepped out of the alcove he'd been hiding in to nail a Sophomore girl in the back of the head with a well-timed shot from his pistol. He instantly spun on the spot, his coat billowing behind him like blue wings, and fired a pair of shots at an upcoming group of students. Before the students could react, he drew back and fled down a dim pathway.

A whistling sound alerted him to imminent danger, and he threw himself on the ground, drawing the shotgun as he fell. A large dart spun past his head, slamming into the far wall with a resounding thud. No supplementary fire was forthcoming, however, so Martin assumed it was a misfire.

He peered intently around the corner, tagging a large figure he hoped was Chris in the back of the neck. He quickly retreated down another hallway before he could be caught, smiling inwardly.

Of all things in the world, Martin loved the thrill of Dart Tag. It helped him stay alert and ready. He spun around a corner, ducking a small dart and shooting its owner in the stomach. What angered him, however, was that the person he had tagged brought his gun down on the back of Martin's head.

Stars exploded momentarily in front of his eyes and he staggered back, blinking quickly to rid his eyes of the spots that plagued them. He threw himself sideways, colliding with the wall of the maze as the gun was swung at him again.

Rather than risk another blow to the head, Martin rounded on the figure and came up behind it. He gripped the person in a headlock, forcing the gun down and away until it clattered harmlessly to the floor.

He pushed the student away, picking up their gun and fleeing with it. *Your loss, my gain pal...*

He quickly examined the spoils of his small victory: a tiny one-shot pistol that operated off of whistling darts. With a small smirk, he loaded the gun with one of his own whistlers and held it in front of him. It was time to attempt to break his old score. He heard movement behind him, and crept into one of the small alcoves that dotted the maze. He primed the firing chamber of the small gun and waited.

A figure passed him in the dark, and Martin saw the face of the girl from lunch, her face illuminated by the glow from the back of her gun.

Martin fired the shot, the dart smoothly striking the pressure plate on her back, and her gun shut down with a low moan. Before she could react, Martin was gone, dashing down the corridor.

However, the girl was not done with Martin Spire. Not just yet...

Chapter 4: A Secret Revealed

"Martin!" called the girl, and Martin instantly rotated on the spot, his shotgun raised in a firing position. He sneered through the darkness at her.

"What do you want?" he spat, lowering the gun for a moment. He kept it trained on the target point on her belly, rather than averting it. He'd dealt with people who'd tried to scam him this way before.

"Want to team up?" she asked, indicating the small icons on the side of her gun.

"No." Martin turned on his heel and walked off, leaving the girl in the maze. He allowed himself a quick shake of the head. Teammates were troublesome. If he had a teammate, he had to focus on making sure they were alright... he didn't have time for that.

Besides... Chris was undoubtedly in the maze somewhere. Martin had a healthy dose of payback for last year. Chris had nailed him full in the eye with a large dart, almost permanently blinding him.

He checked the shotgun, priming the firing chamber. He rounded a corner and sank a pair of darts into the back of one of the students he found there. Before anyone in the hallway could make a sound, he drew his commandeered pistol and fired it down the hallway, striking one of the oncoming students with the dart.

A sound behind him alerted his senses, and he ducked to avoid something much larger than a dart. His eyes pierced the darkness, and he realized that someone had swung the back end of a gun at the back of his head.

Martin backpedaled quickly as a dart came whistling his way. He dove to the side, his shoulder colliding painfully with the wall of the maze. Pain rocketed through Martin's shoulder, and he heard a familiar snicker.

"Having fun, Spire?" asked the unmistakable voice of his quarry, Chris. The gigantic boy was wielding a pair of Shoulder-Fired Dart-Launchers that had the word "Brute" emblazoned along the sides. Judging by the size of the dart, these guns were aptly named. Each one was as long as his forearm and about as thick.

Martin ran forward, his pistol held at the ready. Chris, however, had other plans. The gigantic cannon swung down, as opposed to firing, and the thick plastic caught Martin full in the face. Warm blood trickled from his nose as he collapsed to his hands and knees for a moment. He stood up, holstering his gun as he faced Chris.

"That was uncalled for," he stated. The blood had trickled past his lower lip, and was giving him a ghastly smile as he leered at Chris. It seemed almost as though he was enjoying himself. The launcher came swinging his way again, this time aimed for his ribs. Martin jumped backwards, pushing the launcher out of the way with the flat of his hand and lunging forward to punch Chris in the stomach.

The brutish student stumbled backward, dropping one of the launchers on the ground. Martin quickly kicked it out of reach before Chris could pick it back up. He wiped a smear of blood from his face, grinning down at Chris.

"Stop!"

He rolled his eyes as the girl he'd just tried to lose in the maze came speeding up to them. She put herself between the two boys, facing Martin. "Stop this – now!"

Chris looked up at her, his eyes glittering in the darkness. "You're new here, eh?" he asked, holding his stomach from where Martin had hit him. She looked over her shoulder and nodded.

Chris stood up, nodding at her. "Then you don't know what *that* is, do you?" he asked, pointing one of his thick fingers directly at Martin. The girl followed his finger and looked at the boy standing there.

"Him? What about him?" she asked. Chris grinned wickedly.

"Little monster, he is," he offered, "Antisocial as they come, and friendly as a cactus. Watch out for him – he'd likely rape you as look at you."

Martin sighed. "Chris, what are you talking about? Is your Reflected-Appraisal Syndrome acting up again?" Chris sneered at him, and Martin probably guessed Chris had no clue what he'd said.

"Whatever you say," snickered Chris, "I'm not the one who has a whore for a mother."

Martin's eye twitched slightly in the darkness, and the girl immediately stepped aside. The boy in the Loden coat looked ready to charge.

"What..." he gritted, "...did you just say?"

Chris waved his hand, "I said your mother was a whore. Everyone knows exactly how you were conceived, you little accident-"

Before Chris could move, Martin had whipped a small thin object from beneath his coat. It looked almost like a thin drumstick, but thicker about three-fourths of the way up. Martin was holding it just below this thicker part, pointing a tapered end at Chris.

"I'm warning you," he snarled, "You have NO idea what I'm capable of!"

Chris looked at the stick with surprise, but quickly began to laugh. "Ooh," he chortled, "Are you going to turn me into a toad, Merlin?"

"Keep this up and I just might," retorted Martin. He reached out his left hand and made a motion as though he was holding onto a cord of some kind. He closed his eyes and pointed the rod at Chris again.

"Xidul!"

The girl saw nothing come from the 'wand', but Chris was lifted from his feet and hurled against one of the maze walls. Martin turned the thin piece of wood on himself, muttering something again. With a half-grin, he looked at the girl.

"Blink and you'll miss it," he taunted, dashing forward. He seemed to blur through the maze, heading straight for Chris. Before the gigantic boy could fully right himself, two fists smashed into his stomach, knocking over one of the maze walls and hurling him from the labyrinth.

Martin stood up, dusting off his hands and putting the stick away again. "So much for you..."

The girl ran up to him, panting in fright, "What... are you?" she asked, directing her gaze at his face. He turned his slate-colored eyes on her, looking down at her with an imperious air.

"What do you think?"

She stared at him, her jaw hanging open in surprise. "A... magician?" she offered slowly, looking at the place in his coat where she knew the rod was. Martin blew air through his nose in irritation.

"When you say it like that," he muttered, "I sound like I belong at a carnival."

She straightened up, putting her hands on her hips. "Then what do *you* call yourself?"

"A Tzen," replied Martin simply.

"What is a Tzen?" she asked. Martin, however, was looking out his newly-made exit to the maze.

"Not now," he said, "I'll tell you some other time."

Before she could react, Martin was back inside the maze without leaving a trace other than the gigantic hole in the wall.

Martin leaned against one of the walls in the maze, checking to make sure he was alright. *Stupid... stupid... stupid...* he chanted, almost knocking his head against the wall in frustration.

It wasn't magic he used – he hated it when people confused it with such a mundane and childish thing. Martin merely drew on that which already existed – energy. It was what made him a Tzen.

His breathing slowly returned to normal, as did his heart rate. Performing Xidul indoors was a stupid thing to do. What was even dumber was to chain it to another 'spell'. He sighed, massaging his temples. He knew already what the extent of Chris' injuries was. After spending at least three years honing that particular skill, he knew already what it could do. Chris had at least two broken ribs, and probably a collapsed lung.

He pulled out his Tzen Rod and examined it, running his fingers up and down the shaft of smooth wood. How something so simple could contain such power, he himself barely understood.

From what his teacher had taught him, he was using his own body to complete something similar to an electrical circuit. He looked around, smiling inwardly. One of the reasons he could see so well in the darkness was because it was illuminated for his eyes alone.

Threads of greenish-white energy drifted like gossamer webs within the maze. They intersected with various other colors, forming a rainbow of thin strings that seemed to go through the sides of the labyrinth.

Martin reached out and touched a fiery orange Thread, closing his fingers around it. A familiar warmth filled his chest as he drew upon what could only be the Fire Energy flowing through the Thread like water through a pipe. He released the Thread, closing his eyes as he heard footsteps approaching. He pretended he was a part of the wall, praying he wouldn't be found.

"There you are!" chirped a familiar voice. *So much for joining the clergy...*

"Yes..." he said, his voice flat and listless. He looked down at the girl in front of him. "...I didn't get your name."

"Alena Steward," she said, extending her hand. Martin declined it, leaning back against the wall.

"Why did you come?"

She shrugged, "After seeing someone get blown through a wall, I think I want answers. Talk."

Martin hastily checked the maze tunnel for any students, but found none. He almost wished someone WOULD come so that he wouldn't have to explain anything. He let out a sigh and began to speak.

"The Art you call 'magic' is merely the manipulation of energy that flows naturally around the planet," he stated as though quoting a textbook, "Different elements produce different variations of energy, and these can be harnessed by those sensitive enough to utilize it."

Alena nodded as he spoke. "So... is there a way to make someone sensitive enough?" she asked after a moment of silence.

Martin was quiet for a very long time; it felt like hours to Alena. Just when she was about to ask him if he'd fallen asleep, he spoke in his deep baritone voice again.

"Yes."

Alena restrained herself from punching the air in excitement. "Can you teach me?"

Martin shook his head vehemently. "I think not."

She pouted, glaring at him. "And why not? Am I not good enough?"

Martin chuckled, but it sounded more like he was choking on something. "I am not strong enough. I'll take you to my teacher someday, perhaps *he* can help. There are..." he seemed to look for the correct word, "...problems," he said delicately. She arced an eyebrow, and he continued.

"I said I was a Tzen, right? Well, Tzen are a close-knit group of individuals, there are probably around twenty or thirty of us right now. If you looked up my name, Spire, in the phone book, I am not listed because I live with them."

Alena shuddered, "So... I would have to live with them as well?"

Martin pondered this for a moment. "I was introduced to the Tzen when I was four, and I have no parents. I have an uncle, but I won emancipation in court when I was sixteen. Perhaps that's why it doesn't bother me. You're what, seventeen? Perhaps they'll make an exception..."

Alena looked thoughtful, but finally her curiosity got the better of her. She nodded, "Can you talk to them on my behalf? Please?" She gave him what would probably have qualified as 'puppy-dog eyes', but Martin was not affected by such actions.

"I will," he said, "But they will probably ask to speak to you directly. When could you come to the old North Bridge?"

Alena was quiet for a moment, but eventually spoke. "I can come tonight, probably around nine or ten. Is that okay?"

Martin smiled through the darkness. "Excellent choice of timing. You will meet my teacher then; he has those hours. His name is Dais."

Martin drew his Tzen Rod and held it out toward her. "Go on," he said, "Take it. I have another – Dais supplied me with a few extras after I combusted my first one."

Alena laughed at the picture of Martin attempting to launch a fireball only to have his wand explode into flames. Martin found nothing about the action amusing, however, and merely glared at her.

"Don't forget to come. I'll be there too."

And with that, Martin was gone, walking silently down the corridors of the maze.

Chapter 5: Meeting Dais

Alena parked her bicycle next to one of the stone pylons that supported the old North Bridge. She leaned against the pillar, her eyes looking around waiting for Martin and his teacher, Dais.

"Dais will be here shortly," said a smooth voice next to her. She jumped and staggered away as the shape of a familiar coat-clad student seemed to shimmer out of the darkness. Martin laughed at the expression on her face.

"It's not funny!" she shouted, putting her hands on her hips. "You scared the crap out of me!"

Martin shrugged, "Likewise. You realize you almost hit me with the bike as you pulled up?"

Alena blushed, and Martin could feel the heat radiating off of her. She was hotter than the Fire Energy Threads that were running near his left hip. Suddenly, there was a loud crash and a string of expletives and a third figure came staggering into view.

"Good afternoon Dais," deadpanned Martin. Dais ran a hand through his messy black hair, smiling sheepishly at the two adolescents. "Hi..."

Martin turned back to Alena. "Dais has a habit of tripping over all stationary objects," he explained. Dais frowned, his chagrin easily visible on his thin face.

"Hey now," he muttered, "You're the one who wants me to make your girlfriend into a Tzen Sensitive, don't forget it."

Martin twitched unpleasantly, and his hand actually jerked towards a thin sheathe at his side where he was undoubtedly holstering another Tzen rod. "She... is not... my girlfriend..." he gritted, glaring unpleasantly at Dais.

Dais ignored him, turning to Alena. "I've made a decision, miss... ah..."

"Alena," she supplied.

"Alena, lovely name... I've made a decision. Martin and I are going to have a brief duel to demonstrate what you will one day be capable of. When we are through, you can choose if you still want to become one of us."

He faced Martin, pulling out his own Tzen rod. Martin already had his out, his face unreadable. Alena took several large steps backward, unsure of what she was going to see.

"Ibleuz," said Martin, swinging his rod like a sword and sending a semicircle of bright white light toward his teacher, "Kuzan!" No sooner had he spoken, a second assault; a laser of pale light, streaked away from Martin's Tzen Rod.

Dais dodged the first assault easily, but the beam of light sizzled past his ear closer than he would have liked. He grimaced, looking back at Martin.

"Trezin!"

A golden-red sphere of light burst from Dais' rod, and Martin hurled himself sideways as it streaked past him and into the night sky. Alena watched the two men battle it out, hurling spheres and rays of energy at each other for the better part of twenty minutes before Dais signaled it was time to stop.

Alena was breathless. Something like this belonged in a fantasy movie, not in real life. Magic and/or energy manipulation was something she had never even dreamt was real!

"So Alena," remarked Dais as breath returned to his lungs, "Are you still ready to do this?"

Alena nodded without hesitation, a smile on her face. Dais looked helplessly toward Martin as if begging him to change her mind. Martin had already holstered his rod, and was standing about two yards away with his arms crossed. He shook his head at Dais and closed his eyes in annoyance. "Just do it."

Dais looked back toward Alena. "Please forgive me for this, ma'am..." he said sheepishly. He pulled out his Tzen Rod and grasped her shirt by the hem. He lifted it up, exposing the bare flesh of her flat belly. Before Alena could react, he had pressed the tip of the rod against her and muttered one word.

"Ciduu!"

Alena collapsed to the ground, screaming and writhing in pain as a flaming red mark spread from the point he'd touched the rod to until her entire body was glowing a fiery red. After a moment which seemed like an eternity, the glow (and the pain) receded until it was only a small red tattoo on pale flesh.

Gasping, Alena stood up and looked around. She could see the Threads that wove in and out of the ground and pylons that supported the bridge. After catching her breath, she looked at Dais.

"What... what did you do to me?" she asked, clutching the spot next to her navel where the rod had burned the mark.

"I did nothing," said Dais matter-of-factly, "All I did was imbue your body with the sensitivity to both see and harness the energy that flows naturally around us."

"Why did it hurt?" she asked in confusion. Dais shrugged, "It always does – it ain't my fault..." he ran a hand through his hair again.

Martin decided to intervene. "Tomorrow," he said, "You will meet me at the school. I will be waiting by the front door."

Alena was about to tell him it was Saturday tomorrow, but he silenced her by holding up his hand. "I know it is the weekend. I will be taking you to our home to get you acquainted with the training grounds. That is all."

Martin seemed to shimmer for a moment, and after a split second of blinking, Alena found that the boy in the Loden Coat had faded from existence. Dais had also gone, leaving no trace that they had ever been there.

"...how handy..." she muttered as she mounted her bicycle and began to pedal home.

As she left the bridge area, two pairs of eyes watched her depart. The first, a pair of lead-gray eyes, turned to face the second pair.

"Dais, will she be alright?"

The second pair of eyes, electric green, turned to face the speaker. "Why do you care, Martin? Going soft? Care about your little girlfriend?"

Martin's dead eyes looked away in disgust. "I thought I'd explained I'm not into that sort of thing."

Dais' eyes crinkled cheerfully in the darkness. "I didn't know you swung on that side of the line, Martin."

Martin's eyes flared up at the statement, and for the next few minutes any passerby would have heard the two men scuffling like children in a schoolyard. Finally, Martin sat on Dais' chest until the older man cried uncle.

"Ow... geez, that hurt. You didn't have to elbow me in the jaw, you know," said Dais as he sat up. Martin snorted at his statement, but said nothing. "I don't get why you're so afraid to live a little. Normal people have relationships at seventeen. What about you? You barely have a relationship with yourself!"

Martin's eyes glared at Dais. "I do not want a relationship. End of story."

Dais shrugged, "I'll remember that when you come to me for dating advice in a few weeks."

"Do you WANT me to elbow you in the mouth again?" growled Martin as Dais began to laugh. Dais shrugged at the statement. "I'm not itching for a fight, but if you want one, we can clown around all you want back at The Hall, okay?"

With that, Dais seemed to fade away, much like he'd done to get away from Alena. Martin lingered a moment longer, thinking over the day.

What the hell is wrong with me in the first place? I'm Martin Spire! I'm the pride-and-joy of the Tzen, not some hormone-soaked teenager. I've already made enough mistakes for one lifetime... last thing I need is to make more.

And why the hell did I help Alena out at breakfast this morning? I really must be going soft. A few years ago, I probably would have crushed her glasses, not given them back... or at least ignored the confrontation entirely.

This is stupid... utterly stupid. Not only did I help her, I later on got riled up over that bloated buffoon Chris! I usually keep my cool... I'm losing my touch.

Martin decided to head back to The Hall. It was more comfortable in his personal bedroom as opposed to sitting on a piece of rubble with a segment of rebar poking him in the back. He stood up, stretching to loosen up his muscles as he felt several joints pop.

Martin suddenly felt a spike of energy, and his head whipped around so fast he thought he'd slipped a disc. Something was happening a few minutes east of him.

I'll be damned if I'm not going to check that one out...

He drew out his Tzen Rod and pointed it at himself, hastily grabbing one of the lighter green Air Energy Threads and focusing on transferring its power to him. With a gust of wind, Martin was hovering in the air, channeling the energy out the soles of his leather shoes.

Let's see here...

There! There was the energy spike again. He angled his body and took off like a shot, soaring over the ground beneath him like a bird. He quickly masked his energy signature with a simple Earth incantation, rendering himself invisible to a fellow Tzen or Energy Manipulator.

This wasn't necessary. It turned out the energy spike wasn't the problem. It was Alena. Martin wanted to moan as he saw her predicament. Some fool had lodged a branch in her bicycle tire, causing her to crash. Whoever this cretin was, he now had Alena pinned by her wrists to a nearby tree and was forcing his knee between her legs.

A strange and alien sense of possessiveness swept over Martin. He cancelled all the energy in his body, dropping to the ground. He quickly grasped one of the reddish-orange Threads and ran up to the figure.

"Get your hands off her!" he snarled, grabbing the offender by the collar and hurling him away from Alena. "I should have known better than to let her ride home in the dark!"

His rod was out in an instant, and Martin knew instantly that whatever incantation, he cast was going to be lethal. He pointed the rod at the thug as he stood up, feeling the Fire Energy coursing through his veins.

"Kodom-tzintasa!"

Wave after wave of flames poured from his Tzen Rod, engulfing the form of the street thug in seconds. Martin snapped the rod to the side, canceling the effects of the incantation, and eyed the pile of ash that had once been a human being.

"Are you alright?" he asked, turning to Alena. She nodded briefly, and then reached forward and hugged him.

Chapter 6: Glimmer

Martin stiffened to the point where he thought he was going to snap his own spine. Almost out of reflex, he wanted to push Alena away. He suddenly realized, however, that she was crying. Martin's rigid posture slowly relaxed.

What the hell? What am I supposed to do?

He tentatively put one arm on Alena's back, patting it reassuringly. "Uh... it's alright. He's gone."

Alena let out a sob into his chest, and Martin mentally kicked himself. *Sure... bring up the fact that she was almost raped...*

"I'll take you home," he said after a few moments.

He shifted around until she was hugging him from behind. He channeled the Air Energy into himself again, lifting them both from the ground. Alena gave a startled gasp, and he felt her clutch him tighter.

"Relax," he said, "I won't let you drop."

Since when did I know how to be reassuring?

Alena relaxed slightly, and Martin felt the pressure on his ribcage slowly lessen. *That's better... oxygen is always a good thing...*

"Alright, I need you to show me where you live," he said quietly. Alena peered around him as she began to survey her surroundings.

"T-two blocks fr-from here..." she choked, pointing in the direction she was referring to. Martin slowly began to take her in that direction.

For some reason, this feels oddly nice. No... I am Martin Spire. Nice isn't in my vocabulary. She was just hurt. She'd cling to anyone who just saved her...

Resolving himself to this fact, he set her down on one of the streets. He turned to her as best he could, seeing as she was clinging to him like a limpet. "Which way from here?" he asked softly. He tried to keep the usual edge out of his voice.

Alena looked around, and finally pointed to a red brick house at the end of the street. Martin slowly shifted her onto his shoulder and began walking, keeping an arm around her waist for support.

"T-thank you..." she choked, wiping her eyes. "I was-"

Martin shushed her. "It's alright."

Alena gave him another hug, and Martin fought down the instinct to push her away again. She released him after a moment and walked up to the green door of her house. She looked back at him with a small smile on her tear-streaked face. "Would you like to come in?"

Martin's eyes shifted nervously around, "Won't your parents mind?"

"They're in Panama for a week," she explained, "I'm in charge for now."

Martin sighed and walked forward, stepping through the door and into an ornate foyer area. Before his sight could adjust to the dimmed lights, there was a growl and something large pounced on him from the side.

"Charlotte! Down!" Alena reprimanded, pulling a large black Labrador retriever off of Martin. The dog whined but sat down obediently next to her master. Martin pushed himself up from the floor, looking first at the dog and then at Alena.

"Nice dog," he remarked dryly as he brushed dog hair from his coat. Alena smiled at his nature. A few weeks ago, when she had transferred to this school district, rumors had floated wildly concerning an untouchable vampire of a student at the local High School. Who would have thought said vampire would be standing in her foyer engaged in a staring match with her goober of a lab?

"Can I get you something?" she asked, moving toward the kitchen, "Water? Milk? Wine?"

Martin looked at her oddly. "Wine?"

She grinned, "So you were paying attention."

Martin barely refrained from rolling his eyes. Instead, he contented himself with reaching into a pocket of his coat and clutching a small roll of paper. This was one of his many secrets; something he'd never shown anyone. A thin roll of paper with the words "*DO NOT SHOW EMOTION*" printed neatly on them. It was a reminder to himself to remain as impassive as a statue.

"Water will be fine," he said after a moment, "Thank you."

Alena vanished into the kitchen, leaving Martin alone with 'Charlotte'. The boy turned and glared at the dog. She was now preoccupied chasing her own tail in the adjoining living room.

I still don't trust you...

Alena returned and passed him a glass of cool, crisp water. Martin accepted it with a nod and sipped at it. Alena watched him from over a glass of lemonade.

"Thank you again," she said. Martin looked at her over the rim of the lead-crystal glass his water was in. She was visibly calmer; no doubt the initial shock of her ordeal was over. Martin had to admit she was a strong person to recover this quickly. Something akin to admiration flickered within his chest, but he quickly squashed it.

"I already told you you're welcome," he said, "Just let me know if you need anything."

The grandfather clock in the living room let out a chime, and Martin's eyes looked to the ornate brass face.

Ah crap...

"Well, Dais is officially going to kill me..." he muttered as he finished the water. Alena raised an eyebrow at him.

"He wanted me back at The Hall by midnight, but it's now one... I'm screwed."

Alena had a hard time believing that Dais was going to do anything to Martin. Just based upon less than twenty-four hours of knowing him, Martin seemed to be unfazed by anything anyone could do. Nothing, that is, unless she counted that incident with Chris in the maze...

"Martin, why did you get so riled up at Chris?" she asked as she set down her lemonade glass. Martin coughed, looking at the floor.

"Calling my mother a whore is an insult to her memory... and to my existence."

Judging by the look in his eyes, Martin was not going to continue this conversation. Then again, he rarely even engaged in conversations.

"What's 'The Hall'?" she asked after a moment. Martin looked at her for a moment before answering.

"The Hall is the cavern the Tzen are using as a base," he said slowly, "I'll take you there tomorrow." She nodded, and was suddenly overcome with the fact that it was already one in the morning. A yawn slipped unbidden from her lips. She thought she saw Martin's face soften, but it may have been a trick of her tired eyes.

"Go on, go to bed. I'll see you tomorrow..." he said, turning to leave. "Remember, I'll be by the school. Don't leave me hanging, Alena..."

With that, he was gone; back out into the cool night air. Alena looked out, but he was nowhere to be found. Undoubtedly he had used some form of Energy Manipulation to vanish.

***

Martin stepped through the archway of The Hall; Dais waiting for him against a pillar. Their eyes locked as soon as Martin entered, and Dais was instantly ready to have a confrontation with his pupil.

"So, have fun?" he remarked dryly. Martin snorted and tried to walk past his teacher, but Dais put a hand on his shoulder.

"Come on Martin, at least give me something to feel good about. At least tell me you used protection!" he said, his face cracking into a smile. Martin's glare could have stopped a clock at that point, and he was directing all the intensity at Dais. "Do you mind getting your hand off my shoulder?" he gritted, shrugging it off roughly. Dais held up his hands in defense, the irritating smile never leaving his lips.

"Touchy," he remarked, "Go on then, hit the sack. Everyone else is out already anyway..."

Martin was already gone, his coat swishing behind him as he walked across the massive hallway that served as the entryway to the Tzen Refuge. He stalked angrily down the wide hallway, passing the circular doors on his left and right. He was grateful that his shoes were making no sound against the simple beige carpet that stretched down to the end, lest he wake one of his touchier teammates. He pulled a chain from his neck, inserting an attached key into one of the doors on the sides of the hallway and pushing the door open.

He was greeted by his room – the one place he felt he could truly relax. Both sides of the room were symmetrical, each containing a bed, a desk and a small nightstand. A lamp was attached above the bed, and a small dresser was parked near the door. A series of pegs lined the back of the door he had just opened, and a pair of mannequins displayed what looked like a partial suit of lightweight armor. One of the bed-lights was on, illuminating his roommate, Douglas Reaves, in the midst of reading an engrossing novel. He looked up as he walked in, grinning like the Cheshire cat at Martin.

"Martin!" he said jovially, putting aside his novel and standing up, "Dais said you finally got laid!"

Martin made a solemn vow to murder Dais when he saw him the next morning, but proceeded explain to his roommate, that *no*, he hadn't slept with anyone and that *no*, he was not dating at the time. He also made his intentions to kill Dais known.

"Ouch," said Douglas as he rubbed the back of his blonde head sheepishly, "So Dais was just being himself as usual then?"

"I'm surprised you fell for it," muttered Martin as he hung his coat on one of the pegs on his side of the room, "You were here before me anyway – you've known that moron longer than I have."

Douglas shrugged, going back over to his bed and collapsing onto it with a sigh. He turned a pair of cerulean eyes on his partner, grinning again. "So tell me, is she cute? Does she have a sister?"

He was silenced as one of Martin's pillows landed on his face. The lights in the room went out, and he heard Martin shift over in his bed.

"Yes. No. Good night, Douglas," gritted Martin.

Douglas was dumbstruck at Martin's admittance to thinking someone was 'cute' – seeing as he seemed to be the type that kicked puppies for fun and ate babies three meals a day. Shrugging it off, Douglas burrowed down beneath his blanket and closed his eyes, rapidly falling asleep.

Chapter 7: The Hall

Martin was ready to explode. He'd been waiting at the High School for the past half-hour, and Alena still hadn't shown up. Not only that, but the Gods seemed intent on punishing him, and there was now a curious girl from the High School Paper poking around, wondering what he was doing here on the weekend.

"For the last time," he said as he fought to keep his voice level, "I am meeting someone here. Yes, I know there is a football game going on back on the north field – I'm not interested. Please leave now."

The girl in question was too busy saying things that Martin was trying his hardest to tune out. He was in one heck of a foul mood right now. His Loden Coat was draped around his shoulders, and the sun seemed to have a mind of its own. The damn thing was beating down on him with all the intensity of a June drought; and it was the beginning of September.

"Why are you wearing a coat in this heat?" asked the bouncing girl, fanning herself with a pad of lined paper. Martin would have dearly loved to make her eat it – she was bouncing upon his nerves something terrible.

"Because I feel like it, now piss off," he snapped, his anger welling inside. If Alena didn't get here soon...

"Martin!"

Speak of the devil... Martin turned as Alena jogged up to him, sweat pouring down her face. The girl who had been bothering him raised an eyebrow at his choice of company.

"I'm sorry I'm late," panted Alena, "My bike chain snapped, so I had to jog."

Martin nodded, turning to the newspaper girl. "Now that you've seen that I'm not planning to blow up the school," he said icily, "You can leave."

The girl haughtily threw a braid of blonde hair over her shoulder. Martin had a strong urge to choke her with her own hair after her next words.

"I guess even a freak can get a girlfriend."

Martin felt a vein pop in his forehead, and before he could respond, something frightening happened.

Martin never knew what hit him.

"Yes," Alena said cheerily. She danced over to Martin and threw her arms around his neck. "He got a girlfriend. Big deal! At least he did better than someone like you!"

Before Martin could react to anything being said, a pair of soft lips covered his own. He just barely managed to keep his impassive air about him, seeing as his reflexes were screaming to jerk his head away. A flash blinded his eyes for a moment, and Martin had the strongest urge to kill someone.

The girl was running off, her camera clutched tightly in her fist.

Martin quickly broke away from Alena, running the back of his hand across his mouth. "Pardon my French, but *what the hell do you think you were doing?*" he said, his voice seething with suppressed shock. Alena snickered, jerking a thumb toward the retreating figure of the newspaper girl.

"I got her to go away, didn't I?" she asked, smiling cheerfully. Martin gave her an exasperated look, his slate-colored eyes betraying nothing in the way of emotions or thoughts. They might as well have been stolen from a corpse for all the warmth they showed.

"And now that will be in the school papers. Happy? I hope so..." he turned and motioned for her to follow him. "Come. The Hall isn't that far away from here."

It took about a half an hour to get to the entrance of 'The Hall'. At first, Alena didn't see anything. The entrance was cleverly disguised beneath a large rock situated in some woods. Although the stone was heavy, it was also easy to move if you had the right tools; namely a Tzen Rod and basic knowledge of Air Energy.

"After you," Martin said, gesturing toward the revealed trapdoor as the massive stone floated overhead. She gave it a nervous glance before descending the metal ladder beneath the hatch. Martin followed, lowering the rock into place.

They climbed down in silence, the ladder seeming to continue downward forever. After what felt like an eternity of climbing, Alena finally felt solid ground beneath her feet. She pushed away from the ladder as Martin released the rungs, dropping the last yard or so onto the floor of a tunnel.

"The Hall is just ahead," he explained, motioning for her to follow him. The dim light of a few torches and a Fire Energy Thread cast an ethereal orange glow in the tunnel, and Alena could see it was once a mine. Tracks still ran along the ground, although they were rusted and disused. The wooden supports had been replaced, however, and Alena was willing to place bets it was the Tzen who were responsible. They walked down the tunnel for a few minutes before Martin halted in front of a large steel door. He turned around to Alena, his face half-lit by the dancing flames.

"Beyond this door," he said, "Is The Hall. You can tell no-one what you've seen in here, alright? Some of the things that are down here are beyond even our understanding, such as why this place exists. We do not know everything. Just remember not to intentionally insult anyone and you'll be fine." Martin turned and pushed open the door, motioning for Alena to pass.

She stepped over the threshold into a large cavern, ogling at its size. The roof of the cavern stretched high above them, barely visible at such a distance. The sides of the cavern must have been several miles across, and a large lake covered the bottom. Jutting from the standing water were several islands, each connected by bridges that looked suspiciously like they were made from bones. From somewhere above them, a blue light lit the area, dancing off of large stone and glass structures that dotted the islands.

Alena could only stand there, her mouth hanging open in wonder. A city beneath the surface of the earth; if possible, it surprised her more than the fact that some form of magic actually existed.

Someone ran past her, and Alena was only aware of a shock of red hair before the figure was gone. She was about to ask Martin who it was when a second figure ran in front of her, long black hair trailing behind.

"You nitwit!" screeched the second figure, "Get back here! This is your fault!"

Alena raised a questioning eyebrow, curious as to what was whose fault. Martin walked up next to her, his face impassive as usual.

"That was Michael and Donna. They're two of our low-ranked Tzen, but they have a knack for causing each other problems."

There was a crash, followed by several profanities. Michael came dashing back into view, his face a mask of horror. Martin watched as he tore past, willing his legs to move faster as Donna came running after him, a lump visible on her forehead.

It was only then that Alena noticed something. Both Michael and Donna were wearing identical coats to Martin.

Long, knee-length navy blue Loden coats that they left unbuttoned in front.

"Are the coats like your uniforms?" she asked, nodding at Donna who had caught Michael and was proceeding to beat him into a bloody pulp. Martin shrugged, "Sort of."

A familiar figure walked across one of the bridges toward them, waving as he approached. Alena smiled as Dais walked up to them, the grin obvious on his face.

"Well, this is a fine sight," he said jovially, "Showing your girlfriend the ropes, eh Martin?"

Alena had the strongest urge to kiss Martin again to see what Dais' reaction would be, but decided now was not a good time. It was at least a sixty-foot drop into the lake below from her current position. Martin easily resembled the type to shove her off if she irked him.

"For the last frikin' time," bit Martin irritably, "She's not my girlfriend!"

Dais smiled, "Denial."

Martin took several deep breaths before responding to his teacher. "Listen here, all I'm doing is showing a fellow Tzen where she can come if she needs us, alright?"

Dais nodded, accepting the answer until he had something else to mock him over. "Why don't you give her the guided tour? You know, shower her around?"

"Let me find a container for my joy..." muttered Martin sarcastically, but he motioned for Alena to follow him anyway. Dais waved as the pair walked off, shouting something about playing nice with the other Tzen.

"...idiot..." grumbled Martin into the collar of hic coat. He stopped, pointing at a large egg-shaped building that looked as though it had been carved from marble. "This is the Deep Shaft," he explained, "It leads deeper into the cavern. I'd suggest you steer clear for now, as several tunnels are unstable. We're working on that..."

He continued, pointing out buildings that Alena would need to know. He also taught her where the bedrooms were, just in case she ever wound up staying for an extended period of time. When he'd given her the tour of the current island they were on, he walked her over to a balcony that overlooked the cavernous chamber they were in.

"Most of the islands here are identical," he deadpanned, sweeping one of his hands out for emphasis. "The only difference is the main island over there, which also has a museum, library, and palace. We haven't been able to fully explore over there yet because the bridges are down, and there are no Air Energy Threads this deep."

Alena was looking off the balcony in wonder. Fireflies were flitting in and out of a cluster of shelf fungi that were growing on the side of the island, and their light was illuminating the sheer rock face of their perch.

"It's beautiful down here," she breathed, looking all around. Normally, she wasn't the type for caves. This, however...

"I'm glad you like it," he remarked flatly, "Now I'll introduce you to the members of this island's bedding chamber."

He pressed his finger against a switch, which let out a shrill cry. Alena assumed it was some kind of intercom. Within moments, her hypothesis was proven correct as no less than six of Martin's acquaintances came over and stood at attention.

"Alena, this is my 'family'," he said calmly, jerking his head toward the assembled Tzen.

Chapter 8: Family

Martin faced the Tzen that had arrived at his call. "This is Alena," he said sharply, "She is one of us now, alright? Give her any crap and you're answering to me, understood? Now, on to the introductions..."

The first boy stepped forward. He was smaller than most adolescents, and his frame was wiry, bordering on unhealthily thin. His skin was chalk white, similar to Martin's, but his eyes were the most striking thing about him. They were the most unusual shade of violet Alena had ever seen in her life. They danced with an inner mischief, and she instantly knew who the prankster of the lot was.

"I'm Jason," remarked the violet-eyed boy, brushing absently at his black hair, which was pulled into a loose ponytail, "A pleasure to meet you. I'm the Information Specialist of Team Twelve."

Martin leaned over to Alena, "This is island number twelve, so we're Team Twelve," he informed her. She nodded, looking at the next Tzen.

"I'm Donna," said the girl as she rubbed the goose-egg forming just below her bangs. She was what most people would call 'plain but pretty', with just the right skin tone and average green eyes. Alena surmised she could pass you in a crowd undetected. "I'm the Maintenance Officer around here. The fool with the red hair is Michael, my assistant."

Michael waved hello, nursing a split lip. He was pale, like most of the people she'd seen, but it wasn't his skin tone that drew attention to him. No, it was the fact that his left arm ended at the bicep. The sleeve of his Loden coat hung empty and lifeless at his side, and Alena could make out the outline of the stub within the blue fabric.

"Hi," he muttered with no small amount of resentment in his voice. He glared at Donna, as if he wanted to shoot her on the spot. Alena nodded in greeting as the next person stepped forward.

"Hey," he said cheerfully as he waved to Alena, "I'm Derrick." He flashed a smile that belonged somewhere on the silver screen, his perfectly straight teeth brighter than usual in the dim light of the cavern. His brown eyes seemed to light up, and his entire demeanor seemed optimistic. "I run the gondola to the next island," he explained, pointing at a rickety looking device that hung from a thick cable. "You ever need a ride, you let me know, hear?"

Alena nodded, smiling at the exuberant boy.

"I'm Douglas; Martin's roommate," said the next boy, smiling at her. His blond hair was tousled; sticking wildly in all directions as if he had put a finger in a socket. His eyes seemed cheerful, but something about his demeanor simply shrieked that he had a guarded attitude.

"And that leaves me, I guess..." deadpanned another girl off on the side. Her red hair was cut shoulder length, framing a thin face that seemed to have died long ago. She looked almost like a redheaded counterpart to Martin, and her attitude seemed just as dour. "I'm Terra."

Alena smiled, waving at the last girl, who took no notice of the gesture. She turned back to Martin and was surprised to find him gone. "Where'd he go?" she asked, turning back to the Tzen only to find Jason remaining. He smiled at her, pointing at one of the buildings.

"Ran in there like the devil was chasing him," he said with a small smile. She thanked him and walked over to the building. Just as she was about to open the door, she heard a sound from inside.

"Goddamnit!" swore someone who sounded like Martin, "We can't send anyone else down there right now!" Alena pushed open the door and peered inside. Martin was standing with his back to her; a headset perched on his ears. He was tapping his foot impatiently as whoever was on the other line spoke.

"Listen here you piece of-" he started, but was cut off by the other person. He finally sighed and responded with a curt affirmative into the microphone before taking the headset off of his head and hurling it with considerable force into the far wall where it broke. He turned around, and spotted Alena by the door. He shook his head and walked over, opening the door the rest of the way.

"C'mon," he grumbled, "We've got work."

"Work?" she asked, tagging along behind him, "What kind of work?"

He guided her into one of the buildings and handed her a Loden Coat, "Try that on," he instructed. "Blasted lizards running loose in one of the tunnels we're trying to clear out. I'm about ready just to kill someone..."

"How are lizards a problem?" she asked, shrugging on the coat. It was too tight around the shoulders, and Martin quickly handed her one with a wider measurement.

"Think Monitor Lizards with bad tempers," he replied as he perused a shelf of strange devices. He finally selected one that looked somewhat like a misshapen egg and slipped it into his coat pocket. He tossed one to Alena, who managed to get her hands out of the sleeves fast enough to catch it.

"That's a grenade," he stated, and Alena almost dropped it. "Since I haven't had time to train you with that Tzen Rod yet, that'll have to do. C'mon."

Alena followed Martin as he stalked out of the Supply Room. She could feel the anger rolling off of him, and she had every intention of *not* getting in his way... for now. He stopped at an old mining elevator, motioning for her to climb inside. She did so, and he followed without a word.

After manipulating a small control box, as well as giving it a good punch to relieve stress, Martin and Alena were descending deeper beneath the ground. Martin was leaning against one of the walls; two of his fingers massaging his temples in agitation. He'd finally given up on breaking that habit.

They disembarked the lift, stepping into a red-lit tunnel that seemed to twist and coil like a gigantic snake. Somewhere, Alena could hear the sounds of people yelling and explosions. Martin quickened his stride, almost jogging down the passageway toward the din. He rounded the corner, his hand flying to his Tzen Rod only to find it missing. He quickly patted his pockets before sighing in agitation.

Fine then... let's do this the old-fashioned way... He stomped forward, his eyes watching for his quarry. Something darted in the shadows, and he held up his hand, palm outwards. His other hand, his left, grasped the glowing Fire Energy Thread near him.

"Trezin!"

The familiar amber sphere exploded from his palm, raising blisters on the skin as it fired into the darkness. There was a shriek and one of the lizards toppled from its hiding place. Its head was seared into a stump.

Martin turned around and doubled down the tunnel, making sure Alena was following.

"When we find more of them," he stated, "Grasp a Fire Energy Thread and point your Rod at the enemy. When you feel warmth in your belly, clearly say the word "Trezin" to launch a fireball. Got that?"

Alena was about to say yes, but there wasn't any time as a large scaly lizard hurtled toward them both. Martin ducked, and suddenly realized his error. By ducking the charge, it would be heading straight for Alena. *Shit!* He raised his blistered palm as the lizard flew overhead; he rammed his hand upward, striking the lizard in the chest.

"Sunakare-dicharis!" he spat, and there was a bright flash of blue-white light as the lizard fell to the side. He wiped his hand on his pants, grimacing slightly. God how he hated that incantation. Still, it seemed useful for something...

"What did you do to it?" asked Alena as she nudged the corpse of the lizard with her sneaker. Martin looked over his shoulder at her.

"I pumped enough ice into its body to freeze its heart. Why do you ask?" he said. His voice carried all the emotion of the stone walls that surrounded them. Alena shuddered, reminding herself not to get on Martin's bad side.

"I think we should split up," he stated calmly, "We'll get this done faster. Just make sure to kill around five of them and we should be good. Okay?"

Alena did not like the thought of taking on one of those tiny dragons by herself, but took a calming breath and nodded.

"The magic word is Trezin, right?" she queried, making sure she knew how to kill the lizards in the first place. Martin nodded and turned around, striding down the tunnel.

His mind was running at seventy miles per hour, thoughts racing through it like light through a fiber optic cable. So much was happening. Normally these lizards were a nuisance, not a threat. The message stated someone had been mauled. That was *very* unusual.

Secondly, his freezing incantation was partially repelled by something. He looked down at his hand. The blisters had popped from the cold, and were hanging lifelessly from his palm. He scowled, wondering what he could have done with his Rod. He was certain he'd had it with him when he entered the lift.

Another lizard came slithering from the darkness, and Martin wasted no time in dispatching it with an icicle through the head. He allowed himself a small smile. Ice incantations had a variety of uses, and it was one of his favorite branches of the Art he had been immersed in.

Pain shot up his leg, and he looked down to find the teeth of one of the lizards piercing his calf. He swore loudly, grabbing the reptile by the head and muttering the words for an Earth incantation. The creature's head imploded under the force exerted on it, and Martin dropped the carcass to the ground with a disgusted look.

In contrast to Ice incantations, he thought, Earth was barbaric. Whereas Ice had a clinical precision to it, used mainly for long-range attacks executed by the launching of icicles, Earth was close-range and harsh. It consisted of the ability to amplify the gravity near the area the incantation was cast in, causing the enemy to be crushed. On the flip side, Martin could also lower his own gravity to float or make impressive leaps through the air. Of course, he could just use Air incantations for the same thing, so he usually remained set in his ways of avoiding Earth unless it was necessary.

He heard a hiss and decided the time would come to reminisce about his choice in incantations later. There were lizards out there to kill. A smirk spread across his aristocratic features as he dove deeper into the tunnels. Why not try out that little spell he'd learned earlier...

Chapter 9: The Revelation

Martin limped as quickly as he could around one of the corners in the tunnel. His leg was hurting like hell at this point, and his hand was beginning to throb. He cursed his luck, as well as anything else he happened to think of at that moment. He turned another corner and was confronted with a dark shape. He was inches from icing it six ways to Thursday when he realized it was Jason.

"Jason, how is the extermination progressing?" he asked, his voice curt and clipped. Jason grinned at him in the darkness.

"Your girlfriend is kicking ass down there," he said slyly, "She's already nuked eight of those things."

Eight?!

"Are you sure?" asked Martin, although his face failed to convey his surprise. When Jason nodded, Martin pushed past him and began to walk deeper into the cavern.

"You'd best watch out down there," said Jason, "I'm guessing they've got a nest nearby."

Martin waved a hand distractedly as he kept walking. *A nest, eh?*

If there was a nest down here, and he could empty it, the lizard problem would be solved. He felt his pockets one more time, checking for his rod. Nothing. He sighed and kept going, looking for more of the lizards.

A yell tore through the hallways and a second dark shape came hurtling toward him. In the dim light of the cavern, Martin recognized Alena's terrified face. He was about to stop her and ask what was wrong when a lizard came around the corner.

Oh shit.

In comparison to the other reptiles in the cavern, this one was enormous. Its back was scraping the ceiling of the tunnel, bringing down rocks and dirt in showers to glance off armored scales.

Martin readied himself, pointing the index and middle fingers on both hands at the lizard. He grasped the nearest Thread and began to mutter the incantation.

"Aburasi-Dokumaray!" he said, firing an icicle from the four fingers pointed at the behemoth. To his dismay, the icicles merely glanced off the scales. He lowered his hands, drawing a pocketknife from his coat.

This is suicide...

He felt something stirring inside him, and realized instantly what was going to happen. He mentally apologized to Alena before rushing forward, flicking the blade of his knife out as he ran.

He never even got close. He heard Alena scream as the reptile's claws raked across his chest, lifting him into the air and hurling him backwards into the wall of the cavern. He slumped to the floor, his body aching. The blade of his knife was snapped off, having embedded itself in the palm of the lizard's hand.

"Bastard," he muttered as he forced himself to his feet. His body felt like someone had beaten it with a hammer, and he could feel one of his ribs was probably broken. He winced, glaring at the lizard. It had now taken to roaring at Alena. He grinned inwardly at the display. It was only trying to intimidate her at this point.

He staggered forward, walking toward the gigantic creature in shaky, tottering steps. The claw lashed out again, and he was hurled against Alena as they both collided with the hard floor of the tunnel.

Martin lay still for a moment, feeling his body pulse with a familiar energy. He closed his eyes, wishing he could control what was about to happen. Alena scrambled out from beneath him as the Threads in the cavern began to weave around his body, cocooning him in their vibrant essence.

"Martin?"

He heard her call out to him, but it was barely understood. His body was rippling, and he twisted around inside the cocoon of Threads. He felt his skin pulse, running across the surface of his body like water. He knew what he was.

The Threads dissipated, and Martin stood in front of Alena again. He looked almost identical to how he had before, but there was one main difference. Something about the way

74

he carried himself – it was more hunched, almost ape-like. His eyes burned vibrantly, glowing pale green in the dark tunnel.

"Stay!" he snarled, and Alena recoiled at the sound of his voice. It sounded harsh and guttural, almost animalistic.

Martin lurched forward, aiming for the lizard. Before his foot touched the ground, however, he was gone. Alena felt a gust of wind sweep past her and turned around in time to see the lizard recoil from a strike to the jaw. It shrieked, shaking its head from side to side as Martin landed on its back.

"Again!"

The same guttural voice tore from his throat, but it was followed by a punch to the back of the reptile's skull. The sheer force of the blow slammed its chin against the floor of the tunnel.

Martin leapt in front of it, grabbing the nearest cable he could reach; a blue-white Ice Energy Thread.

"Aburasi-Dokumaray!"

This time, the icicles that shot from his hand pierced the lizard, nailing it to the far wall of the cavern. Blood erupted from its throat and nostrils as it twisted and fought for freedom, but failed. Eventually, its eyes clouded over and it hung there lifelessly.

Martin grasped a red Fire Energy Thread and pointed his hand at the lizard's corpse.

"Trezin!"

The fireball that erupted from his hand was large enough to turn the walls of the tunnel into glass, burning the corpse until nothing was left except a blackened wall spattered with dark red blood.

Martin stood there for a moment before the cocoon of Threads encased him again. In less time than it took for Alena to step forward, the shell was gone. Martin turned and looked at her, and his eyes looked strange. Not glowing green, but sad.

"...sorry..."

He collapsed at her feet; facedown on the hard floor of the cavern. He was breathing, Alena could see that, but it didn't look like he was in the best condition of his life.

"Martin?" she asked, rolling him over. His eyes were closed, and his face looked oddly calm. Alena noticed that there was a hint of a smile on his lips.

"Someone!" she shrieked, "Help!"

In response to her cry, Jason game hurtling around the corner, looking from Martin to Alena, "What the hell happened?"

"He... he did something... killed the lizard..." she said, pointing to the wall and at Martin for emphasis, "Now..."

Jason scooped up his teammate, slinging him over his shoulder. "C'mon, let's go find Terra. She's pretty much the medic around here…"

The pair of them jogged back through the tunnel to the elevator. Jason dropped Martin into the corner and pressed the 'ascend' button on the lift. He looked at his comrade and then back at Alena.

"What did he do?"

Alena looked at Martin with worry etched into her features. "He… something with a cocoon…" she said uncertainly. Jason, however, reacted in an opposite way to what she expected. She thought he'd call her crazy, but instead he sighed in annoyance.

"So… our friend lost it again, eh? Fine… Terra'll fix him up all right. He's fine; don't worry your pretty little head about him…"

Alena looked up at Jason, "What happened, though? He…"

Jason smiled sadly. "You just saw the reason he doesn't have a family other than us. I think he'd be the best one to explain it. It isn't really my place…"

Alena nodded, swaying slightly as the elevator ground to a halt.

"By the way," Jason said as she opened the door of the elevator for him, "You look good in a Loden Coat."

Alena smiled at him, "Thanks…"

He dragged Martin over to one of the buildings and kicked the door as hard as he could. "Terra! Open the door! He went and did it again!"

The blank-faced girl opened the door and looked down at Martin. She sighed in exasperation, massaging her forehead with two fingers. "Again?"

Jason snorted in agreement, and Terra stepped aside to allow them access. "Just put him in one of the beds."

Alena heard her mutter several curses that seemed to revolve around Martin and his lack of control, but didn't think it was wise to say anything. Instead, she busied herself eying several computer screens that lined the far wall. One of them was on, and a green label flashed at the bottom: Spire, Martin K.

Above his name, a thin line continued to spike, showing his heartbeat. A computer turned on next to this one, displaying the outline of Martin's body as he lay on the bed behind them. His head and ribs were color-coded as red, while his hand and left leg were in orange. The rest of his body was colored green or blue.

Several graphs next to the body outline continued to change as the computer terminal received data feedback from Martin's body. Alena turned around to see that Terra had inserted a needle into his arm and was watching the screens with interest.

"Good," she said calmly, "He didn't get hurt badly..."

Alena looked at the screen and then back to Martin.

That's not bad?

Chapter 10: Nighttime Meeting

Martin felt ill as he opened his eyes. They swept slowly from side to side as he began trying to recognize where he was. The computers to his right hummed softly, and he could hear the steady pinging of the heart monitor. He shifted slightly, wincing as pain shot through his ribs.

What in Hell's name happened? There was that... thing... and then... I...

Shock dilated his pupils. He had lost control. Jason... Alena... were they alright? Had he killed them along with the lizard? He tried to sit up but found something heavy in his lap. He looked down to see Terra; her head resting on his leg. She looked dead tired.

Carefully, so as not to wake her, Martin scooted his leg from beneath her cheek and swung his legs carefully over the side of the bed. Pain shot through his left leg, and he bit his tongue to keep from moaning. That wasn't something Martin Spire did regularly.

He tested his leg on the ground carefully. Terra had done a good job healing his leg, it seemed. The patch-job she had performed on his leg was excellent, and there was Earth Energy was holding his rib together well. He still couldn't feel his right hand, and his head felt like a midget was swinging around a hammer in there. He shook his head groggily, wincing again as the motion aggravated what felt like a migraine. He limped over to the door and slid it open, staggering outside.

The bluish glow that lit the cavern seemed hauntingly bright, and the luminosity stabbed at his eyes like needles. Something almost feral in him wanted nothing better than to hurl a fireball at that light, but something else told him it wouldn't do any good. He averted his eyes, taking shaky steps out of the medical bay.

"You shouldn't be up…" muttered a voice from his right. He turned his head sharply, instinctively grabbing it between his hands as the jerky motion sent a pang of agony through his skull. Jason was leaning on the wall, his arms folded across his chest. His normally cheerful eyes were downcast, and he was fixing Martin with a venomous glare.

"Alena…" rasped Martin, shocked at how dry his throat was. "…is she… did I…?"

Jason shook his head, and the gray-eyed youth let out a breath he didn't know he'd been holding. He then looked up at his comrade, "Where… is she?"

"She's in your bed in your room," stated Jason flatly, "Douglas is watching over her. Martin…"

Martin waved a dismissive hand at Jason, limping toward the doorway that led to the sleeping quarters. "I don't… want to hear about it… not now…" He continued his shambling walk toward the doorway until he practically fell against it. His sore head connected painfully with the metal, causing a myriad of colored lights to swirl before him. He blinked, trying to rid himself of the illusion.

"Martin, listen!" said Jason, pushing himself from his perch and walking over. Martin wound up collapsing into his arms, his vision blurring and his head pounding. "Listen to me! You've got to stop! She's fine, okay? Just relax!"

Martin struggled feebly in Jason's arms. Unfortunately, in his weakened state, even the wiry prankster was stronger than him. He cursed himself for his weakness. "Lemme go..." he muttered. His words were barely coherent, and his tongue felt like it was thick and puffy.

"No," stated Jason as he pulled him through the doors Martin had been fumbling to open. "I'm gonna put you in my room for now. Just shut up and take it like a man, Martin. You got your ass whooped. Just calm down until tomorrow, okay?"

"What time... is it..." mumbled Martin. Jason stopped and fumbled with his key for a moment.

"It's around eleven," he said calmly, lurching through the door as he dragged Martin backwards into the room. He dumped him onto one of the beds, wiping his hand across his forehead. "Lay off the beef jerky for a while, pal. You're not such a light guy..."

Martin muttered something incoherent as he began to succumb to blackness; the combination of exertion and a comfortable pillow worked against him to drag him into slumber.

***

When Martin's eyes flickered open for the second time, his head felt worlds better. Gone was the pounding, and his ribs and leg felt much better. He sat up, looking around. Jason's bed was neatly made; the white sheets pulled taut over the plain mattress. Martin pulled himself from the bed, smoothing the sheets out until they looked decent enough for his critical eye.

He stepped out into the hall, and immediately backpedaled to avoid being mauled by Douglas as he came jogging down the corridor. His roommate jerked to a halt and looked at him oddly.

"Eh... hi?" he offered, looking at Martin as though he was going to be eaten. "Nice morning, isn't it?"

Martin looked back at him, barely comprehending the conversation. Apparently there was a long road back to coherency for him. He nodded dumbly and then began to walk toward his room. He fought with his key, cursing it until it fit into the lock on his door. He gave it a sharp turn, hearing the click as the tumblers in the lock released.

Alena was still lying on his bed, her glasses on his nightstand. There was a slight frown on her features, making her look... dare he say it... almost cute. Martin berated himself for saying that word. Martin Spire found the word 'cute' fit very little in this world...

After a few moments of writing in his journal while comfortably seated at his desk, he was aware of a pair of eyes watching him. He closed the notebook and looked over at Alena. She was awake, her eyes watching him curiously. He noticed that her glasses were back on her face – how did that motion escape him. He attributed it to his headache.

"Good morning," he said, pushing some of his raven-black hair out of his eyes, "Are you alright?"

Alena nodded, looking at him with an expression he knew all too well: fear. He sighed, absentmindedly twirling his pen dexterously between his thin fingers. "I'm sorry."

She shook her head, rolling over and facing the ceiling. Martin watched her intently, attempting to gauge her reaction. It never came. Just as she was about to open her mouth, the door banged open. Martin's headache returned as Jason walked through, looking for all the world as though he'd just won the lottery.

"Guess what?" he sang, his violet eyes roaming onto Martin, and then Alena. Martin massaged his forehead, sighing again. "Humor me..." he said, calmly, "What?"

"Breakfast is ready you two! Go on – Douglas is pigging out down there already."

Martin nodded before turning to Alena. "I would wait here, but I am not certain of your state of dress. Therefore, I will wait for you outside the door. I will then escort you to the dining hall."

With all the formality of a butler, he rose and followed behind Jason, exiting the room. He turned around and leaned on the wall opposite the door, staring intently at the imperfections in the metal. After a few moments, Alena walked out clad in the same attire from the day before, including the Loden Coat. It was lightly dusted with dirt, undoubtedly from the caves below them, but to his surprise it wasn't ripped. His was missing two buttons and the underarm had torn wide open. He wasn't much for sewing, so he left that to Douglas. He snickered inwardly. Douglas, for all his macho attitude, had what he considered the most feminine hobbies. He'd even found him knitting once!

Of course, Martin wasn't much better. All the Tzen had some kind of strange hobby. Jason collected and categorized bugs, Terra liked to fish, and Michael and Donna both shared a love for machines. Douglas seemed to love working with fabric, Derrick was always messing with some formula or another, and he himself folded origami.

He gestured for her to follow him and began to walk toward the gondola. "The only island with anything worth using as a dining hall is Island Nine," he explained. Derrick was standing there next to the gondola, his notepad out as he scribbled furiously with his pencil. Not wanting to get wrapped into another theory about how to calculate various energy outputs, he decided to step onto the lift before tapping his distracted comrade's shoulder.

"Eh?" he muttered, looking up at him. "Oh! You're here already. Great; let's get moving."

Derrick climbed into the gondola with them, turning a crank that set the rickety device into motion. It ran smoothly along the thick iron cables, swaying slightly as its motion gave it momentum. Alena looked over the edge, gazing into the waters below.

Schools of bioluminescent fish swam around, occasionally breaching out of the water like tiny whales to catch fireflies. A large predator resembling a shark circled a good distance away, eying the glowing fish hungrily. She looked back at Martin curiously.

"How come all this can remain hidden?" she asked, gesturing around for emphasis.

"I'll answer that," Derrick smiled. "We're too deep. Mining regulations state that without proper reason, mine shafts can only be dug down fifty feet in this area. They dug down and found nothing, so they abandoned the shaft. We're down about a mile, though..."

He looked up at the ceiling, "I'm actually quite impressed myself. I thought the seismology on the surface would be different, but it's not. It's like this cavern doesn't exist at all if you live on the surface..."

Alena smiled at him. Derrick grinned back and pointed past her into the water. She turned and looked at what seemed to be a large eel swimming along.

"Terra's gonna have a fit," he said, "She's been trying to catch him for ages. Bastard keeps stealing her bait. She'd probably need a wire as thick as her arm to catch that monster though... but it'd feed us for a while..."

He let the sentence trail off. Martin blew air through his nose in irritation. "Can't this piece of junk move any faster?"

"You ask that every time, don't you?" asked Derrick as he glared at his fellow Tzen. "We're almost there. Quit your bitching..."

Martin's eyebrows shot up in outrage. "Bitching? Who's the one who sniveled when his toolkit got lost? Hmm? Who was bitching then?"

Now Derrick was furious. "You..."

Alena watched them argue different points back and forth from opposite sides of the elevator. It only ended when, much to Martin's chagrin, the lift hit the ledge on Island Nine and the door opened. Unfortunately for him, however, he'd been leaning on said door and was sent sprawling onto his rear, glowering at both Derrick and Alena for having the audacity to laugh as heartily as they were.

"Dining hall's just up ahead," he muttered walking off. "Come on..."

Alena jogged after him, while Derrick brought up the rear. "Oh man," he howled, "You should have seen your face! You practically had a 'WTF' stamp on your forehead..." the sentence trailed off into more laughter. Martin glared at him, his pride sinking slowly.

"Just shut up before I dump you off this island..." he bit, walking away. For some reason Derrick went pale as a sheet, glaring after him.

"Low blow..." he muttered, glowering darkly.

"Why?" asked Alena, looking from Martin to Derrick.

"I can't swim."

Alena smiled at him, "It's not so bad – just don't drown!"

"Haw haw haw..." he muttered walking ahead of her. "Hurry up or the hash browns'll be gone..."

Chapter 11: Information

Martin pushed open the doors to the dining hall, walking inside with his usual air of indifference. He knew there were people staring at him. They obviously knew he'd lost control again...

He pulled out one of the metal chairs, the legs scraping against the floor, and sat down next to Douglas. His roommate looked up at him, his mouth half-full of hash browns. "Whazzup?"

Martin gave him a withering glance. Douglas swallowed his mouthful painfully, wiping the back of his hand across his mouth and turned to his teammate.

"Look, I know what happened..." he started, "...but it's no big deal. Nothing-"

Martin slammed his fist down hard enough to dent the surface of the table. "No big deal?" he said, the calm in his voice masking his fury. "I could have killed two of us when that happened, and you say it's no big deal?"

Douglas took one look at Martin's eyes and realized he'd lost this battle. "Okay, just listen," he pleaded, "Alena was pissing herself over you last night. Did you at least go say good morning?"

Another withering glance was sent his way, and this time it was laced with contempt. "Yes."

Douglas decided to let Martin brood without an interruption for now. It wasn't wise to piss him off right after he'd lost control like that. He turned back to his food, noticing dully that his appetite was gone. He pushed the plate away and stood up.

"I'm gonna go train. See ya around," he said, forcing a smile to his face.

Martin nodded, his gray eyes never leaving the table in front of him. He was staring intently at the tabletop. Martin Spire didn't eat on Sundays. It was just a ritual he did. Every weekend without fail, he skipped three meals. The following day, however, he ate enough to put everyone else to shame.

After a while, Martin seemed to wake up and began to glare at the Tzen on his left and right who were giving him cautious glances. After he'd finished, he stood up, popping his shoulders to alleviate the tenseness that had taken up residence there.

He walked over two tables to where Alena was sitting. It seemed she'd made fast friends with some of the Island Nine girls, and was busy chatting away with them. Martin tapped her on the shoulder, and the girl looked up into his eyes with surprise.

"Are you ready to begin training?" he asked her dully. She looked back at her new friends for a moment before nodding. Martin walked away, hearing Alena stand and follow him. They exited the dining hall and walked down one of the narrow Island Nine streets that crisscrossed the area.

"We'll use the Island Nine training ground for now," he said calmly, motioning to an area that had been fenced off and populated with practice dummies. Douglas was already there, nailing one of the burlap human replicas with knives made of ice.

"Before we begin," Martin said, "I'm going to give you a basic rundown of what each Elemental Thread is capable of, if that's alright with you."

Alena drew out the Tzen Rod he had given her and nodded, a smile on her lips. Martin sensed her eagerness, and felt something quiver in his chest. Being over-eager was what led him to disaster when he began training in the first place.

"Fire Element Threads," he said, grasping one of the orange Threads, "Carry the essence of heat. These can be harnessed for use as fireballs, or shaped using the natural 'Neutral' energy that flows through your body. That, however, takes years of practice..."

He pointed his rod at the nearest dummy. "Trezin!" The dummy caught fire and burned for a moment before collapsing from its stand and lying on the ground.

Martin released the Fire Energy Thread and closed his fingers around a greenish-white cord instead.

"Air Energy Threads carry the essence of air itself. They can be used to fly, like I demonstrated day before yesterday, but also as impact incantation or blades."

He looked around, sighting an unused dummy. He pointed his wand at it and muttered "Xidul!"

A familiar impact spell knocked the dummy from its cable, sending it into the dirt with a thud. Martin then sheathed the wand, turning to Alena with a grimace.

"You don't NEED the wand," he said, "But it is preferred. Anything other than those ebony sticks tends to incur the wrath of the element you're summoning."

To prove his point, he opened his mouth and focused on the Air Energy in his body. Rather than directing it to his hand where the wand would normally be, he directed it to his tongue.

"Garahno!"

There was an explosion of wind that issued from Martin's mouth, sweeping the fallen dummy from the ground and hurling headfirst into Douglas, who was watching intently.

Martin nodded an apology to his roommate as he turned back to Alena. "For now, practice with Fireball and Impact, alright? They're the easiest incantations of Fire and Air."

His speech was slurred, and his tongue felt heavy and dead again. He moved it around in his mouth to restore feeling, "And use the wand. Any other focus point is a bad idea for a novice."

He turned around and walked back toward the gondola. Alena watched him for a moment. Something about her taciturn friend was amiss. Ignoring his orders to train, she crept after him.

Martin activated the gondola, riding it back to the other side. Alena watched from Island Nine as he walked toward the sleeping chambers. When the gondola returned, she rode it after him, her mind ablaze with curiosity.

Martin was either unaware that he was being followed or just plain didn't care, Alena realized. He opened the door to his room and stepped inside, leaving the metal portal slightly ajar. She peered through, careful not to lean on the metal lest it squeak.

Inside the room, Martin drew out two objects. The first was a candle surrounded by a gleaming glass hurricane lamp, and the other was a square object covered in a small white cloth. He lit the candle, placing the hurricane lamp protectively around the small flame, and set the covered object next to it on his desk. He sat down in front of the two objects, and for a moment it looked like he was praying.

Alena almost panicked as he stood up to leave. Instead, however, she ducked into the room next to Martin's. She heard him leave, his leather shoes making soft thumps against the carpeted floor. After she heard the metal door at the end of the hallway close, she crept out and reentered his room.

The candle was still burning innocently on his desk. The other object, however, was what held her attention. She carefully walked over to it and slowly drew the small white cloth off of the object.

It was a picture set in an elaborate silver frame. There were five people shown; four girls and a young boy. Alena smiled at the image. It was obvious who the boy was. The gray eyes were unmistakable. There was one major difference in this picture, however, and that was the smile. Martin Spire was smiling.

The date in the corner was faded, but Alena was able to tell that the picture was at least seven years old. Martin would have been eleven. He was standing with an arm around two girls on each side of him, his smile radiating the innocence most young people seem to possess. The background looked to be a park or carnival of some sort, with bright green trees and blue sky intermittently populated with fluffy white clouds. His gray eyes were no longer dead and lifeless, but sparkling with energy and vigor. Alena noticed that he was still wearing that Navy Blue Loden Coat in the photograph.

The girls, however, were a mystery to Alena. The first, on the far left, was small and frail. She had thin brown hair and striking green eyes. She certainly wasn't much of a looker, that was for sure. Alena grinned. Since when was she

one to judge? She was a nerd, after all. This girl, however,

with her almost hawk-like features and scrawny build, looked

as though a well-timed gust would blow her over. Hanging

around her neck was a silver rosary, with the figure of Jesus

Christ crucified on it.

The second girl was also thin and wiry, but with

stringy blond hair and piercing blue eyes. A pair of wire

framed glasses rested on her nose, and her smile revealed

slightly crooked teeth. A scar was obvious above her right

eye, and it looked like she had split her head open on

something like a desk. She was playing absently with a small

blue mood ring on her hand as the picture was taken.

In the middle of the photograph was Martin, his arms

around the four girls in the picture. To his right, now, was a

girl with long brown hair. It was similar to the first girl's in

style, but it looked silkier and had more shine. Brown eyes

stared out of a pair of oval glasses at whoever it was taking

the picture, but her face radiated happiness. She was

apparently enjoying herself.

The fourth girl was leaning on the third, pinching

Martin's left hand between the third girl's shoulder and her

back. She was smiling at the camera, her straight teeth

stirring a twinge of jealousy in Alena. Her black hair was tied

back in a ponytail that reached down to her waist, and

freckles spotted her nose and cheeks. Vivid blue eyes peeked from below elegant brows, and a plain choker, modeled after ivy, was wrapped around her neck. Her arms were folded across her chest, almost signifying defiance.

Alena smiled. Martin at least had some friends somewhere.

"What are you doing in here?"

Alena jumped a full foot in the air to face Douglas, who had walked in on her. She smiled sheepishly at him, looking at the floor shortly after. "I... er..."

Douglas tossed the book he'd been carrying over onto his bed. "That's Martin's stuff – he's gonna be pissed if he finds you messed with it..."

He walked past Alena and replaced the white cloth over the photograph, hiding the young Martin and his four friends from view. He then turned back to Alena.

"What is it?" she asked before he could speak, pointing to the candle and the photograph. Douglas looked down at it, and Alena could see him thinking. He finally decided to speak.

"A memorial..."

Alena blinked, not quite comprehending what had just been said. "Come again?"

Douglas rubbed the back of his head self-consciously. "Those girls... they're dead. They were Martin's best friends. They died in a fire about six years ago. That's why Martin wasn't eating today. Today... Sunday, that is... is the day they died. It's his way of paying respect."

Alena looked at the covered photograph, remembering how Martin's childlike face radiated energy and life. Her mind compared it to the Martin she knew now. Other than the Loden Coat and gray eyes, she wouldn't recognize the two as the same person. "How... did they die?" she asked carefully.

Douglas looked nervously at the door, as if expecting Satan himself to come bursting through. "Martin... he was working with some Solar Energy... it went wrong. The orphanage they were staying in burned to the ground. Probably about thirty people died. Of course, someone blamed arson... but Martin's been beating himself up over that forever. It was him. As harsh as this sounds, he killed them. I think nothing short of a miracle is going to jar him awake, though..."

Alena was watching in dumbstruck silence. "Martin... he killed them?"

"Unintentionally, of course... more manslaughter than murder, I suppose..." muttered Douglas as he looked at the floor. "Damn... Martin's gonna fricassee my head if he finds out I told you about this..."

Alena smiled at him. "Don't worry," she said, "I won't tell."

"Tell what?" asked an all too familiar voice. Alena
and Douglas turned to the door to see Martin leaning there,
his eyes watching them. "Tell me that you told her about my
past? Douglas... I'm surprised..." his voice was glacially cold,
and it seemed to slice through the room like a sword.

"Er..." Douglas looked ready to wet himself. Martin
was practically glaring through him. Alena realized that this
was inches from coming to blows. She had to do something
before Martin killed Douglas.

"I asked first – he didn't willingly divulge that
information," she said quickly. Martin's steely gaze quickly
turned to her, and Alena had a half-second to wonder if she
had done the right thing before Martin spoke again.

Chapter 12: Zerolytes

"Do I look like I care?" he asked her calmly. He was obviously angered beyond most forms of measure, but his face refused to show it. It remained as impassive as if it were chiseled from stone. His gaze shifted back to Douglas.

"Douglas, when I'm through with you-"

Luckily for the blonde, the threat was unfinished. A ringing noise filled the air, and Martin's left eye gave an involuntary twitch. He swept past both Alena and Douglas over to his desk and picked up a thin cellular phone. He flipped it open with practiced ease and held it to his ear.

"Spire," he snapped into the phone, "What do you want?"

Whoever was on the other end of the line spat something very fast and very loud, causing Martin to wince. Martin turned around to face the other two occupants of the room, leaning on his desk.

"Yeah, we cleaned out the lizards," he said after a moment. He closed his eyes and massaged a spot on his forehead. "I know, I know, but we..." there were a few seconds of silence followed by what sounded to be expletives. Martin sighed in exasperation and hung up, looking up at Douglas and Alena. "I'll deal with you two later," he spat, "We've got some company."

He opened one of the desk drawers, pulling out a few objects. One was a Tzen Rod, the other was a silver gauntlet. He threw the cell phone into his pocket, his face remaining impassive.

"What kind of company?" asked Douglas as he walked over to the armor mannequins that rested along the far wall. He drew off the armor for the chest and right arm, sliding it on as he spoke.

"Zerolytes," said Martin dourly, "They've been seen in the East Caves. We're gonna go kick them out."

Douglas finished applying his armor, fitting his Tzen Rod into a socket on the gauntlet. It pointed away from his arm, aimed wherever he pointed his arm. He put on his coat over the armor, letting his left arm hang at his side rather than going through the sleeve.

Martin, in the meantime, had strapped on the metallic gauntlet over his right hand and pushed his rod into his pocket. He adjusted his coat over the shining glove and turned to Alena.

"Stay here," he explained. "You can wander around Island Twelve, but don't go to any of the other islands. I'll explain in details when I get back."

He walked past her and out the door, Douglas on his heels. Michael and Donna came jogging towards them, both suited similarly. Michael was grinning from ear to ear, showing a thin mouthpiece clenched in his teeth.

"Let's go," he said; his voice only slightly hampered by the device. "I call point!"

Michael led the way out of the bedding chambers, with Martin right behind him and Donna and Douglas chatting in the background about the safety of some of the machinery. Douglas wanted to build a gondola over to the 'mainland shelf' on the side of the cavern, but Donna was hesitant because of the frailty of some of the spare cables, saying they needed all the solid cables they could get.

"Would you both be quiet?" asked Martin as they drew near the gondola that would lead them upwards toward the entrance to the East Caves, "Do you *want* them to hear us? Are you, perhaps, trying to give them a chance to set up one of their defenses?"

Michael snickered, looking over his shoulder at his fellow Tzen. "We're gonna just observe them for a second before attacking; find out what they're doing here and so on."

Martin nodded in response, adjusting his gauntlet absently. "Let's just get in there."

The gondola trundled slowly up the cables, clanking softly in the quiet of the cavern. Douglas and Donna had even grown quiet, their adrenaline flowing in anticipation of the upcoming conflict.

"Donna," said Martin, "You take care of reconnaissance. Douglas and Michael, creep around and get on the enemy's blindside. I'll take the center. I know you wanted point, Michael, but you're more useful on the side."

"Who made you boss?" sneered the one-armed boy, his displeasure at the comment obvious. Donna's hand connected with his head rather harshly, causing him to swear profusely.

"He's boss because he can kill you if you revolt, got it genius?" she bit, nodding at Martin. He nodded his gratitude back, but said nothing.

Michael looked up at Martin, and noticed his 'commander's' grey orbs locked on him. "Hey! Stop staring! What, do I have something on my face?" he spat.

"I was merely looking at you."

"Well look somewhere else!" retorted Michael, turning and looking over the edge of the gondola as it rose higher above the lake surface.

"Then stop whining loud enough to make my ears bleed."

"I'm gonna make much more than your ears bleed, pal!" snarled Michael without turning around. Martin smirked at his comrade from behind. *As if...*

The gondola clanked to a stop, and Martin pushed open the door. He stepped out onto an uneven rock ledge that protruded below the mouth of a cave. He walked forward into the dimly lit cavern, motioning for his teammates to follow him.

After a few minutes of walking, he heard familiar sounds. One was the swishing of silk; he identified it as the black silk robes worn by the Zerolytes he was about to confront.

The second sound he heard was a masculine voice, but it was too low to make out actual words. It sounded more like the rumble of distant thunder. His eyes narrowed; it had been a long time since a Zerolyte had come into the cavern.

He ducked behind a stalagmite, watching the other three Tzen. Donna crept to his right, sneaking up directly behind the enemy. Martin looked around the stalagmite at her, and noticed her holding up four fingers.

Michael and Douglas had crept to his left, crawling up a narrow ledge to position themselves directly above and slightly behind the Zerolytes. Martin took a deep breath and then walked around the stalagmite into full view of the trespassers.

"I'd suggest you keep your voices down," he said calmly. One of the Zerolytes took a step back at his sudden appearance, two drew out their wands, and another merely stood and gaped at him. At least, Martin assumed he was gaping. The hood he wore obscured his face, but he was facing Martin and making no move to attack.

Two fireballs sped toward him, and Martin smiled inwardly. He stepped sideways, watching as the two fireballs smashed into the rocks near him, coating his entry point in smoke. The fourth Zerolyte began to speak, and Martin recognized the masculine voice. He hurtled out of the smoke, leaping forward and smashing his metal gauntlet into the face of the first Zerolyte. There was a shriek and the black-robed figure collapsed to the ground.

"Now!" he cried, throwing himself flat as a fireball sizzled close to him. He quickly pushed himself up into a handstand, bringing both heels down on the skull of the unfortunate Zerolyte in front of him. There was a dull crack, and muffled cursing.

Before the remaining two Zerolytes could react, Martin had grasped one of the Ice Energy Threads that flowed through the area. He held up the gauntlet, praying his theory would hold.

"Akashik!"

A burst of white light exploded from the palm of his gauntlet, solidifying into an arrow made of ice and piercing one of the Zerolytes through the shoulder. The hapless creature flew backwards only to be nailed to the wall.

"Yahoo! Take that bastard!" shrieked Michael as he vaulted into the battle. Martin could see that he had clenched an Earth Energy Thread between his teeth and was preparing to send an incantation toward the fourth and final Zerolyte.

It would have been the fourth, though, if one of the two Martin had knocked down decided to ram a knife through Michael's leg, causing him to stumble and fall.

"Bastard!" shrieked Donna as she readied her wand, "Abornimaz!"

The ground beneath the offending Zerolyte parted, and a gigantic pile of rocks and earth were jolted upwards. The unsuspecting victim was launched into the air high enough to smack against the ceiling with a surprised yell.

Douglas, on the other hand, was readying the deciding factor in the fight. His wand was pointed at the fourth Zerolyte, and the entire rod was vibrating with one of the more powerful energies – Light.

"Lennocma–Oduparon!" he called, and a sphere of light floated into the cavern, hovering in the air like a will-o-wisp. "Everybody get down!"

Martin, Donna, and Michael all threw themselves flat. Martin especially had seen what this technique could do.

"Ahniot!" cried Douglas, and the sphere exploded into thousands of needles, each one ricocheting around the room. They pierced through the flesh of the Zerolytes, killing two of them instantly. The third collapsed to the ground, heaving as his lungs were punctured again and again.

The last Zerolyte saw that the battle was lost. He grasped an Air Energy Thread and began to chant. Michael lunged forward as best he could on his injured leg and grabbed the creature around the neck. Startled, the Zerolyte drew away, leaving Michael with a pendant in his hand. The black-robed figure, however, faded away.

"Damn!" swore Michael as he threw the pendant away. Martin caught it before it belted him in the eye, examining it carefully. It was an ornate silver amulet, emblazoned with the carving of a Monkshood plant. Martin's eyes narrowed.

"It's a warning," he said to Michael as Donna helped him stand upright by looping his arm around his neck. Douglas looked at him oddly, and Michael snorted.

"Yeah – they're gonna hang us with jewelry, right?"

Martin resisted the urge to brain his friend with the amulet. "Monkshood plant; Beware, a deadly foe is near; chivalry."

Donna nodded appreciatively, "Symbolism, huh?"

Martin pocketed the medallion, turning to leave the East Cave. "Let's get back to Island Twelve. Dais'll want to hear about this for sure." They climbed back into the gondola, Michael complaining about his 'damn leg' the whole time.

"Would your leg hurt less if I flung you from the lift?" snapped Martin after a few minutes. Michael stuck his tongue out immaturely, but said nothing the rest of the ride.

Martin's hand remained in his pocket, his thumb rubbing over the smooth metal of the amulet. His mind was a tempest of possibilities. Zerolytes hadn't shown in the cavern for at least two years. Why were they showing up now?

"Donna," he said without turning around, "Why do you think the Zerolytes are here now?"

She looked up from scolding Michael and blinked a few times. "What the hell? How should I know?"

Martin closed his eyes, tilting his head back so that his face was angled toward the roof of the cavern. "I was just asking for a theory."

Donna folded her arms across her chest. "I really have no clue, sorry..."

Martin nodded, still refusing to turn around. When the gondola stopped at Island Twelve, he was the first to leave as he stalked toward Dais' bunker. His eyes were their usual dead gray, but a small spark had awoken within his mind. That spark was called curiosity.

Just what the hell were they doing here, and why were they in the East Caves?

Chapter 13: Two on One

Martin nonchalantly threw the pendant to Dais as he walked past, ignoring the look on his face. He strolled quickly to the bedding chambers and opened the door, only partially surprised to find Alena still there. He nodded at her, his face drawn with exertion.

"I suppose I should take you home," he said after a moment, "You've been down here all night and most of both yesterday and today – you're probably longing for the surface."

She smiled at him, and Martin felt an alien surge of warmth in his chest. He quashed it with his iron will and motioned for her to follow him. "We'll take the escape shaft – it's faster."

Martin led Alena to a large tube that stood against the far wall. They both stepped inside, and Martin pressed a switch on the far wall. They heard hissing beneath their feet, like a bed of snakes, and Alena looked down expectantly.

"This is a steam-driven escape pod," explained Martin as he saw her curious gaze, "It thrusts us upwards into a powerful electromagnetic field where we are drawn up into a cushioned ceiling. This dulls the blow, obviously, and prevents us from dying upon impact. We'll exit the lift after that."

No sooner had he said this, there was a small explosion beneath their feet and Alena felt her stomach lurch horribly as the capsule was launched upwards. There was a sickening moment when it felt like the pod was going to fall back down again before the electromagnetic field kicked in and they were hauled upwards once more.

After impacting the cushioned ceiling, Martin pushed open the door and motioned for her to step outside. Alena blinked in the bright sunlight, turning to face their exit. She was impressed to see it was camouflaged in the base of a large tree, and upon closer inspection it was revealed to be a very clever fake of a dead fir tree.

"Clever exit," she commented as her eyes adjusted to the sunlight. Martin nodded, pointing to the main road that lay not far from them. "Shall I walk you home?"

She looked at him incredulously, "Huh?"

Martin rolled his slate-colored eyes in exasperation. "Is it that hard to believe I would offer to walk you home? I'm antisocial, not evil."

Alena stared at him, smiling at his attempt at humor. Martin arched an eyebrow, still expecting an answer.

"Well," she said after a moment, "I suppose I could *deign* to allow you to accompany me home." The false arrogance in her voice did not get past Martin, who smiled wryly.

"Of course, madam, there might be knaves along the road," he countered, offering her his arm. She linked arms with him and walked off. A few feet down the road Martin realized his position.

Shit!

Here he was, linking arms with a girl he'd known for less than seventy-two hours. His eyes narrowed, remembering the blonde-haired newspaper girl from yesterday. At least he had something to look forward to – tomorrow's school newspaper.

"Alena," he said as they walked across the street toward her home, "We still need to discuss the problem of the photograph that will undoubtedly appear in the paper tomorrow."

She smiled at him, and Martin instantly didn't like the look in her eyes. "What's so bad about it, huh? Come on – nobody'll care."

That's what you think... "Look, I seriously think it would be a good idea to come up with a backup plan-"

"Nobody's gonna hurt me for it," she retorted, her smile faltering slightly. "Look, it was just a way to scare off an annoying person – that's what we'll tell them, alright?"

Martin closed his eyes and nodded, "Alright..." *I hope you know what you're getting into... why the hell do I care anyway?*

He opened his eyes and continued to walk. They passed a park with a cluster of small children climbing in and around the structures built in the patch of woodchips. Martin's eyes hardened. If there was one thing he didn't like, it was people. Children, however, were the seeds of humans in his opinion.

Worthless little... he thought idly as one child tripped and fell, scraping his knee on the sidewalk next to the structures. Martin continued walking, but Alena tugged his arm toward the child.

"Come on, let's help him."

"It will resolve eventually," he deadpanned, "No need to get involved."

They argued for a moment before Martin gave a satisfied smile and pointed at the child. Alena turned to see his mother come over and wipe the scrape clean before applying a bandage. She kissed his knee and ushered him off toward his friends.

"See?" he said coldly, "It was resolved – we didn't need to get involved."

Alena gave him an equally cold gaze but continued walking anyway. Martin sighed, inwardly shrugging. Why would anyone want to get involved in someone else's problems? What good could come of it?

Yeah... especially for someone like me...

Martin walked after Alena, catching up in a few strides. They walked in silence until Alena made an observation that chilled Martin slightly.

"We're being followed, you know."

Martin quickly cast his mind around and settled on two points of energy behind them. *The hell... how did I miss THAT?*

"Damn..." he muttered, flexing his fingers as they hung at his side. "Do you know who they are?"

Alena shook her head, and then pulled his collar down to her level. "Hang on," she said in an audible voice, "You've got something on your ear."

Martin had been with the Tzen long enough to know a ruse when he was confronted with one. He bent down and played along, allowing Alena to blow softly in his ear and make shooing motions. For some bizarre reason, the feeling of her warm breath on his skin made an electric burst fire up his spine. He resisted the oncoming shiver, wondering if it was worth it.

"Well, if it ain't the freak!" said one of the two points of energy as they caught up. Martin looked up with no expression on his face at the two people. Chris' best friends and right-hand men, apparently, wanting revenge for hospitalizing their 'leader'.

"Hello you two," he said calmly. The first boy, Deagan Rivers, sneered at him. He brushed a strand of sickly black hair from his eyes, licking his lips nervously. Martin resisted the urge to smile. At least this person knew it wasn't going to be an easy battle.

The other boy, and Deagan's brother, Jonathan, merely folded his arms and remained silent. His auburn bangs fell to his forehead, giving him a profile almost reminiscent of a Neanderthal.

"What brings you two here," asked Martin genially, staring at the two. The genial tone in his voice didn't quite reach his face, which remained blank. Deagan wasted no time in responding.

"You hurt Chris, you know, and now you're gonna get it!" he spat, clenching his hands into fists. Martin shook his head sadly.

"As much as I admire your loyalty, I am afraid I cannot let that happen. You see, I offered to walk this young lady home."

Jonathan spoke up, his voice low and menacing enough to send a shiver up Alena's spine. "Don't worry," he said, "We'll 'walk' her home." There was no denying that this boy's mind was in the gutter, and that he was undoubtedly going to harass Alena if Martin failed to drive them off.

Where the hell did THAT thought come from?

Martin sighed, taking off his Loden coat and handing it to Alena. "Please hold this," he said, dropping it into her arms. She looked at him in confusion before realizing what was going on.

"Come on, then," said Martin as he stepped forward, "Which one of you wants first hit?"

Deagan charged forward, pulling his arm back to punch Martin square in the face. The raven-haired youth, however, immediately put his analytical mind to the task. The hand was pulled back, meaning it was going to be a straight punch. However, due to the bend at the elbow, the blow would come from his right. As soon as Deagan was within range, Martin raised his arm up, blocking the blow with his forearm.

"Worthless," he said calmly, planting his foot in Deagan's chest and heaving him away. "Learn to punch properly. Keep the fist close in to your body."

Deagan stood up, rage written all over his features. "Bastard! Don't mock me!"

"Mock you? I was trying to help you!" said Martin, feigning hurt. "If you wish to continue your rabid-monkey fighting style, be my guest."

Deagan launched himself at Martin, this time aiming to knee him in the groin. Martin raised his leg, blocking the knee, and quickly grabbed Deagan by the collar and arm, hurling him to the side. "Nope – sorry. Try again!"

Deagan lay on the ground for a moment, his black hair sprawled around him. Jonathan was watching in something akin to surprise and (Martin suspected) at least a sliver of admiration.

"Are you going to get up or give up?" asked Martin without turning to face Deagan. It was then that he saw what Deagan was doing. A Swiss Army knife was in his hand, and he was breathing hard as he rose to his feet.

A knife? This changes the scope of things a bit, doesn't it?

Martin saw the knife coming and twisted his body out of the way, feeling the knife slash one of his belt loops off. He frowned. *Damn! Those are my good pants!*

He tripped Deagan, letting the boy's own momentum turn against him as he sprawled to the ground. Unfortunately, Deagan wasn't done yet, and hurled the knife at Martin.

Martin remembered hearing somewhere that when you throw a knife, it spins vertically. As anyone knows, a vertical (or horizontal) circle has 360 degrees. With a thrown knife, only 90 of them can pierce you.

Today wasn't Martin's lucky day. The blade sank into his shoulder before he could react, and red began seeping into his white dress shirt. His knees gave out from shock as he fell to the ground, his hand involuntarily grasping the wound.

"...ass..." he muttered, forcing himself back up. Deagan was wearing a satisfied smirk on his face. He readied another punch and charged. It was then that Martin saw the value in the throwing of the knife. By disabling his right shoulder, he could no longer guard this punch.

Like hell I'm gonna let him hit me...

Martin threw himself forward, bulling into the other boy's legs and tripping him again. Deagan let loose a stream of colorful words strung together in creative patterns as he collided with the ground.

Jonathan decided it was his turn, and a boot swung out of nowhere to collide with Martin's head. For what felt like the hundredth time, stars blinked in front of his eyes. He rolled to the side before another strike could hit him and forced himself to his knees. He stood up shakily, his knees weak, and he felt the effects of blood loss beginning to take hold.

Not done... not yet...

Chapter 14: Back to Square One

Martin was never, not on pain of death, going to admit how much that knife in his shoulder hurt. It just wasn't going to happen. He wasn't stupid enough to pull the blade out either, which left him in a rather awkward position. The wound was effectively plugged by the blade. Yes it was bleeding, but it wasn't as bad as it probably looked.

"Nice throw," remarked Martin as he had to fight to keep his face from showing how much pain he was in. Three inches of sharpened steel were embedded in his shoulder, and part of him was itching to use it against Deagan. "However, it won't be enough to carry you through this."

Deagan and Jonathan were standing shoulder to shoulder, leering at him. Deagan's face split into a wide smile. "I told you – we could've done this the easy way – without the knife."

Martin allowed himself to frown slightly. "What, you wanted me to say 'sure – beat the living crap out of me and do undoubtedly perverted things to the young lady I'm escorting home'? You're both insane."

The effects of blood loss were becoming more apparent as Martin was having a harder time focusing on his targets. *Damn...*

Before he could react, Jonathan was standing right in front of him. A fist connected with his jaw, knocking him to the floor. The boot came swinging at him again, this time catching him squarely in the chest. He was actually lifted into the air, coming back down to roll slightly on the ground. A cough tore its way from Martin's lungs, and a slight coppery taste filled his mouth. Blood.

"You must love the freak a lot if you're willing to wear the same cheap trench coats he does," Deagan said. Even though Martin wasn't facing him, he knew he was talking to Alena.

Bastard! Get away from her!

Martin forced himself up on all fours, only to be kicked in the stomach. The wind left his lungs, and he collapsed again. It was horribly uncomfortable, to say the least, seeing as his right shoulder was propped up by the knife embedded in it.

He gathered all his strength and rolled sideways, pushing himself to his feet as he did. He stood in front of Jonathan, his legs spread apart for balance as his right arm hung limply down in front of him. It was worthless to move it and risk causing more damage with that damn blade stuck in there.

Jonathan looked at him in surprise. "I have to hand it to you," he said after a moment, "You've got a lot of guts to keep standing up."

Martin nodded at him, "And you've got a nice kick. Now – we have a fight to finish."

Jonathan barreled forward, and Martin instantly recognized the stance. The only reason someone would run with their legs splaying out to the side was to deliver a running roundhouse kick.

I highly doubt he has the training for that, but it looks like he's gonna try.

Martin stepped to the side as Jonathan drew close, slamming his left elbow down on his back. Jonathan collapsed to the ground and slid a little bit, facedown in the dirt.

"Look, I know you're pissed..." Deagan was saying as he kept stepping closer to Alena. She suddenly noticed Martin standing behind him.

"Pissed is an understatement," she said, "Try the epitome of enraged!"

Deagan sensed something was wrong and turned around to find himself facing exactly what had been described. "Hello," snarled Martin, driving his knee into Deagan's groin and causing him to emit a very shrill sound as he collapsed to the ground.

Martin made no move as Jonathan walked over and began dragging his brother away. The look on his face could probably have killed, but he knew when to give up. Deagan was still clutching his livelihood and moaning curses and insults.

Martin's head swam, and it was as if someone opened the floodgates in his mind. The pain of the knife in his shoulder seemed to intensify tenfold. He buckled to his knees, and he knew he had to do something before he fell unconscious.

"Alena!" he gasped, reaching into his pocket, "Call... Terra..." he handed her his cell phone, his eyes beginning to droop. "Explain..." his head hit the ground as his body succumbed to blood loss.

Alena wasted no time in dialing opening his contacts list and finding Terra. She quickly pressed the call button and held the phone to her ear. After two rings, Terra answered.

"Yeah?" she muttered, her voice bland. Alena almost shrieked into the phone what the problem was, but managed to retain some degree of self control.

"Martin's been stabbed," she said, "We're on one of the side roads outside the base... we just passed a playground of sorts, if it's any help."

There was silence on the other end before Terra responded. "En route."

Alena paced back and forth, wondering if she should call the police and report armed assault. The problem being the chain of events. Why had they attacked Martin? He had attacked their friend. If she explained that, she would have to explain the Air Incantation he had used. *That* would go over really well.

Terra showed up a few moments later with a medical kit. She sighed when she saw Martin lying on the ground.

Alena had rolled him over so that the knife wouldn't be worked even deeper, if that was possible.

"Alright," said Terra calmly. She kneeled down next to Martin and slipped a pair of cold fingers against his throat. When his pulse was confirmed as weak but present, Terra asked Alena's help to drag him back to the base. The only problem was that they would be near the main road, and dragging a comatose figure would look suspicious.

"Alright..." sighed Terra, massaging her forehead. Alena inwardly wondered if it was some kind of Tzen thing. It seemed like they dealt with a lot of stress, and thus wound up massaging their temples regularly.

"We'll have to drag him around the back way," muttered Terra after a moment. Alena raised an eyebrow in curiosity. "Back way?"

Terra sat back on her feet, looking down at Martin with something akin to worry. "There's an old quarry in the woods about ten minutes from here," she explained. "One of the tunnels in it connects to The Hall."

Alena grasped Martin by his shoulders, slinging his Loden Coat across his stomach so she wouldn't have to carry it. Terra grasped his ankles and heaved him into the air. Before anyone could see them, they quickly dove deeper into the woods, carrying their unconscious friend with them.

***

The quarry was, indeed, abandoned. There were still pieces of broken machinery strewn about, and it looked like someone had set off a large explosive in the immediate vicinity. An old bulldozer was flipped onto its roof, the treads torn completely off. Alena's eyes widened, and she made a mental note to come back and examine the area closer later.

Terra, in the meantime, was having a slight dilemma. She had let down Martin's ankles and was standing in the middle of the quarry scratching her head. Three pathways were in front of her, and it didn't take a genius to figure out that she had forgotten which one was correct.

"Damn..." she snarled, kicking at a rock in frustration, "Which one was it?"

She looked back at Martin with another look of slight worry in her eyes. Martin had stopped bleeding, but that knife in the wound wasn't going to be good for him in the long run. She looked back at the three tunnels, racking her brain for an answer.

"Alena!" The girl in question ran over, looking at the three tunnels with apprehension. Terra turned to her with her usual mask of indifference in place. "Pick one, and hurry."

Alena looked at the tunnels and selected the far left one. Terra walked back over to Martin and hoisted him by the ankles again. Alena jogged over and hefted him up by the armpits again.

"Hey Terra..." she asked as they walked toward the opening they'd chosen. The medic made a sound showing she was listening. Alena took a deep breath and continued. "Why doesn't Martin like anyone?"

Terra made a sound that might (by a stretch) be considered a chuckle. "Martin has never liked anyone," she explained. "He forced himself into a façade to punish himself for what happened in the orphanage seven years ago... I know you know about that... and now he's numb to everything around him. I, personally, think he likes it that way."

Alena looked down at Martin, saying nothing. "That's stupid... it wasn't his fault, was it?"

Terra made that aggravating sound again. "Yeah it was. He was the one messing with Fire and Solar Threads. He was the one who tried to use a discarded incantation in the hopes of making it work. He was the one who set the orphanage on fire. He was the one who killed thirty plus innocent people."

Alena frowned at Terra's back. "But it was an accident!"

Again with the sound, "Try explaining that to him. Do you realize how it looks? He experiments with something that fascinates him. When Martin is fascinated, nothing should get in his way. Anyway, he's fascinated, and suddenly his project kills all those people. That, my friend, was his fault."

Alena looked back to Martin and then up at Terra. "But-"

"No buts," snapped Terra. This was one of the few times Terra had openly shown any kind of emotion other than apathy. She swiveled her head around to look at Alena as they walked down the dark tunnel. "Guess what? One of my friends died in that explosion! Could you forgive someone who had done that to your friends?"

Before any more words could be exchanged, the tunnel they were in opened into a familiar blue cavern. Terra sighed and shook her head. "Nice choosing," she said dryly as they walked onto one of the gondolas. She pulled the start lever, allowing the small contraption to trundle down into the cavern. When it reached the end, Terra stepped off and hauled Martin's body into the medical bay.

"Sorry," she said to Alena as they entered, "I shouldn't have snapped at you…"

Alena waved it off, but kept the information she'd learned today filed in her mind for future reference. A small part of her wondered if she should tell Martin when he woke up, but the rest of her decided against it. He didn't need to know something that would hurt him – not unless it was necessary.

She sighed, and before she knew what she was doing, she found herself massaging her temples. She allowed herself a small smile. *Looks like I'm one of the family now…*

She looked back at Martin before turning to Terra. "I'm gonna head home, alright? That's where I was heading when Martin was attacked."

Terra nodded, turning to her medical table and snapping on a pair of rubber gloves. "I'll take care of him, don't worry," she said calmly.

Alena nodded, leaving the medical bay. Terra, in the meantime, turned back to Martin's body. With her gloves in place, she quickly drew the knife out of Martin's shoulder. The wound began to bleed again, and she quickly pressed a gauze pad over the wound. Luckily, while the wound was deep, it wasn't large. She debated on whether or not to use stitches, but quickly decided against it and grasped an Earth Energy Thread. She placed her hand on Martin's shoulder, using the gravitational energy of the incantation to draw the wound together again.

When she was finished, she took a moment to admire her handiwork. Apart form the disgusting bloodstain on his nice shirt, Martin looked as good as new. She unbuttoned the shirt, taking it off and wrapping the wound in medical tape in case he tore it open again. With a last backward glance, Terra left the medical bay, tossing her gloves into a wastebasket near the door.

Chapter 15: Changing

Martin's eyes flickered open, taking in his surroundings. He was remarkably calm for someone who had just been stabbed and dragged halfway across his hometown of Steilacoom. He took a quick look around, slowly moving his head so as not to make himself dizzy. *Good, I'm back at The Hall.*

He pushed himself up into a sitting position, closing his eyes but not sleeping. He turned his gaze inward, focusing on himself for a period of quiet meditation before he got up. Terra was bound to be around somewhere, and once he was released it was hard to find quiet anywhere in The Hall.

His mind touched on the past few days. For some bizarre reason, he felt an extremely alien surge of happiness when he thought of them. The past three days were the happiest he'd been in a long time. Someone, namely Alena, wasn't scared to the point of urinating herself when she saw him. He wondered if that would hold true if she saw what he was truly capable of.

The rest of the Tzen knew it. Heck, even Chris knew it. Chris, however, couldn't tell anyone because they'd commit him to a mental asylum as soon as he began speaking. It wasn't something easily believed without having seen or experienced it. Even then it was still hard to come to terms with.

Martin sighed, his closed eyes giving a slight twitch. Alena would uncover the truth sooner or later. Even in his catatonic state he had heard parts of the conversation between her and Terra. What she didn't know was the reason he punished himself wasn't the crime, it was his own reaction, or lack thereof.

He wished he could feel things like remorse. Perhaps it would have helped the healing process after that accident. An accident that should have claimed his life but instead only warped his body chemistry beyond recognition, hence the transformation in the tunnel a day and a half ago. He frowned, but still didn't open his eyes.

People thought he was stupid because he didn't talk. When he had first heard that rumor, he had wanted to laugh. The problem, however, was that Martin had almost never laughed in his life. He guessed he either couldn't or didn't know how. No, he was highly intelligent, and far from stupid. The prime reason he didn't speak, however, was because he spent most of his time in his own mind. He indulged in quiet introspection and thought, fueling himself off of the machinations of his mind.

The other reasons he rarely spoke included the fact that he never said anything unless it was imperative to the situation or extremely important. Jokes, humor, and the like were lost on him, so people naturally assumed he was stupid and didn't get them. In reality, although it seemed to be lost

on him, Martin understood every word. Some things,
however, just didn't register as funny.

Prime example, he once had noticed, was the long-
standing joke of kicking a male in the groin. It was brutally
effective in a fight, yes, but not something to be made a joke
of by any means. People didn't make jokes about shooting
people, did they? And why mock someone for being over or
underweight? The golden middle was difficult to attain
anyway.

The door to the medical bay opened, and Martin
opened his eyes to see Terra walk in. She looked up at him,
her face barely registering the fact that he existed.

"It's good to see you're awake," she said, but her
voice didn't sound at all happy by the fact. Quite the opposite,
in fact, but it didn't bother Martin.

Martin had known for a long time that Terra held a
grudge against him, but didn't exactly know why. He always
shrugged it off, ignoring it like he did the rest of the world.
After subconsciously eavesdropping on the conversation
yesterday, however, he understood a bit more about his
apathetic teammate.

"May I leave?" he asked quietly, gingerly testing his
shoulder. It stung slightly, and felt a bit stiff, but other than
that seemed fine. Terra nodded, and he hopped off the bed,
noticing his lack of shirt. He mentally shrugged it off and
walked back to his bedding chamber to retrieve a new one.

He walked into his bedroom and drew out one of his white dress shirts. He sighed, pushing his arms through the sleeves and beginning to button it up. Did Deagan know how expensive these things were? It helped that the Tzen all shared a funding pool, but it was still no excuse. It was one of the reasons the Tzen didn't use electricity – it would cost too much. Besides, why risk being traced and discovered when a Lightning Energy Thread could produce the same results and offered much more control?

He finished buttoning the shirt up and opened his closet, eyeing the six Loden Coats that hung inside. He selected one that was almost identical to his old one, drawing it quickly around his shoulders. The air in The Hall could get rather chilly, he reasoned, and he was going to take a walk.

He exited the bedding chamber, his unbuttoned coat swishing behind him. He let his hands fall to his side, checking for the Tzen Rod. It was there, thankfully. Martin had been willing to bet it would have fallen out of his pocket during the fight with Deagan. Miraculously, even after being dragged all that way, it was still with him.

He got on the gondola, pushing the lever into position and beginning to move. Derrick, while he ran the gondola, was rarely around to do it. It was more a position of convenience. He was their frontline strategist as well, and spent a lot of time with Dais planning fortifications for the lower levels. Martin gave an involuntary shudder.

The last time he'd seen the lower levels, he'd had nightmares for a week. It was enough to scare even him. He cast a furtive glance to the north wall of the cavern. There, nestled among the rocks, was the entrance to the lower levels, as well as the 'Mainland Shelf' of The Hall – a place that had yet to be seen. It was another area shrouded in mystery.

Screw that... this whole cavern is shrouded in mystery. Who built it? Why did they build so elaborately, with ivory, marble and crystal? Also... what happened to them?

Martin pushed these thoughts into his head as he crossed the expanse of land known as Island Nine. He nodded a quiet greeting at a redheaded boy who was practicing some kind of karate or judo on a training dummy. The boy nodded back before continuing to beat the stuffing out of the humanoid burlap sack.

Loden coat swishing behind him, Martin boarded the next gondola, pulling the lever and trundling toward Island Six.

The islands were arranged in four 'spokes' radiating from the Mainland Shelf. In the first spoke were islands One, Four, Seven and Ten. Spoke Two consisted of Islands Two, Five, Eight and Eleven. The third and final spoke consisted of Islands Three, Six, Nine and Twelve. The main pathways were what characterized the spokes, but multiple smaller pathways connected the islands to each other.

130

He passed Sasaki Miyagi, a Japanese boy who had once been on Island Twelve before moving to Island Six after he moved above ground as well. It turned out that the chute that led to Island Six was closer to where he was moving to so he began taking that chute instead. Eventually, he was moved into the sleeping chambers and given 'citizenship' there.

"Hey Martin!" he called cheerfully, "Long time no... hey... what's wrong with your eyes?"

Martin regarded him coolly for a moment. "Why? What is it?"

Sasaki hauled him into the bedding chambers of Island Six, showing him a mirror that hung on the back of his door. Martin leaned forward, examined his eyes, and then stood back up.

"No idea. This is the first time I'm seeing them like this."

Martin's eyes had changed colors, and he didn't like it. The gray color he was used to seemed vacant. Instead of the familiar slate color, they were now orange. As if that wasn't bad enough, the tangerine irises were flecked with a red color identical to blood. He blinked a few times and then looked in the mirror again. They were still there.

Did Terra put contacts in my eyes while I was out?

He rubbed his eyes, checking for contact lenses. None were present, leaving him stumped.

"Thanks for telling me;" he muttered to Sasaki, "I'll go see Terra about them."

Grumbling about his walk being cut short, he walked back to the gondola and rode it to Island Nine. Luckily, he didn't need to go much further as he found Terra conversing with the 'medic' of Island Nine. They were deeply involved in a discussion about bones and bone density when Martin approached.

"Terra," he asked when she looked up, "Can you take a look at my eyes?"

Martin was glad Terra had one of those no-questions-asked policies unless it was obviously necessary. She nodded, motioning him over to a position where the light was brighter. He complied, standing with the abominable blue light shining directly in his face. His pupils shrank until they felt like they were almost closed.

"What the heck did you do to yourself?" she asked after a moment. Martin looked at her in surprise, although his face was carefully trained to conceal it. "What do you mean?"

Terra had her hands on her hips, eyeing him warily. She looked around for a moment before calling back to the other medic. "Hey Kat, get over here and look at this!"

Martin felt somewhat irked at the fact that she was ignoring his question, not to mention treating him like an attraction at a carnival, but there was obviously wisdom in asking a second opinion.

"Coming!" Catherine Hawkins was one of the better medics in The Hall. In Martin's opinion, she was second only to Terra. She jogged up, pushing a strand of black hair behind her ear as she leaned in to look at Martin's eyes. As soon as she saw the color she recoiled.

"What the hell?" she asked, looking from Terra's serious expression to Martin's confused visage.

Terra shrugged. "I guess now would be a good time to have a real doctor down here. We're good for fixing cuts and breaks, but *this*..." her sentence trailed off as she looked at Martin. He was tapping his foot in irritation. "So you're saying you have no idea what this is?" he asked after a moment, pointing to his eyes, "And for all I know it could kill me tomorrow?"

Terra looked at him with her usual apathetic aura in place, while Kat snorted at him. "I doubt it will kill you, but you'd better be cautious. Neither of us knows what that is, but..."

Both Terra and Martin waited for her to continue. After a moment, she looked up at them both. "Well... they look almost familiar, like I've seen them before. I'm gonna go check the Steilacoom Library for info, okay? I'll get back to you."

Content with the fact that something was, at the very least, getting done, Martin decided to resume his interrupted walk. More than anything, Martin loved to take random strolls around The Hall. It helped clear his mind. In light of both the Zerolyte attack and now the changing of his eyes, he needed all the clarity he could get.

Martin also loved the air in The Hall, he reasoned as he breathed deep. It carried the scent of the standing water below, along with the earthy smell of the walls. The scent also carried something else. It was... Martin cast his mind around for the correct word before deciding on 'age'. Something about the cavern had the aged smell like an attic. Attics, to Martin, meant those undiscovered generational treasures hidden away by grandparents who saw it as no more than clutter. A small smile flitted across Martin's face. He was a fine one to talk – his grandparents had died before he was born.

That wasn't the point, however. The point, Martin reminded himself, was that he loved the air in the cavern and was going to 'his spot' to do a bit of thinking. It was one of the only other places outside the medical ward he could find some quiet.

Chapter 16: School

Martin was at his favorite thinking place. On Island One was a precipice that had once been connected to the Mainland Shelf via a bridge. The expanse was now void of any means of transport, the bridge having long since collapsed into the water below. Martin was currently sitting on the hard stone, his legs hanging off the edge to dangle freely in the empty air.

His gaze was on the various buildings that sat comfortably on the other side. To him, it was almost like they were mocking him. He could practically hear the voices of the stones on the other side, saying 'we're over here and you're over there' in that mocking, singsong voice he envisioned them to have.

He sighed, shaking his head. Here he was personifying rocks when he was supposed to be trying to think of a way to get to the other side. It was a puzzle that had yet to be solved, and Martin wanted to be the one to solve it. He hated, *hated*, it when something remained unsolved. It was like one of those itches. The kind that after twisting yourself in all directions you realize there's no way to reach.

The first thought he'd had was to swim across. However, on their expedition down there, they'd caught sight of several enormous eels that looked rather fierce. Terra had advised them *not* to take a dip in the water, and the team had heartily agreed. Not to mention that the water was both stagnant and freezing cold.

Martin leaned forward slightly, resting his elbows on his knees. He *was* going to get to that ledge over there if it killed him. He snorted, something he'd been doing a lot of lately, and stood up. Perhaps he could convince Michael and Donna to give up a cable or two.

He stood up to leave when his eye caught movement. His eyes widened in shock. Of all the places movement could be, on the Mainland Ledge shouldn't be one of them.

He dashed down onto the Island One plaza and told the first person he saw, telling them to spread the word. He then bolted back to Island Twelve as fast as he could to report to Dais. By the time he got there, he was barely able to gasp out the news.

Dais regarded his pupil thoughtfully for a moment before responding. "It is possible that there is another chute leading down onto the Mainland Ledge," he said at length, "But it would be most prudent to find a way over to there from below ground."

Douglas, who had been in Dais' office when Martin had burst in, nodded solemnly. "I was talking to Donna about that when we went to hunt those Zerolytes," he said, "Donna said we didn't have enough secure cables to make it, though, as we need all we can for-"

Dais rounded on him quickly, "So we have the cables?" he asked excitedly, "Go tell Donna and Michael that someone's been spotted on the Mainland Ledge and that it is top priority that we get over there and investigate."

Douglas nodded, "Pardon my impudence, but why wasn't it top priority to explore over there?"

Dais leaned back in his chair, folding his arms behind his head, "As long as there was no threat from that front, it was considered secure. A hasty assumption, I know, but we made that choice when we first moved in here. Later, as we worked on fixing things up, we ran out of resources. At least, I thought we had... but if Michael and Donna actually have the cables, we can get over there."

Martin nodded, turning to leave. He was stopped by Douglas' hand on his shoulder. "What's with the eyes?"

Martin cast a furtive glance at him before responding. "Kat of Island Nine is checking on it as we speak."

Douglas looked at him oddly for a moment before removing his hand. Martin decided it was time to go lie down. His body was tired from sprinting all the way from Island One, and he needed his strength tomorrow. Tomorrow was Monday – and Martin Spire hated Mondays.

***

His eyes flickered open the next day, staring at the ceiling above him. He sighed, forcing himself out of bed and onto the carpeted floor. He quickly drew on his usual black pants and white shirt before slipping his bare feet into some dark dress socks. The Loden Coat was placed around his shoulders, and he jammed his feet into his dress shoes. He grabbed for the briefcase as he left the room, making sure to turn to lock the door behind him.

The chute he took from The Hall put him at about a fifteen minute walk from the High School. Martin, however, usually made it in ten or twelve. He walked calmly across the main road, passing the gas station where most of the Seniors smoked after school and walked down the narrow, tree-lined path that led to his school.

The grayish building loomed in an ocean of darker gray parking lots. The building was built similar to a federal penitentiary. It had a large, boxy appearance to it and seemed to squat over the parking lots like some kind of monster. The double doors below were propped open, much like a mouth, beckoning him to come inside.

Pushing the mental image of a glowering beast to the side, he stepped inside. The air conditioned hallways were colder than usual, and the area seemed almost lifeless. His eyes narrowed. *Where are all the students?*

He checked his watch. He was five minutes early, but there were usually a few students here ahead of him. He walked over to the bulletin board in the commons area and ran a thin finger down the events posted there.

Aha... there's an assembly in the gym today...

He settled for lurking outside the gymnasium rather than going inside. It never failed to make his stomach turn when he was amongst so many people. If Martin hated anything, it was people in general. He put his briefcase on the ground next to him, seating himself comfortably on a tabletop while waiting for the assembly to end.

Unfortunately, it didn't end for another hour. Martin was bored out of his mind by the first twenty minutes of waiting and discovered that making entries in his digital journal did little or nothing to alleviate the boredom. He sighed, closing his laptop and stowing it back in the briefcase. He snapped the lid shut, twirling the golden dials to seal it tightly.

Man... I hate this place...

Martin looked around the tiny area outside the gym. This entire school, in his opinion, was a monument to the stupidity he dealt with every day. People behaved one way and spoke another – that was contradiction. They claimed to be in love, when in reality they were merely lusting after someone. That or they were lusting after more than one person and thought it made them 'cool'.

Several times, Martin had been told he was a geek, nerd, misfit, and a variety of other things. He smirked as he pushed his hands into his coat pockets. Did they really think such infantile behavior bothered him? He closed his eyes, wondering briefly if they were still orange. *Undoubtedly...*

His eyes suddenly flickered open. He was in a school – a school with six-hundred plus students. Of those six-hundred, two were friendly (himself and Alena) while the rest were either neutral or enemy 'units'. How would they react to the change in his eyes?

Probably think they're contact lenses...

Deciding to take the matter in stride, he got up and decided now was as good a time as any to go use the bathroom. Making sure to take his briefcase with him, he pushed open the swinging door and stepped inside, locking it behind him. After taking care of what needed to be taken care of, Martin exited the bathroom to find most of the students filing out of the gymnasium already. *I thought I was early... I guess the assembly started earlier than school normally would...*

He spotted a Loden Coat as it passed him, and his face flew to the wearer. Alena. So she was here, dressed in the coat? She was asking for it now. If anyone saw her like that...

"It's not healthy to emulate freaks, Alena," said a voice from up ahead. Martin's orange eyes flickered to the speaker, recognizing Deagan. Jonathan wasn't present at the moment, and Martin was glad for that. He didn't really fancy another two-versus-one battle.

"It isn't any of your concern how she dresses," he said, walking forward in step with Alena. Deagan shot him a surprised look, evidently surprised that he wasn't in the hospital from the stab wound, but quickly recovered. He muttered something that sounded like 'monster' before Martin reached him.

"Well, I'd be defensive of my girlfriend too, seeing as it's in the School Paper," he leered, holding out the yellow-colored packet of papers to Martin. He snatched it away, looking at the photo on the front page. A picture of Alena and himself in what seemed to be a very passionate kiss was centered on the page, the caption below reading "Beauty and the Beast" in big bold letters.

"Catchy title," drawled Martin as he tossed the paper to the side. He tried his hardest to ignore the fact that students were filing past him on his left and right. He was effectively circled by them. If Deagan was to strike him now, they would merely circle them literally and begin the usual chant of "Fight, Fight!"

Deagan was grinning like a fool at Martin's expression, which looked as though he'd swallowed a quart of lemon juice. Alena had stopped to witness the exchange, standing behind Martin's right shoulder. Deagan peered at her for a moment before giving her a very suggestive smile.

"Did he personally 'take your measurements'?" he asked with a grin. Martin's eyes burned for a moment. "That's enough!" Martin positioned himself directly between Deagan and Alena. "I gave her the coat yesterday because she was cold. You don't honestly think I own only one, do you?"

Deagan was momentarily shaken off balance by the fact that Martin's nose was inches from his own. It suddenly dawned on him how intimidating he actually was – especially up close.

"I didn't think you could afford more than one cheap trench-coat-" he started, but was cut off by Martin's hand closing around his throat and pushing him against one of the soda machines.

"Deagan," he said, his voice dripping false sweetness, "This is a Loden Coat. On average, they cost between nine-hundred and two-thousand dollars... hardly a cheap trench-coat... and I think that makes it worth more than your measly life!"

Deagan's eyes bugged out from his head, his hands feebly clawing at Martin's arm. Martin gave him a distasteful look and released him, walking away with his coat swishing behind him. Deagan sat on the floor for a moment before standing up. A Freshman next to him snickered.

"Heh, he got you good, didn't he?" laughed the boy, covering his mouth with his hand. Deagan, his pride and ego shot to pieces, retreated to his first class.

Alena, meanwhile, was walking next to Martin. Her eyes were downcast, and it was several minutes before she spoke.

"You didn't need to do that..." she said quietly. Martin looked at her for a moment before answering.

"A few years ago, I wouldn't have," he said calmly. He then turned his gaze back to watching where he was going. He had a bad habit of losing himself in thought and ending up in all sorts of places. It wasn't particularly unpleasant, other than the fact that it made him late for classes.

Sighing, Alena took the stairs leading up to the second floor while Martin walked ahead to his reading corner in the cafeteria. He propped his feet up on the dilapidated desk and pulled out his book, flipping to the bookmarked page, and beginning to read.

Chapter 17: MIA

It was almost lunchtime when Martin's cell rang. Sighing, he put away his book and pulled it from his coat. He checked the caller I.D., frowning slightly. Dais. The other Tzen knew well enough not to bother him unless it was necessary. He flipped open the phone and held it to his ear.

"Spire, and make it quick," he snapped, leaning back in the chair.

"Martin? Oh good, I was afraid you wouldn't answer. Listen, Alena's energy signature just winked off. Is she alright?" asked the man on the other end of the line. Martin's eyes narrows.

"What do you mean?" he said quietly, "Someone's energy doesn't just wink off."

Dais sighed on the other end of the line, "Just keep an eye out for her at lunch. That's coming up in about fifteen minutes, right? Keep a sharp lookout for her."

Martin affirmed the request and snapped the phone shut. He leaned back to continue reading but was interrupted by the intercom speaker. His ears perked up at the sound of a familiar name.

"Alena Steward, please come to the main office. Alena Steward..." Martin's eyes flickered up to the stairs Alena had ascended, waiting for her to come down. Two minutes passed. Five. Martin's eyes began to narrow into slits. Something didn't feel right.

"Alena Steward, please come to the main office. Alena Steward..." the announcement repeated itself at the seven minute mark. Martin threw his gear together and ascended the stairs two at a time. The hairs on the back of his neck were standing erect – and he'd long since learned to trust them.

He reached the top of the stairs and almost ran over Travis. He skirted around the guard before questions could be asked and moved quickly down the hallways. He wasn't allowed to run, per se, but he was allowed to walk as quickly as possible. He reached the center of the hallway and quickly cast his mind around.

Come on, Alena, come on...

Nothing. There wasn't a trace of her familiar, warm energy anywhere on the upper floor. He doubled back, descending the stairs in leaps and bounds until he reached the lower floor. Again, he cast his mind around only to come up empty handed. He frowned.

Two things could cause an energy signal to vanish: either the person's death or the person leaving the immediate area. Martin figured he'd have known if Alena had met an untimely death, so he figured she had left.

But why? Why would she leave campus in the middle of a school day? The office doesn't know about it, or they wouldn't be paging her...

He flicked open his cell phone again and dialed Dais' number, retreating into the Men's Bathroom as the dial tone rang in his ear. Finally, Dais picked up the phone with an irritated sound.

"She's not here," said Martin, "Her energy signature is not in the building – not even a trace of it. It's like she was never here."

Dais swore into the phone, "I'll get Jason on it A.S.A.P. – you know him, he's bound to know something – and if he doesn't he'll try to figure it out."

The line went dead, and Martin quickly pocketed the device before he could be caught. Cell phones were supposed to be prohibited at school, but just because it was forbidden didn't stop Martin from bringing his. Besides, if people knew what he was capable of, they wouldn't interfere with him in the first place.

Alena... where are you... he thought anxiously. He tapped his foot on the cool marble tile in the bathroom before his old self took over. *Why the hell do I care in the first place? She's just an acquaintance – even if she IS a fellow Tzen.*

Martin left the bathroom, discreetly signing himself out at the front counter before anyone could ask questions. He jotted down his reason for leaving as a dental appointment before exiting the building as fast as he could. He practically ran all the way to the rock that covered the Twelfth Chute before lifting it with Air Energy and descending the ladder.

The rock dropped loudly into place, causing him to lose his grip and fall a few rungs before he regained his grip. His knee banged harshly on the metal, eliciting a curse from the normally stoic boy. A throbbing pain began to work its way up his leg, but since it wasn't broken he continued to climb down.

As fast as he could he made his way to Dais' chambers, pounding thrice on the door and not waiting for a response. Dais looked up in surprise, having been in the middle of interrogating Jason.

"What do we know?" he asked, walking in as though this was his chamber and not Dais'. "What happened to her?" Dais cast him a withering look that was on par to some that Martin doled out, but remained silent. Jason, however, took the initiative.

"We do know that there were high energy levels recorded in the area twenty minutes before her disappearance. Around the time the energy winked out, these energy levels climaxed and then began to abate. Around five minutes later, the energy was gone altogether, including residue."

Martin massaged his temples. Finding lost Tzen was easy, he'd done it several times. Finding lost Tzen with no energy to trace was not as easy, and had to be done the old-fashioned way. "So we can infer that whatever caused the energy caused her to disappear too?"

"When'd you grow a brain?" asked Dais snidely, "Yeah, that's about it. We don't know what caused any of this yet, but we've got Terra looking at the energy particle patterns to see if we can figure out what kind of energy it was."

Martin nodded curtly, deciding to ignore the jab placed at the beginning of the statement. He turned around to leave, but someone spoke.

"Just because you're worried about her doesn't give you the excuse to do something stupid, Martin." Surprisingly, it was not Dais, but Jason who had spoken. Martin turned and regarded him with his burning eyes. "I know. I wasn't planning on it."

He turned and practically flew down to the medical bay where Terra was undoubtedly working. He almost skidded into the door before pounding on it with all his might. Terra opened the door after a moment, allowing him in. He opened his mouth to speak, but she beat him to it.

"The energy patterns that appeared are most unusual," she said, gesturing toward several printouts and computer monitors, "They behaved almost like 'wild' energy, rather than the restrained elemental energy we're used to. I'm going to hazard a guess and say it has to do with the

Zerolytes, but I'm not sure. Last time I checked, they were working on harnessing natural energy."

Martin looked at a printout comparing natural energy to this new energy. Remarkably, only two points on the graph matched. The new energy was of a much higher density, and inevitably power, than the other. He frowned.

"This reeks of something familiar..." he muttered as he began to leaf through the various printouts, occasionally checking them with data on the screens. Terra retreated to her workspace and began working on an attempted synthesis of the new energy. Perhaps it would help them track it down.

"Is there any chance Alena's energy was converted into some other kind of energy?" asked Martin without looking up. Terra shook her head firmly. "That kind of transformation would pretty much be the end to all of us, if the Zerolytes did, indeed, do this. If they did, they could convert a Fire Thread into an Ice Thread – and that's never good. It could upset the global balance."

Martin was not a staunch believer in a God of any kind, but found himself offering a quick prayer to whatever deities were left that this wasn't the cause. He continued rifling through the various papers; checking and re-checking the data with what was on the computer screens. Everything matched – but that was the problem. What was being inferred here was impossible.

"Terra..." he said after about an hour. He had rolled over a chair and was sitting in it, his face buried in his hands, "...this isn't making any sense!"

Terra indulged in a sigh before responding. "I know, Martin, but we have to try! If the Zerolytes are behind this..."

Martin stood up, attempting to remain calm. He walked over to the door, pushing it open. For the second time, someone made an out of character comment – this time Terra.

"If I didn't know better, I'd say you like her, Martin."

Martin's face contorted into his infamous glare as he looked at the door. "I do not!" he said firmly, walking out the door. Terra sighed, returning to her energy synthesis.

Martin, meanwhile, was trying to rid himself of the seed Terra had just planted in his brain. *Me? Like anyone? Heh... that's a real laugh!*

He looked up at the roof of The Hall, his golden eyes narrowing. *I am heartless. I am not meant to indulge in such things as 'liking' someone – period.*

He continued walking, almost running over Jason as he walked toward the escape chute. His mind was operating at high speeds, attempting to formulate a way to locate Alena without an energy trace. He stepped inside the chute, closing his eyes as he waited for the steam pressure below to reach the critical point.

High-density natural energy... why does that ring such a bell... it's so familiar it's frightening...

A frown creased his normally calm features. He had been working on something like that a long time ago. His eyes snapped open as he remembered. That was the project he'd been working on when the orphanage had burned. If the Zerolytes were behind this, how dare they disgrace the memory of the orphanage by reawakening that cursed project?

And just who were the Zerolytes anyway? They'd appeared about four years ago, wielding similar energy to the Tzen. Martin had assumed they were fellow energy manipulators, but had been quickly shot down as he realized that the energy they wielded was of a different wavelength, and most often fused with another type of energy.

If we could figure out how to do that... we'd be next to invincible.

The pod he was in shot upwards toward the surface, lurching as the electromagnetic field caught the metal capsule. Martin sighed heavily as he continued to rocket upwards. There were three choices to find Alena now. The first was waiting for a ransom note of some kind, but that was never guaranteed. If she had been kidnapped for another reason other than ransom...

The second choice was to comb every inch of the surface and all of the underground tunnels for any trace of

Zerolyte activity or Alena herself. That, even, wasn't guaranteed to turn up results. It had been proven multiple times that those black-robed manipulators were good at hiding their tracks.

The third and final option was Martin himself. If he used his modified body to the extreme levels, it was possible he *might* pick up energy levels that were too low for even machines to detect. Unfortunately, to do that, he would need to give up control to the so-called beast lurking within him. The same beast, actually, that had saved Alena's life in the caverns a few days ago.

Another variable Martin wasn't keen on dealing with was Alena's parents. They would be returning from Panama soon, and if their precious daughter wasn't back by then, they'd call the police. Very likely was the fact that they'd be led to him. Martin shuddered. Police had seen him several times, and often that was enough to land him jail time. He didn't intend to smudge the name of Tzen by landing himself in the slammer.

Martin resolved himself to using option three. Even if he gave up all control, he was going to find Alena. The pod stopped, the door opening as Martin made his decision. He stepped outside, closing his eyes and readying the incantation that would rely only upon the natural energy in his body – and possibly kill him if he botched it up.

Chapter 18: The Lower Levels

"Erhaz-Ahatamz," said Martin as he began channeling the energy through his veins. It felt as though various barriers in his body began to drop, allowing the energy to flow freely into those previously blocked areas. The coiling strands twisted around his heart, his lungs, and around his windpipe. He felt the familiar tightness as the energy began to take root there. The incantation was almost ready. Martin took a deep breath.

"Nutapriel-Askil!" he muttered, watching his arm for the first sign of change he knew would come. Sure enough, the skin near the crook of his arm began to ripple. Thin black strands leaked from enlarging pores, crawling down his arm toward his hand like spider's legs. The sensation was odd, but not really unpleasant. The whippy tentacles sank into his skin with no pain whatsoever, hardening and twisting amongst each other like living things until his forearm was completely black, as hard as diamond from the armor he had released.

This was one of the forbidden techniques of Energy Manipulation. He sighed, watching as the tentacles continued to crawl up his arm, hardening along his bicep until they reached his shoulder. This was the one good thing that had come out of that explosion in the orphanage. Solar Energy, if only he had known, was highly unstable. The slightest twitch could destabilize everything within a thirty-foot radius. Unfortunately, at the time, that included him.

Now, as tendrils of neutral energy laced their way along the right side of his chest, he was the abomination of the world. It was one of the reasons Martin made such an effective shock trooper for the Tzen; he didn't care if he died. As a matter of fact, it probably would have been better. With this *thing* living inside him feeding off of excess Solar Energy, he deserved death.

A faint smile crossed his lips as the dark tubes crawled up the side of his face. The creature he shared his body with wasn't entirely unpleasant – it was what had kept him alive in more confrontations than he could count. It was just a period of adjusting to the fact that there was a second consciousness inside him. It wasn't intelligent by any means, but it was sentient and operated off of basic instincts for survival. It couldn't communicate with him – he didn't 'hear voices in his head' as Jason often joked, but it made him a formidable adversary.

The tentacles now covered his right arm, half his torso, and his head. It left off before covering his mouth, nose, ears or eyes. It was now working its way down his left side, the tendrils reaching across his chest to meet with the other side as more reached down his legs.

The creature protected him valiantly. He was, after all, its host body. If he was killed, the creature died as well. It operated simply, however, and was not a complex life-form. It remained dormant in his chest cavity, held in check by various barriers of energy. When the situation was dire, or Martin deemed it acceptable, he lowered these 'gates' and fed the creature his leftover Solar Energy mixed in with liberal amounts of neutral energy. This, in turn, caused it to react as though the situation was dire (as it usually was) and protect the host, namely Martin.

It had often bothered him why the transformation started at his right arm, rather than somewhere vital such as the head. It never really mattered, however, as the creature always got the job done. Now, as Martin stood in the glade clad from head to toe in black tentacle armor, he wondered if this would help him locate Alena's energy source. True, the creature gave him 'gifts' of sorts, but it wasn't anything truly special beyond enhancing his reflexes and natural senses.

"Unexesael," he said, allowing the energy to crisscross his augmented body before flowing into his mind. He narrowed his eyes, tightening his focus on the familiar energy signal and prayed it would work. His eyes closed all the way. By robbing himself of one sense, his others increased to compensate.

There! It was faint, but the familiar warm energy Alena usually gave off was coming from a point a few miles west of him. Martin's eyes opened, but closed halfway in a grimace. She was about three miles away – trying to cover that on foot would be pointless. By the time he got near her current destination, her captors would have moved on.

He monitored the energy for a moment longer. It seemed that she was descending, but not rapidly. He focused all the neutral energy he could muster into his back, channeling it once again into awakening his parasitic companion. Slowly... painfully slowly... a set of 'arms' began to grow from his back. This was the one other advantage of the creature he carried. While these new limbs would vanish after he cancelled his incantation, they (and anything else he wished to create) could augment his body as if they were actually a part of it.

The 'arms' slowly began to take on a different shape, growing larger and wider. Gaps were filled with thin, dainty tentacles that wove between each other as though under the guidance of a textile master. Before long, a pair of wings was resting comfortably on Martin's shoulders. He sighed, letting out the breath he'd unconsciously been holding as the appendages formed.

Time to get to work...

He flapped the wings once, watching as leaves and twigs were blown away from him. He beat them again, rising slightly into the air. He flapped them again and again until he was hovering several feet above the forest floor. He quickly masked himself by distorting the air around him with a basic Air Incantation before flying straight up. He positioned himself in line with Alena's energy and flew rapidly in that direction, hoping he wasn't going to be too late.

***

He arrived above Alena's position in less than ten minutes. He opened his wings as air brakes, slowing his flight into a hover. He looked down. The area below him was a swamp - any pathway put here would have sunken in the quagmire long ago. He quickly thought of The Hall, realizing that this swamp was probably close to the Mainland Shelf.

Snarling, he doubled back and kicked open the pod he'd exited. He folded up his wings and squeezed inside, allowing the pod to take him back down. He disembarked at the bottom, opening the wings and soaring over to the Mainland Shelf. Gritting his teeth, he began to look around.

The buildings over here were toppled and ruined, rubble littering the streets. The only door that looked promising was one that stood off on one side, made of plain oak wood with a simple metal handle. Judging by the fairly new scratch marks it had left on the ground; it looked as though it had been used recently.

Martin pulled the wings back into his body, frowning slightly. His enhanced sense of smell picked up an unpleasant coppery smell from beyond the door. He knew the smell as if it was his name: blood.

And boy is there a lot of it...

He kicked the door as hard as he could, knocking it open and destroying one of the hinges. There was a small pool of blood on the ground, and Martin knelt down and put his fingers in it. It was dry, and this meant Martin could safely infer that it was old. How old was impossible to say.

The blood pool was adjacent to another pool, and he frowned. This one was smaller than the first, and looked almost like a large drip. Another lay beyond that. Martin wasn't a fool – he knew exactly what this was. It was a trail. The light was dim, and Martin really didn't like the atmosphere. It reminded him of the Lower Levels. He snorted. This area probably connected to those damn passageways.

The Lower Levels were tunnels that ran deep beneath The Hall. The last time Martin had been down there, he had seen all sorts of abominations. It looked as though someone had used it as a combination of torture chamber and laboratory.

He shook images of mutilated corpses from his mind. Now was *not* the time to be hesitant. He focused his energy again, and realized he was technically on top of Alena. Not only that, but there were four other energy sources – probably Zerolytes.

He bared his teeth, walking past the blood pools and up to another door. He tried the handle, but found it locked. He rolled his eyes. *I should have known...* With a grunt, he channeled all his energy into his foot and kicked the door down. The impact tore it from its hinges and it fell about ten feet before hitting the ground beneath it with a loud thud. Martin stuck his head through and looked around.

His suspicions were proven correct. This area *was* linked to the Lower Levels. He peered down into the cavern below him, recognizing the First Floor chamber. The area consisted of a raised wooden walkway, now soaked in blood and slathered in entrails of supposedly human origin. Below the pathways was darkness, out of which came an ominous hissing. Martin could see the snakes in this form, his augmented eyesight proving useful beyond measure in the unnatural darkness.

Thousands upon thousands of snakes were slithering amongst each other. He couldn't tell if they were poisonous, but really had no desire to find out. He jumped down from his perch in a high doorway onto the pathway below. He looked back up, wondering who the idiot who designed this chamber was. The door was built practically on the ceiling, with at least a ten foot drop onto the platforms below. One thing was for certain – he wasn't leaving that way without his wings or Air Energy. Currently, however, none of the Threads could be seen. Only a few dark purple Threads wove their way through the area – Dark Energy Threads.

That suits me just fine...

He stepped over what looked like it had once been a liver as he climbed a small flight of stairs. The smell around him was horrendous, assaulting his enhanced sense of smell with brutal ferocity. The air carried that coppery tang of blood, while something else seemed to hang in the air like a curtain. It smelled almost like formaldehyde and bodily fluids. Martin couldn't help but wrinkle his nose in disgust.

He passed what seemed to be a Crow's Cage. Inside was a skeleton, hanging from the roof of the cage by its feet. Large metal hooks were pierced through the bones, and Martin pitied the poor soul that had received this punishment.

And Dais thought the Mainland Shelf was safe...

He crossed his arms as he walked, something he did out of nervous habit, and seeing the amount of blood and gore splashed across the floors and walls made him extremely nervous. Even wild animals didn't cause this much carnage. He drummed his fingers on the tentacle armor he was wearing. Despite the obvious carnage, it was quiet. Where was the creature that had done this?

Martin suddenly felt a wave of nausea overcome him. He frowned, leaning against the wall. That was highly unusual. It wasn't the blood making him nauseous, nor the organs strewn across the ground like confetti. Something else....

The rocks he was leaning on felt odd, almost false. He gave one a push and found that it moved rather easily.

With curiosity reigning supreme in his mind, he pushed the rocks aside and peered through.

Several corpses lined the walls, each one burned and charred. A single corpse, however, stood out from the rest. It was relatively fresh, and hadn't been burned. Evidently, however, the unfortunate victim had met his death by having his head taken off his shoulders – it was lying a few feet away in a pool of blood.

A silver hook sword was clenched firmly in the corpse's hand. Martin looked down at it for a moment before stomping on the dead fingers, breaking them and causing them to release the sword. *He won't need this... not anymore...*

Martin held the sword against his back until the tentacle armor formed a makeshift sheathe for it. He spent a few minutes looking around before leaving. Apart from a few empty Crow's Cages, there wasn't anything else in this area. Martin turned to leave, almost stepping on the beheaded corpse on his way out. He frowned again. Whatever did this was sick – just plain sick.

Chapter 19: Descent

Martin walked past the false rocks only to discover, much to his dismay, that the pathway he had come down was one of three possible routes. He had come from the left, but there was a path in front of him and to his right. Martin weighed his options at this point. He had found evidence of what seemed to be mass murder. Dais had said that in situations like this it was best to have a teammate. It would probably be wise to go back for help.

The only problem was the creature dwelling in him. Because he had it, he could armor his body the way he did. The rest of the Tzen did not possess this ability, and Martin didn't want to be the cause of any deaths. Resigning himself to this, he forged ahead down the path in front of him. He hadn't gone more than ten feet when he ran into the first inhabitant of the caverns.

The hook sword was drawn from its sheathe as he dodged a swipe of claws. The beast he had encountered resembled an abnormally large skeleton; bits of flesh still hanging from the bones. The right hand had become enlarged, and was topped with long claws. The beast let out a screech that reverberated in Martin's head.

An Animation Incantation?!

Martin dodged a full body charge and surveyed the creature. Whenever someone did an Animation Incantation, they transferred Dark Energy into an inanimate object at a certain point. This point was the weakness of the animated object. In this case, it was the glowing purple patch on the back of the head. Martin waited until it charged again before severing the head. Quickly, before the head could reattach, he jammed the sword through the violet area. The skeletal creature faded away as though it had never existed.

The pathway continued for a bit, past a few more brutally mutilated corpses before ending at a similar door to the first two. Martin pressed his ear against it, and could make out a faint rustling and clicking. His eyebrows furrowed; he seemed to be doing a lot of frowning recently. He quickly debated whether or not to open the door, but eventually decided that if Alena was anywhere in this cavern, he would have to go through whatever else lay in it anyway.

Spiders. Millions of spiders. Large and black; with abdomens the size of basketballs, they were crawling all over a narrow ledge that encircled a tall chamber. The bottom of the chamber was hidden from sight, but an extreme heat was rising out of it. Martin immediately began swinging the sword and stomping on the spiders as he walked around the ledge, surveying his surroundings. When he reached the other side of the chamber, having killed most of the arachnids on the ledge, he noticed a stone floating in the air.

What the hell?

There were no Air Energy Threads – how could this rock be floating? He reached out to it and poked it once or twice. When it didn't go hurtling into the darkness, Martin gingerly climbed onto it.

From his new vantage point, a second stone platform was visible beneath the first one. Muttering curses, Martin lowered himself down onto it. He kicked a spider that was lurking there off the edge before looking around. More of those floating rocks were hanging in the air, suspended all over the place like ornaments. As he descended, the heat increased until there were virtually no spiders. That suited him just fine.

The bottom of the chamber was covered in lava. How deep it was, Martin couldn't guess, but the heat was extreme. A large ledge was hanging in the middle of the chamber, and Martin made his way over to it. He wasn't really afraid of falling. The bottom of the chamber was still a good fifty feet below him – more than enough time to summon his wings and break his fall.

The center platform was bare with the exception of a single human skull. Martin frowned and kicked it into the lava. Much to his surprise, a small ruby fell out from beneath it. He knelt and picked it up, frowning slightly. It was a dainty red stone, set in a gold plate shaped like a triangle. Deciding it would be a waste to let it sit here in a spider-infested chamber, Martin quickly pocketed it.

He summoned his wings and ascended from the chamber, grateful for being able to escape the infernal heat. His feet touched down near the door he had entered by, and his quickly opened it and exited the area before any spiders could follow him.

The slamming of the door awakened a horde of bats he hadn't noticed earlier. Each one was the size of a small dog, and they flew down at him. It seemed they were extremely upset over the sound. They beat their massive wings in his face, and Martin had no choice but to resort to an undignified flailing of his sword. After driving the bats away, killing some, he sheathed the sword and took the final unexplored pathway.

This is taking far too long.

Martin winced as his cell phone rang. *Insert another delay...* He answered the phone, holding it to his ear.

"What the hell are you doing in the Lower Levels?" barked Dais with all the intensity of a drill sergeant. Martin sighed, debating whether or not to just hang up the phone.

"Dais, Alena was taken down here by a troupe of Zerolytes. She shouldn't be much farther down."

"Martin! Get your ass out of there now! You're not to go further without a team!" reprimanded Dais, sternly.

"Go to Hell!" spat Martin viciously, "If we delay she could die! Besides, I'm the one suited for solo missions. The others will get in the way!"

"Martin! Don't-" it was too late. Martin had closed the cell phone, hanging up on Dais, and turned it off. He jammed it in his pocket, his brow furrowed into a frown.

Me... on a team... I think Dais has been drinking again...

Martin kicked down another door, glad when he found stairs leading down. He quickly descended them deeper into the cavern. The walls around him still showed signs of carnage. Blood was spattered haphazardly along them like a bad paintjob, staining the area crimson. Torches were lining the walls, their light throwing eerie shadows off the bloodstained walls.

An involuntary shiver ripped its way through Martin's body. He was getting closer to Alena – he could feel it. However, he was also getting close to something else – a something else with an unbelievable energy source. His golden eyes narrowed into slits. That was Solar Energy unless he was greatly mistaken.

What is Solar Energy doing this deep?

He reached the bottom of the stairs, almost running into an iron door. This one couldn't be kicked down, he realized, but luckily for him it was unlocked. He grasped the semicircular handle, giving it a push. With a screeching sound, the door swung inwards. So much for stealth...

The room he had entered was enormous. It was so large, in fact, that he couldn't see the far walls. Instead, an eerie red glow illuminated the ceiling and floor. The darkness seemed almost alive, squeezing him from all sides.

"Let me go, damn it!"

That, unless he was sorely confused, sounded like Alena's voice. She had to be close. He charged through the doorway, mentally checking the position of any Threads in the area - three Dark, one Earth, and one Fire. That suited him just fine.

"Alena!" he yelled into the depths of the cavern, hoping for a response. Instead of her voice, however, a fireball rocketed out of the darkness. It struck Martin full in the chest, lifting him into the air and throwing him against the door he'd just come in. He slid down the wall, his body aching. Before his attacker could follow up the fireball with another incantation, Martin had rolled to the side. An icicle embedded itself in the wall where his head had been moments ago. Whoever this was had extremely good aim.

He grabbed a Dark Energy Thread in each hand, bringing his hands up in front of him in a fighting stance. He felt the chill racing through his body as the energy was absorbed. It polluted his insides like a gripping fear, twisting and coiling within his belly like a den of snakes.

"Show yourself!" he commanded, feeling his body continue filling with Dark Energy. He began channeling the leftover energy into his hands in preparation for the battle that was sure to come.

A figure stepped out of the darkness. It was a Zerolyte, and a high ranking one at that. The robes were the classic midnight black, but there were golden patterns sewn along the edges. The hood completely obscured the face, as was customary in the Zerolytes, and the sleeves hung empty at the figure's sides.

"Martin Spire."

It was the first time a Zerolyte had addressed him by name. He tightened his focus, making sure to keep his guard up. The Zerolyte was standing less than ten feet away from him. It made no move to attack.

"Where's Alena?" he snarled, pushing all the pent-up Dark Energy into his hands. They began to burn with purple fire, giving him an otherworldly appearance. "Tell me!"

The Zerolyte raised both empty sleeves to the sky, and a second figure stepped out of the darkness. It was another Zerolyte. Before Martin could attack, another appeared. This pattern continued until no less than twenty black-robed figures were barring his path.

"Die."

The Zerolyte wasn't one for conversation, Martin decided as he dodged a hail of icicles. Each Zerolyte seemed to be able to telepathically communicate with the others, synchronizing their attacks with brutal perfection.

Martin summoned his wings again, folding one over his face to block a particularly nasty fireball. He grimaced as the incantation burned at the armor. Seeing as it was technically a part of him, a small part of his consciousness reigned in any appendage he grew.

Time for retaliation!

He held his black-armored hands forward, pointing at one of the Zerolytes. "Somesacael!" he said, watching as a series of the black tentacles grew from his wrists, speeding toward his target. They struck the Zerolyte in the chest, knocking him backward into the darkness, and ricocheted off of him into the next victim. This one, however, jumped backward to avoid the assault. Martin sneered, moving his arms like a puppeteer, directing the flow of the tendrils.

"Die already!" he cursed, smacking another one in the face. There was a scream as the tentacles snapped his neck, dropping on the ground. Eighteen Zerolytes remained. Martin retracted the tentacles, his arms jerking slightly from the recoil as the tendrils slammed back into his wrists.

The first Zerolyte, the one who had addressed him by name, was laughing. It hadn't moved from its spot, but was merely watching the battle with some kind of detached interest.

Martin rushed forward, purple-hued hands at his sides. The Zerolytes instantly converged upon him, attempting to stop his mad rush. He grinned, although there was no mirth in it.

He leapt into the air, striking one in the jaw, kicking another in the legs as he landed, tripping him. They collapsed to the ground. The first one was dead from the force of the blow. He ran forward, double punching the next Zerolyte out of his way, sending him careening into one of his partners. He literally ran over the next Zerolyte, making sure to stomp his head in as he passed over it. He leapt off of the dying Zerolyte's shoulders before whipping one of his arms like a flail and punching what looked to be the leader in the face. He landed on the Zerolyte's chest before quickly rebounding and landing behind it.

Chapter 20: Rescue

There was silence in the chamber. The remaining Zerolytes had formed a circle around Martin and the leader, watching with rapt interest. The head Zerolyte forced himself up, reaching inside his hood and feeling his face. A hollow laugh reverberated throughout the massive chamber.

"You've broken my nose," it said mirthlessly.

"You've pissed me off!" snapped Martin, channeling more of the Dark Energy into his hands in preparation for another fight. The Zerolyte laughed at him, serving to further infuriate Martin.

"Fine then. Since you have struck me, let's fight!" Martin barely managed to shield his face with his wing before a fist broke his jaw. He snapped the wing open, catching the Zerolyte in the chest and knocking him backwards. The figure landed gracefully on its feet, arms stretched out in front. "Lanatoatzen!"

Seven spheres of violet energy shot from the Zerolyte's hands, heading straight for Martin. He slammed both wings around himself like a cocoon, feeling the dull thumps as the energy struck him. A dull ache filled his wings, causing them to slacken slightly.

"Bastard!" he snapped, "Where's Alena!"

The Zerolyte danced out of the path of a fireball, "The girl?" it asked, calmly, "She's with us now."

"Go screw!" snapped Martin hotly, "She's coming back to The Hall with me!"

The Zerolyte laughed again. It was that same, hollow laugh he'd heard a few seconds ago. "Oh that is rich," commented the figure, "You? You're going to defeat all of us and bring her back? You don't even care about her!"

Martin felt anger rising in his body. He knew it was going to end badly for both parties, but at the moment he didn't care. So what if this Zerolyte was speaking half of the truth. It wasn't that he didn't care, he didn't know *if* he cared.

"I thought I told you to go screw!" he bit, readying his hands again. "Come on, then, try to stop me!"

The Zerolyte had lost all mirth. It was staring at Martin with a mixture of curiosity and loathing – as one might examine a two-headed slug.

"What do you want with her, anyway?" it asked, summoning a fireball into its hand, "Is she your pet?"

Martin snapped. He hurled himself forward, heedless of the fireball, and punched the Zerolyte hard enough to lift it into the air. It flew backwards, landing on its back on the hard floor with a grunt.

"Bastard!" Martin yelled, summoning all the energy he could grasp in his body. He began storing it in every available pocket within his being, causing his body to begin emitting a faint light.

The Zerolyte immediately recognized the technique. Roughly translated, it was "Supernova."

"Retreat!" it called, watching as the Zerolytes began to melt into the shadows. Unfortunately, they weren't fast enough.

"Zesrosimiel!"

Martin seemed to explode, casting rainbows of energy in every direction. The Zerolytes that hadn't managed to escape, including the supposed leader, were vaporized instantly. The ceiling above was scorched black, and bits of it were burned away entirely.

When the incantation ended, Martin was lying facedown on the ground. He'd used up the energy stored in his tentacle armor, causing it to retreat back into his system until later. Not only that, but most of his body's natural energy was spent as well, leaving him exhausted.

After resting for a moment, Martin forced himself to his feet, staggering slightly. He felt extremely naked without the armor. His commandeered hook sword had been melted – it was now a silvery puddle on the ground a few feet away. Sighing, he began walking deeper into the room. He flicked open his cell phone, turning it on and dialing Dais' number with practiced ease. After the customary three rings, Dais answered the phone.

"Dais," he said calmly, "I'm about four floors down. Alena's nearby. I'm going to bring her back, but I need you all to prepare a way for me to get off of the Mainland Shelf. Is that understood?"

Dais affirmed the decision after Martin explained the loss of his armor. After hanging up the phone, Martin broke into a jog, crossing the enormous room in about half an hour and reaching a large door. It simply screamed suspicious. It was a simple oak door, inlaid with iron symbols and surrounded by spears that pointed accusingly downward toward Martin.

Sneering, Martin grasped the handle and pushed the door open, feeling a cold draft sweep across his exposed skin. Gooseflesh sprouted along his arms, even beneath his Loden Coat, and the hairs on the back of his neck stood at attention.

Beyond the door was a garden, or so it seemed. A false sun blazed in a false sky, shining down upon a green, lush field. It all seemed idyllic, like a child's dream. In the middle of the garden were two more Zerolytes, and between them was Alena. A nasty grimace shredded Martin's normally calm features.

"Hands off!" he yelled, rushing forward. He leapt onto the first Zerolyte from behind, much to its surprise, and bore it to the ground. He kicked it in the face before rounding on its companion. The second Zerolyte had dropped Alena and was raising a jewel-encrusted axe to finish her. Martin swore.

He lunged forward, catching the axe by the haft as it descended. Before the Zerolyte could react, the weapon was wrenched from its hands and buried in its chest. The axe was ripped out with a sucking sound and hurled at the second Zerolyte. It took its head clean off as it sailed through the air to land in a gazing pool.

"Are you alright?" asked Martin, offering his hand to Alena. She nodded, taking his hand and standing up. She was staring at the ground in shame, like a scolded child.

"What?" he asked, looking at her in confusion. Her eyes looked up at him for a moment before looking back down at her shoes.

"I should've fought back..." she muttered. Martin resisted the urge to hit her, but remembered that it wasn't right to hit women.

"You haven't been properly trained," he explained, "It was to be expected. Come. I'll see if Dais can train you properly starting tomorrow. For now, let's get the hell out of here."

He flicked open his cell, dialing Dais again. "Yeah, I've got her."

Dais was overjoyed, and so was Martin (even if it didn't show on his face) when he was told that a working lift had been established between Island Twelve and the Mainland Shelf.

"We're getting out of here," he said to Alena. He grasped her by the hand and began to run, crossing the enormous room in half the time it took initially and opening the iron door. They ascended the stairs in silence, both of them thinking about how nice it would be to leave this hell of a cavern.

Alena clung tightly to Martin as they crossed the few floors above them that were littered with flayed corpses and discarded organs. This, of course, was after she finished emptying her stomach in a corner. Martin wrinkled his nose in disgust. "It's just a dead body," he explained, "We're all going to die – no use getting disgusted by it."

Alena shook her head, "Not like that, no..." She was referring to a corpse that had been stripped down to the muscle before being split open like a dissected frog. Martin eyed the display in distaste.

"Alright," he conceded, "That *is* disgusting. But let's just focus on getting out of here."

The problem, however, was something he'd forgotten. The door he'd kicked in had fallen ten feet, as had he. There was no way to ascend back up the trapdoor. After calling Jason and requesting a rope ladder, they had little to do but sit on a pair of crates and wait.

"I wonder what this place was..." Alena wondered aloud, looking around in disgust at the torture devices and corpses. Martin was drumming his fingers on the crate, hoping it wasn't going to be long before they could get out of here. The smell of body fluids was starting to get to him.

"A torture chamber for the palace district, perhaps?" he offered. Alena became very quiet, staring at her hands. Martin sighed, "You don't need to be ashamed," he said. He was trying to sound comforting. Unfortunately, it came out sounding like he needed a laxative. *I need lots of practice at this whole being nice thing...*

"Why did you come for me?" she asked after a moment. Martin looked up, fixing her with his golden eyes. "You even have to ask?"

She nodded, "It's because Dais ordered you, huh?"

He blanched, looking at her as if she'd grown not one but two extra heads. "The hell? Dais can't command me!"

She looked at him in confusion, but before she could say anything else, a rope ladder dropped down to rest on the wooden platform where they sat. "C'mon lovebirds," sang Jason from his vantage point above them, "Let's get outta this hellhole, yeah?"

Martin motioned for Alena to go first, and she quickly ascended the ladder. Once she was safely out, Martin shimmied up after her, stepping into the fresh air of The Hall. He took deep breaths, filling his lungs with that familiar earthy smell as opposed to the smell of rotting bodies.

"It's good to be out," he said after a moment. He turned to Jason, who was standing nearby with a knowing expression on his face. "When are we going to pursue study of the Mainland Shelf... what are you grinning about?"

Jason shrugged, putting his hands behind his head and whistling as he walked toward the newly constructed bridge. Martin stared after him for a moment before turning to Alena.

"Let's go report to Dais," he said quickly, motioning for her walk ahead of him, "Ladies first."

Smiling, she bowed in thanks and crossed the bridge. Martin, however, turned and gave one long look at the Mainland Shelf. Ever since he'd joined the Tzen, he'd wanted to know everything about whoever had built his place. Seeing the extent of the depravity in that dungeon, however...

He shook the thoughts from his head, catching up to Alena. Now was not the time for those kinds of thoughts. He *was* going to solve the mystery of the Mainland Shelf. He would solve it if it killed him. He walked behind Alena, thinking quietly.

Jason was waiting for them on Island Twelve, his usual cocky 'I'm-better-than-you' grin firmly plastered on his face. He pointed toward Dais' chamber. "Boss is waiting for you," he said, gesturing for Martin and Alena to go ahead.

Martin sighed inwardly. He was going to get the reaming of a lifetime for disobeying Dais... not to mention telling him to go to hell...

Alena walked up and knocked on Dais' door, waiting for an answer. There was silence for a moment before they both heard Dais' voice tell them to enter. Resigning himself to his fate, Martin followed Alena into the chamber ahead of them.

Dais looked like he'd taken Martin's advice and gone to hell and come back. His hair was standing up in all directions, and Martin recognized the mission reports from their first trip into the Lower Levels. He sighed again, looking up at Dais and waiting for his punishment.

Chapter 21: Punishment

Martin stood before Dais' desk, hoping fervently that whatever punishment his superior meted out would not be too severe. The dark-haired man was staring intently across the desk with anger concealed behind his eyes. Alena was standing off on one side, scuffing at the carpet with the toe of her shoe.

"Martin..." sighed Dais exasperatedly, "...what on earth am I going to do with you? First you go and reveal our secret to the outside world, and then you go gallivanting off into the Lower Levels. What's next? A date?"

Martin frowned, but said nothing. It seemed his quiet personality surfaced occasionally, and this was one of those times. Dais looked intently at him before continuing to speak. This time, his voice was edged with barely concealed anger.

"You're one of the best Tzen out there. I can't have you killed. I'm removing Ms. Stewart from your custody for the time being and confining you to Cavern Arrest until further notice."

Martin looked up indignantly. "I never knew she was in my custody in the first place. Also, you can't confine me to the Cavern as I need to return to the surface before those nincompoops at the High School begin to wonder as to my whereabouts."

Dais regarded him coolly for a moment. "You are permitted to leave for High School purposes only," he said after a moment. "This does not give you excuse to go creating chaos for Alena – is that clear?"

Martin blew air through his nose in annoyance. "I never caused trouble for her in the first place!" he snapped. His voice was completely cold, retaining that usual glacial quality the Tzen all knew was a part of him.

Dais stood up, pounding his hands onto the desk. "You were the one who left me no choice but to turn her into a Tzen in the first place!" he thundered. Martin's eyebrows rose; one of the only indicators he was feeling anything at all. "If you hadn't lost your goddamn cool, we wouldn't be in this position in the first place!"

Martin walked up to the desk, slamming his own hands down as well. His face was inches from Dais', and his voice was just about as loud. "What position are we in?" he yelled, "We're in virtually the same position we were in before Alena joined... unless you're not telling me something."

Dais' face became visibly white, and Martin smirked at him. "I thought so. Now, what have you been keeping from me?"

Sighing in defeat, Dais slumped back into his chair. "The Zerolytes know that Alena has high energy levels to begin with," he said slowly, "And we believe they are looking for her because of it. Terra is suspecting it has something to do with Solar Energy, like what you were doing seven years ago, but we have no proof."

Martin sighed, rubbing his temples. "There was a large burst of Solar Energy while I was in the Lower Levels," he said quietly, "Just before I encountered around twenty Zerolytes."

Dais nodded, "I assume you already know about the corpses and experiments down there, am I right?"

"Corpses, yes," replied Martin, "Experiments, no."

Dais drew out several sheets of yellowed paper. Sketched on them were maps and charts of the first three of the Lower Levels. "The entire area down there is a highly fortified base," he explained, "The true purpose is unknown, but there was a lot of EM Modification going on at the time..."

Alena piped up at this point. "What is EM Modification?"

Dais regarded her for a moment before continuing. "EM Modification is the use of the higher energies, namely Solar and Lunar, to disturb the natural energies within the cells of the body and forcing them to mutate."

Dais slid over a few Polaroid photographs, which Martin quickly passed to Alena. "Those are images of one of the experiments my team found about two years ago when we went into those damn caverns."

The photographs showed something roughly humanoid, with a wide chest and thick, gnarled arms. It was dead, but it also looked extremely formidable. Spines ran down its back, and there were the beginnings of a tail beginning to grow near the posterior. Four pale eyes were situated on the head.

Most striking of all, however, was the lack of symmetry. Most creatures retained some form of it. This 'experiment' had none at all. The right side was enlarged and bloated, with two arms and one leg. The left side of the creature was small and shriveled, with only one arm and one leg. The four eyes on the head were placed with three on the left and one on the right. The nose had been completely shifted to the right, and the mouth was angled on the face.

"What the hell is it?" asked Jason, who had been peering over Alena's shoulder. Dais shrugged noncommittally, which irritated Martin somewhat. "Shouldn't we be clearing the caverns out? Now that a bridge has been built, they could feasibly attack the Islands."

Dais nodded at him, "We're having a team seal the cavern for now. Later on, when more of our Tzen have attained higher skills, we can attempt to eradicate these abominations."

Alena felt extremely out of place. She was about to leave when Dais turned to her. "You had best return to your home," he said, "I'll have Jason watch over you from a distance to make certain you're safe, don't worry."

She nodded, and noticed Martin giving Jason the evil eye. As the black-haired boy passed him, Martin caught his shoulder. He leaned down, whispering in his ear. "If you touch her, consider yourself dead."

Jason smiled, leaning back up to whisper in Martin's ear. "Somebody's jealous..."

"Somebody needs to shut up," retorted Martin hotly.

He straightened up before Jason could give him any more snide remarks, facing Dais. "Should I return to quarters for the time being?"

Dais nodded, and Martin turned to leave. "Don't even consider sneaking back into the caverns, alright?"

A strong urge presented itself to flip Dais the bird, but Martin fought it down. He nodded instead, leaving the room. Dais leaned back, folding his arms in his lap as he stared into space. It had been an eventful day. Part of him wanted to retire to his room for the night, but he had to log some of the information into the databases.

***

Martin sat down at his desk, pulling out his journal. He entered a few paragraphs before rapidly becoming bored. His mind floated around, looking for things to do. A stack of his origami paper caught his eye, so he began to fold something.

Several minutes later, a crane emerged from his hands. He used a nearby Air Energy Thread to create a small tornado, suspending his new creation in it. He returned to his stack of paper, folding it into a triangle to begin the next crane. Halfway through, the door opened. Douglas poked his head inside, before calling out a greeting. Martin didn't respond; he just continued to fold. His blonde companion walked into the room, closing the door behind him.

"Heard you got reamed by Dais," he remarked offhandedly. Martin made a 'hn' sound to show he had heard, but otherwise said nothing. Douglas frowned, hopping into his bed. "Did he come down on you hard?"

"Cavern Arrest," muttered Martin, finishing his second crane and tossing it carelessly into the miniature whirlwind. Both birds fluttered around inside the cyclone, looking almost as if they were alive.

Douglas let out a low whistle, watching the birds spiral in the wind. "So you're stuck here?" he asked, watching Martin's pianist fingers beginning to fold a third piece of paper. Martin nodded, "With the exception of school, that is," he said after a moment.

His roommate sighed in relief, "I don't know if I could deal with you brooding around me all this time. How long is it for?"

"Until further notice..." muttered Martin as he tossed the third crane into the cyclone. He watched them dance in the wind for a moment before drawing a fourth sheet down from his stack.

Everyone knew that when Martin Spire made cranes, it was best to stay away from him. Only Douglas, the one person he even *barely* trusted, could get near him without an incantation knocking them away – usually something painful like Xidul.

Martin made the cranes because he was thinking. Several people asked him where he learned to make them – mainly because they had one 'flaw' in their design. While the wings were supposed to fold outwards on the cranes, a slight defect made them turn in slightly. This gave them a very angular look. When asked, the questioner usually was met with a cold stare.

Douglas had once asked the question because he was curious. Martin told him, quite plainly, that if he ever asked that question again he would be cursing the day his father met his mother. Douglas had wisely decided to drop the interrogation.

The true reason Martin made his cranes with this variation was that it had been one of the four friends who had died in the orphanage fire who had taught this version to him. Oh Martin knew how to make the 'normal' cranes just fine. However, the sentiment behind these 'warped' birds was something even his cold heart couldn't shake.

Amanda, the girl who had taught him, said that any old person could make a regular crane. It took someone truly unique and special to make one of these cranes. It was the same way in the world. She had said anyone could make a difference – but it took someone truly special to make a positive difference.

Martin, therefore, only made these 'edited' cranes. He did it to honor her memory, and (to a slightly egotistical extent) to honor himself. He believed he couldn't really make a positive contribution, but he could at least keep the memories of his old friends alive, couldn't he?

Douglas was watching him with rapt attention as another crane flew into the whirlwind. "Are you done yet? Dais is gonna kill you for wasting all that paper."

"This paper was purchased from my pocket," was the frosty reply, "And I highly doubt Dais could kill me."

Douglas knew he was probably right. Martin's skills as a Tzen certainly surpassed any of the others living on the Islands. Dais and Steven, however, two of the 'chaperones', were extraordinarily talented. Douglas wasn't one-hundred percent convinced that Martin could fight them, but he knew his roommate wasn't going to be easily killed by either of them. There were two main reasons to this. The first reason was that neither Dais nor Steven had it in them to kill unless the situation was absolutely necessary.

The second reason was because of Martin's tentacle armor. That stuff could probably block a Solar Energy Saber without sustaining a scratch. Secretly, Douglas envied the technique. However, he understood the price at which it came. Martin had virtually sold the souls of thirty people for that ability. Douglas shuddered. *That* was something he could never do.

He watched as Martin began folding yet another crane. He leaned back on his bed, thinking of the various things that had happened today. He'd heard about Martin going AWOL and delving into the Lower Levels to save Alena. That, he knew, was highly unusual. If it had been any other Tzen, Martin could have cared less. He was more a solo player than a teammate anyway.

He'd heard from Jason about Martin's confrontation at the school before going into the lower levels. When he heard what that Deagan kid had called him, he wanted to laugh. Monster. If anything, Martin was more of a supermonster than a monster.

Chapter 22: Cavern Arrest

Martin's crane collection had risen to thirty by the time Douglas had convinced him to stop. Derrick, the gondola operator, needed assistance in rigging a more secure ride to the Mainland Shelf. Seeing as there was nothing better to do until the following day, Martin finally tossed in the last crane and followed his teammate.

"How hard can it be to rig a gondola?" asked Douglas as they walked towards the construction site, "I mean, it's just some cables and winches, right?"

Unfortunately, that wasn't the labor Derrick had in mind for them. He needed them to go gather the materials he needed from the warehouse on Island Five and transport them here. That, however, entailed a good deal of heavy lifting. One length of cable, or around ninety feet, weighed around one-hundred pounds.

After several hours (and a good deal of sweat, blood and a large amount of cursing from Douglas) the materials were stacked neatly next to Derrick's building site. The exuberant blonde thanked them, and promised to put in a good word for Martin the next time he saw Dais. Martin decided to take what he could get and left.

He meandered around the cavern that was to be his prison 'until further notice'. He let out a sigh as he approached the precipice on Island One. He sat down, allowing his legs to dangle from the edge to swing freely above the chasm below.

"Someone's looking dejected..." sighed a voice from behind him. Martin didn't need to turn around to know it was Jason. He stared pointedly at the standing water below him and said nothing.

"C'mon Martin, face it. That Alena girl... you like her."

Martin resisted the urge to punch Jason solidly in the mouth, continuing to stare at the water as he replied, "No."

"Yeah you do – just admit it," came the calm remark from the usually cheerful joker. Martin snorted, but continued to keep his silence.

"You know you like her, Martin. You think about her all the time, don't you? Why else would you kick your way to the Lower Levels to save her?"

"Because she's a fellow Tzen," snapped Martin hotly, "I'm not exactly what you'd call boyfriend material anyway. I'm nothing more than a teammate."

"Do I detect a hint of wistfulness in your voice?" teased the violet-eyed boy with the hint of a smile in his voice, "Do you, perhaps, wish you *were* more 'boyfriend material'?"

"Go bug someone else," muttered Martin. He was glad his back was to Jason, as he felt an unusual heat rising into his cheeks. His face was slightly flushed with a rare shade of pink.

"Tell me what you think of her," asked Jason, ignoring the order to leave and sitting down somewhere behind him. "Just go on – let it all out."

"She is a nice, caring person with a bit too much of a good heart. She seemed to have a bit of a problem with the common sense category, seeing as she's trying to help me in one way or another."

Jason grinned, "Oh, you picked up on that, eh?" he asked, shifting his position on the ground to something more comfortable, "I thought you never watched anything other than those damn Threads."

Martin twisted his head to give him a death glare, saying nothing.

"No, it's just that you're always training or messing with those old notebooks," he offered, trying not to annoy his teammate, "You've never once taken part in anything social, why don't you give it a try?"

"And what, pray tell, am I going to do?" bit Martin, "There's not much I can do outside of school events, is there?"

Jason stood up, brushing dirt from his Loden Coat. "I'll give you a hint – it involves two people moving rhythmically to the beat of a song."

"Dancing? What the hell does that..." the thought clicked. There was a dance coming up at the High School in about three days. He looked back at Jason. "How the heck do you know that?"

Jason shrugged, "Don't forget what I do, Martin."

Information Dealer... right...

"Alright, but what the hell am I supposed to do? I dance waltzes, not nightclub stripteases, which seems to be popular these days. Besides, all I have are my Tzen-issue clothes."

"Since when does the great Martin Spire worry about anything?" pushed Jason, "It's not like she cares. You know she likes you."

Martin snorted, "Yeah, right..."

Jason walked up and whacked Martin on the back of the head. Martin let out a surprised sound, clutching at his raven black hair. "What the hell?!"

"Wake up and smell the roses," barked Jason, "She's liked you since she saw you at the school, alright?" He was staring intently at Martin as he spoke, almost as if he was daring him to respond. Martin rose to the bait.

"How the hell do you know these things?" he asked, glaring defiantly at Jason. "What're you, some kind of psychic?"

"Information Dealer," supplied Jason, "It's one of the things I do best." He grinned, knowing exactly which one of them had won this round.

"Hmph. So what do you want me to do? Show up with a rose in my teeth and serenade her?" muttered Martin, turning back to stare out into the cavern with his orange eyes. "Besides, I doubt there'll be anything close to classical I can dance to."

"You leave that to Derrick and me," supplied Jason, "I know the DJ who's going to be selecting the songs." He grinned at Martin's back as the other boy blanched.

"You've got to kidding me!" said Martin, turning around and standing up to be on eye level with Jason. "You have got to be kidding me!"

"Naah, I wouldn't do that," assured Jason. He thought for a moment, "Oh, and her parents get back tomorrow night. See you around."

Jason took off before Martin could weasel any more information out of him. He stood on the precipice, running one of his delicate hands through his dark hair in exasperation.

Me? Dance with Alena? Is he nuts?

A small part of him admitted that it would be nice, but he quickly squished it. That was something he shouldn't have even had floating around in his head in the first place. He shook his head, ignoring the incessant voice of Jason telling him what to do.

Finally, after pacing around and gnawing on his tongue for the better part of twenty minutes while weighing the possible outcomes, he flipped open his phone.

Fudge... I don't have her phone number...

He sighed, massaging his temples. Although he was confined to The Hall, he figured Derrick owed him a favor. He jogged back to Island Twelve, poking the gondola operator on the shoulder upon arrival.

"Whassup?" asked the boy in question, looking up from assembling a winch, "Need something?"

"Actually, yes," said Martin, surprising Derrick, "I need a phone number. You're not confined to The Hall, you see."

Derrick straightened up, popping his knuckles, "Okay, whose number do you need?"

The next words to leave the stoic boy's mouth shocked Derrick almost to the point of speechlessness. "Alena Steward."

Derrick blinked a few times before nodding, "Sure, no problem. Dais'll have her number on record, I'll see if I can get it for you."

Martin nodded, indicating his pocket with one finger, "When you get the number, give me a call, alright?"

Derrick nodded, "First though, I'm gonna need to fix this damn winch. Stupid piece of shit popped open on me."

Martin nodded, turning and walking off. If he was going to go through with this, there was going to be a lot of preparation. He stepped into his bedding chamber, pushing the closet open. Inside hung all of the clothes he owned. This, however, was almost thirty copies of the same outfit: white shirt, black pants, black shoes, and the Navy Blue Loden Coat.

He drew out the pants, shirt and shoes, wondering if he should take an Onyx Black Loden Coat to compliment the pants. After a moment, he drew it out and tossed it on his bed. He laid the clothes out as though they were on a body, checking to see if it would look alright. It passed his scrutiny, so he carefully draped the clothes over the armor mannequin that stood in the corner of his room.

That done, Martin let out a sigh. *Jason, if I end up stuck at a dance with nothing but rap music playing, I'm gonna kill you.*

He pushed the thought from his mind. He had enough worries right now. He checked his watch, wondering what time it was. It was almost eleven. His eyebrows rose a fraction of an inch – one of the few ways anyone could tell if Martin was surprised. Time had flown, it seemed. He had signed himself out of the school at 12:15, and that much time had elapsed?

He mentally checked his day. The hours seemed to match up, and the realization made Martin extremely tired. A yawn slipped unbidden from his lips, and he shook his head to clear it.

He sat down at his desk, drawing out his journal and making an entry. Seeing as he felt like he had a bit of energy left, he decided to check one of his old notebooks. He drew a notebook out of his desk, making sure he had the right one. It was silver with a black spine, along with several interesting symbols that looked like a cross between Japanese Kanji and Western Lettering.

He opened the book, running his finger down several of the pages until he found what he was looking for. These notebooks contained all his observations about the long-term effects of using the Threads. Something had been bothering him since noon.

He almost gave a triumphant shout, but the door opening to reveal Douglas kept him quiet. He snapped shut the notebook, a triumphant grin visible on his features.

Lunar Energy, while rare, is the third most powerful of all the Elemental Energies that encircle the planet. The only energies that are more potent are Solar and Time. Lunar Energy can begin to mutate the body through extended use, as can Solar. Repeated contact with a mutated individual can cause the Natural Energy in the area to either drop or become spiked with immense quantities of high-density energy. This theory is known as the Theory of Energy Conservation. The

high-density energy has unique properties, and prolonged
exposure can prove fatal.

So that settled it. Something or someone in that
school had been exposed to a lot of Lunar or Solar Energy.
The reaction had been to spike the surrounding area,
effectively masking Alena's Energy Signature so the Zerolytes
would be able to kidnap her.

Martin grinned triumphantly as he took off his
clothes, climbing into bed. In the morning he would show the
notebook to Dais, hopefully earning him a slight reprieve in
his commander's eyes. For now, however, sleep was a very
tempting option. Besides, he had to be well rested for the
dance in three days.

He closed his eyes, focusing on the blackness. A
small smirk found its way onto his visage. He, the sin-soaked
Martin Spire, was going to be taking a girl to a dance. The
world was truly coming upon the Apocalypse. What next? Was
he going to... god forbid... take Alena on a *date*? He snickered
inwardly at how much like Dais he was beginning to sound
before slipping into his usual dreamless sleep.

Chapter 23: Meet the Parents

Martin's cell phone awakened him sometime around eight. He answered, smiling slightly as Derrick read off Alena's number to him. He quickly thanked his comrade and hung up, dialing the seven digits as quickly as he could. The phone rang twice before it was answered.

"Jack Steward," said a male voice. Martin frowned, but quickly forced a more-or-less pleasant expression onto his face. He knew from experience that the facial expression seemed to carry through the phone line. "Hello, may I speak to Alena, please?"

"She's at school, what do you want?" snapped the voice. Martin decided to drop the faux happy-ass act and speak plainly. "I wanted to take her to the dance in two days."

There was silence before the voice spoke again. "Who is this?"

"Martin Spire, a friend of Alena's from school," he answered calmly. Although he was dropping the happy act, he was trying to keep the ice from his voice.

"Well Mister Spire," said the man on the other end, "I happen to be her father. If you wish to take my daughter to the dance, you will have to go through me first. Five-o-clock, my residence. I'm sure you can find it if you have her phone number." The line went dead, and Martin snapped the phone shut, cursing everything he could think of at that moment. *Why me?*

He sighed, looking at the clock again. Eight-twenty. He figured now was a good a time as any to go see what was cooking in the breakfast hall before talking to Dais about the notebook. He tossed on his usual set of clothes, sparing his nice set for the dance, put the notebook in his coat pocket and left the room.

After feasting on some scrambled eggs, Martin went to Dais' chamber. He knocked on the door before entering, finding his superior looking over several documents. He looked up as Martin entered, his eyes fixing on the blank expression.

"I know how the Zerolytes were able to kidnap Alena so easily," said Martin quietly. "I'll tell you, but I need something in return."

Dais was on full alert, sitting up straight and leaning forward slightly toward Martin. "Go on, name your price."

"I want freedom two days from now. After that, you can put me back on Cavern Arrest. I also want to be able to leave the Cavern to meet a contact at five."

Dais thought it over before nodding once. Martin tossed his notebook on the desk and left, leaving Dais to read it on his own. Now he was fully ready for the dance. He cornered Jason and made certain there would be music he could dance to before checking his watch again. Eight forty. He sighed. *Time hates me...*

He meandered across the cavern for the next three hours, doing odd jobs for people to help pass the time. He played handyman in the medical ward, scrubbing several syringes and laundering some of the cleaning cloths before helping Michael work on a project to develop a 'Tzen Knife' for close combat.

Finally, at eleven thirty sharp, Martin left the Tzen Refuge with his briefcase clenched tightly in his fist. Lunch was in thirty minutes, and after that came his first class.

Oh yeah, I don't get to return until I feel like apologizing. Oh well. I guess I get some free time.

It was no secret that Martin's pride was second only to his power as a Tzen. If someone requested an apology for anything, they could just as well forget it. His pride was so great it wouldn't allow it. It was extremely rare that Martin would ever deign to stoop as low as to apologize to what he viewed as a disgusting creature; namely a human being.

He walked into the school just in time to hear the lunch bell ring. He quickly made his way over to the line, checking what today's special was. Nachos. That suited him just fine. He purchased a dish and sat down at the table he usually inhabited. He took up his usual hobby of scaring the wits out of anyone who walked near him by glaring evilly at them, his death glare amplified by his orange and red eyes.

After both lunch and his math class had ended, he walked down to the front office and filled out a counselor form. If he was going to be hurled out of math for speaking his mind, they could keep the class. He was taking it as an elective anyway. He'd placed highest on the placement tests – technically he didn't belong in High School but in College, but he still had to wait until his Graduation Year.

Sighing, he dropped the slip into the counselor's drop box and sat back down to read. Only when he became aware of a presence did he look up. Alena was standing there, staring at him as if he'd lost his marbles. He raised an eyebrow, prompting her to speak.

"My dad just called," she said. Martin concealed his emotions well, as none became visible. Inside; however, he was cursing fate. "He said you wanted to take me to the dance. Is that true?"

Martin looked back to his book, "If you would like to go, of course."

She sat down near him, leaning on her chin on her hands as she watched him. In no way would she deny he was handsome. Unfortunately, his personality was less than kind to those he didn't trust. She got the distinct impression he barely trusted his fellow Tzen.

"I'd love to go," she said after a moment. Martin nodded.

"Your father has requested a meeting with me at five-o-clock today," he said monotonously, "I'll be coming over for dinner, it seems."

Alena admired his intelligence, she'd admit that, but it was slightly unnerving. Of course her father would have him over for dinner – it was almost a rite of passage – but Martin seemed to have gleaned that from the time of their meeting alone.

"How do you do it?" she asked after a moment. He looked up from his book, blinking several times at her, "Oh, deduction?" She nodded, and he shrugged, turning back to his book. "It comes naturally, I guess... I never really thought about it."

The two continued to have a very one-sided conversation until the 'School's Out' bell rang. Martin tossed his book into his bag, glad that he was almost finished with it, and nodded slightly to Alena. "I will see you in two hours."

He turned and left, leaving Alena standing by the table. Someone looked from her to Martin's retreating back before shrugging it off. Alena watched the observer continue onwards, heading toward the bright yellow school busses that were parked in front of the building.

***

Martin straightened his Onyx Loden Coat as he stood on Alena's doorstep. He cleared his throat before ringing the doorbell. A rich, melodious sound echoed from within the house before a middle-aged woman opened the door about a foot. She glanced suspiciously at him before speaking. "Yes?"

"I'm here for a meeting with Jack Steward, ma'am," he said courteously, "Is he in? He told me to meet him here at five."

"Jack honey! The boy is here!" called the lady, leaning back into the house and calling for the man in question. *Judging by the suffix, this is Alena's mother.*

A tall, imposing figure opened the door the rest of the way. Martin had to admit this man knew how to make an impression. He was around six feet tall, with graying salt-and-pepper hair and a sharp nose. His blue eyes were hawkish, set in an angular and ruddy face. He was dressed in a suit and tie, both midnight blue, and one of his large hands was playing with his moustache.

"So you're Martin Spire?" he asked carefully, continuing to stroke his moustache. Martin nodded, offering his hand. Jack took it, shaking it firmly. Martin's grip was strong, but not strong enough to hurt the man. Not that he was trying.

"Won't you come in?" he asked, motioning for Martin to come inside. As he passed the large man, he felt someone whisper in his ear, "Nice coat."

He looked at the woman, who was smiling slightly. "I'm from Austria," she explained. "Genuine Loden, hmm?"

Martin nodded, hanging it on a hanger she offered him and parking it in the hallway closet for the time being. He felt extremely naked without it, but tonight was about impressing Alena's parents, not worrying about his own childish apprehensions.

"Dinner's almost ready," said Alena's mother, walking back into the kitchen. "If you'll sit on the couch, I'll call when it's done."

Martin looked around for the family room. Even though he'd been inside their house before, Martin had to make it seem like it was his first time. After locating the sofa, he sat down gently, folding his hands in his lap and waiting.

Jack walked in, sitting on one of the seats across from Martin. He eyed the youth carefully, as if willing him to do something wrong. Martin regarded him with neutrality, watching the older man equally as warily.

"How did you meet my daughter?" asked Jack at length. Martin's hands moved ever so slightly in his lap; an indication that he was upset at the question having been asked.

"We were both in the cafeteria, and were both victims of foul play by a group of young ladies," said Martin. Jack eyed him again. Martin was rapidly tiring of this game. "Did she not tell you?"

"We just got back from Panama last night," said Jack, "Wonderful place, really."

Martin nodded, "I've only ever seen it in photographs," he said. "My uncle is in Turkey though, and he says that's lovely countryside as well."

Jack was impressed, "I'm sure it is. Now, where are your parents? Isn't it customary for them to accompany the child who hopes to date my daughter?"

"Both my parents are dead," explained Martin, "They died when I was six. I lived with my uncle until I was sixteen. On my sixteenth birthday I won my emancipation in court."

Jack's gaze had become interested, almost bordering on shocked. "Where do you live now?"

"9708, Onyx Drive," he said calmly, "It's the single-story blue house in the cul-de-sac near the High School."

This was partially true. Dais had funded a small house for Martin since he acted as the above-ground contact for the Tzen. If anyone was asked where he lived, he was to give out that address.

Jack nodded, looking up at his wife, "Is it ready?" he asked. The woman nodded, "I'm Camilla, by the way," she said, extending a thin hand toward Martin. He took it, shaking it firmly but gently so as not to hurt her. That would NOT leave a good impression.

"Alright then," said Jack, standing up and rubbing his hands together, "Alena!"

The young lady in question came down the stairs, smiling at Martin and at her father as she entered the room.

Her father gestured to the adjoining dining room, "Shall we eat?"

Martin made a great show of being polite. He held Alena's chair out for her, pushing it back in. This earned him an approving look from Camilla, but something suspicious flickered in Jack's eyes.

"Alright, then," said Jack, "Let's eat."

Without saying a blessing, for which Martin was glad, they began to eat. The only reason Martin detested prayer was because he didn't believe in a God. That and he didn't know any. He sighed in his mind, looking down at the lobster bisque Camilla had prepared. *Good thing I love seafood.*

Chapter 24: Permission and Treats

Little was said over dinner. Martin wasn't certain if this was customary or if they weren't used to having guests. Either way, the silence suited him just fine. After he had finished, he dabbed his lips with a napkin, nodding toward Alena's mother. "The bisque was very good, ma'am," he said quietly. Camilla smiled at him.

"Now then," said Jack pointedly, leaning across the table slightly, "We've got business to discuss. Why would you like to take my daughter to this dance?"

Martin straightened. Now this was an attitude he could appreciate – an almost blunt straightforwardness. "Apparently, my intervening in the cafeteria earned her some negative publicity. I wanted to make it up to her."

Alena's face turned fiery red and she shrank slightly in her seat. Martin mentally kicked himself in the head. That wasn't the intended reaction. Camilla leaned forward toward her daughter, "Alena, honey, what happened?"

Alena was quiet for a moment before responding. "Some girls picked on me," she said softly, "One of them hit me, and Martin interfered."

Jack sighed, "Why were they mad at you?" he asked, temporarily forgetting Martin was seated at the table. The raven haired youth found this suited his tastes just fine.

"They were cheerleaders," she said, "I called one of them a tramp after she called me a crazy bitch."

Camilla looked over at Martin, "Thank you," she said quickly. "Jack, I don't see the harm in him taking her to one dance, do you?"

Jack was quiet, and Martin could feel the hesitation emanating from him. It was quite typical for the father of a young lady to have misgivings about a young man who was coming to take her on a date. Martin understood this – he was certain that if he ever had a daughter he would be the same way.

"After all, Jack," continued Camilla, "You said you thought she should go to more social events."

Jack finally seemed to cave, turning to Martin. "Alright, you can take her," he said. "I'm warning you though: try any funny business-"

"Do I strike you as the type?" interrupted Martin. He had remained calm, even though Jack was almost yelling at him. His orange-red eyes were fixed unblinkingly on the man's ice blue ones.

"And take out those damn contacts!" snapped Jack after a moment, staring at his plate, "Kids these days..."

"These are not contact lenses, sir," he said, "They are my true eye color."

Jack's face looked up in surprise, but he said nothing. After a few moments of tense silence, the large man seemed to acquiesce. "I think we're done with dinner," he said awkwardly, "Er... if you want to leave you can," he said looking at Martin.

Nodding his thanks, Martin quickly retrieved his Loden Coat from the hall closet and pushed his arms through the shoulders. "Would you like me to give you a cell phone number, sir?" he asked before he left. Jack seemed to like the idea, so Martin scrawled his number on a scrap of paper and handed it to him.

"Have a nice night, Mr. Steward," he said, nodding politely to him. He turned around and walked out of Alena's home, the chilly night air blowing across his features. He disappeared into the gathering night, heading in the direction of his 'Alibi Home', just in case Jack got suspicious and followed him. Besides, there was a connecting path to The Hall from the backyard.

He arrived at the single story blue house at around eight, barely managing to see well enough to fumble a key out of his pocket and unlock the door. Thanks to the high-powered ventilation system, there was almost no dust in the area. Rather than bask in the indoor warmth, however, Martin walked out the back door and opened one of the large fir trees there, descending into The Hall.

***

He reentered The Hall to find Jason smirking at him. He sighed, rolling his eyes at him. "What do you want?"

"Well, the DJ is gonna play some Mozart and a little bit of Tchaikovsky for you and Alena to dance to. He'll also toss in a bit of Gershwin here and there. Of course, this is a four-hour dance, keep in mind. There will be a lot of that mindless crap people think is music these days."

Martin nodded his thanks and walked off to report to Dais. He heard Jason begin snickering from behind him. He paused, turning back to face the Information Dealer. "What's so funny?"

"Just the way you handled yourself at Alena's tonight," he snorted, "You acted like Little Lord Fauntleroy in front of her parents!"

Martin's brow furrowed, but he ignored it. "How was I supposed to act?" he asked, "Give them both a hug and a kiss?"

Jason blanched at the mental image, "Er, I don't think so."

"Then keep your nose out of my personal affairs, thank you very much." With that haughty statement, Martin turned around and walked into Dais' chambers.

Much to his surprise, he found Alena waiting for him there. He barely managed to conceal his shock. "How did you get here before I did?"

It was Dais, however, who spoke. "This girl, Martin, is an absolute genius," he proclaimed, "Not only has she earned herself the rights to study under *Steven*," the commanding Tzen cast Martin a reproachful glare, as if asking why it hadn't been him to receive the honor, "But she found a previously deactivated tube leading from the Lakewood Park to the East Caverns!"

Martin nodded to Alena in congratulations, but said nothing. "So, what do I do now? I'm still on Cavern Arrest for two more days, right?"

"Not at all," said Dais with a sweep of his hand, "As a matter of fact, I think Alena had something to ask of you."

That shocked him. He looked over at the girl with his usual stoic face plastered on his visage. "You needed something?"

"Let's go get some ice-cream," she said. "My parents just gave me the 'helpless girl versus pervert boy' speech. I need something to calm me down."

"I don't eat ice-cream," Martin responded flatly, trying to sound untouched by her offer. In reality, he was quite stunned by her question, and something in his insides jumbled. Now where in the world had THAT come from? *Don't tell me she's becoming fond of me... that would be ridiculous... I am most certainly NOT becoming attached to HER!*

"Come on," she continued, "I bet even YOU have a favorite flavor..." she smiled at him and Martin felt a part of his insides melt. The girl's smile had suddenly become a catalyst to his well-kept emotions. Martin found this fact absolutely appalling... *Despite how cute her smile is. Rgh, I did not just think that.*

"I told you before, I don't eat ice-cream," he replied, much to Alena's disappointment.

"You meant you *don't* eat it, or you've never *tried* it?" she asked in curiosity. Martin found he had nothing to say, not really knowing how to retort. It was common knowledge among the Tzen that he spent all his free time training or reading, and had never spent his time on silly or childish things like ice-cream.

Alena's eyes widened all the more at Martin's hesitation and the realization of the truth. "You're kidding me," she gasped, "You've NEVER tried ice-cream before?" Her delicate fingers flew to her mouth, curtaining her lips.

Martin's glare intensified at her surprised outburst. So what if he hadn't tasted ice-cream before? He wasn't too fond of sweets, nor was he interested in trying the cold dessert. It was merely a child's treat, one that no adult should be eating as well. He shouldn't have felt embarrassed.

And yet here I stand, reddening like a tomato.

"That's it," said Alena, "We're going. My treat, alright?" she beamed at him with a hint of authority he hadn't seen from her. He was slightly taken aback. *As in... a date? Is she asking me on a DATE?*

"Forget it," he muttered angrily, "I don't want any." He shrugged his shoulders and leaned against the wall, glowering at Dais. *Bastard probably planned this whole thing... thinks he's funny or something...*

"I'm *famished* though, Martin!" she complained, trying to give him the puppy-dog eyes.

"You'll survive," he grunted, focusing anywhere but on her pleading face. For some reason, he didn't think he'd be able to resist this time. *Please stop pestering me!*

"Come on, Martin, just ONE cup, alright? I promise I'll leave you alone after that? Deal?" she pleaded with him, causing him to grit his teeth. He accidentally locked his gaze on hers. *DAMN her! Damn her and those eyes!*

"Woman, are you insane?" he said, "It is nighttime. It is cold. Ice-cream, as I understand it, is meant to be eaten on a *hot day*, not a *cold night*!" He grinned inwardly. *Ha! Beat that logic!*

Her grin suddenly intensified, and Martin felt something squirm inside him. Why did her grin make him so nervous?

"Cold times are the BEST times to eat ice-cream!" she said, "You can savor it longer because you don't have to rush to eat it quickly. It won't melt as quickly as it would on a hot day!"

Martin pondered this for a moment before inwardly (DEEPLY inwardly) applauding her logic. What she had just said made perfect sense, although he would rather lick a recently vacated public toilet seat than admit it.

The stoic boy tapped his teeth together impatiently, in obvious consideration of her offer. Alena bit her lip to keep her smile from growing. She knew she was slowly winning him over.

"I hardly consider anything with a high sugar content to be very nutritious..." he said, letting the sentence trail off. He was silently cluing that he had surrendered. Alena let out an excited squeal and jumped over to him, wrapping her thin arms around his neck. Their cheeks wound up touching.

"Oh, you won't be disappointed!" she exclaimed. She was displaying all the vigor of a little girl who had gotten a pony for Christmas. Her grip tightened and Martin couldn't help but feel overwhelmed at her sudden act of affection.

She hugged him.

No normal person had the *GUTS* to touch him.

How could something as small as agreeing to go eat ice-cream with her make her so overjoyed. However, before he could ponder that any further, the girl was already dragging him out the door, her excitement making Martin work doubly hard to suppress a smile. Something about the simplicity in the things that made her smile was refreshing to him. He couldn't quite put his finger on it.

Alena was checking the pockets of her pants for money. Finally, Martin decided that as long as he had to do this, he would do it right. He pulled out his wallet. "I'll pay..." he muttered. Although *she* was the one who wanted to make him eat this stuff, he wouldn't dare make her pay for it. His parents would be rolling in their graves if he let her pay for his meal. It just wasn't... gentlemanly. *Since when do I care?*

The only thing he hoped for was that she wasn't a big or exotic eater...

"I don't want anything too extraordinary," he said as she hauled him into one of the chutes that led to the surface. For some reason, he felt as light as a feather, as though he could escape The Hall without the use of the chute.

"That's fine," she said, tugging at the sleeve of his Loden coat. "Come on."

Chapter 25: Ice-Cream

Martin peered at the menu, instinctively checking the prices. He let out an inward sigh as he realized they weren't too expensive. He only had fifty dollars, had he wasn't exactly sure how much an ice-cream cost. *Heck, I barely buy anything above ground outside of the school...*

He had no idea such a place existed in Steilacoom. The room was rather small, and yet it radiated warmth despite being an ice-cream restaurant. The style was simple, with booths, leather seats, and red-and-white checkered tablecloths. The walls were painted a light yellow, and the furniture was a lighter shade of brown than what he was used to seeing. Overall, it was a nice place with a good feel. For some reason, he felt rather comfortable here.

Best of all, he didn't see anyone he recognized. No acquaintances meant the probability for trouble to start became extremely low.

While gazing at the choices, Alena kept sneaking looks at him and smiling as if she were more than happy he had decided to come. It was caught, of course, by his sharp vision, and he was very surprised that his coming had made her so ecstatic.

"I'm not too fond of sweets..." he muttered, "I'll just get vanilla."

Alena's eyes widened slightly. "Wow... I was just going to order that. I'm not too big on sweets either..."

"Why were you so set on getting ice-cream then? You LOOKED like the sweet-loving type," he said flatly. She just smiled at him, and then he remembered her words from earlier. *Right... to distract her from her parent's ramblings...*

"Two vanilla, in cups," said Alena as she signaled the waiter on duty. When the cups were set in front of him, Martin eyed his as though it was about to explode and turn into a Zerolyte.

"Go on, try it!" urged Alena, watching him closely. He gave her an annoyed look. "You were the one who was so thrilled about coming here," he muttered quietly, "You eat first." Still, the dessert looked temptingly delicious, and he had to work to suppress the childish excitement that had bubbled from within him and wanted to surface.

She made no oppositions, and began to eat the ice-cream, savoring the delectable treat. While she ate, Martin couldn't help but notice the male waiter eyeing Alena from where he stood in the corner. He frowned. That guy, probably still in High School, was staring at her with a lustful expression on his face. He was checking her out.

Feeling a sudden wash of protectiveness, Martin gave the young man a deadly look before placing his clenched fist near her hand, so that it would appear they were dating.

The boy gave a disappointed and irritated look before resuming his chores.

Unable to figure out exactly why he had done that, he began eating his ice-cream. He admitted it was good, but wasn't about to let Alena know that. When she asked, however, he merely deflected the question into different forms of Energy Manipulation.

Alena was watching him as intently as he'd been watching her. Martin hadn't really picked up the scope of her gazing, for which she was glad. She watched him use his thin hands to illustrate the proper shape for a Lightning Incantation. When he spoke, she could hardly recognize him as the cold-hearted boy she'd met at the High School a few days ago. His words entranced her, and his intelligence astounded her. *How is this guy NOT swarmed by an army of drooling girls?*

One thing she concluded, however, was that she would treasure the friendship she had with the boy... no, man... in front of her. She decided that he was something special... in a good way, of course.

There was a quiet moment between the two, although it was anything but awkward. They just stared at the table, almost like they had fallen asleep or died on the spot. They stat there for a moment, just glad for the other's company. As quickly as the moment had come, however, it left, and the awkwardness awoke once again.

Suddenly, the male waiter walked past their table, and there was an odd clattering sound. Instinctively, the two looked up. Behind Alena's chair, the waiter had clumsily juggled a tray full of empty glasses while attempting to place a full glass on the table. He wobbled a bit, but despite his efforts, the idiot's clumsiness dominated.

The glass came tumbling down...

...right onto Alena's Loden Coat.

"Oh God, I'm SO sorry," exclaimed the waiter as he dove behind the counter for paper towels and a rag. Alena didn't seem bothered at all. She was staring at her shirt as if someone had told her there was a piece of lint hanging on it. The waiter returned and began by cleaning the mess off the floor. Martin's eyebrows furrowed.

This man was beginning to wear on his patience. First the lustful looks and now the giant spill. *If I didn't know any better, I'd think he was trying to get Alena's attention...*

Martin's eye barely refrained from twitching as the waiter stood up to wipe Alena's front. *Quit touching her!*

He was inwardly screaming at the young man who was running his fingers through Alena's chocolate-brown tresses as he cleaned them. He knew better than to yell possessive things like that in public, though, so he settled with seething quietly at the man instead.

However, when the pervert's hands began to stray to close to Alena's breasts with the rag Martin decided it was time to intervene. His hand shot out, clasping the waiter's wrist – hard. "I think you had better go get some more paper towels," he gritted, giving the boy a full-on death glare. Martin released his arm, giving him one more death glare for good measure. "The floor's sticky."

Alena, meanwhile, was too busy with dabbing at the coat to notice the sparks flying between the two men. They were as territorial as two stray dogs fighting over a piece of meat. The waiter finally acquiesced and fled back behind the counter away from Martin. The black-haired boy let out an inward breath of relief. He didn't like that waiter. If there hadn't been an elderly couple sitting in the corner, Martin probably would have beaten the crap out of him.

"You alright?" he asked, trying to suppress his irritation with the waiter. *Is everyone in Steilacoom a pervert?!*

"...smells like watermelon..." she muttered. Martin took off his Loden coat, draping it around her shoulders in an instinctive maneuver. Alena inhaled his scent, committing it to memory. To her, the coat smelled like roses and cinnamon. He then gave a glance to the empty ice-cream dishes before carelessly discarding them in a nearby wastebasket.

"Shall we go?" he asked. Alena smiled, trying to take off the coat. He put his hands on her shoulders, preventing the coat from being removed. "Just keep it on for now, alright? I'll get you another coat back at The Hall..."

"I couldn't..." the look he gave her booked no argument. She sighed. Martin drew out his wallet, walking over to the counter. *Even if she had her wallet, I wouldn't let her get near that pervy waiter...*

He felt slightly reassured in the fact that with both her and his coats on, she was covered enough to keep that pervert's eyes from wandering. He put the required fare on the counter, paying in exact change. It was a bad habit he'd picked up from Jason.

He motioned toward the door, holding it for Alena. Just before he left, he sent the waiter one last glare, effectively scaring the young man witless. He left, feeling slightly small without his coat on. *At least it's being put to good use...*

He kept a wide distance between himself and Alena on the way back to her home. For some reason, he felt extremely awkward. He activated a minor Ice Incantation, creating a tiny mirror in his hand. He quickly checked it to make sure Alena was still behind him. She was, and was staring at the back of his head with a hazy smile. At the sight of that smile, a part of him melted.

Oh crap... what have I gotten myself into...?

He shook his head. *Correction... Dais, what have YOU gotten me into?*

Unfortunately, Alena wanted to stop at the grocery mart as well. She had brought her debit cart, much to

Martin's chagrin until he remembered it had been his *offer* to treat her to ice-cream.

That was how the impassive Martin Spire found himself inside the grocery mart with Alena. In the midst of his bitter resentment, there was one thing that baffled him the most. Why had he even bothered entering the building with her?

He pondered this, among other things, while he walked with her. Some things were understandable. *Why did my heart beat fast in that ice-cream parlor?* That was easy, he figured. He wasn't used to being in public with anyone, let alone someone of the opposite gender.

It had taken an enormous chunk of his ego to admit that he had actually *liked* spending the time with her. Around her, for some reason, he had actually *wanted* to smile. Of course, being who he was, he suppressed the urge. After several long minutes, he finally managed to whittle down all his 'symptoms' and convince himself that anything that was between them was merely friendship.

"Hey, Martin!" a feminine voice broke through his thoughts, "Stop sulking already, we're almost done!"

Sulking... he thought *...was I sulking?* For some reason his face colored slightly. She smiled at him. "If you're embarrassed to be with me..."

"I'm not embarrassed to be with you." The words had come out of his mouth in the same amount of time it had taken his mind to call him a liar. He shoved his conscience into dormancy again, rubbing the back of his neck in concealed frustration. "I... I just have a reputation to uphold."

Damn...

He knew what the problem was with that statement. Even though his ego had gone down from admitting he liked her... *slightly*... it was still blocking many useful parts of his body: for example – his brain.

At the moment, to quote Derrick, he felt like the biggest asshole in the world. Worse yet, however, was the fact that he couldn't do anything about it... not without Alena discovering many things he didn't want her knowing.

Martin checked his watch. Nine-thirty, on the dot. He sighed. "Alena, are we almost done here?"

"Yeah, I just need some tuna and we're outta here," she replied cheerfully. She all but danced down the next aisle before returning with a blue can of tuna fish clenched in her hand. She tossed it into the basket before smiling at Martin. He gave a breath of relief. Nobody had seen him with a...

"Martin... what are you doing?"

...girl.

He turned around, resisting the urge to punch Jason in the mouth. The information dealer was standing right there, trying his hardest not to laugh. "You..."

"Jason," remarked Martin coldly, "If one word about this gets out, you're going to be the next victim of my Trezin spell, understood?"

Jason grinned at him, "Are you sure you'd do that while your girlfriend was around, cuz right now you two look damn near inseparable!"

Martin felt heat rise into his face, and forced it back down. "I'm serious, Jason."

Jason knew he was serious. Heck, since when was Martin ever anything else. He also knew Martin wouldn't kill him if he kept his mouth shut. However, if Dais knew...

He turned and walked off, ducking into an aisle full of baby food and masking himself with an Air Incantation. While invisible, he drew out his cell phone and turned on the video capture setting. Grinning evilly, he came around the corner and began filming the two Tzen as they walked to the checkout lanes.

Martin knew exactly what Jason was doing. Did the information dealer really think he couldn't sense him there? Unfortunately, there was nothing Martin could do. He couldn't exactly punch thin air, exposing it as a seventeen-year-old boy with a penchant for Energy Manipulation, in the middle of a crowded Quickie Mart.

For the second time in three hours, Martin wanted to drown his head in a sewer as Jason kept on filming him and

Alena – close enough to fit onto the same screen of a narrow cell phone camera.

Chapter 26: Patrol

Martin stared at Dais with horror on his face. Taking Alena out in public for ice-cream was one thing, but this... "You want me to do WHAT?"

Dais smirked at him, sliding a manila envelope toward him. Martin snatched it up and flicked it open, his orange eyes scanning down the page. There was no doubt about it. Steven had authorized this one personally. Martin allowed his head to fall until his chin touched his chest. "Yes sir..."

He tossed the envelope back onto Dais' desk, striding out of the room. It wasn't bad enough that Jason had shown the cell phone's video to Dais, who had in turn told all of the Tzen... no, his torment couldn't just stop there, could it? *Why me?*

***

Guard duty. That was the one chore around The Cavern Martin actually hated. He could even deal with picking up litter near the entrances – all fifteen of them – but guard duty was downright boring. Not only was he strolling aimlessly around waiting for something to happen, Dais had assigned him to investigate the Mainland Shelf while on duty, making sure it was 'free from hostiles'.

Alena had gone to Island Two to train with the elusive Tzen, Steven, leaving him in the clutches of Dais. He pulled on his Loden Coat, cursing Dais in three different languages as he crammed his Tzen Rod into his coat pocket, fervently hoping Dais suffered a debilitating aneurism within the next twenty minutes.

Jason was having the time of his life. He followed Martin all the way to the lift that would take him to the Mainland Shelf, nagging him about proper dating etiquette. Martin had to dig into inner reserves to prevent himself from throttling the exuberant youth.

"Jason..." he gritted after a moment of silence, "Go away."

Jason decided to comply running off to pester one of the Island Nine girls who happened to be on Island Twelve for medical training from Terra. Martin boarded the gondola, jerking the lever into the ON position and trundling across the chasm that separated him from the ever-mysterious Mainland Shore.

***

It was quiet – that was the first thing Martin noticed. It wasn't the 'nice' quiet he appreciated when the rest of the Tzen were excavating the South Tunnels. It wasn't the deafening silence he felt sometimes in his sleep. This was a different quiet – like a crypt. It felt as though some invisible hand had strangled all the sound, rendering the area mute.

Martin closed his eyes and inhaled deeply through his nose. The air even smelled different over here. Whereas the Twelve Islands smelled like earth, this area still carried that lingering scent of blood – undoubtedly wafting from the door to the Lower Levels.

Two other Tzen were waiting for him at the entrance to the Palace District. Martin recognized one of them from his training days – Frank Dearing. Frank was an intelligent boy with blazing blue eyes and pale blonde hair. His personality closely mimicked Michael; wanting to help people in any way he could.

The other boy was Richard Thorne. His red hair was standing in all directions, much like Douglas', and his eyes were lime green. They held no warmth, but his face was split into a wide smile. Martin had never actually *met* Richard, but had heard of him and his habit of disobeying commands. While a talented Tzen, Richard had a habit of using incantations in unorthodox ways – often getting the job done but injuring himself and his comrades in the process.

"So, we're all pulling GD?" asked Frank, smiling at Martin. Martin nodded back, dispensing a small smile of his own. Frank was a trustworthy ally, and one Martin would have rather been tied to instead of Douglas. Unfortunately, Douglas' abilities made up for his slight shortcomings, and thus they became a team. Frank was now partnered with some girl named Mary-Anne Rogers over on Island Three.

"Yes," said Martin. His usual clipped voice was even sharper today, and he saw Richard raise his eyebrows at the curtness of the statement. Still, the redhead refused to say anything.

"We're each going to split up," said Martin after a moment of thinking, "I'll take the large marble building in front of us. Frank – you take that sprawling building with the iron gates. Richard – you go ahead and check through that archway over there – inside the building lit by blue lights."

The three shared a nod before each going their separate ways. Martin strode up to the large building, marveling inwardly at the complexity of the outside structure. It was a rectangular construction, with pillars supporting a gently curving roof. The doors were elegant, having been wrought from bronze. There were letters on the handles, but Martin found he couldn't decipher them.

Sighing in annoyance, he pushed on the doors. Much to his surprise, they opened. A dank, musty smell drifted from inside, along with the unmistakable smell of blood. There wasn't as much in this building as in the Lower Levels, but the smell was still there.

Drawing his rod, Martin quietly stepped inside, looking around. There were bookshelves everywhere, but any literature had long since rotted away. What little remained was unreadable, as it crumbled when he touched it. His frown deepened. *Just how old is this place?*

The 'library' was empty. There was a large, central column with stairs winding up around it, leading upwards to a higher level. Martin was about to ascend when his keen hearing picked up a sound. It sounded like something scratching at wood. Before he explored further, he was going to figure out what that sound was.

But there is no way I'm doing it alone...

He left the library, closing the door behind him. While a lone wolf at heart, Martin had no intentions of running into something he couldn't handle. He weighed his options between choosing either Frank or Richard for this mission. It was a no-brainer - he tilted his head back and yelled for Frank. What use was it calling for Richard if he probably wouldn't come anyway?

In moments, the blonde came running up with his wand out. Martin explained about the sound and Frank was eager to help – as usual. Martin gave him his gratitude – something he rarely gave to anyone – before opening the door again and stepping inside.

The sound was louder now, and both boys tightened their grips on their Tzen Rods as they walked. Frank walked backwards, his back pressed against Martin's. After a moment, they pinpointed the sound as having come from above them. They nodded to each other before quietly ascending the stairs.

The upper level was much the same as the bottom. Bookshelves lined the walls, their shelves empty and bare.

Frank gave a shudder, "I really don't like this." He muttered, "No... I don't like this at all..."

"Let's just keep moving," replied Martin, hoping to hide the slight tremor in his voice. Whatever was making those sounds was close – he could *feel* it. The hairs on his neck were standing at attention like soldiers, and every nerve in his stomach was screaming at him to run.

They stepped off the stairs onto the marble floor of the second level. They stuck close to each other, checking down aisles and behind bookcases for any signs of recent activity.

"Something's bothering me," said Frank after a moment. Martin looked up from examining a fallen bookcase to stare at his partner. "The whole time we've been here, we've heard something, right?"

"Yeah, that's why I called you," replied Martin, standing up and walking over to his comrade.

"But whatever is in here has left no footprints in the dust – the only set is ours."

Martin suddenly realized his mistake. The curved roof of the building was most likely either made of wood or lined with it. Whatever this was wasn't on the ground at all – *it was on the ceiling!*

"Frank! Get under something!"

The blonde dove beneath an elegant iron table as something landed on the tops of a row of bookshelves across the room from them. Martin dove beneath a leaning bookcase, his eyes focusing through the gloom at the source of the sound.

A large, low-slung, hairy body was perched precariously atop four spindly legs. It was perfectly symmetrical with the exception of the humanoid face leering at them from one side of the bulbous, furry body. The eyes were swollen and glowing, emitting a yellowish glow, which pierced the darkness like knives. The mouth was twisted into something like a combination of a scream of pain and a ghastly smile. Martin's wand was in his hand in a flash, his eyes searching for a Thread.

Crap!

There wasn't a single Thread running through the library. Not one. That would explain why this building still housed this abomination – unless it had moved in recently.

"Frank! I'm gonna distract it! You go get Richard!"

Frank nodded and dove for the stairs. The creature lunged for him, but Martin was already in its path. He grabbed it by the front two legs, flipping it sideways. It wasn't heavy, despite being larger than him, and Martin suspected it was merely an oversized insect. Frank, in the meantime, had made his getaway and could be heard screaming for Richard.

Martin stepped away as the creature righted itself. It seemed to be an odd process for the symmetrical beast. It hoisted itself up on its legs, despite the fact that its body was upside-down, and then flipped two of the legs over the top like an acrobat, thus righting itself.

Martin's eyes cast around the room for anything that could be used as a weapon. Apart from the bookshelves lining the walls and the table Frank had scuttled beneath, the room was bare. Cursing, Martin watched as the creature slowly walked forward.

It had a bizarre, lilting gait, the body swinging from side-to-side as it walked. The very sight of it unnerved Martin. In a flash, the face's mouth closed. It reopened a moment later, and Martin barely had time to pull his coat up to block a spray of something sticky. Martin surmised it was likely some kind of poison or paralytic acid. The stench was horrific – it smelled like week-old fish.

He heard the door beneath open, and Frank came charging up the stairs with one of the egg-shaped grenades in his hand. "Suck it!" he crowed, throwing the projectile directly at the spider-like abomination. It struck dead on, emitting a flash of light. A screech filled the room, deafening Martin for a moment.

As his hearing returned, he could hear Frank and Richard throwing curses at the creature, along with several rocks. He normally would have laughed at how childish it looked, but without the Threads they were virtually helpless. Martin shook the fog from his mind and climbed up a bookshelf, bracing his back against the wall. The other Tzen might have been helpless, but he wasn't going to resort to throwing rocks like a fourth grader. He pushed with his legs, feeling the bookshelf give way beneath him and fall forward.

There was a sickening thud as it hit the body of the creature, knocking it out. Martin quickly grabbed the nearest thing he could reach, surprised as it came away in his hand. The leg of the table had come completely off. Snarling, Martin proceeded to beat the spider-thing around what he assumed to be the head until he was quite certain it was deceased.

He drew in a breath, tossing the bloody table leg to the side. Greenish-yellow pus oozed from the various wounds he'd inflicted, but other than that the spider was relatively unharmed.

"Thanks for your help... Let's leave it here for now," he suggested, "We'll cart it to Island Seven later – we all know how much Lisa will love something like this..."

Lisa was the biologist in the cavern. Although she looked to be no older than seventeen, she was actually twenty-nine. She had named, observed, and categorized more than fifty creatures since her first trip to The Hall a year ago.

Both boys nodded in concurrence before Richard spoke. "If a spider inhabits a library, I wonder what inhabits a museum..."

Martin's face lost what little color it had.

Chapter 27: Museum

The part of the Mainland Shelf that Richard had called the museum definitely deserved the name. There were rows of glass cases along the walls, and a few artifacts seemed to have survived. Mostly, they were items with metal parts such as swords and shields. Martin gave an inward shrug, watching the dim blue light dance across the blade of a sword. At least if something *did* inhabit this place they wouldn't be unarmed.

Richard was poking around near a display case full of cut gemstones while Frank had gone off to examine a wall covered in various shields. Martin sighed, looking around. There were stairs on the opposite side of the room from the entrance leading downward to a lower floor. The air smelled coppery, but it wasn't the smell of blood.

"I don't think anything's living here," said Martin after a while. Frank looked away from the shield display. "Huh?"

"The air doesn't smell like blood," Martin informed him; "The library had a faint trace of it, which I think can be attributed to that creature."

Richard stood up from the gemstone display, "I'm not so sure," he told Martin, "There is evidence of a struggle in this area. It's faint, but it's there."

Martin immediately began to look around as Richard explained. "The case containing a few spears is tipped over, and it looks like it would normally take a lot of force to do that."

Martin walked over to the fallen case, examining the spears as they lay jumbled across the floor like chopsticks. "Also, the central pillar has lots of cracks, almost like something hit it with incredible force."

Again, Martin had to admit that Richard was right. A large marble column, probably fifteen feet thick, was rising from the floor to the ceiling. It was cracked almost all the way through, but still resting upon itself.

"That is strange," said Frank after a moment, "I'd attributed most of that to age."

"Think," snapped Martin as he looked around for more evidence, "How can age tip over a stone-and-glass display case?" Frank looked at the case for a moment before shrugging.

"Oh shit..." Martin looked over to Richard, who had begun descending the stairs. "Guys, you might want to see this."

Martin walked over and stood next to Richard, Frank following suit. The stairs suddenly ended in a large cylindrical pit. It looked as though it had been carved by a machine; the walls were perfectly smooth. Frank tossed a small stone down, listening for the sound of it striking the bottom.

After five minutes with no sound, he gave up. "Well, we know that it's deep…" he said calmly, backing away from the shaft. "I'm *not* going to be the one to jump down first."

"I don't think any of us are," said Richard, also backing away, "Let's get out of here. There's obviously nothing left here for us to explore."

"First we should grab a weapon," said Martin. He was the only one to turn his back on the pit and walk away rather than back up. "We don't know what's in that third building – it's a good idea to be prepared."

Unfortunately, this was easier said than done. Martin would have preferred a sword, but had to settle with a spear. Whatever had broken the case open was extremely strong – not even all three of them could kick through the glass. He hefted a light spear, twirling it experimentally.

"I feel like I've gone back in time," he muttered, "Spears aren't going to do us much good if our enemy can use Energy Manipulation…"

Frank chose a large iron spear; thick around as his arm, and lay it across his shoulders. "It doesn't matter," he said, "I don't think anything down here *can*. Have you noticed the complete lack of Threads?"

"Maybe that's why this group of individuals died out," suggested Richard. He hefted the remaining spears, testing one for balance.

"Probably not – there are Threads on the Twelve Islands, remember?" supplied Martin as he walked toward the door, "Come on, let's check out that last building."

With one last glance around the trio departed. They crossed the Palace District courtyard and strode up to the iron gates that encircled a third building. Martin inserted his spear into a small gap and forced the gates open, snapping his spear in the process. He scowled, tossing the broken shaft away.

"Here," Richard handed him another, and Martin twirled it again, "Good. Thanks."

Before they went inside, Frank asked if they could stop for lunch. They each decided to return to their respective islands to collect their lunch pails before exploring this building. Martin rode back with his two teammates, but they parted ways as he went into the bedding chambers.

He fetched the lunch pail, making sure it was full of the usual non-perishable items it was required to store before walking back out and waiting at the gondola. Frank came back first, his pail clutched tightly in his fist. "Oh hey, you're fast," he grinned, leaning next to Martin, "So, what's in the pail? Last time you hid a few grenades in there."

"I do not have grenades in my lunch pail," deadpanned Martin.

"Then what's in there, goddamnit?" pestered Frank, staring eagerly at the lidded pail as if it contained the secrets of the universe.

"My lunch."

"Oh..." Frank felt like the largest dolt in the cavern at that moment, but was saved as Richard came up with his pail slung over his shoulder. He nodded at his comrades as they stepped onto the gondola, pressing the lever and beginning their ride back to the Mainland Shelf.

A few days ago, I never thought I'd be using a gondola to the Mainland Shelf as easily as I travel between islands...

He stepped off, walking over to the building they had yet to enter. He pulled out a packet of meat from within his lunch pail, unwrapping it and tearing a small section off. He bit into it, relishing the juicy ham as he chewed. He swallowed it, watching his teammates eat their lunches as well.

Frank had brought a simple PB&J. As any Tzen knew, that was his all-time favorite meal. Along with the sandwich, he had also brought a soda and a bag of chips. It was a simple, yet effective lunch for on-the-go people. Martin figured being a Tzen qualified him as an on-the-go person. It was one of the reasons he was in such good shape.

Constantly running around the cavern, training, and using Energy Manipulation left his body little time to acquire fat reserves. Not only that, but Martin also had resolved himself not to eat too many unhealthy foods – hence the reason he was sticking to a plain sandwich roll, a bag of jerky, and a small packet of ham.

Richard, on the other hand, was opening a can of tuna and spreading the contents on a cracker. Next to him on the ground was a single-serve bottle of sparkling cider, as well as a bag of potato chips.

They ate in silence, each one preoccupied with their own thoughts. It was unusual. Seeing as the Tzen were split up among twelve islands, mealtimes were usually loud, filled with the latest gossip and information from the neighboring islands.

Finally, Frank broke the silence. "I hear you asked that new girl to the dance."

Martin eyed him warily, wondering where he was going with this. "Yes, I did. Why?"

The blonde grinned, turning to Richard, "Look at that," he said, "Our little Martin's all grown up now…"

Martin resisted the urge to kill him, but instead resumed eating the ham. "What of it?"

"Well, how are you going to approach this?" asked Richard, putting down his tuna and crackers and staring at Martin intently. Martin looked up at him, easily masking the confusion that wanted to take up residence on his visage. "Huh?"

Both boys sighed in exasperation. "Let's start with the basics," said Frank, "What are you wearing?"

"Wait!" Martin put down the empty packet of ham, reaching for the beef jerky. "Since when are you two dating experts?"

Richard leaned forward, "I'm not, but Frank reads enough about human relationships to qualify. Me? I just read romance novels."

Martin quietly contemplated the pros and cons of strangling the two into silence, but decided to go along with it. It wasn't as if he *had* to listen to what they were saying. "I'm wearing my usual attire, replacing my blue coat with onyx black."

Frank gaped at him, "Are you nuts? You want to make a good impression, don't you? It's a formal dance, yes?"

Martin frowned, "Yes."

"That's it. When our shift is off in forty minutes, we're going to drag your ass to the Towne Center and buy you a suitable outfit." Richard was staring at Martin as if he'd never seen him before.

"What does it matter?" asked Martin, popping a piece of jerky in his mouth, "Nobody cares, do they?"

Frank slapped his forehead, "Girls like Alena care *a lot* about that sort of thing, you know," he supplied, "And they call you a genius..."

Martin said nothing, filling his mouth with another strip of jerky. Truth be told, he was incredibly unsettled by the whole prospect. He was, by definition, a simple person. He liked things that made sense. Someone caring about clothing... just didn't make sense to him. Clothes were meant to be practical and functional, weren't they? You wear a coat when you're cold, not for image...

I'm a fine one to talk... I never take off my coat even when it's 80 plus outside...

Frank was chattering with Richard about different styles of clothing for formal dances. Martin finished his jerky without a sound, watching the two talk about it as if it were the end of the world. Finally, he spoke.

"And if I choose not to listen to your 'advice'... then what?"

Frank stared incredulously at him. "Richard, help this dork grow a pair of balls, would you? He needs to do this – the girl..."

Richard promptly clamped a hand across Frank's mouth. "He needs to figure that one out on his own, Frank."

More confused than ever, Martin popped the last of the jerky into his mouth, chewing it as he watched his comrades. "What about Alena am I supposed to figure out?"

"You'll see," said Richard, removing his hand as Frank gasped for air, "That is, I hope you will. You're pretty dense."

Martin felt a vein in his forehead twitch slightly. *Dense?!* He frowned, tearing a bit of bread from the dinner roll and popping it into his mouth. *I'm not dense...*

"And you sulk."

"What the hell does that have to do with anything?" snapped Martin, looking up from his roll. "I do not!"

Richard was grinning at him, exposing the gold incisor in his mouth. Martin sorely wanted to punch it into his throat, but took a few breaths to calm himself. "Fine. We'll go to the Towne Center after our shift is done. I would request, however, that you not make fools of yourselves."

The two clapped themselves on the back for a job well done while Martin watched, silently wondering what he'd gotten himself into.

Chapter 28: A Different Dance

Martin stood outside Alena's door, debating whether or not he should just turn tail and flee. His pride stopped him, however, and he reached forward and pressed the doorbell. He fumbled absently with the clothes Frank and Richard had chosen for him. He was dressed in a tuxedo, and he felt as if he looked like a penguin. Still, the tux suited his normally stiff demeanor.

"Ready to go?" he asked as Alena came to the door. He refrained from gawking, although he felt the almost irresistible urge to do just that. She was dressed in a maroon sleeveless, spaghetti-strap dress that came just to above her breasts, teasing viewers with a hint of cleavage.

He offered her his arm, focusing on her face instead. She was wearing contacts instead of her usual glasses, and she was lightly made-up so as not to look too tacky. She smiled and accepted, and he walked her down to the vehicle they would be taking. Dais had offered to play chauffer, and Martin had decided to accept.

"So, to the school?" asked Dais as the two teenagers stepped in. Martin nodded, and Dais put his foot on the gas, driving away from Alena's house. "You know, if I didn't know who you were, you'd look just like a normal boy," said Dais after driving in silence. Martin thanked him, but his eyes betrayed him. He was displeased with the statement.

They disembarked outside the school, Martin offering Alena his arm again. They walked around the side of the school, entering the gymnasium from the parking lot doors. Martin instantly felt several eyes on him as he walked in. A few of the people near the door who recognized him were muttering to themselves.

"What is that *animal* doing here?" asked a girl with blonde hair. Martin ignored the statement as he usually did – they were right, after all. The next statement, made by the girl's dancing partner, infuriated him.

"Who cares – check out the chick!"

Martin forced himself not to blow the boy away, resolving to keep walking. They walked around the side of the gym toward the refreshment table, where Martin decided he would wait until some appropriate dancing music played. Alena agreed – she didn't like attempting to dance to rap music.

Martin sipped at a cup full of some kind of punch, watching several students make fools of themselves on the dance floor. One boy was 'dancing' in a manner that involved groping his dance partner as if they were in bed, not in a gym. It made Martin sick.

Finally, Mozart's *Violin Sonata #12* began to play. Several students booed at the musical choice, moving off the dance floor. Martin allowed himself a minute smile. The vacating of the dancing area suited him just fine. He placed his glass of punch down on the table, motioning for Alena to come with him.

They walked out into the cleared area, Martin patting Alena on the shoulder as he felt her stiffen. People were staring at them both, some in open-mouthed surprise. Someone muttered something along the lines of "Who actually dances to this shit?"

Martin took Alena into his arms, murmuring softly in her ear how to position her hands. She nodded almost invisibly, placing her arms correctly around his thin shoulders. Slowly... ever so slowly... they began to dance.

Although Alena seemed to be enjoying herself, Martin had other problems. A few students had actually taken a step forward toward the dancing pair, and Martin looked up to fix them with a full-throttle glare. The students in front stopped, looking uncertainly at each other before deciding it would be in their best interests not to interfere.

Why?

Martin watched as the students ran off to get something to drink from the refreshments table.

Why can't they just piss off and leave Alena and myself alone?

He swayed gently back and forth with Alena in time to the music, feeling himself slipping into the moment. He fought against his urge to sigh contentedly.

I never did anything to any of them...

He broke away from Alena as the song ended, walking back over to the refreshments table to pick up his punch. His paranoia kicked in, and he decided to fill a different cup.

They were afraid of me the first day I came here...

He sipped from it, looking at Alena. "You did well."

That was high praise coming from someone like Martin. He sensed her smile next to him and for a moment gave in and allowed himself to feel content and pleased.

He put down his punch cup as he realized it was empty. He listened to the current song, trying to discern if it was one of the ones Jason had told him would play. Unfortunately, it was merely a classical song with rap lyrics. Cursing whoever thought such an abomination was a good idea, he refilled his cup and took another sip.

"Thank you."

Martin looked over at Alena. She had abandoned her punch in favor of a glass of ice water. He nodded at her, perplexed. "For what?"

"You took me to the dance, didn't you?" she looked at him with something akin to happiness dancing in her eyes. Martin nodded, looking back at the writhing mass of humanity that was 'dancing' in the gym.

"Nobody ever asked me out before..." she trailed off, watching the people dance spasmodically. Martin snorted.

"I can't see why not."

I shouldn't have asked her to come... this will make her reputation worse...

Alena blushed, and Martin could almost sense the heat radiating off her face. He closed his eyes, picturing her visage in his mind. For some reason, it brought him a sense of calm.

I'm insane.

"You're welcome," he said after a moment. Alena looked over at him, a smile on her lips. Martin noticed how plump and full they looked in the dim light of the gym. He wondered how they would feel against his in a willing kiss, not a surprise, faux kiss.

What the hell? Where did that thought come from?

He was grateful for the darkness, it helped hide the fact that a tinge of pink rose into his ivory cheeks.

Bad Martin... that is a very bad thing to think...

Sighing, Martin wondered if he was just flat out stupid for allowing such a thought to permeate his mind. His ears perked up at the sound of classical music, and he recognized one of Beethoven's Symphonies. *Thank you Jason!*

He led Alena back out onto the dance floor, his orange eyes gazing around to deter any potential hazards. Thankfully, the students weren't paying attention anymore. At least, that's what it seemed like.

Something tapped him on the shoulder as he danced, and a gruff voice spoke up. "Mind if I cut in?"

The voice was somewhat familiar, but still alien to Martin. That didn't mean he was going to acquiesce – especially when he saw the look on Alena's face. Whoever was behind him was scaring her. He turned to face the speaker.

"Who-"

A fist shot out of nowhere, striking Martin in the left eye and knocking him over. He stood up, clutching his face and glaring at the smug face in front of him. Chris.

"I didn't think you'd be out of the hospital that fast," he bit, standing fully upright. His eye throbbed painfully, and the dull ache seemed to pierce to the back of his skull. His cheekbone felt broken, but he couldn't be sure. It hurt to blink on that side of his face.

Chris grinned at Martin, "I heal quickly," he said, cracking his knuckles menacingly. Alena rushed to Martin, glaring at Chris. "You just don't know when to give up!"

Chris snickered at her, "Looks like the monster nabbed himself a first-class whore," he said maliciously, "You're probably in his bed just as much as he is!"

Martin's face contorted into a vicious snarl. "You bastard! Keep her out of this! Come on! It's time for a different dance!" he lunged forward, but Chris struck him across the jaw, knocking him to the ground again. Martin suddenly realized how helpless he was without the Threads nearby. *Wait... there were Threads here before... where are they now?*

A shoe came down on his head, causing lights to appear before his eyes. He cursed, twisting away from the pain and rising to his knees. He glared at Chris with anger. Sight was virtually gone in his left eye, but his right held all the fury of a hurricane.

Chris was watching him intently, "Come on then, show me that animal side of you we all know you have!"

"Never!"

I'm not going to give in to him...

In a heartbeat, Chris' fist shot out, connecting with Martin's chest and causing him to stagger backwards again. He sank to his knees, gasping from pain.

"Why?" he croaked, clutching his chest in pain. His mask was slipping, and rapidly. "Why can't you just leave me ALONE?"

With a savage yell, he lunged forward, only to be met by the fist again. He crashed to the ground; a sickening crack echoing through the gym. Everyone was silent as Martin lay on the ground like a limp pile of laundry.

Chris watched his adversary for a moment. "Not so tough are you, shit-head."

The pile on the ground began to shift, forcing itself up again. Chris' eyes widened slightly. "Still going?"

"Damn... right..." Martin's breath was coming in gasps now, and blood streamed from his nose. It had impacted the floor directly. One of his teeth had been chipped, and the point had dug into his lip, drawing even more blood.

Chris kicked him again, knocking him down. He then proceeded to kick him repeatedly. Several students cheered him on. Alena rushed forward to stop Chris, but a few students held her back, despite her kicking and screaming. Martin, however, wasn't feeling the blows. His mind had mostly shut down.

Shit... where did I go wrong?

The blows ceased, and Martin took a deep breath. *I'm not done... not yet...*

He forced himself up on all fours. He had always prided himself on his ability to keep going after a brutal blow. This time was no exception. *Why can't I hit him? Normally he's not this hard to strike!*

Martin stood shakily before Chris, his entire body feeling bruised and broken. One of his ribs was likely shattered, but he forced himself to take no notice of it. It was then that he saw his mistake. Chris was no longer standing in his default offensive-assault stance, but had shifted to a defensive-countering stance.

Oh... that explains a lot...

Now the problem became how to get around the giant's guard to actually hit him. Martin took a deep breath.

He wasn't completely helpless without the Threads. He channeled almost all of his Neutral Energy into his right hand. His left felt broken.

"Chris!" He looked over at the large boy, forcing himself not to choke on the blood in his throat as he spoke. "I'm not done yet!"

The giant lunged forward, and Martin threw the punch, aiming directly for Chris' face. Although it struck, knocking two of Chris' teeth from his head and the boy unconscious, the other's punch impacted with *his* face as well. Martin was lifted from the ground and hurled into the wall. His head struck the concrete with a resounding *CRACK*. He slid to the floor, the world around him becoming hazy.

Shit... he could see Alena running over to him *...sorry...*

His thoughts continued to disassociate, leaving him to succumb to the inky blackness he knew so well. The last thing he consciously was aware of was Alena pulling his cell phone from his pocket.

Chapter 29: Halved

One of Martin's amber eyes flickered open. A white ceiling, decorated only with a crack, was what met his eye. Sighing, he surmised Alena must have called a Tzen or two to get him back into The Hall. Bandages surrounded his head, covering his left eye. His ribs and chest were tightly covered in the white cloth as well.

The fingers on his right hand were broken from the knuckle down, and his left hand was in a fitted cast. He couldn't even budge the fingers if he tried. Sighing, he leaned back in the bed only to find that the back of his head was coated in some kind of form-fitting plaster.

What the hell did that bastard do to me?

Martin gave himself a mental once-over. Half of his face; the left side, had no feeling at all. Both hands were broken, as was at least one rib. His sternum had a nice crack, but fortunately for him it was healing thanks to Terra's knowledge of Earth Incantations. Apparently his head was cracked too, based upon the plaster.

It's a miracle I'm alive...

He shifted slightly, and almost jumped as his movement provoked a response from a figure in the corner. He squinted through the dim light and realized it was Douglas. "Hey."

Douglas grinned weakly at him, walking over to the bedside. "How're you feeling?"

Martin shook his head, looking up at his roommate. He noticed an IV drip trailing a clear fluid into his arm. He shook his head, resolving to ask Terra how she procured the medical supplies she needed. "How long have I been out?"

Douglas pulled up Terra's desk chair, seating himself in it. "About three days. Dais forged a note to the school explaining the accident in the gym. Chris is under police guard, and Alena's back at her house. You... you're here."

"And how bad am I?" he asked, fearing the response. The bandages over his left eye were itching slightly, but his hands were both broken so he couldn't scratch at it.

"Well..." Douglas nervously looked at his roommate as though he was going to explode. Martin sighed, wishing he could massage his temples. "Just say it."

"You've lost your left eye."

That got Martin's attention. "What?!"

"Terra said that whatever hit you in the eye disrupted the optic nerve, and badly. The eyeball itself was popped in one or two places, leaking vitreous into your skull. She had to remove the eye entirely."

Martin mentally checked his skull. Sure enough, there was an alien emptiness where his left eye should have been. "You're going to be out of commission for at least a month," said Douglas gloomily, "And don't start in on me – I have to pick up your slack."

Martin wanted to laugh. He wanted to do *something* other than sit in the bed in disbelief. *I'm half-blind?!* "Fine..." he managed to mutter, staring across the medical bay at his reflection in the mirror that hung above the sink. *Give me a fife and a drummer boy while you're at it, eh Fate?*

The bandages above his left eye were only itching because there was a large stain of dried blood on them. He cursed, wishing he could have done something equally as bad to Chris.

"When's Terra going to discharge me at least?" he asked, hoping for a good response. Douglas, at last, gave him a smile. "Well, you're going to be discharged tomorrow. Your fingers should have healed by then, according to Terra, and after that it's just a process of adjusting to half-sight until you're mission-ready again."

Martin nodded wordlessly. "And what about the eye socket?" he asked, "Did she sew it shut?"

"No. There was far too much blood to see anything clearly, and she didn't want to risk it... are you going to be okay?"

Martin was staring at the ceiling, his remaining eye clouded. "Yeah, I'll be fine."

Douglas stood up, brushing himself down absentmindedly, "I'm gonna go tell Dais you're up, okay?"

Martin nodded again, saying nothing. *Why? First I have to fight Chris in a maze, then Zerolytes attack, and then Alena disappears. Within the span of a day or two, Mainland Shelf opens, and now this! Why can't I be like Jason – nothing interesting ever happens to him...*

He blinked for a moment. He knew exactly why it always seemed to happen to him. Because of the power he carried; namely the parasitic creature he shared his body with, the energy levels near him were higher. This attracted all sorts of unwanted attention from other Energy Manipulators.

The fight with Chris in the maze was a fluke – that was probably not intended to happen the way it did. He had blown his cool, and almost wiped Chris off the map. Now, looking back, he figured he should have finished the job. *Hindsight is always 20/20...*

The Zerolytes had come to deliver a warning, although it still hadn't come to pass. A powerful foe... that was nobody he knew. While Chris was strong, he wasn't strong enough to merit the attention of the Zerolytes.

Alena's disappearance had been his fault. Because he'd been present at her 'initiation' beneath the bridge, a part of his Solar Energy Aura had become a part of her. Thus, she attracted the attention of the Zerolytes.

The Mainland Shelf incidents, however, were bothering him. First it was the Lower Levels, now a spider-thing in the Library, and that deep shaft in the museum. What the hell went on over there in the past?

And, of course, the present incident was also his fault. Had he finished Chris when he'd had the chance, Chris wouldn't have been able to forcibly wreck his eye. Scowling, Martin raised his head and slammed it back down onto the pillow. Needles of pain shot through his damaged skull, causing him to wince slightly as Dais walked in. Terra was at his side, watching him with her usual apathetic expression.

"It's good to see you up," said Dais. For once, Martin got the feeling that he was actually relieved to see him. Normally Dais didn't seem to care one way or the other, but this time he seemed genuinely happy to have his pupil back.

"Indeed," offered Terra, "I assume Douglas has briefed you on your status?"

"One eye missing? Yeah... he told me about that one already." Martin's sole surviving eye was fixed on Dais and Terra, flicking between the two of them. Finally, he spoke. "What's going to happen to me?" he asked after a moment. "I know you're probably already considering my removal from the Mission Teams for good, right?"

"It was a possibility..." trailed Dais, "...it depends on how well you adapt to limited eyesight."

Terra nodded from her position next to Dais, "You'll be out of here tomorrow, but I don't want you using Incantations. The strain on your body would be too much; it would probably reopen wounds or damage the nerves leading to your brain. Wait about a week at best."

Martin closed his eye, envisioning Terra combusting on the spot. It wasn't her fault, he knew, but it still was nice to visualize for the moment. After a few seconds his eye reopened, staring at Terra intently. "How is Alena? Does she know about this?"

"She called us," said Dais with a small grin, "Said you'd been in a fight and gotten hurt."

"Truth be told," said Terra, "I thought she was joking. Normally you don't come away from too many fights with injuries that make Alena panic like she did."

She panicked?

"However, she doesn't know about your condition..." trailed Dais, "...I'll let you get some rest. It'll help your body recover. Just take things easy, okay? I'll have Jason contact Alena and let her know you're alright."

"Thanks." Martin closed his eye, focusing on his Neutral Energy. After the fight, he had noticed it had become strangely disrupted. It was now disassociated and free-flowing, and he needed to recombine it into his system or he'd lose control of the parasite. Soon after reestablishing some semblance of normalcy in his altered body, Martin fell into a dreamless slumber.

***

Something jolted Martin awake, and that wasn't something he liked. Terra was standing over him with some kind of shiny medical tool in her hand. It took Martin a moment to realize that she had drawn out the IV tube, and that was what had woken him up.

"You're free to go," she said, "You're hands are pretty much healed, just don't hit anyone or they'll re-break. Lay off of training for at least a week, got that?"

Martin sighed, nodding and swinging his legs from the bed. His entire body felt like it had been crushed between a pair of cogs, and he knew exactly which muscle-bound brute to thank for *that*.

I swear, when I get my hands on that piece of...

His thoughts were interrupted by Terra tapping his shoulder. "Do you... want to take the bandages off your head?"

His eye winked at her, but it had actually been a blink of surprise. "Uh, is it safe?"

"Yes... for the most part."

"Fine. I'd like to see the damage firsthand anyway..." he walked over to the mirror staring at his reflection as Terra undid the bandages surrounding his head.

Beneath the bandages was an empty eye socket, and the fresh air felt strange inside it. He closed his eyelid, and it felt extremely empty without the eye there. Finally, he stepped away from the mirror. "That's... unusual..."

Terra shrugged, "I'm not sure how it feels, no offense."

"None taken." Martin walked out of the Medical Bay with slightly unsteady steps. His legs felt painfully heavy, and he wanted to get to his bedding chamber and lie down – perhaps sleep for a week.

Michael almost walked past him until he saw the empty eye socket. "Holy *SHIT!*"

"Thank you," said Martin as he turned to look at his fellow Tzen. "Anything else you'd like to say?"

He could only see half of Michael's face the way he was standing, so he had to turn his head slightly to capture the full image of what was actually in front of him. Michael just stared at him for a moment before plastering his usual grin on his face.

"Welcome to the Amputee Club," he joked, drawing the stump of his left arm out from inside his coat.

Martin winced at the sight of the severed appendage. If it hadn't been for his carelessness when he had first become a Tzen, Michael would still have both his arms. It had been a routine mission when a Zerolyte had fired an Air Blade at him. Michael knocked it away, but at the cost of his arm.

"I still haven't repaid my debt, have I?" asked Martin as he stared at the arm. Michael shrugged, "Nah, don't worry about it. 'Sides, if I want to do something stupid like save your life, I can only do one thing: get drunk."

"Michael... you're seventeen. You're not allowed to drink." Martin eyed him carefully, "At least... not legally."

"I know. C'mon, what's a couple of cold ones in the grand scheme of things?" Michael was grinning at him, and Martin suddenly felt nauseous. "Ugh... I'm gonna go lie down. Sorry, I'm not used to the whole one-eye thing."

"You'll get used to it," said Michael, "I'll help if you want. I got over the loss of an arm okay, didn't I?"

"Yeah..." Martin allowed a small smile to appear on his lips, but then hid it as soon as Michael saw it. It was his way of displaying thanks. "...you did..."

He turned and walked toward the bedding chamber. His sense of depth perception was shot to hell, and he actually tripped over flat ground once or twice on his way to his comfortable, familiar bed.

Upon arrival, he didn't even bother to take off his clothes. He crashed onto the bed and rolled over, facing the ceiling. Suspended above his bed was a mobile with a few different origami models he'd made. He smiled, closing his remaining eye. *I'll get over this... I know I will...*

Chapter 30: The Palace

It took Martin only three weeks to adjust to having only one eye. With his field of vision halved, he had to compensate by turning his head more than usual to see what was in front of him. During training sessions with Douglas, he had to move much more if he was going to dodge, as he couldn't see if he'd actually made it out of harm's way.

It was during one of these training sessions that Alena appeared. She had been shocked to learn that Martin's eye had required removal, but gradually got used to it. In her mind, one eye missing didn't change the person. She was coming to the Island Twelve Training Grounds for something important today, and it was obvious that Steven had sent her.

"What is it?" asked Martin dully, noting the roll of paper in her hand. She smiled her familiar smile, holding the paper out to him.

"See for yourself!" He accepted it as if it would bite him, sliding the red ribbon off the parchment and unfurling it gingerly.

"...oh..." Clasped in Martin's hands was an official order from Steven to examine a newly-cleared area of the Mainland Shelf; a supposed palace. A door had apparently been revealed by a recent mudslide in one of the green zones, and Martin and Alena were to investigate. They were allowed to bring one other Tzen with them. Martin nodded at Douglas, who eagerly accepted.

Stamped at the bottom of the scroll was a number, which Martin eyed suspiciously. The number was an indicator as to how difficult this task was projected to be. Ten was an easy rank, and one was nigh-impossible. This mission was a four.

"Alright," he said, handing the scroll back to Alena, "When do we set out."

"Steven said we're setting out whenever you're ready – he said to gather up anything you think you'll need." Alena was grinning ear to ear, and it suddenly dawned on Martin that this was her first mission as a member of the Tzen. *But... why would Steven send her on a Level Four mission first? I started with Level Ten, just like everyone else.*

"Why are you coming on such a high-level mission?" he asked. *I guess I'll just find out the old-fashioned way.*

"Steven says that with his training I'm close to the level of any other Tzen at this level," she answered. Her eyes were gleaming behind her glasses at the prospect of finally being counted as one of the Tzen.

Douglas was grinning, and wrapped an arm around both of his comrades. "Aww, we get to spend some quality bonding time exploring some murky old ruins!"

Martin elbowed Douglas in the stomach, causing him to let go with a muttered 'oomph'. Alena was blushing furiously, doubtlessly from Douglas' comment about 'bonding time', and Martin gave her a reassuring nod.

"I'm going to go collect my belongings," he informed Douglas. He turned to Alena, "This is your first mission, correct?" she nodded, "Then let me give you some advice; try not to die. My first mission I learned a valuable lesson: listen to the leader at all costs."

"That's good advice," she said, smiling, "Alright, who's the scroll say the leader is?"

"Me – that's why I'm telling you this." Alena nodded, "Okay. I trust you."

Martin felt a large part of him shift. It felt as though his intestines had morphed into a bed of snakes. *She what?*

"Er... alright... Meet me by the gondola when you're ready." Martin suddenly felt like chastising himself. Why was he *stammering*? Because she said she trusted him? What happened to the old Martin?

I don't care. I'm Martin. Always have been, always will be. Now, let's focus on this mission...

He walked back to his bedding chamber, checking drawers and shelves for equipment. A few flash grenades were placed gingerly in a hip satchel, and his Tzen Rod was strapped onto his thigh. He placed a small knife inside one of his pockets, in case something jumped them in close quarters, and dropped a small medical kit into another inner pocket. Last but not least, he picked up a flashlight and tested the batteries. If the palace was anything like the library, there would barely be any light. It would be a good idea to bring something like this.

He walked out, almost running over Donna on his way to the gondola. After a hasty apology and several rude statements from his teammate, he finally managed to lose her and make his way to the lift. Alena was already waiting for him. Sighing at Donna for wasting his time, he climbed onto the gondola. Douglas was standing next to her, tapping his foot impatiently.

"Gee, who peed in your Wheaties?" asked Alena as she climbed in next to him. Martin gave her a withering glare, "I hope that was a joke."

Alena laughed, the sound making Martin's head feel considerably lighter. "Of course it was a joke!"

Martin nodded, "I know – I was being sarcastic."

They rode the gondola the rest of the way in silence. Upon disembarking, Martin swiveled his head to look at Alena with his good eye. "Where is the entrance to this place?"

"It's a few blocks past the Mausoleum," she explained. Seeing the confused look on his face, she mentally hit herself, "Oh, you go past the Museum and through the Residential District to find the Mausoleum. Once you find it, you go left."

Martin muttered something about needing to have Jason draw a map of the explored areas of the Mainland

Shelf, but proceeded toward the Museum he, Frank and Richard had located.

"Hey Douglas," asked Alena once Martin was out of earshot. The blonde looked over at her with a 'hmm?' sound.

"What was Martin like? I've only known him like this – but what was he like?"

Douglas made sure Martin couldn't hear him before continuing. "Martin... he's always been Martin, I guess. There was always a part of him that just didn't do well with people – period. He was a natural-born Tzen, and people hated him for it – called him a witch's son and things like that. Because of things like that, he grew resentful."

Douglas had not removed his eyes from Martin's back the entire time. He wanted to make sure that the glacial Tzen wasn't going to turn around and kill him. "Most of the time, the threats he makes to us, the Tzen, are empty. They're meant for the shock value, I guess. He wouldn't ever hurt one of us. He's loyal, not to mention sharp as a tack, and we're his only family."

Alena was watching Martin. The black-haired boy was walking briskly through the Residential Area Green Zone with his usual haughty stride. "Dais," continued Douglas, "Found him when he was three – Martin's parents were his good friends – and helped train him as a Tzen. Later, when his parents died, it was Dais who helped him win his emancipation in court. His uncle, while nice, had no clue how to care for a son."

"This was after the orphanage fire, right?" asked Alena. Douglas nodded, "Martin used to help out at an orphanage to earn extra money. That's where he met his four closest friends: Amanda, Katie, Sarah, and Lisa. They're the four girls you saw in his photograph. They, of course, later died in the orphanage fire."

Alena was silent. She was contemplating what it must have been like for Martin. Douglas was grinning at her, "You like him, don't you?" he asked without looking directly at her. When she nodded, he gave an almighty sigh. "Well then, it's the beginning of the end for you, Alena."

She looked at him in confusion. "Martin, apparently, believes that anyone close to him is going to die. He cites the orphanage fire and his parents as proof. I think he's just unlucky, but..."

He looked at Alena, "...are you really willing to take that chance? You've barely known the guy for a month."

Alena looked at Martin. "I want to help him – he helped me..." her mind flashed to the first night of her being a Tzen. "Yeah – I want to help him."

She looked at Douglas. The blonde was staring at her as if she had eight eyes. "Well, it's your funeral..."

He began humming a very upbeat tune as he walked off after Martin. After another few minutes, the trio arrived at a large gateway that was partially buried in mud. Martin sighed, kicking the gate experimentally. While he had not expected it to swing, it still caught him off guard when it snapped clean off its hinges and landed with a squelching sound in the mud.

"Okay…" he muttered, "Let's go."

Douglas looked at the large palace that dominated the wall near where they were standing. Elegant towers of rock seemed to point upwards like the fingers of some colossal golem, each one tipped with a conical roof. The palace itself wasn't a new discovery – many Tzen had seen it upon their recent excursions to the Mainland Shelf. It was the discovery of the door being revealed that was exciting.

The first door they found was extravagant to say the least. It stood at least fifteen feet high, and seemed to be made of stone and gold. Figures were carved in square panels set into the door, which prompted Martin to kneel down and begin examining them.

"Who made these?" he wondered aloud, brushing his fingers across the figures carved on the door. The most current one depicted a person with wings emitting some kind of brilliant white light. Below the figure were countless creatures, each one flinching away from the light as if it actually burned them.

"Martin," said Douglas tentatively, "Our mission was to examine the *inside* of the palace, you know. Dais and

Steven were thinking of moving us all to the Mainland Shelf and leaving the Islands for maintenance work, but first we need to make sure it's safe."

Martin stood up, nodding. "Alright, let's go in."

The door was heavy, not to mention large, and it took all three of them pulling on the large door handle to get it open wide enough for them to slip inside. After a good amount of heaving on the door to get it to open, they were rewarded with a thin line of darkness.

"Alena, shut the damn door!" barked Martin suddenly. A black mist had begun to creep from within the palace. The three of them forced their weight against the door, slamming it shut. The mist was now sealed back inside the palace.

"What the hell was that?" asked Douglas. Martin was standing at the door, frowning and glaring at the crack between the doors where the mist had issued from.

"I have no idea. Come on – let's find another way in. It's a pity there are no Threads nearby – I'd have just fought that stuff."

It was now Alena's turn. "How can you fight black fog, Martin?"

The glance he shot at her for a split second was enough to scare Alena slightly. "Some incantations, such as Wind and Fire, can blow or burn away things like mist, you know."

Sighing, he brushed past his teammates and walked around the side of the palace, checking for a window of any kind. After at least an hour with no results, Martin gave up and returned to the entrance. "Well, that's that. Other than the front door, there's no other way inside."

Douglas was twirling his Tzen Rod between his fingers, "Why can't we just run past the mist?" he asked.

"An idiot to the end, aren't you?" said Martin in his usual deadpan voice, "We don't know what it is. It could be even more lethal to us than arsenic. We need to find some way to get around it."

Douglas was resentful of being called an idiot, but nodded nonetheless. "Fine."

Alena, however, couldn't shake from her mind the image of the fog as it crept from within the palace. It acted, dare she say it, like it was almost *alive*. Martin, also, couldn't remove the image. The movements it made were too deliberate – they weren't random. Another thing he noticed was that they seemed to behave like his tentacle armor.

With another sigh, he began to examine every inch of the front of the palace.

Chapter 31: Tahadoazleh

Finally, after what seemed like years, the three Tzen encountered an alternate route into the palace... or so they hoped. It was a classic, overused escapade they were going to attempt: going through the sewers. Alena had located a hatch that was embossed with a water drop, and they agreed it was probably the sewers. Therefore, the three of them spent even *more* time wresting the top off the hatch.

"Who wants to go first?" asked Douglas as he peered down the revealed hole. There were spider webs all over the walls, and the ladder looked rusty and frail as it descended into the darkness.

"I'll go," offered Alena as she eyed the hole. Martin's eyebrows rose several millimeters, showing that he was surprised. He stepped aside, allowing her access to the hole.

"Hey Martin," Douglas said as Alena climbed down the ladder. Thankfully, it was holding her weight. The Tzen in question turned and faced his teammate to show he was listening. "What do you think we're going to find?" Martin gave him a baleful glance. "How should I know?" asked Martin. Any further discussion was cut off as Alena shouted up that she had reached the bottom.

***

Martin splashed into water that seemed to by inky black, and most likely was. It rose to his hips, making walking difficult. The walkway had long since cracked and crumbled in several places, and rubble littered the remaining areas. Martin snorted in annoyance as he realized that the only way they were going to go anywhere was sloshing through what felt like four billion years of manure.

Douglas landed in the murky water behind him, cursing as the liquid splashed up onto his Loden Coat. "Get over it," snapped Martin irritably, "I know – it smells like-"

"Shit?" finished Douglas with a humorless smile, "Yeah, I know."

Martin snorted again, "Let's go."

Alena walked between the two boys as they made their way down the dark tunnel. Martin's flashlight lit up the area, exposing it as more of a catacomb than a sewer. Rusted metal grates rested along the walls, and a few rats and spiders scurried along the ruined pathways.

"After this is done," moaned Douglas, "I'm gonna bleach myself and take a blood oath never to come back here."

"Keep talking, Douglas," said Martin, "You might eventually say something smart."

Douglas said nothing, but the incensed aura around him was almost palpable. He glared daggers at his teammates back, but refused to dignify him with a response of any kind.

"Are we there yet?" he whined after a moment. Martin turned and shone the light in his eyes. "Does it look it? Shut up and quit asking stupid questions?"

"Geez, is it that time of month?" muttered Douglas as he rubbed his eyes. Martin spat in the already filthy water. The air was leaving an unpleasant taste in his mouth. "I'll ignore that. Let's just hurry this up and get on with it. We've still got a ways until we're under the palace."

"How the hell do you know?" returned Douglas. Martin pointed up toward a manhole cover. "We're still in the Residential District."

Feeling foolish, Douglas decided to be quiet. Alena, however, was not. "Let's play a game while we walk," she suggested. Martin wanted to bash her with the flashlight for her immaturity when he suddenly realized it would help keep his mind off the stench. Resigning himself to the fact that Fate hated him, he muttered an affirmative.

"Alright – let's play Questionnaire," suggested Douglas. The wink he shot Alena was almost (but not quite) masked by the darkness. She suddenly understood.

"Martin, you first," she prompted. Sighing, the one-eyed youth thought for a moment before asking his question. "Why did you want to become a Tzen?"

She coughed a few times to clear her lungs of the filthy air before answering him. "Who wouldn't? It's so cool!"

Aah…

"Okay, your turn then, I suppose." Martin was beginning to regret agreeing to play this.

"What were the exact circumstances of the orphanage fire seven years ago?"

Martin whirled around; creating small eddies in the murky water. His orange eye bore down on Alena with savage intensity. "Why do you want to know that?"

She refused to cower from his intimidating glare, "Curiosity."

He sighed, facing forward again and walking down the tunnel. "I was experimenting with Solar Energy. I was trying to bind it into myself in place of Neutral Energy. Needless to say, I blew up half the orphanage in the process."

"Yeah," Alena was giving her next question serious thought. It could potentially get her killed, but she was just curious enough to ask it.

"Douglas," asked Martin when he realized it was his turn to ask, "What do you think of Terra?"

Douglas' blush was practically lighting up the tunnel. "Er... why do you ask?" he said after a moment of hemming and hawing. Martin smiled slightly, although it was utterly hopeless to try to see it in the dark. "You cannot answer a question with a question – it's against the rules."

"Aw chickenshit," muttered Douglas, "Fine, I like her. Big frikin' deal." He folded his arms defiantly across his chest before asking *his* question. "My turn – what do *you* think of Terra?"

"She's apathetic and cold, not to mention slightly overbearing when you're in the Medical Bay," was Martin's sharp reply, "My turn again – Alena, why am I putting up with this stupid asinine game?"

Alena grinned – one thing she would easily admit to liking about Martin was his personality, even if it *was* a bit rough at times. "You're just humoring me so we can pass the time. My turn again – how did *you* survive the orphanage fire?"

Douglas interrupted before Martin could answer. "That's a damn good question," he said thoughtfully, "It's kinda strange that you, the person at the epicenter, would be unharmed. I'd have bet you'd be the first one to die."

Alena hadn't been expecting him to answer this one. She had prepared for everything from him attacking to him just quitting the game. An honest answer didn't seem likely, but there it was.

"I didn't escape unharmed," said Martin, "While I succeeded in replacing a good sixty-percent of my Neutral Energy with Solar Energy, the containment process was flawed. I did cause the explosion, but the remaining Solar Energy fused with me, creating the thing that lives inside me. It's the same thing that created my tentacle armor and the same thing that transformed me against the massive lizard."

"So that's why you're so guarded about losing control?" she asked. Martin seemed to forget the rules of the game, namely the one stating one question per person, and answered her anyway. "Yes. If I lose control, that 'Solar Parasite' awakens. My body enters some kind of trance-like state – I have zero control during that time. That's why I was shocked to find that I'd not killed you or Jason that day in the tunnels."

He looked at the water swirling at his thighs as he walked, "If I'd known that my little experiment could go *this* wrong, I would never have attempted it." His voice was laden with regret. "Of the thirty that died that day, I only claim sadness for four of them. The others..." he paused as if searching for the right words, "...were an acceptable sacrifice."

Alena's jaw fell open, and Douglas made an odd sound behind him. "You're not serious!"

"Dead serious," said Martin. He shone the light ahead of him, spotting the ladder with a plaque next to it. He heaved himself out of the water onto the shattered remnants of the pathway and brushed dirt from the engraved letters.

"Crap," he muttered, "It's some kind of hieroglyphics."

Douglas pushed past him, examining the lettering. "Damn right it is. Alena, look at this."

Alena peered between the two boys, gazing at the plaque. For some reason, the symbols looked familiar. Suddenly, Martin seemed to remember something. "That's not hieroglyphics," he said, "That's Alintean!"

Both of his teammates stared at him as if he was insane. "Er... what's 'Alintean'?" asked Alena after an awkward silence.

"The Alintean Race was here billions of years ago," he explained, pointing to the plaque, "Their language forms the base for our incantations. An example would be Xidul, which is the Alintean word for 'Impact'.

Douglas nodded, "As far as we know, they were the ones who built this cavern. They vacated it about four billion years ago. Some of the records we've found indicate some kind of conflict with another species, and they were eventually driven away entirely. Where they went is a mystery."

Alena was staring at the plaque. Her eyes flickered over to Martin, "Can you read it?"

"I'll try..." he leaned closer, examining the lettering closely. The first symbol looked like an inverted triangle with a spiral inside. "That means 'seal', as in lock," he translated, pointing to it. He ran his finger onto the next one. It looked almost like a bowling ball, complete with the three holes, but a crack ran from the bottom to the halfway point. "This one means 'barrier'."

"So we've got a sealed barrier?" asked Douglas. Martin nodded. "This one is 'Tahadoazleh'. I'm not sure what it means." The symbol looked like a thunderbolt surrounded by three circles arranged like a bulls-eye. Spokes radiated out, two on each side, to touch the farthest circle.

"Then how in the world do you know it means Taha-whatever?" asked Douglas hotly, "For all we know…"

"Shut it," snapped Martin, "I know Alintean ten times better than *you* do, Douglas." The blonde growled something like 'stuck-up bastard' before leaning against the wall. Martin proceeded to scrutinize the tablet for several more minutes before stepping away.

"*Barrier, Seal, Hide, Tahadoazleh, Protector, Palace, Entry, No*," read Martin. "Roughly translated, it *should* mean something like: 'The Barrier is Sealed to Hide the Tahadoazleh; the protector of the palace. Do not enter.'."

"So, is it saying it's a bad idea to go in?" asked Douglas dryly.

"I guess we're gonna find out," said Martin, ascending the ladder until he was positioned directly beneath the hatch. He pulled out his knife and began to work the rust out of the hinges. The reddish powder rained down like sand, coating the floor in a rich blood-red color.

There was an audible snap, a curse, and a thud as Martin landed on his back in the fallen powder. His hand was still wrapped around one of the rungs of the ladder, which had broken off in his hand.

"No matter," he said, tossing the iron bar into the brackish water, "I've got it loosened anyway. Now, let's get going, shall we?"

He grabbed the rungs, testing them gingerly before suggesting they ascend one at a time. With that piece of advice, he was gone, pushing open the hatch and stepping into the palace. Before Douglas could put a foot on the rung, he heard Martin's voice.

"Well shit..."

Chapter 32: Within the Palace

Douglas and Alena rocketed up the ladder, entering what seemed to be a courtyard. Although there was a menagerie of dead plants, the ceiling was closed off. Apparently the door they were trying wasn't really the front door if this was any indicator. Insects, most likely some kind of cicada, buzzed and hummed in the still air around them.

The plants and the bugs weren't the cause of Martin's exclamation, though. It was the host of Zerolyte corpses that littered the area. There must have been at least two hundred; their robes were clawed and bloody, and body parts were removed from their hosts, strewn about carelessly like confetti. Martin looked at the corpses with something akin to curiosity, while Douglas staggered over and began heaving into a stone planter. Alena was merely watching the bodies with horror.

"What the hell happened?" asked Douglas after he was finished emptying his stomach onto an unfortunate plant, "What did this? I mean, they're our enemies and all, but still..." he looked at a corpse that had been sliced in half from crotch to neck, the organs spilling out onto the floor in a bloody puddle, "...even they didn't deserve this..."

Martin stepped over one of the bodies, walking purposefully toward a door on the far side. "It's cruel, but it's a fact of life. I'm more worried about what they were doing here in such large numbers." Martin's voice carried no emotion, but there was something under the calm exterior; Alena could tell. She seemed to be awoken from a daze at his words, "Yeah – why were they here? This area was recently uncovered, after all..." she trailed off as she picked her way across the room to follow Martin.

Martin tried an arched door, surprised to find it unlocked. "Douglas, are you coming or are you making friends with these guys?" he asked, waving his comrade over. Douglas grimaced and carefully walked over to where his teammates were standing.

"The blood isn't too old," said Martin. Douglas had just stepped in some, and was leaving a trail of grisly footprints, "It's still in a liquid state. These Zerolytes died recently."

He walked through the doorway, Alena and Douglas on his heels. He had been prepared to use his flashlight, but the room was already lit with torches. He put his light into a pocket; the weight pulling his coat slightly off balance. They were standing in another plant-filled room, this one containing a few more Zerolyte corpses.

"Well, we know there's someone who doesn't like Zerolytes," muttered Douglas as he eyed a corpse that had been flung against a wall and impaled on a torch bracket. "Whoever it is, though, is rather brutal in their methods."

"Hello Captain Obvious," said Martin, the sarcasm dripping from his voice like honey, "I thought that was clear by now."

Alena was crouched near one of the less-mutilated corpses. "What makes a wound like this?" she asked, looking up at Martin. The Tzen turned and knelt by the corpse, admiring the deep gash that crossed the Zerolyte's torso. It was clean, like a scalpel wound, but far too wide to be any kind of blade he'd seen before. He gave a shrug, "Beats me."

Martin looked up, surveying the room. "Douglas," he snapped, drawing his wand, "Get ready!"

Alena drew out her Tzen Rod as well, "What's wrong?" she asked, pressing her back to Martin's. He gave a snort, "The bugs stopped their song – something disturbed them. They were still singing when we left the room, so it wasn't us."

Alena was impressed by his observational skills, but had no time to say it. As she opened her mouth, the ground beneath them quaked slightly. Martin's eyebrow rose slightly, Douglas cursed, and Alena looked at the both of them. "Uh... what was that?"

Martin grabbed both of them by the collar, "Get going!" He kicked open a door, forcing them through and following them. The door was slammed behind them, and the three immediately pushed the nearest object they could find against it – a stone planter similar to the one Douglas had used as an illness bucket.

The ground quaked again, and Martin looked around to ascertain their surroundings. They were in a blue-lit room with a waterfall in the corner. Several tables were situated in the room, and ivy grew up and down the walls. A pair of bookshelves rested on either sides of the door, each one laden with jars, urns and bottles.

"Let's go!" he said, the edge in his voice sharp enough to cut steel, "There's another door!"

He heaved the metal door open, snapping one of the ancient hinges as he did. Alena went first, followed by Douglas. They hadn't gone more than two steps when the barricaded door gave an almighty lurch as something impacted it. A roar issued from the other side, causing Douglas to go pale and Alena's eyes to widen.

"Just go!" snapped Martin, closing the door behind them, "I don't know what it is, but I'm guessing it's not friendly."

There was a sound like a keg of dynamite being set off, and they ascended the stairs three at a time, hoping they were fast enough. Douglas screeched to a halt, drawing out a grenade. "You guys go," he said, "I'll stun it and follow!"

Martin hit him in the head; none too softly, "Stop playing the goddamn hero and get moving!" Douglas glared at him, but tossed the grenade down the stairs anyway. There flash lit the entire stairwell, and a glass-shattering screech filled the enclosed stone shaft. Martin clamped his hands over his ears, doubling over in pain at the sound.

"What the hell is it?" asked Douglas, recovering from the pain and running ahead. Martin pushed Alena ahead of him and followed, "That's probably that thing we read about – 'Tahadoazleh'," he explained, looking over his shoulder. There was still no sign of their pursuer, but Martin could hear it coming up the stairs. It sounded as if it was quite a ways off still.

They ducked onto a landing, opening a wood and iron door and closing it behind them. Martin looked around instinctively for an escape route. "Out the window; quick!" They ran over to the broken window, and Martin kicked it until it came loose from the masonry and fell out.

A narrow ledge ran along the windowsill, and Martin grimaced at the sheer height of their position. They were at least a hundred feet off the ground; probably more. "Come on!"

He stepped out, balancing on the ledge and beginning to shuffle along it; his back to the wall. Alena came next, and Douglas brought up the rear. Martin found himself wishing for a Thread so he could fight this thing, but the entirety of the Mainland Shelf seemed devoid of them. *I wonder why that is...*

There was another roar, and Martin felt his head swim slightly. *Not a good time for this.* He continued to balance along the ledge until he came to another window. He elbowed it in, climbing inside as hastily as he could. He helped Alena and Douglas through, looking around carefully.

They were in a ballroom of some kind, the floor being made of polished marble and the walls and ceiling inlaid with gold and precious gemstones. "Whoever made this place wasn't going to skimp with the extravagance," noted Douglas. Before Martin could respond, the wall itself seemed to bow inward, and it didn't take a genius to figure out why.

"Damn! Everyone, get to the far side of the room!" Douglas was almost bowled over as Martin forced him back, pushing him against the wall. He was about to make one of his usual snide remarks, but the wall seemed to cave in, exposing what as behind it.

A human-sized, scaly body was crouched in the opening. Each hand was twice the size of the vaguely amphibian head, and ended in three hooked claws. Needle-sharp spines ran along the body, and the teeth were equally as pointed. There were no eyes, and two clawed legs supported the body, as well as a tail that ended in yet more spikes.

"What the hell is THAT?!" asked Douglas, trying to recoil only to be stopped by the ornate wall. Martin readied a

fighting stance, preparing to use the only energy available –
Neutral. "That, my friend, is undoubtedly Tahadoazleh."

Tahadoazleh crossed the ballroom in seconds, the
clawed hand burying itself in the wall as Douglas dodged. He
rolled across the polished floor, cursing heavily. Tahadoazleh
removed its claw from the wall, rounding on the nearest
target: Martin.

"Hey! Ugly! Over here!" something struck it in the
head, causing it to divert its attention to the source. Alena
had thrown a stone and was arming another. With a roar,
Tahadoazleh began to run forward. A bright flash stopped its
progress, causing it to reel drunkenly before collapsing
against a wall.

Martin hastily pulled another flash grenade from his
pocket, holding it cautiously as he watched Tahadoazleh right
itself. The scale armor it was protected by was undoubtedly
too thick to pierce with anything *normal*...

"Erhaz-Ahatamz!" he called, channeling the Neutral
Energy into his system to lower the protective barrier
surrounding the Solar Parasite. "Nutapriel-Askil!" The tentacle
armor seemed to cover his body, stemming not only from his
right arm but issuing from his empty eye socket as well.
Hesitation gripped Tahadoazleh for a moment. The massive
reptile soon decided that it was in no danger and attacked.

"Somesacael!"

The tentacles exploded from Martin's wrist, just like before, and struck Tahadoazleh in the chest. The sheer force pushed it back, slamming it into the wall. However, the pointed ends of the tentacles had failed to pierce the scale armor.

Martin muttered a few four letter words, dodging a downward slash from Tahadoazleh by wrapping himself in a sphere of tentacles and rolling out of the way. He righted himself as a grenade from Douglas struck the creature in the face, causing it to stumble about blindly again.

"Hahiel-Somesacael!" The tentacles shot forward again, this time from both arms. They struck Tahadoazleh in the stomach, and there was an audible crack as several scales seemed to crumble from the force of the blow. The lizard-creature was thrown against the wall like a rag doll, hissing in rage.

"Now get the hell out of my way!" Martin's voice was bizarre, seeming to come from two entities at once. The spiral pattern that had been formed when the tentacles came from Martin's eye socket seemed to ripple for a moment before twisting open, and both Douglas and Alena fought back the urge to scream.

Beneath the tentacles was an eye, but it wasn't Martin's. It was dead black, with a white slit of an iris. In the center of the white slit was another black spot, most likely the pupil itself. Tahadoazleh stopped hissing, staring at the eye as if it was the last thing on Earth.

The two sets of tentacles launched forward, piercing Tahadoazleh through the stomach. The reptile was lifted into the air before being casually hurled from the window. It took a good portion of the wall with it as it flew. It seemed to hover in the air for a moment before gravity remembered its duty and the body fell from sight.

"Ohdaec," said Martin, and the armor retracted back into his body again. The haunting eye seemed to fold in upon itself until it disappeared entirely. Martin went down on one knee for a moment before righting himself. "Let's continue, shall we?"

Both Tzen looked at him as if he was crazy, but nodded. "Er... should we radio Dais and tell him we've encountered and neutralized at least one hostile?" asked Douglas, pulling his cell phone from his pocket. Martin nodded.

"Martin?" Alena was standing next to him, a question forming on her lips. "If that thing killed all those Zerolytes, how did we escape?"

"We knew it existed," he said matter-of-factly. A faint smile tugged at the corner of his lips, "And you've got me."

Chapter 33: Crystals

Martin grinned openly as he discovered a cache of gold, but the smile quickly turned into a frown as he realized it was worth little more than pocket lint to the Tzen. Alena failed to understand this logic. With a pained sigh, the one-eyed Tzen began to explain it to her.

"If I took this to the surface to sell," he said with his usual patience, "It would raise some questions as to its origin. Then, to prove I haven't robbed a jewelry store, I would have to show this place to investigators. Before I can say, 'whoops', archaeologists will be crawling all over this place like flies on a carcass. Does it make sense now?" He finished his statement by slamming one of the chests full of gold shut with a resounding thud. "Still, I might have a use for it later. Best mark its location on the map, Douglas."

Douglas had found that it was easier to map out the Palace than to get lost, and had since been detailing every minute detail on a large roll of paper. Currently it was spread out on a table that had once housed relics. These relics were now neatly lined up on the floor next to the blonde as his pen scratched away at the parchment.

Finally, with the 'Vault' added to the map, Douglas stood up with a triumphant look on his face. "Good," said Martin, examining the paper as it was presented to him, "Let's continue."

The trio proceeded down a long hallway, peering into each room they passed. The first room looked like it was from the same time period and design style as the Bedding Chambers back on the Islands. The ceilings were etched with murals, and the beds were almost identical. Martin even saw the familiar holes in the walls that were used to house Rods.

"Why don't we rest here for a moment?" suggested Martin, seating himself on a chair, "We've still got a lot to do."

Douglas wholeheartedly agreed, plunking himself down on the bed with a relaxed sigh. Alena walked over to the other bed, seating herself on it quietly. She was obviously thinking about something, and neither Douglas nor Martin wanted to stir her out of it.

Why do I have a heart all of a sudden? Martin was deep in thought as well, his hand on his fist and his remaining eye closed. *Since when do I care about anything... or anyone?*

He also knew why he hadn't. His mind was in a position of mistrust. As far as other people went, they were worth trusting as far as he could throw them. *Yeah, and I should be able to trust her a lot. With my Air Incantations, I could throw her for miles... not that I would.*

He frowned deeper than usual, the action partially opening his empty socket. He winced as the cold air came into contact with the sensitive lining of his eye and quickly closed it again. *Then again, what harm could this do? It's been seven years since I've loved anyone... I might as well make a stab at being human again...*

His common sense was having a fit over his decision, but Martin quickly pushed it back into his mind. It was, after all, his choice. However, he had no idea how to begin being nice to a girl like Alena. All he knew was that she liked ice-cream.

Okay, at least it's a start... now what to do about it.

Finally, after their allotted rest time expired, the three Tzen continued exploring the palace. When they found a chamber full of crystals, Martin was intrigued at the expression on her face. It looked like elation to him. *Ah, so she also likes crystals...*

Douglas turned to Martin, noting his quietness. "You've been *much* more somber than usual... what's going on?"

Martin seemed to wake up, shaking his head slightly. "Nothing..." *Crap... if Douglas found out I was going soft, I'd never hear the end of it.*

"Nothing..." he was still watching Alena. She was examining a large pink quartz crystal carved into the shape of a wolf puppy. "I don't think anyone will care if you keep one, if you'd like," offered Martin, slowly. *Damn... I'm not used to this whole 'being nice' thing.*

Alena beamed at him, clutching the little wolf to her chest in happiness. "Thanks!"

Don't even know if it was my place... "You're welcome." The smile she gave him made a small part of his consciousness get up and dance like a moron. The rest of him wanted to follow suit, but an order from Martin's ego, the command center, kept his body the way it was. Instead, he allowed the edges of his mouth to curl up ever so slightly.

Martin almost never smiled. Seeing one from him was testament to the fact that miracles still existed. His face rarely showed such phenomena – even on a small scale. Smirking was commonplace; he did it whenever provoked. A true smile, however, proved that there was still a tiny vestige of humanity within his shell.

Alena seemed to recognize this fact, nodding at him. "Alright, so I've earned a smile from you... sort of... now I'll work on a laugh," she proclaimed, hugging the crystal with one arm and pumping the air excitedly with the other.

Martin shook his head in mild amusement while Douglas looked on in confusion, not quite comprehending the situation. Finally deciding it wasn't worth it, he opted to continue mapping out their current position.

***

Finally, after what felt like days, the trio had several rolls of paper which formed the basis for Douglas' crude maps. He eyed them scornfully, knowing how bad they looked. Jason would definitely laugh at him for even attempting cartography.

"Ignore him when we get back," said Martin as if he had read Douglas' mind. He then turned to Alena. "When's your formal initiation going to be?"

The girl looked up from her crystal wolf think for a moment, "Thursday," she said after a moment, "Steven said it would be in the Great Hall on Island Three."

Martin nodded, his fingers subconsciously rubbing the back of his right hand. After the initiation, Alena would see what was there... that she would. He tilted his head back as the familiar earthy smell of The Hall washed over him. The palace behind them was forgotten for the moment.

Behind them, perched on a makeshift sled, was the body of the lizard-creature; Tahadoazleh. Martin intended to leave it near the lift and get Lisa to look at it. A Zerolyte corpse was draped on the sled as well; Martin wanted confirmation that it was, indeed, Tahadoazleh that had performed the murders.

They boarded the gondola, leaving the corpses behind, and rode to Island Twelve without a sound. Douglas had recently gotten over his mild apprehensions to dragging the corpses behind them, and was breathing great sighs of relief. Alena was too preoccupied with examining her wolf pup carving to speak at the moment, and Martin didn't feel the need to talk; therefore he didn't.

Lisa met them at the gondola. Apparently Dais had told her they'd encountered a hostile, and she was banking on it being close by. She was dressed in a snow-white Loden Coat, and it seemed to amplify the lab-rat image. A pair of wire-framed glasses rested on a thin nose, shielding her green eyes. Long brown hair hung to her mid-back, pulled into a messy ponytail. Beneath the coat she was wearing a simple green blouse and a skirt that hung to her knees. A pair of matching green high-heels completed the ensemble.

The biologist was prepared, carrying a large satchel full of her standard examining equipment. Martin gave her directions to the corpses and proceeded to escort Douglas and Alena to Dais' chamber. Douglas handed over the maps, much to the amusement of Jason, before retreating to his bedroom.

"You've done well," commented Dais as he studied the maps. "You're free for now – play nice."

Martin's stomach seemed to find this an appropriate time to growl, reminding him that he hadn't eaten in a while. He'd missed breakfast that morning and dinner the previous night. Alena giggled next to him as he buried his face in his hand out of mortification.

"That seems to settle the matter of what to do next," chirped Jason happily, a grin on his impish face, "Why don't you two go get something to eat – I'm sure Alena's hungry too, eh Martin." He threw the older boy a suggestive look as if screaming 'take her on a date, dumbass'.

As Martin turned to leave, Dais decided to interject one last time. "Martin, after you're done, I'd like to speak to you. I'll be expecting you to drop by the Island Seven Auditorium at midnight, alright?"

Concerned as to the secrecy, Martin nodded. He wasn't stupid, and knew that there would likely be someone else interested in what Dais was going to tell him; namely Alena. He'd have to be careful to prevent her from leaving Island Twelve.

He walked back over to the desk, leaning down to Dais' level. "Tell Derrick of this, and have him shut down the gondola after I'm across, alright?"

Dais nodded, waving a dismissive hand in the air. He glanced worriedly at the stack of information Donna was bringing through the door. "That's not paperwork, is it?" he asked with a groan. The mechanic shook her head, "It's a list of parts we need to bring The Hall to one-hundred percent efficiency." Sighing with relief, Dais began to leaf through the papers.

Outside the door, Martin was inwardly fighting himself to find the right words to say. He hated to stutter, and therefore made certain all his words were in their proper order before saying them. Finally settling on an arrangement that didn't make him look like an ass, he turned to Alena.

"You must be hungry. Would you like me to fix you something to eat?" he asked, fighting the urge to die on the spot.

Alena gave him a dumbfounded look, "You can cook?" she asked incredulously. He frowned slightly, "Has someone told you otherwise?"

She snickered slightly, "Steven said you lived off of cold teriyaki for two months after first coming to the Tzen."

Martin sighed, "Trust him to bring *that* up..." he moaned, "Yeah, I did. After a while, Donna took pity on me and showed me a few dishes. I found out I liked to cook and it just sort of went from there. Now, I even substitute in the kitchens... on occasion..."

She smiled at him, and his chest seemed to be less constricted. *What the hell is wrong with me?* "I'd love to dine with you," she said, the smile never leaving her face. She extended a hand to him, and Martin took it. He quickly analyzed how her hand felt in his – smooth and creamy – before deciding to just go with the moment.

"It will be an honor," he said, leading her to one of the surface chutes, "We'll use my surface house – it has a better kitchen."

She walked next to him as they crossed Island Twelve. Douglas had emerged from his room with a stack of laundry and promptly dropped it at the sight. There was Mr. No-Emotions Spire leading, of all things, a *girl* across the

Island. Not only that, it didn't look like he wanted to commit ritual suicide for doing it.

Martin motioned for Alena to enter the chute first before turning and giving a nonchalant wave to Douglas. The blonde mindlessly returned it, staring incredulously as his teammates vanished to the surface. He shook his head, clearing it.

If Spire can do it, why can't I?

He boldly walked into the Medical Bay where Terra was working. "Hey Terra," he called, seeing the apathetic redhead snap her head up from the desk to see who was calling her, "Need any help?"

With a grateful nod, she motioned to a stack of medical implements that needed to be cleaned, "I'd be pleased as punch if you'd..."

Douglas grinned, "No problem, leave it to me!" With the image of a half-smiling Terra ingrained in his mind, Douglas took the medical tools to the sink, donned the protection gloves, and began washing the various scalpels and syringe needles in their bath of steaming sterilizer.

Not quite a romantic candlelight dinner, but a man's gotta take what he can get. "So Terra," he asked, "How was your day?"

Chapter 34: Dinner

There was a curse, a clang, and several more curses as Martin finally wrested his pan from beneath the counter. Apparently the house itself was against him tonight, and there wasn't a thing that had gone right. First the door had stuck, and then the potatoes had spoiled. Now he realized his pot was somehow pushed into a cabinet far too small for it and he had to brace a foot against the next cabinet over to wrench it free.

"Finally," he moaned, tossing the pan on the stove. The one-eyed boy gave it a quick spray with a butter solution and turned the dial to 'HI' before leaning back against the counter. His Loden Coat had been shed in favor of a plain white apron. There was no catchphrase such as 'kiss the cook' on it – Martin never went out into the realm of the gaudy. If anything, his apron would have read 'kiss my ass'.

The kitchen was simple, furnished with white cabinets topped with a granite counter. After an ample space, there was a row of hanging cabinets that ran along the three walls of the room; each one filled with measuring cups, storage containers, and glassware. The oven was the only thing that still remained from the old house. Yellow and mottled with a few patches of rust, Martin had never seen a reason to rid himself of it as it still worked perfectly.

"I'm sorry," he said to Alena. His teammate was sitting in the adjoining living room on one of the spacious sofas. "I know it's boring because I have no television." The pot began to steam and Martin walked over to the stove and cracked a pair of eggs on the counter, dropping them into the steaming pan. "And I guess I won't be fixing you Chili-Potatoes after all..."

Alena looked up from the magazine she was reading to smile at him, "That's fine. I'm stunned that you'd offer to cook for me. It... just doesn't seem like something you'd do normally."

Martin's eyebrow rose, but he said nothing. Rather, he turned back to the pan and gave the eggs an experimental poke with a spatula. Seeing them ready, he flipped them neatly over in the pan. They landed rather lopsidedly, and Martin swore under his breath and carefully remedied their awkward position without breaking the yolks.

"So, we're having eggs?" asked Alena, walking into the kitchen. Martin nodded wordlessly, watching the whites of the eggs bubble slightly from the heat. "They're almost ready."

Alena patted him on the shoulder, "Thanks."

Martin looked at her in silence for a moment before responding with a muttered "You're welcome."

He scraped the eggs out of the pan and dropped them on an awaiting plate. He handed one to Alena, moving to sit down at the table in the family room. He always laughed at the name. He lived alone, thanks to Dais' good graces, but never had anyone over to share it with. It was more a solitary-room. Alena was the first guest to ever enter the house other than Douglas. His last visit had been over a year ago.

"You know," Alena said after a moment of chewing on her eggs, "You're not a bad person."

Martin looked up from staring at his egg yolk to fix her with his solitary orange eye. "Hmm?"

"I said you're not a bad person," Alena repeated, putting down her fork. "You're a bit rough... kinda weird and antisocial... but nonetheless you're kind of nice as well."

Martin gave a small sound and looked down at his plate. "Thank you." The reason he'd looked down before speaking was to hide the tiny amount of color that had spread on his cheeks. A few years ago, he would have died to hear those words. Now they filled him with no end of sadness. He pitied Alena to some extent. The other Tzen knew what he could do... she didn't, and that's why she had no problem saying that.

"Alena," he spoke up after staring at his egg for the better part of ten minutes, "You say I'm a good person, but I killed over two dozen people. How can a good person do that?"

Alena's fork clattered to the plate, "It was an accident, wasn't it? That doesn't make you evil, Martin."

"I knew the risk," said Martin, "I knew the possibility of an explosion, but I thought I knew what I was doing as well. I thought... I thought I could contain it. I failed to heed the warning Amanda gave me before I started the experiment. She told me it would happen..."

His disfigured face looked at her from across the table, "I killed them, Alena. There isn't really an alternative explanation. I should have never tried the experiment I did. I should have been happy with the gifts I'd been given."

Alena was silent for a long period of time before she spoke again. "You were what, twelve?"

"That doesn't matter," Martin snapped, "I still killed them. If I had been four, eight, or forty-eight, murder is still murder!"

"Douglas even says it was more unintentional manslaughter than murder!" said Alena quickly. She was aware that her voice was rising, but decided it wasn't important right now.

"That's loads better," spat Martin, "My friends are still dead, Alena. Have you ever lost a friend?"

"Yes, but-"

"Did you see them come staggering out of an inferno, their body burning to ash as they screamed for you to help? Did you do nothing but stand there in shock as they

collapsed, screaming and writhing and dying? Did you do
nothing but stand there as an entire orphanage *caved in* to
kill scores of children, some no older than *four*?" Martin was
irate now, his fists clenched. It was in times like these that he
cursed himself for showing emotion. He was supposed to limit
it. He took several deep breaths to calm himself before
focusing his eye on Alena. "I'm sorry... that was out of place. I
did not mean to yell at you."

Alena gave him a weak smile, "It's alright, Martin..."

Martin hurriedly finished his egg, scooping up his
plate. "Would you like me to walk you home?"

Alena gave him a look he couldn't quite decipher. He
hoped it wasn't fear. He didn't want her to be afraid of him.
Finally, her face relaxed into a smile. "I'd like that."

***

"I'm going to give you a warning," Martin said as
they walked toward Alena's house. Neither had wanted to
break the companionable silence between them, but Martin
had something he needed to say. "After your Formal
Initiation, there will be a tournament. Dais has expressed
wishes to put us on a team, but I need to know if you trust
me enough to fight by my side."

She was silent for a moment, leading Martin to
wonder if she'd heard him at all. Just as he was opening his
mouth to repeat the question, she answered. "My answer has
not changed."

Something about her had, though. Martin could sense it. His eye narrowed in the darkness, even though Alena couldn't see it. "Are you sure? You may... discover things you might wish you hadn't. Are you willing to take that risk? I'll tell Dais to cancel the plan." Secretly, he was rejoicing at the idea of fighting by her side. For some reason, he saw her as an equal – something he'd long considered impossible.

"I'm fine," she said, "If I 'discover' anything, it will be up to me to decide my reaction."

"Now you're sounding like me," he muttered dourly, folding his arms behind his head as they approached her house. "Don't go down that road, I'm telling you it's a bad idea."

She smiled. Martin could feel it in the darkness. Long years spent more beneath the ground than above it had honed his senses to the point where he could tell if you flicked a finger in a dark room. Most of the tunnels had been plunged into inky darkness.

"Well," Martin said as he walked up Alena's front steps, "I'll see you tomorrow, then?"

She nodded at him, holding out her hand. He shook it, but on an impulse brought the slender fingers to his mouth and pressed them against his lips. At the same second, he clasped his other hand around an Air Energy Thread, murmuring the masking Incantation he knew so well. In the middle of kissing her hand, he faded from view as though he'd never existed in the first place.

Alena was standing on the porch, her hand still outstretched. Martin stood perfectly still, not wanting to alert her to the fact that he hadn't teleported or some such action. She slowly drew her hand in and looked at it, as if expecting it to come alive and attack her. A small smile, sincere and from her heart, crossed her features.

She looked out into the night one more time, her eyes actually stopping on his hiding place. For one wild moment, Martin wondered if she could see through his sight barrier. Of course, this was ridiculous. She turned and walked into her house almost as quickly as she had looked at him.

A small smile flitted across Martin's lips for a moment as he recalled the texture of her smooth, butter-cream skin against them. Deciding he would *not* show his face in The Hall looking like a love-sick fool, he made several laps around a nearby park to clear his thoughts before returning to the Tzen base. When the chute emptied out beneath the ground, he was greeted by none other than the pony-tailed information gatherer himself. Jason gave him a knowing grin.

"Real smooth, Spire," he said. Martin frowned, the action causing Jason's grin to enlarge to ludicrous proportions. *How does this little rat always find things out so fast?* Martin's hand extended forward, catching Jason in the stomach. Before the information dealer could make a sound, Martin spoke.

"Xidul!"

Jason was tossed backward, barely catching himself against the wall of the medical bay before he impacted headfirst. He hung there for a moment before dropping to the ground, his grin still firmly in place.

"Save it for the Arena," he said. His eyes crinkled in his usual sardonic smile, "I hope I get paired with Alena – she's got quite a pair of knockers." He dodged a fireball and sped off laughing at Martin's indignation and red face. *Bastard!*

Martin shook his head to clear it before heading to his room. There were at least two hours before he was expected to meet Dais, so he figured a few entries in his journal couldn't hurt. After writing them in his neat cursive, he turned his attention to the looming stack of Origami paper that rested on the desk. *Why not, eh?*

A square base emerged from his skilled fingers not a minute after he'd picked up a sheet of gold foil. From the square base, he quickly formed a frog base before continuing the pattern and repetition to produce a lily. He set the delicate flower off to the side, drawing a green foil sheet down from the stack to make something else.

***

Martin's clock struck eleven forty-five before he left the room. He tiptoed silently out of his bedroom and down the hallway of the bedding chambers. Derrick was waiting by the gondola. After Martin was safely across, he turned the key in its slot to cancel the lift until he turned it back on. He leaned against the winch, pulling out a book and flicking through the pages until he reached his bookmark. With a contented smile, he began to read.

Martin crossed all the way to Island Seven Auditorium, leaning against the lectern as he waited for Dais to appear. At five past twelve, his commander came creeping into the room, slinking along the walls like a shadow and coming to stop at Martin's side. With a sigh, he began to speak.

Chapter 35: Arrangements

"I want you to answer me honestly," said Dais, "The response you give me determines your partner at the Arena on Thursday." Martin nodded wordlessly, not turning to face his commander. "When you were in the Lower Levels, what did the room you rescued Alena from look like?"

"A garden." The response was curt and honest, causing Dais to blink for a moment. "A garden?" Martin nodded, his gaze never leaving the far wall. The empty socket was closest to Dais, and it was beginning to unnerve the elder Tzen. "Describe it, if you would," pushed Dais. Martin took a deep breath and began to speak.

"It was an island, surrounded by water. I could not see the end of the water; it was hidden in some kind of mist. I had come from some kind of pyramid, and in front of me was a large tree. A pathway wound between two gazing pools, each one filled with polished stones. There was an abundance of plants, but the most important thing to me at the time was the two Zerolytes with Alena... I may have missed something."

"Most likely the Garden of Nubason," explained Dais solemnly, "Nubason was an Alintean King said to have found the Path to Hell. It's a bunch of old legends Donna dug up while excavating the South Tunnels – I doubt most of it is true. Still, if Nubason's Garden exists..." he was silent for the next several minutes.

After what seemed to be an eternity, he spoke again. "Martin, I am going to give you a gift. This is something Michael, Donna and I have worked very hard on. Please accept it." He produced a pair of gold bracelets. They were thick, at least two inches wide, and looked heavy. Each one had a phrase written in Alintean carved on its surface: *Elseniol Narcestahiel*. Martin accepted the bangles, eying them suspiciously. "Why?"

"These will halve your Energy Levels, but enable you to control the parasite within you. They work by channeling stored Lunar Energy into your body. As you know, Lunar energy opposes Solar, so they cancel out. This numbs your Energy Levels, but you can control the parasite."

Martin slipped both bracelets over his wrists, feeling the cold metal against his wrists. Within seconds, his body began to feel fatigued. His muscles ached as if he'd run for days, and his naturally high stock of Neutral and Solar Energies seemed diminished by at least half.

On the plus side, however, an immense clarity began to pervade his mind. It was as if the world was sharper; clearer. Colors stood out from each other more than before. The smells of the cavern seemed intensified, and the earthy aroma seemed to fill his entire head.

The ornaments were heavy, hanging on his arms like shackles. "And the phrase, Elseniol Narcestahiel, what does it mean?" he asked, looking up at his teacher.

"It will remove the binding, enabling you to use one-hundred percent of your Energy Levels. I'm warning you, though. If you do that, there is a good chance you'll lose control of your little buggy friend."

Friend? Friend my ass...

"Understood." Martin shifted his hands awkwardly within the bangles. "Will I fight next to Alena?" he asked, looking at his teacher. Dais nodded, "Yes. Now, go to bed. Do *not* take those bangles off unless your life depends on it, is that clear?"

Martin nodded, twisting his arms side-to-side to rub along the insides of the bracelets. It was unusual. The only jewelry he usually wore was an old mood ring that no longer worked – a gift from Katie, one of his friends who had perished in the fire. It was a miracle it still fit him.

He turned and left the auditorium. Although everything around him was sharper, it took some getting used to before he could walk a straight line. His entire body was exhausted – something he was going to have to get used to in the days to come. The day after tomorrow was the Arena Tournament. There was no way he was going to lose – not while Alena was his partner. She deserved the honor. She

was the first 'artificial' Tzen accepted in over fifty years, as
Dais had told him.

He staggered back to where Derrick stood reading
his book. He took a deep breath and whistled, calling his
comrade's attention. He quickly started the gondola again,
letting Martin come back to Island Twelve.

"I'm dead," he muttered as he passed Derrick, "I'm
in the bedding chamber if anyone needs me. Where's
Douglas?"

"Your roommate's puttin' the moves on Terra," he
said, smiling amusedly, "I wish him the best of luck."

Nodding feebly, Martin walked awkwardly back
toward his bedding chamber. He collapsed onto his bed,
wondering how some simple gold bangles could feel like they
weighed several tons. With that thought in his mind, Martin
caved in to his need for sleep.

***

Martin was awoken by someone poking his forehead.
Growling slightly, he forced open his orange eye, fixing the
intruder with the most fearsome glare he could manage while
feeling as though he had gone to hell and back. His gaze fell
on none other than Douglas; grinning as though he'd won the
lottery.

"What do you want?" asked Martin, sitting up and
feeling the poking come to a halt. He blinked a few times,

ridding his eye of sleep, before fixing his orange gaze on
Douglas.

"Do you have any idea how long you've been out?"
he asked, moving away from the bed lest Martin decide to
blow him away. Martin stared at him wordlessly, and Douglas
took this as a sign to continue. "You've been out for at least a
day. Alena's Initiation is in two hours. She asked me where
you were. Are you gonna come or not?"

Martin forced himself from the bed, feeling the
weight of the bangles on his wrists. He slipped on his Loden
Coat, making sure the sleeves hid the jewelry from sight at
least partially, and then walked after Douglas. For some
reason, the hallway in the Bedding Chambers seemed longer
than usual.

Upon finally reaching the Island Seven Auditorium,
where he had been the night before, he saw that every Tzen
in The Hall had gathered there. They were sitting on the stone
benches that rested in a wide semicircle around a central
raised platform. Standing on the platform were three figures.
The first was Dais, tapping his fingers against the podium.
He'd never been good at public speaking.

The second figure was Alena, decked out in her
Loden Coat and looking as happy as anyone could be. The
third figure was Steven. The 'Tzen Lord' as others referred to
him, always masked himself with a partial Air Incantation.
Nobody knew why. All Martin could tell was that he was a

male standing about a head taller than himself. Any other details were washed away by the heat-haze that seemed to swirl around him.

"Ladies and Gentlemen," said Dais after checking his watch, "I'm going to keep this brief, if that's alright with you. Alena?"

He turned to Alena and she stepped forward, now standing between Dais and Steven. Martin watched from the doorway he had entered from, leaning on the doorframe.

Dais and Steven both drew out their Tzen Rods, placing them against the smooth skin on the back of Alena's right hand. They both muttered something, and Martin saw Alena wince as if she had been stabbed. A glowing symbol flared to life on the back of her hand. It was in the shape of two obtuse triangles, each one connected on one corner, and their apexes pointing down. From these apexes, two parallel lines descended down to meet her wrist.

"Alena Steward has received the MIN," proclaimed Dais, "We hereby recognize her as a fellow Tzen until the day she leaves this world. *Mahnyou Ji'it Tansamas!*" The remainder of the crowd, Martin included, repeated the chant. *Mahnyou Ji'it Tansamas*: For the Future.

"And now," said Steven, his hollow voice echoing throughout the Auditorium, "We shall proceed to Island Eight. The Arena awaits us. Every one of you shall fight your best against each other. I have taken the liberty of distributing a field across the Arena to insure no deaths occur this time."

With that reassurance, Steven faded from view entirely. Martin knew he was probably on his way to Island Eight. With much murmuring, the assembled Tzen began to move as one toward the Arena. Upon arrival, they all were required to pair off and draw a number. This number was their team number that would be used in pairing them off with their opponents.

"Well," said Martin to Alena, "It looks like we're Five." He looked at her for a moment, "Are you alright?"

Alena was breathing hard, and she shook her head to clear it. "Sorry – my hand still stings."

Martin held up his own hand, showing her the MIN glowing there. "It's how we Tzen I.D. each other," he explained. "Only a Tzen can see it. Congratulations."

"First Match: Four versus Nine!" Dais was standing on a large precipice above the Arena. The massive building was built similar to the Roman Coliseum, but not as decorative. It was a simple, circular building with a sand-filled central area. Littering this central point were large stones, pieces of furniture, miscellaneous trash, and a variety of objects. They were there to help Tzen think on their feet and use the available surroundings to their advantage.

Benches lined the inside walls for the spectators, and there were two gates leading into the arena. Spectators followed a trail down to these gates where they were briefed on rules and then sent into battle. Crisscrossing the Arena floor were various Threads; almost every type except Solar was present.

The Arena, while considered a sport by some of the Tzen, was also a functioning training zone to many. It was all fine and good to train against those on your island, but eventually you came to know them too well; began to anticipate their moves. The Arena was a chance to pit yourself against a Tzen from another island; thus varying your training.

Martin walked with Alena up to the stands. He chose them a seat near the pathway so that they could access the gates easier. With a small smile, Martin sat down on the plain stone bench and began to watch.

Team Four consisted of a blonde girl and her black-haired male partner. They were both standing at attention as they faced their opponents. Martin recognized them. The blonde was Amy Smart, a girl from Island Twelve, and the black-haired boy was a message boy from Island Four, James Richter. He relayed this to Alena while she watched the opposing team enter the Arena.

Much to Martin's surprise, Douglas was on Team Nine. He waved at Martin, seeing his roommate in the crowd. His partner was Frank, the boy Martin had worked with on the Mainland Shelf.

Steven was standing in a large box above the Arena, watching the teams walk forward to meet in the center. With his dead voice, he began to speak. "TEAMS, RETURN TO YOUR SIDES!"

Both teams bowed and walked over to the gates they'd entered from. Steven spoke again. "ON MY MARK..."

Team Nine and Team Four crouched down into their offense positions. Martin leaned forward as Steven said the words '...GET SET...' in his uninterested tone.

"GO!"

The two teams lunged forward, ducking behind rubble as their opponent fired various incantations at them. Douglas rose and fired a stream of blue-white light as Amy, who caught it full in the chest. She was lifted off her feet and hurled backwards, her body striking the side of the Arena with a resounding THWACK.

"ONE!"

Martin turned to Alena, "Each player has three strikes against them," he said, "You have to strike each opponent three times while avoiding their attacks. First team to do so wins. If you're struck three times, you are removed."

His explanation was forestalled by a loud (and rude) exclamation from Douglas as he mirrored Amy's movements, catching a Xidul in the chest and landing in an undignified heap on the floor. Steven roared out the call "ONE" again. Both teams were matched.

Chapter 36: J'tavit

"TWO!"

Martin watched with disinterest as Douglas righted

himself and lifted Amy with a Dark Incantation before hurling

her back against the wall. Frank lunged in, firing a spear of

light that struck her in the stomach. Due to Steven's

incantations, it didn't pierce her.

"THREE!"

Amy flipped Douglas and Frank the bird and walked

out of the Arena, leaving her partner to face their wrath.

James looked extremely angry that his partner had been

defeated, but didn't seem to see it as too bad of a loss. Martin

smirked. *No teamwork at all.*

Instantly, James grasped hold of a Fire Energy

Thread, "Trezin!" Douglas dropped to the ground, letting the

fireball race through the area he had been occupying a

second before. He leapt to his feet, bounded across the Arena

and buried his fist in James' gut. The black haired boy

wheezed and collapsed as Steven yelled "ONE!"

Martin was analyzing Douglas and Frank's strategy.

It seemed they were focusing first on one enemy and then on

the other. It was a good strategy, but not very efficient

against an army of foes. Martin made mental notes on ways

to counter it. The winner of this round fought the next

contestant. The last group standing won.

"ONE!" Frank had taken a direct hit with a spear of fire. Martin knew the incantation: Kodom-Akashik. Roughly translated it equated to "Burning Spear". It was generally a high-power incantation, and Martin wondered how James had managed to learn it at all, much less be able to actually *use* it.

Frank seemed to be thinking the same thing as he stood up, glaring evilly at James. The black-haired boy snorted at him, raising his hand. "Kodom-Dokumaray!" Needles of flame leapt from James' fingertips, thudding into Frank with high intensity and volume. The blonde was catapulted through his teammate, landing both of them on the floor. Martin's eye narrowed. James was a far better Tzen than he let on.

"TWO!" James seemed not to hear Steven as he rounded on his enemies. He reached out, grasping a Fire Energy Thread. Seeing as it was the third time he had done this, Martin concluded he stuck mainly to Fire Incantations. That would leave him open to Earth and Water, but he'd be able to power through Dark and Ice. Martin, thankfully, leaned more toward Air and Ice, so he was only halved. He could technically manipulate any Energy – all Tzen could – it was a matter of personal preference.

A great pillar of fire leapt from beneath Douglas and Frank, launching them into the air before either had a chance to react. Steven counted off "THREE" and "TWO", seeing as

James had struck both opponents. Frank slouched out to the edge of the Arena, nursing a wonderful goose-egg on his forehead.

Douglas pulled himself upright, pawing at some blood that ran from a split lip. He dove to the side as James fired another Burning Spear at him, righting himself in time to cast his own assault. Unfortunately, the only Thread near him was Ice. He swore and dove away as another spear impacted the wall behind him.

Hm... Douglas isn't half bad... thought Martin as he watched the battle.

There was a yell as Douglas was hurled through the air by a fireball, and Steven rang a large gong signaling Team Four as the winner. James gave a glance around the Arena for a moment until his pale gray eyes settled on Martin. He raised his wand into the air. "J'TAVIT, MARTIN SPIRE!" His wand glowed and fired a streak of blue light into the sky. James was smiling and pointing at Martin with an outstretched finger. A hush fell over the crowd as people looked at James in awe.

"James Richter has called J'tavit on Martin Spire," said Steven. He was irked at having the Arena proceedings interrupted like this, but J'tavit was an old custom – dating back to the Era of the Alinteans.

"I do." James' voice was cold, his unfeeling eyes rivaling Martin's placid gaze as he stood on the sandy floor of the Arena. Martin rose and, disregarding rules about going through gates, jumped over a low barrier into the Arena.

Alena quickly turned to the Tzen next to her. "What's J'tavit?"

"J'tavit is a challenge – it's issued only during Arena matches. It's a brutal fight with the loser forfeiting his life." Alena looked down into the Arena in horror. *A fight to the death... like the Roman Blood Sports...*

Steven waved a hand behind his protective shimmering barrier, and the air itself seemed to come undone. The barrier preventing death was lifted. Martin stood at ease before James, his hands in his pants pockets as he regarded his opponent with mild disinterest.

"And why, James, would you call J'tavit on me?" he asked. His voice was flat; carrying all the emotion of an iceberg.

"You're a monster," spat James. There were several murmurings in the Arena, but ironically no one contradicted the statement. Alena was in shocked silence. Martin shrugged, "If that's what you believe, I've no reason to contradict it. And you think you're going to kill me, right?"

Jason drew out his rod, pointing it at Martin. "I'll give you a quick death – more than what you gave the children of the orphanage!"

Martin frowned. "I do not deny my involvement, but their deaths mean nothing now. Why do you bring up the past?"

"My *brother* died there!" screamed James. His calm façade shattered, "I've waited seven years to finish you off! I've never been strong enough... not until now. Kodom-Akashik!" Martin moved out of the way as the spear of flames raced past him. While powerful, Burning Spear was relatively easy to predict. He drew out his own wand, mentally checking the positions of the required Threads for incantations.

He was near a Dark Thread, but that would do him no good. An Air Thread lay beyond that, so that was his intended destination. His orange eye watched James recoil from the blast of his incantation, turning to Martin's new position.

"Think you're funny?" he asked, twirling the wand, "Well I'll fix you. Kodom-Va'aka!"

Martin's eye bolted open. *Kodom-Va'aka?!*

The incantation spread from the tip of James' wand, the fires taking shape until a great winged serpent was birthed from the end of the Tzen Rod. Martin glared at the fiery dragon for a moment before it twisted through the air like a missile, heading directly for where he stood. As a last ditch effort to avoid being vaporized, Martin threw up his wand, grasping an Earth Thread. "Ihrtan-Emonael!"

320

A wall of rock rose up from the floor of the Arena, rising until it blocked Martin's view of the dragon. There was a horrible explosion of sound, light, and heat as the great serpent slammed against the rock, immediately bursting like a bomb. Martin, even from behind his shield, felt the heat. It was great enough that he buckled to his knees.

When the smoke cleared, he realized his wall was gone. James was still intact as well, but his wand had snapped in half from the concussion blast of such an extreme incantation. Martin's wand had broken as well. Biting back a curse, he looked around the Arena for a weapon.

James drew an old longsword from the sand, throwing it to Martin as he pulled a second from the rocks. Martin caught it, twirling it experimentally. He liked swords – they were easy to use, and functioned like an extension of himself.

He parried a thrust, twirling the sword around as he blocked a punch with his arm. Their swords rang against each other, the metal flashing in the dim light of the cavern. Martin slashed his sword at an angle, attempting to catch James beneath his guard. The other boy slammed the sword away, driving the point toward Martin.

With a gasp, Martin recoiled as the sword nicked his shoulder. It separated the material of the Loden Coat, cutting through the dress shirt beneath and leaving a shallow cut along his left arm. James sneered triumphantly.

"It's just a scratch, don't be so proud of yourself," said Martin as he looked at the thin line of blood on his shoulder. "It barely even tingles."

That was a lie. Like paper-cuts, this was a small wound that hurt in a large way. Of course, there was no way he was going to let James know that. He raised the sword again, pointing it at his opponent. "Let's go."

After another three minutes of parrying, slashing and thrusting their blades at each other, James' sword snapped. He screamed a curse and dove sideways as Martin's blade cleaved the ground. He grabbed an old iron chair that littered the arena floor, hurling it at the one-eyed Tzen.

The chair flew past Martin as he dodged. It clanged worthlessly against the far wall. He winced at the sound. The sounds around him were sharper due to those damn bracelets. He considered taking them off, but wasn't prepared to lose control yet. If he couldn't beat James without his 'buggy friend', he was worthless anyway.

James grabbed another object – a metal rod. Martin instantly recognized that this was a tool that could be very deadly in capable hands. He brought the sword up, ready to go on the defensive if he had to. The pole lashed out, and Martin barely managed to bring the sword up to block it. Unfortunately, the blade broke in two. The rod struck him squarely in the chest, dropping him on his rear in the sand.

The jagged edge of the bar came whistling down, and Martin rolled away as it sank into the sand. He kicked James's legs out from beneath him, hearing the other boy go down. He stood up and looked around for a weapon. Seeing nothing obvious, he backed up; watching his opponent with his solitary eye.

James rose, pulling the pole from the sand. He swung it at Martin, who jumped away. The pole smashed into a piece of rock, and a piece snapped off. Martin snatched up the small metal cylinder, holding it in his hand like a sword. It was only about three feet long, but that wasn't going to hold him back. The next time the rod came his way, he ducked beneath it, ramming his section of the bar into James' stomach.

James coughed, and several drops of red liquid flecked his lips. Martin dodged away as his irate opponent swung the iron pole at him, narrowly missing his face. He felt the wind whistle through his bangs as the end of the rod swung past him. The momentum carried James awkwardly in a semicircle, and Martin lunged forward, kicking his foe in the small of his back. James sprawled in the sand with a curse.

As James rolled over, Martin's foot descended on his chest. The metal bar pointed at his throat. Even if it wasn't as sharp as a sword, it could still kill him. James glared defiantly up at Martin. "Go on then – kill me!"

Martin looked up at Steven, who loudly proclaimed him the winner. Martin looked down at James before throwing the bar to the side. He walked over to the gate he should have entered through, ignoring James' screaming about dishonor. Alena had run down and was on the other side of the gate. The metal bars sank into holes on the ground as she ran through, throwing her arms around him.

"Are you okay?" she asked worriedly, looking at his rumpled clothing and the gash on his shoulder. Martin nodded, jerking his head toward the Arena behind him. "We're next, seeing as I was called in because of J'tavit. Are you ready?"

She nodded, releasing him. Martin sensed some reluctance to let him go. He shrugged it off and faced into the Arena. Most of the weapons were gone, and he felt his pockets for a replacement Tzen rod. Seeing his actions, Douglas whistled at him and tossed him one. Nodding his thanks, he faced the far door and awaited his opponents.

"The next match," Steven announced, "Will be Team Ten!" Much to Martin's chagrin, his opponents were Jason and a girl he recognized as Catherine Hawkins. She lived over on Island Nine. There was no denying she was pretty – she had short black hair that framed a round, heart shaped face. Her eyes, brown as chocolate, were perfectly spaced (if not a little larger than normal), and her lips seemed to not exist at all except as a thin line.

"Jason..." he nodded at the information dealer, "...ready?"

He nodded happily, drawing his Tzen rod, "No time like the present."

Above them, Steven saw their readiness and decided to start the match. "Match Three – Team Five versus Team Ten... START!"

Chapter 37: Five versus Ten

"Breathe, Alena," whispered Martin as the match began. He drew out the borrowed Tzen rod, holding it lightly in his fingers like a conductor's baton. "This is easy compared to some things that will be occurring later."

Alena took a deep breath, gathering her wits. It turned out to be not a moment too soon. Catherine had launched a volley of ice needles at her position, and she barely managed to dodge. One pierced a corner of the Loden Coat she had worn to the Arena. She frowned at Catherine.

Martin, in the meantime, was circling with Jason. The two had moved to another corner of the sandy battle Arena so as not to interfere with their teammates. Now they circled like vultures, each watching the other intently.

Martin grabbed hold of an Ice Thread in one hand and an Air Thread in the other. "Sunakare-Garahno!" From his mouth burst a condensed cyclone of freezing wind; snowflakes whirling within it like tiny white leaves. Jason danced nimbly to the side, wrapping his hand around a bluish-purple Lightning Thread.

"Nonohaismet!" A black cloud issued from Jason's wand, hovering over the Arena like an omen of death. Thunder rumbled in the depths of the writhing mass, and Martin made certain to get away from anything metallic. A lightning bolt shrieked through the air, turning the sand beneath it to glass as it struck. Martin was knocked to his knees by the impact. "ONE!"

Damn! This is going to interfere with Alena! She doesn't know how to counter Lightning Energy!

Martin rolled away as Jason lunged forward. He righted himself, looking for a Thread he could use. A Lunar Thread wound its way nearby; silvery-white in the gloom of the cavern. He wrapped his fingers around it, feeling the familiar sensation of emptiness pour into his body. "Onemsatau!"

He swung the wand like a saber as if to horizontally bisect Jason, and a whitish semicircle of light shot out, whistling through the air. Jason hurled himself flat, barely dodging it. He glared up at Martin. "No fair using Lunar Energy!"

"No fair using Lightning," responded Martin with a jerk of his head, indicating Alena and Catherine who were attempting to fight around the periodic bursts of lightning. Jason grinned at him, saying nothing. It was then that Martin understood.

"She can predict where the lighting is going to strike, can't she?" stated Martin. It was more like he was affirming what he already knew. Catherine and Jason had already gone over this tactic. Alena was in deeper than she probably realized.

Martin jumped forward, knocking Jason over in a surprise lunge, and bounding to the other side. He wrapped his fingers around an Earth Thread as the heavy energy soaked into his being. In his other hand, he grasped hold of a Fire Thread. The warmth spread through his body, mingling with the crisp, weighty feeling of the Earth Thread.

"Aponracia!"

Jason realized instantly what was happening, but it was too late for him to stop Martin. The ground trembled and a large fissure opened, dividing the Arena in half. Steven made a sound of outrage, but it was lost in the din of shouts from the observers.

Flaming rocks, some as large as Jason's head, flew from within the crack. They rained down in the Arena, piercing the artificial cloud cover Jason had summoned and burning it away. They fell fast and hard, and Jason retreated to shelter beneath an archway carved into the side of the pit. When the incantation ended, he poked his head tentatively out from the relative safety of his hiding place to meet with a fist in his jaw.

"Don't try to kill my teammates," spat Martin as he drew the rod back. Steven roared out "ONE!" and then paused, as if thinking, before adding "ONE" to Alena and Catherine's duel. Martin was pleased to see it was Catherine that had sustained the hit. The scoreboard was favoring Martin.

328

"Alright then," said Jason, massaging his jaw, "Then let's play."

Martin's fingers closed over the nearest Thread. Feeling the buzzing entering his veins, he knew it was a Lightning Thread. He quickly sorted through his mental catalogue of incantations for that particular element before deciding upon one.

"Pasroxeir!" There was a burst of crackling energy and a loud yell. Jason was left smoking on the ground, struck full on by one of Martin's more reckless incantations; Spark. It involved electrifying his own arm and belting the foe with it. Martin's hand was still tingling as Steven yelled "TWO, ONE!" It didn't take Martin more than a second to realize that Alena had been hit.

He turned to face her, forgetting that Jason wasn't down completely. He was only aware his foe was still active when he heard a few Alintean words spoken from near his feet.

"Asapih!"

A column of water was launched out of the sand beneath Martin's feet. It lifted him several feet in the air before letting him down, none too gently, in the sand. He glared at Jason, who was on his feet again; wand at the ready. Steven let out a bellow. "TWO!"

"Still going, huh? Alright..." he forced himself up, grasping the Water Thread Jason had used. Water was something volatile, but Martin had a plan in mind. He focused on the rushing feeling in his veins, bringing it into his chest.

"Erlcos-Asapih!" Not only did a water column blast Jason into the air, it spread out across the Arena, sweeping both Alena and Catherine off their feet into the water. They flopped around for a moment like fish while Steven bellowed "THREE" on Jason. The information dealer grumbled good-naturedly and walked over to the loser's bench. He smiled, flipping Martin the bird as he passed, and reminded him they'd duel again soon.

Martin had no time for such things. His plan had to be activated swiftly. The water was clinging to both Alena and Catherine, but it would quickly evaporate. He whistled at Alena. When she looked his way, he let out a yell: "MOVE!"

She lunged away from Catherine, who stood still for a moment in confusion. It was at that moment that Martin's thin hand wrapped around a Lightning Thread, focusing on the electric tingling in his body. "Assnah!"

A lightning bolt shot from his wand, striking Catherine in the chest. The water on her clothes and skin acted as a conductor, amplifying the effect of the incantation. She was hurled through the air, landing in the sand in an ungraceful heap.

"TWO!"

Martin ducked a Burning Spear from Catherine as she stood up again. Evidently she knew James. Alena lunged forward, her hand closing around an Air Thread. "Lipitel-Xidul!"

Martin briefly wondered how she knew that incantation, but his thought process was occupied by watching Catherine sail through the air like a limp rag doll to strike the wall. She slid down it, bruised and cursing, as Steven yelled "THREE! THE WINNING TEAM IS TEAM FIVE!"

Martin bowed to the Tzen assembled and walked off toward the gates. Every three matches the Tzen were allowed a reprieve from fighting to 'freshen up'. This half-hour break involved everything from getting a snack to going to the restroom to chatting up the potential competition.

Martin and Alena wandered over to one of the refreshment stands to get a drink. While Alena deliberated over the available choices of various sodas, Martin leaned casually on the wall to watch the other Tzen. He was very surprised to see Lisa, the biologist, walking in his direction.

"Something the matter?" he asked as she drew closer. She nodded, tugging him away from Alena and the snack bar. With a suppressed curse, he followed her. They walked into a small alcove and Martin resumed his leaning position.

"The thing that killed the Zerolyte," she said, "The one whose corpse you gave me..." Martin nodded as she spoke. "Tahadoazleh," he supplied. "What of it?"

Much to his surprise, Lisa shook her head. "The claws on the 'Tahadoazleh' you brought me don't match the wounds. They're similar, but they're not the same. Whatever killed the Zerolyte didn't use claws – it was Energy Manipulation."

Martin's jaw dropped open for a split second. "But there are no Threads on the Mainland Shelf!" he said after a moment, "How could anyone use EM over there?"

"That's what worries me," said Lisa, running a hand through her brown hair, "I'm going to report this to Dais, but I figured you should know."

Martin nodded again, "Understood. I'll see if I can go back there any time in the future to examine the Palace again. Do you know what type of Energy it was?"

"Either Fire or Solar," Lisa said as she turned to walk away, "The wounds looked like claw marks, but the insides were cauterized by extreme heat. My bet is on Solar, though. It looks like it was stronger than average Fire – it roasted the entirety of the Zerolyte's organs into a pulp."

She turned around and walked off, leaving Martin to his thoughts. He walked back to where Alena was waiting, still trying to decide between a Pepsi and a Coke. He rolled his eyes, settling on a glass of vanilla-flavored milk, and standing against the wall again. There was no point in getting riled up before the Arena battles. If Lisa was his opponent, she might have been trying to worry him into making a mistake.

Like that'll work... he pushed the thoughts of Tahadoazleh and the dead Zerolytes from his mind, focusing on the task at hand. The third fight had finished – that meant seven more to go. He did a quick calculation – it would take him at least three hours to win all seven. He downed the vanilla milk in one gulp, placing the glass back on the refreshment counter. As long as they were on a temporary reprieve, he might as well take care of some basics.

"Alena." The brunette turned to face him as he spoke, "I want you to try something. If an opponent uses Lightning Energy again, counter it with Earth. Each element, obviously, has a counterpart. You can use their opposites to protect yourself."

She thought for a moment, "Fire and Water, I'm guessing," she said after a moment, "Light and Dark, Solar and Lunar..." she trailed off.

"Air and Ice, Earth and Lightning," finished Martin, "Neutral stands alone."

Alena smiled at him, and his heart quickened for a moment. With practiced ease, he crushed the feeling and gazed at her with his unfeeling orange eye. "Now, recite them. I have no use for a partner that will fail me."

"Fire and Water, Light and Dark, Solar and Lunar, Air and Ice, Earth and Lighting, with Neutral standing alone," recited Alena. "Is that right?"

"Yeah, good enough," said Martin. "Just don't forget it. Now, if your opponent fires, for instance, a Fireball at you, don't just use any Water incantation. Use the prefix for Water, in this case 'Batro' with the suffix for Shield, 'Emonael'. So by holding a Water Thread and saying 'Batro-Emonael' you summon a 'Water-Shield'. You see?"

She nodded excitedly, "I get it! So if someone fires a Dark Incantation at me, I use the prefix for Light coupled with the suffix for Shield to form a Light Shield?"

"You've got it now," said Martin encouragingly, trying not to sound false. He was truly excited that she was grasping the concept so quickly. It would make things easier for both of them. "Just remember that this isn't a foolproof defense. If it's a double-incantation, the shield may fail. A very powerful incantation might also do the trick."

She nodded, "But that goes both ways, doesn't it?"

Clever girl...

"Yes, it does. Now, we've got five minutes until the next fight. Before we go in, I'm going to tell you a few prefixes. You know Water, right?"

"Batro," she answered smartly. He nodded. "Light is Oduparon, and Fire is Tre. Remember those, and I'll teach you more in the next break. Just practice using Water, Fire and Light in this next round – get a feel for them. Once you've mastered them, we'll work on some more. Got that?"

She nodded just as Steven's voice permeated the chamber. "MATCH FOUR – TEAM FIVE VERSUS TEAM SEVEN. WILL THESE TEAMS PLEASE REPORT TO THE ARENA!"

He grinned at her, his lopsided smile looking more like a smirk to anyone who didn't know him. Alena saw the adrenaline in his system and for a moment she understood why people called him a monster – he enjoyed fighting a bit too much.

"Let's go, then," he said, leading her toward the gates, "Time is wasting..."

Chapter 38: Five versus Seven

Team Seven was comprised of Terra and Sasaki. Martin grinned inwardly – he'd been waiting to fight Sasaki for a while. He knew Terra specialized mostly in Lunar and Earth Energies, but Sasaki was a mystery to him. Even though they'd shared an island in the past, he'd never seen the Asian boy fight.

Sasaki bowed to him, and Martin returned the gesture. Above them, Steven yelled "GO", prompting him to draw his borrowed wand from his coat. Sasaki already had his out and his brown eyes were seeking out a Thread. Martin watched the gaze as it traveled from Thread to Thread. The eyes flickered momentarily over a Water Thread.

Bingo. He's a Water Manipulator!

Martin immediately sought out a Lightning Thread, making sure it was within easy reach. Seeing it on the other side of the Arena brought a stab of worry into his gut, but he pushed it away. He'd just maneuver over there when he got the chance.

Without warning, Sasaki lunged forward, his hand closing around the Lightning Thread instead of the Water. It was at that moment Martin realized he'd been tricked, and he lunged for the Earth Thread.

"Assnah-Va'aka!"

A serpent, the color of the midnight sky and rippling with electricity, flowed from Sasaki's wand and launched itself at Martin; maw gaping open to reveal teeth in the shape of thunderbolts. Martin lunged away, seeing the dragon swerve to follow him. Fortunately, it was moving too quickly and circled around him, heading back toward its summoner. It wouldn't be long before it could turn around again.

"Ihrtan-Va'aka!" the ground beneath him rumbled, forcing Martin to shift to keep his balance. A massive dragon, born of the sand on the Arena floor, rose up to block its electrical counterpart. The Dragon spread its wings wide, and both dragons vanished in a flash as they collided. All that remained was a mound of glass in the center of the Arena.

Before Martin could rejoice, a stalagmite pushed up from beneath him, spiking him into the air and back onto the ground. He mumbled a curse into the sand as Steven announced "ONE" and stood up, glaring at Terra. She had struck him while dodging Alena's air-based assault.

Clever...

He righted himself, looking around for Sasaki. He found the boy crouching behind a large stone, gathering the Energy from an Earth Thread that flowed past. He rose, pointing his wand at Martin. "Tehitot-Ihmeriat!"

The floor of the Arena cracked open, the jagged fissure speeding toward Martin. With the speed of a wildcat, Martin managed to leap out of the way, and saw the crack heading toward Alena and Terra. Just as he was about to shout out a warning, Terra unknowingly stepped into the path of the crack and wound up hanging from the lip of the chasm. Alena dropped an icicle on her, earning her Steven's shout of first strike.

Martin turned to face Sasaki, who was frowning at his involvement in his teammate's suffering at that moment. Martin spared the boy a conceited smirk. "Not a bad incantation – want to see one of mine?"

He grasped a Light Thread in his right hand, and then pulled a Dark Thread over and put it in the same fist. He closed his eyes – knowing he was putting himself at risk.

"Etlar," he said, and the majority of the spectators in the Arena became extremely quiet.

A pentagram appeared in the sand around Martin's feet, and a matching design encircled Sasaki. A snarl escaped the Asian boy's lips as he sought to step forward, but found that he couldn't. Before another move could be made, five spears of light, one at each of the star's points, stabbed into the ground around him like a cage. Martin was still standing as though he'd been turned to stone.

Waves of Light and Darkness surged from spear to spear, filling the cage (and subsequently Sasaki) with their power. Sasaki's body was not configured for such a high dosage of Energy, and the result was an explosion which left him lying on the floor like a corpse. The stars faded away, returning mobility to both combatants. "ONE!"

"Dohar-Osinus!" Martin quickly shifted the Threads he was holding, exchanging the Light Thread for an Air Thread that floated near his chest. A blackish-gray mist rose up around Sasaki as he tried to rise, only to grip him in the clutches of something far worse than the previous attack.

Everyone in the Arena was quiet now. Dohar-Osinus: Wraith's Mist. It was an Incantation that called to mind the worst thing a person could imagine, forcing them to live it within their minds again and again, until the effects were cancelled or forced loose from the mind. The latter was extremely difficult, however, and Martin doubted Sasaki was capable of doing so. He was right.

A low, keening moan tore its way from the Asian boy's throat. Even Alena and Terra had stopped to watch. Sasaki was curled into the fetal position, rocking back and forth and crying words nobody could understand. Martin stood over him, wand outstretched, with no pity on his face.

"TWO!" called Steven, but the effect was lost. Everyone was focused on Martin and Sasaki. Martin snorted and twisted the wand away. The mist faded, leaving his foe on the floor. He grinned down at him before kicking him hard enough to roll him several feet away. "THREE!"

Sasaki crawled meekly over to his respective gate, tears pouring down his face. Several people booed at Martin, and one even went so far as to throw their drink at him. The cup popped open on his shoulder, spilling soda all over his coat and the side of his head. Martin blinked the liquid from his good eye, glaring into the stands as if *daring* the perpetrator to show himself. Whoever the culprit was, he didn't come forward.

Martin now turned his wand on Terra. Her eyes widened, but she crouched into a defensive stance nonetheless. Martin snorted, pointing at her feet as he grasped a Fire Thread.

"Lipitel-Trezin!"

The fireball that struck the ground did so with the force of a nuclear bomb. There was a shriek as Terra was hurled around inside the explosion before being tossed unceremoniously against the wall. "TWO!"

Something struck him in the back, and he turned to see a ketchup-smeared hot-dog lying on the floor of the Arena. He glared back up into the stands and rounded on Terra again, only to find her gone.

Damn...

A block of ice the size of a small car flattened Martin into the floor. He swore profusely, crawling from beneath it all the while. Terra was hanging from the lip of the Arena, a smug smile on her face. Something about that smile made Martin absolutely furious.

Smile at this!

He grasped both a Water Thread and an Air Thread. He focused all the energies in his body onto a central point near Terra. "Anasapiel!"

A cyclone of raging water pushed its way out of the sand, and Terra's eyes widened in shock as she tried to scramble away, only to find Alena blocking her path. The bespectacled Tzen placed one of her shoes against Terra's stomach and forced her into the waterspout behind her. There was a cry of indignation before Terra disappeared into the whirling waters.

"THREE!"

Martin cancelled the waterspout incantation with a wave of his wand. Terra dropped limply to the ground, her clothing soaked and clinging to her. There was a loud round of booing at Martin, and several people began hurling things at him.

"Shit," swore Martin as somebody lobbed a hard-boiled egg at his head, "Alena, move!"

The pair of them scrambled over to their gate. It promptly lowered, and they scrambled inside, their coats covered in food and drink hurled by irate spectators. Alena was glaring at Martin in silence. After a moment, he looked at her. "What?"

"How could you do that?" she asked, her voice trembling, "How can you possibly sleep at night knowing a technique like that?"

"Simple – it doesn't bother me. It was either I won or he did, and I wasn't going to lose."

Alena slapped him – hard. "At the risk of sounding corny, Martin, winning isn't everything! Show a bit of compassion now and again – you just might improve."

She turned and stalked off to one of the restrooms to scrub some of the food waste out of her coat. Martin stood in the antechamber, his cheek stinging and his teeth rattling in his jaw. He tenderly brought one of his long fingered hands up to his cheek.

Ow...

He heard someone yell his name, and turned to look at the source. It was coming from the Arena. He stuck his head out, looking around for whoever had called his name. A tattered napkin, wrapped around a fistful of expired vegetables, splattered in his face with enough velocity to knock him down.

He pawed the vegetable mess from his face, hurling curses at whoever had done that and demanding they come down and fight him. Of course, nobody volunteered. Hurling one final, vulgar curse into the Arena, he stalked out to do the same thing as Alena – clean up.

He was almost to the restroom when a messenger jogged into the antechamber. "Message," he called, throwing a tightly rolled piece of parchment at Martin. The one-eyed

Tzen caught and opened the paper, reading the letters printed there with disdain.

    Martin,

    Due to popular vote, you are being withheld from all but the final round of the Arena. Your actions against Sasaki are unforgivable. Be thankful you are even allowed to partake in the final round.

    Steven

    Martin rolled up the parchment, putting it into the sleeve of his Loden Coat. Steven's note was blunt and to the point – just like the writer. Alena walked out a moment later, still smelling strongly of food products. When Martin shared the news, she snorted.

    "Serves you right," she hissed, snatching the note and reading it herself. Martin hung his head in frustration. What was the big deal? It was an incantation – just like Trezin or Xidul.

    Of course, Trezin and Xidul don't psychologically scar people...

    Martin decided he was going to return to Island Twelve to change his clothing. It would be at least two more hours until the Final Round, if the fights went quickly.

Upon returning, he also exchanged his current book, *A Tale of Two Cities*, for one entitled *Waiting*. He had finished the former a while ago, and had been forgetting to change it out. Now he figured he had a chance to.

Martin left his chambers, returning to Island Eight. He brought along a spare Coat for Alena – maybe she wouldn't slap him again if he did something 'compassionate' for once.

He smirked at the thought. She'd probably think he was trying to be funny and hit him again anyway. *Damned if I do, damned if I don't...* Shrugging it off as 'one of those things', he boarded the gondola for Island Eight. At least now he had a book to read.

Chapter 39: Finals

The last gong rang, signaling the start of the Final round. Martin pushed himself up off of the floor, sliding his favorite bookmark into his book. It wasn't actually a bookmark; it was an Ace of Spades. It didn't' matter to him – it served its purpose. He walked over to Alena, jerking his head toward the gate leading into the Arena.

Outside, he could hear Steven announcing the teams and their participants. It was himself and Alena on Team Five versus a boy named David and a girl named Deborah on Team Three. He smirked. Those two were possibly the worst team he could imagine right now. David was primarily an Earth Manipulator, while Deborah stuck strictly to Dark.

"Alena," he said as they walked toward the gateway, "You take David. He's big, but he's not that tough. He deals mostly with Earth, occasionally dabbling a bit with Dark. His partner sticks strictly to the latter. I'll deal with her."

Alena gave him a baleful glare that could have rivaled one of his own. "No more psychological scarring, Martin." She walked through the gate, Martin beside her, into the dimly lit Arena. Team Three was already present.

David, as Martin had said, was large. He stood at around six feet, with broad shoulders and a barrel chest. His body supplemented a calculating mind that was hidden beneath curls of brown hair. His face was broad, with the eyes set close together.

Deborah, on the other hand, was a miniscule slip of a girl. She was barely four feet tall, with a thin, wiry frame and pale skin. She was reminiscent of a porcelain doll. Her black hair curled down her back, ending at her waist. Set into her ivory face were a pair of green eyes that stared blankly out at him. Her lips were drawn into a thin line, rendering her mouth almost invisible.

"TEAMS, PREPARE TO BEGIN!" roared Steven from his announcer's box. Martin checked his Tzen Rod, finding it securely in his inner pocket, and saw Alena do the same out of the corner of his eye.

"FINAL MATCH, BEGIN."

David lumbered forward, his wand already out. He was heading straight for Martin. Behind him, Deborah grasped a violet Dark Thread and began to focus. Before Martin could respond to either of them, Alena launched a Fireball at David. This forced the mammoth boy to divert his course, lest he take a hit.

"Karnain!"

Deborah had thrown her gray Loden Coat at Martin, and he was immediately perplexed by the action. It was only once he saw the coat begin to move on its own that he realized what was happening.

Damn! Animation!"

The coat hovered in the Arena like a specter, and Martin watched it with his usual intense gaze. It was connected to Deborah by a single point – the violet patch somewhere on the coat. If he could strike it, it would return the coat to its normal state; a piece of clothing.

It was inside the left sleeve, glowing just brightly enough to be seen. Martin briefly wondered if there was some rule against that, but had to dodge a punch from an empty sleeve. He knew from experience that just because it was empty didn't mean it didn't count as a hit. Generally, this incantation was a decoy maneuver.

Alright, let's play that way then.

He grabbed a Light Thread, feeling the crisp, pure feeling flood his veins. Ducking a punch from the coat, he rolled to the side and stood up, wand at the ready.

"Oduparon-Lanatoatzen!"

A sphere of light appeared near him, shining with the radiance of the sun. Before any of the combatants (or the coat) could react, thousands of needles of blinding light were fired from the orb, nailing the coat to the far wall. Martin lunged forward, stabbing his Tzen Rod through the left sleeve, piercing the Animation Zone. The coat fell limply to the ground as Martin rounded on Deborah.

"You made me waste time," he said conversationally. She frowned at him, bringing her wand up to face him. She grasped the nearest Thread to him – a Fire Thread – and spoke.

"Trehaismet!"

Fire streamed from Deborah's wand, filling the Arena with orange flames and thick black smoke. Martin threw up an arm to shield his face from the abominable heat. While none of the flames were anywhere close to striking him, the incantation effectively stunned him. Firestorms were an excellent distraction. Apparently, Deborah was the illusionist on her Island.

"I know about your weakness," she called out of the smoke, "You hate the heat."

"No shit," said Martin dryly as he waved ash from in front of his face, "How long did it take you to figure out?"

The voice spoke again; this time from somewhere to his right. "As soon as I noticed that you wouldn't touch a Fire Thread unless you had to. That and you stuck mostly to Ice Incantations or Air Incantations."

"Clever girl," said Martin, turning to face the sound of her voice. He couldn't see her, but he was going to have to risk striking in her general direction. He forced his eyes open, looking for a Thread. A Lightning Thread was nearby; it would have to do.

He grabbed it, feeling his hand vibrate from the power contained within the thin cord. Finally, when it felt like his body was going to come apart, he cast the Lightning out of his body.

"Pasroxeir-Tzintasa!"

Lighting leapt from his wand into the ground, spiking up through the sand at irregular intervals. It parted the flames as it crisscrossed the ground in lazy arcs, eventually earning Martin a piercing shriek as it apparently struck Deborah.

"ONE!"

Martin focused again, listening for Deborah. He heard heavy breathing nearby, and ducked a punch that probably would have cracked his jaw. Deborah was standing almost directly in front of him, obscured by the smoke; he grabbed her by the legs and flipped her over his head.

"TWO! ONE!"

Alena!

He dove through the flames, tearing off his Loden Coat as the fire consumed it. Alena was still fighting David, but it was obvious who had taken the hit. Alena had a cut running just below her hairline, and blood was leaking into her face. Her right eye was blinking rapidly as the crimson liquid flowed into it.

"Hold on!"

He threw himself on David's back, punching him solidly in the back of the head. "ONE!"

David, however, had plans that didn't include defeat. He reached over his shoulder, grasping Martin in one enormous hand. Holding him in place, David threw himself back-first onto the Arena floor. His weight bore down on Martin, crushing him.

"ONE!"

There was a moan, and David rolled off. He was clutching his groin in agony, and it only took Martin a moment to realize that Alena was responsible for his pain. He nodded his thanks, looking around for Deborah.

She had been sneaking up on him, but after he spotted her she madly rushed forward, trying to tackle him. He let her hands close on his shoulders. She was planning to head butt him. He twisted his body, slamming her into the ground as her forehead connected with his nose.

"THREE! TWO!"

It was obvious that Deborah wasn't going anywhere, so Martin turned his attention back to David. The behemoth of a Tzen had almost cornered Alena, and apparently he was seeking retribution for the kick to the groin she had given him. Martin threw his Tzen Rod, immediately realizing how stupid it had been to do so. The thin shaft of wood clattered harmlessly next to Alena, but it drew David's attention for a moment.

"Xidul!"

Martin saw the large boy flying toward him, the victim of Alena's Impact incantation. Impressed, he ducked to the side to avoid the flying body. "TWO!"

He wiped blood from his nose, walking over to retrieve his rod from near Alena. He turned to face David, standing shoulder-to-shoulder with her. "You're doing quite well," he said. His voice was flat, but he still saw Alena swell with a sense of pride.

David raised his wand, pointing at the two of them. Martin realized that it hadn't been a good idea to crowd near Alena the way he had. It made them an easier target. "Move!"

Before either of them could do so, however, a tremor shook the cavern. Martin stumbled, catching himself against the wall. He glared at David. "What'd you do?"

"Nothing!" David looked equally as shaken as Martin. He had been pitched into the sand and was looking around for the source of the quake. Alena pushed herself to her feet, leaning against the wall. The tremor came again, this time stronger, and even Martin was forced into the dirt.

Above him, Steven was saying something. His brain wasn't processing it at the moment, so he ignored it. He righted himself again, grabbing Alena by the wrist. "We've got to get out of here!" he said, pointing to the gate, "We're going – NOW!"

He dragged her toward the gate, and he saw David doing the same to Deborah. Martin knocked on the heavy iron gate and dragged Alena through upon its opening. The antechamber quaked again, and bits of rock and debris fell from the ceiling.

"Is The Hall collapsing?" asked Douglas, running over to him. The Tzen were flooding out of the Arena, many confused and somewhat frightened. Martin shrugged, jerking Alena toward the door, "We've got to get out of here!" he repeated.

There was a horrific rending sound, and Martin felt the ground move like liquid beneath his feet. It rippled like water, flowing back into the Arena. Panicked shouting was drowned out by the din, and Martin's head snapped around to look into the Arena.

The entire floor had disappeared; it had caved into an enormous hole in the floor of The Hall. The seating area of the Arena had collapsed and was falling inward, the rocks plummeting down the hole like raindrops. Steven had vacated the announcer's box, and it was fortunate. The box was in several pieces; collapsing into the void below it.

"MOVE!"

The antechamber began to crumble, the floor sliding into the hole as if pulled by some unseen force. Martin began to run. Alena jerked free of his grasp and ran next to him.

Douglas wasted no time in bolting ahead of both of them, working feverishly with the locks on the door.

"C'mon..." there was a loud snap, and the door opened slowly. Martin pushed Douglas and Alena out the door, looking at the receding floor. He ducked out the door, dashing across one of the swaying rope-and-bone bridges onto Island Seven. He looked back at the Arena, watching it buck and convulse in its death throes.

Only one thought permeated his mind.

Why?

Chapter 40: The Invasion

Island Eight's Arena had vanished entirely. After at least an hour of off-and-on quakes, the building had collapsed into the deep shaft that had formed beneath it. All that was left of it was a gaping hole; a pit that seemed to stretch to infinity through the blackness within it. Anything else on the Island had been leveled; and a few piles of rubble remained to stand as testament to the buildings that had once stood there.

Steven was deep in conference with several of his high-ranking Tzen – obviously discussing the source of the quakes. The Hall shook again; minor in comparison to the previous quakes, but still enough to bring down a small shower of dirt from the high ceiling.

"Enemies!"

Martin's head whipped around at the sound of the exclamation. His gaze fell on the pit – at the edge stood four Zerolytes. They were dressed in their usual black robes, inlaid with golden runes, and they all had their hoods drawn low over their faces. The Zerolytes made no move to attack – they merely stood at the edge of the shaft watching the assembled Tzen.

Steven stood up, his shimmering aura hiding any facial expression he may have had. He faced the Zerolytes, and Martin was almost certain he could hear the anger in his voice when he spoke.

"What are you doing here?"

One of the Zerolytes stepped forward. He did not speak, but it raised an empty sleeve to point at Steven. When it did speak, Martin recognized the voice – it was the Zerolyte that had been wearing the Monkshood Amulet. "Sepab!"

A sphere of violet energy was ejected from the sleeve. Steven moved, and the attack collided with a stone spire that was present of Island Seven. The stalagmite crumbled away, showering the gathered Tzen with bits and pieces of rock and dirt.

Steven raised one of his hands in the air; then brought it down to point at the Zerolyte. "Tzen – attack."

There was a collective yell as the Tzen surged forward, grasping at Threads with which to attack the Zerolytes. Unfortunately, the Tzen could only fit two abreast crossing the bridge, which left them as cannon fodder for the Zerolytes.

The Zerolyte raised his hands into the air, chanting something Martin couldn't hear. An arm rose from the pit, then another. Zerolytes were climbing out of the pits like ants, surging into The Hall.

Martin tore the bangles from his wrists, feeling the power of the Solar Parasite flow through his veins. He jammed the bracelets into a pocket of his coat, channeling all the Neutral Energy in his body into his chest.

"Erhaz-Ahatamz!" he murmured, "Nutapriel-Askil!"

The familiar tentacles surged across his body, pinning his clothing against his skin as it defended his flesh from attacks. The wings burst from his back, flapping once to shake the stiffness from them. Martin lunged forward, flying across the gap between Island Eight and Island Seven.

Alena was among the first to cross the bridge, she grasped a Fire Thread, launching a Fireball directly into the mass of Zerolytes that were climbing up the walls of the shaft. Behind her, she heard Steven barking orders to force the Zerolytes back into the pit.

A black figure flew above her, and Alena saw a single orange eye flickering from within a mask of calcium-enriched armor. Wings spread wide; Martin flew low to the ground, sweeping the Zerolytes left and right as he flew through their ranks. Martin flipped around in mid-air, forcing his feet into the chest of one of his foes. The Zerolyte let out a shriek and collapsed back into the pit, waving its arms as it fell.

Alena was so distracted by watching Martin fly she almost let a Zerolyte attack her from behind. She whirled to face it, blocking a fireball with a curtain of water. The Threads that had once crisscrossed the Arena were still present, even if the building was gone.

Douglas was in the midst of several Zerolytes, kicking and punching wildly as he sent one after another into the pit. His fighting style looked undisciplined and random – and it was – but it kept the Zerolytes (or any enemy) from predicting his movements with any degree of accuracy.

Martin launched a sphere of Ice Energy from his hand. The 'gauntlet' formed by his armor protected him from any real harm, while his wings kept him aloft long enough to drop the frigid orb into a knot of Zerolytes. They shrieked in misery, their bodies freezing solid in seconds. He flew through the frozen statues, shattering them with his wings.

There was a loud cry of pain, and Martin's head swiveled to see David, the boy he'd been fighting in the Arena, go down with a knife in his ribs. He snarled. David, while an adversary, was still a Tzen. He re-routed his course and grabbed the Zerolyte responsible for the attack. He lifted the struggling body high into the air before releasing it, hearing his enemy crack against the rocks below and splash into the massive underground lake.

A spear of Dark Energy hurtled past him, barely missing his wing. A Zerolyte was launching spears in every direction, hoping to hit someone or something. Martin folded his wings against his back, going into a steep dive. He folded his arms across his face, protecting himself from the oncoming impact. He slammed into the black-robed figure with all the force of a bullet, smashing it into the rocks.

Alena had backed up to the edge of the pit, and Martin saw the surge of Zerolytes that were trying to push her into the yawning chasm below. He swooped forward, sweeping several Zerolytes out of the way. He dodged a stray fireball, looking around for his next victim. The blood pounded in his temples, and the Parasite was fighting to take control; the adrenaline was helping it. Martin fought down the feral instincts it was trying to force upon him, diving down toward a Zerolyte that was attacking Terra.

No sooner had he dispatched it, he heard a piercing cry. He looked over his shoulder to see that the Zerolytes had crowded right up to the edge of the pit. Alena was nowhere to be found.

"Alena!" He lunged forward, his wings spreading open like the sails of a ship as he bulled through the Zerolytes and leapt off the edge. He flattened all his limbs against his body, diving into the blackness of the pit. Martin could just barely make out Alena's shape plummeting through the dark-drowned shaft.

He compacted his body, falling faster than before. The rock walls of the shaft raced past him at blinding speeds. Alena drew closer and closer by the second, but he wasn't sure how far down the bottom of this hole was. Finally catching up to her, Martin wrapped his arms around her waist and spread the wings to slow their fall. It didn't work. While they slowed down, their combined weight was too great for the wings to support.

Oh hell... Martin barrel-rolled over onto his back, slamming the wings open as wide as he could as clutched Alena to his torso. They slowed considerably. Martin looked over his shoulder to see if the ground was in view yet. He realized at that second that if the tentacle armor didn't protect him well, he was going to die. The ground was less than ten feet away.

He impacted the ground with an explosion of dust and rock, the armor evaporating from his body with the sheer force of the strike. He lay in the crater he had formed, dimly aware of the fact that he was still alive. The shaft was deep to the point where Martin could no longer see their entry hole above him.

Alena was shaking so hard Martin was certain she was going into shock. He rubbed her back soothingly, trying to calm her down. They lay at the bottom of the hole for a few minutes until Alena had stopped shaking.

"Are you... alright?" he asked. His voice was hoarse, probably from inhaling the dust thrown up by his impact. His body ached, which wasn't really surprising, but by some miracle it seemed that the only thing that had happened was severe bruising. The armor was extremely solid.

"I'm fine..." she choked out, separating her body from his, "And you..." she looked at him long and hard in the almost nonexistent light of the shaft. He lay in a four foot deep hole, his body twisted at strange angles. The armor was gone, revealing his porcelain skin; now covered in bruises.

"I'm fine too," he muttered, licking his lips as he forced himself to stand. He stood shakily on his feet for a moment until the ground beneath him stopped tilting in various directions before speaking again. "Now how do we get out?"

They examined the bottom of the shaft, and it was Alena who discovered their answer. The bottom of the hole was connected to a tunnel. Martin, however, was perplexed by the structure. Rather than following the same style as the shaft (a large, vertical column lined with rock) the tunnel was expertly carved. Marble tiles were set into the floor, and large columns of crystal supported the roof. Archways lined with lettering snaked above the columns, sheltering the walkway below.

"I can't read these runes," Martin complained after a moment of examining them, "They're Alintean, but not the kind I know!" His voice carried equal parts of excitement and frustration.

"So, are we going to follow it?" asked Alena, tapping her foot impatiently. Martin seemed to snap out of his examination of the archway to respond, "Yes, but we do *not* want to walk right into a Zerolyte City. Do you still have your Tzen Rod?"

She shook her head. Martin felt around in his pockets, finding his missing as well. He let out a curse, summoning the power of the Parasite to coat his right hand in a gauntlet of black tentacles. At least he could cast incantations without ruining his hand.

"Okay, since you don't have a wand, I need you to stay behind me. I wish we had a light, though..."

She placed one of her hands on his shoulder, and Martin could feel the comforting warmth of her fingers through the thin material of his dress shirt. He reveled in the sensation for a moment before snapping himself out of it. "Alright – let's go." They carefully walked down the pathway, their eyes on the alert for any Threads. Martin and Alena finally gave up after the first half-hour.

"This is stupid," grumbled Martin. "I couldn't find my ass with both hands in this darkness."

Alena snickered, and Martin wished he could glare at her. Heck, he could have flipped her off in this accursed blackness and she would have been none the wiser. He felt his pockets for anything he could use as a light. Nothing.

Just when he was about to suggest they turn back, he ran face-first into a large marble wall. Rubbing his nose, he placed his hands on it and began to feel along it until he found what felt like a doorknob. With a muttered 'eureka', he pushed it open.

A torch-lit passage was beyond the wall. The light spilled out into the hall he'd been standing in. It turned out he was standing in a three-way junction. To one end was the shaft, the second was the torch-lit passage, and the third was still smothered in darkness. Having no want to spend more time in the dark, Martin and Alena both began to walk down the torch-lined pathway.

"It's much brighter now," observed Alena. Martin nodded wordlessly. There was nothing to say. What *could* he say?

"I'm sorry I got you into this," she said.

Martin shrugged, "It wasn't your fault."

The torch-lined passageway let out into what looked like a copy of The Hall above them. Martin's jaw hit the floor. The cavern was filled with a *city*. There was no water that he could see – but a thick red liquid poured from the mouths of gargoyles. A large mansion sat in one corner of the city, while a temple of sorts rose in the middle. All around these two buildings were smaller buildings. This wasn't the most startling thing, however.

"...oh...my...god..." both Martin and Alena murmured at the same time.

The city was inhabited.

Chapter 41: The City

Walking casually through the streets were some of the strangest creatures Martin had ever seen. They stood about seven feet tall, and were bipedal like a human. Their arms had triangular membranous flaps hanging from them, similar to a flying squirrel's 'wings', and their feet had three points; two in the rear and one in the front. Their heads were shaped like teardrops, and a proboscis reminiscent of a moth or butterfly protruded from beneath a pair of bulbous eyes.

Each creature looked identical to the last with the exception of these eyes. They swirled with what seemed to be liquid or gas of varying colors; no two being identical. They all shared jet-black skin; the identical color of tar. From where Martin and Alena stood, it seemed that they were covered with a thin layer of fur, much like a peach. One of them looked up, gazing at Martin and Alena with wide unblinking red eyes. Martin found the creature's gaze to be unnerving.

"It has been a while," it said. This creature was male – the voice intonation was too deep to be female. Martin noticed that, to these creatures, the letter 'S' was pronounced as a 'Z' – thus, the word 'has' sounded as if it had been turned into 'haz'.

Martin blinked at the creature before his brain returned basic actions to him. "A while?" He mentally kicked himself. That was probably one of the dumber things that had come from his mouth.

The creature stared owlishly at him. "It has been a while since we last saw a Vahran."

The words seemed to register in Martin's brain sluggishly. It felt as though his skull was filled with something similar to peanut butter – thoughts were having an incredibly difficult time passing into his brain. "What's a Vahran?"

The creature shrugged his thin shoulders, "It means 'Human'." it said calmly, "Come, we can discuss this later."

The stares that Martin and Alena received were nothing short of frightening. Some of the smaller creatures, their 'wings' not yet grown, took to hiding behind the long legs of their parents as they passed. Others merely stared at them. Seeing as no mouth was visible (Martin surmised the proboscis served this purpose) they didn't exactly gape at them. It was probably the equivalent of slack-jawed awe to these creatures.

"Not to sound rude," said Alena, "But what *are* you?"

"Me? I am Naxis," said the creature. "I did not get your names either."

"I'm Martin Spire," interjected the orange-eyed Tzen, "And this is Alena Steward. What I believe my partner meant, however, was 'what is your species'?"

"Oh!" there was a strange buzzing/chortling sound, and it took Martin a moment to realize the creature was laughing; or something close to it. "We are Alinteans."

Martin stopped in his tracks. *"What?"*

Naxis turned and faced him. His eyes, the color of blood, stared at him for a moment. "We are Alinteans; The Children of the Stars. Is that so hard to believe?"

Martin nodded his head mutely until his voice returned, "I... we... the Alinteans died out over four billion years ago!"

Naxis snorted through his proboscis, the gesture causing it to uncurl and re-curl. "The Purge? We fled; we weren't wiped out."

Naxis turned his back on them again. "Come – we should speak with Balmoch – he'll doubtlessly be glad to answer any of your questions."

"Balmoch?" Alena looked confused.

"Yes, Balmoch. He is our Crowned Star. I supposed you humans would call him a 'Leader' or 'King' – his ancestors helped build this city," he gestured around him, "Long ago when the Purge occurred."

"What is The Purge?" asked Martin, but Naxis had already walked off. He was heading toward the building that Martin had called a Temple.

Inside the so-called Temple it was much more pleasant than the outside. Gilded tapestries inlaid with several gold-sewn symbols hung from the walls on either side of a magnificent black carpet. This rug led all the way up to an elevated dais upon which rested a floating crystal chair.

"That's got to be some kind of EM," he whispered to Alena. She nodded in assent at his statement, but said nothing. Naxis walked forward, kneeling before another Alintean who was sitting on the throne. This one had vivid green eyes the color spring grass.

Naxis made several strange sounds. For some reason, Martin fancied he understood several of the sounds as common words. They just seemed to fit. It was almost as if he knew the language from a past life; or osmosis. The only words he was completely certain of were 'Balmoch', 'Martin Spire', and 'Alena Steward'. Other than that, it seemed that Naxis was merely telling Balmoch of how he had found them.

Finally, the Alintean known as Balmoch leaned forward in his crystal throne. His green eyes regarded Martin and Alena with such intensity that Martin found it almost impossible not to shudder. Finally, after what felt like eons, Balmoch leaned back.

"So you are both Vahran?" he said at length. His voice was low, almost silkily soft. It gave Martin goose-bumps. He nodded his head, to which Balmoch tugged at his proboscis. "And yet I sense you are something else... what could it be?"

Martin decided it would be no use lying to this so called 'Crowned Star'. "It is a parasite."

Balmoch made that chuckling sound again. "So, you are a Carrier of a Solar Parasite then? It is the only parasite that gives off that energy."

Martin was unnerved by the fact that Balmoch knew this, and at the same time relieved that Balmoch wasn't going to kill him outright. He nodded.

Balmoch pushed himself out of the throne, walking back and forth across the dais as he spoke. "It has been over four billion years since a Vahran has made contact with an Alintean... I am honored..." he paused, looking up at Martin. "Yet, this saddens me greatly. The last time such an encounter occurred, so did bloodshed."

Martin felt something twist in his stomach. If this 'Purge' was a great war, there was little doubt that old wounds would be reopened by the arrival of a human in Alintean territory.

"I am sure you have many questions," said Balmoch, "Naxis will accompany you to our Temple. There you will find your answers. Please, make yourselves at home here in Namrah." Martin bowed respectfully, seeing Alena do the same in almost perfect synchronization with his own movements. *Temple? What can we learn at a Temple?*

Naxis motioned for them to follow him. Martin walked next to him, but Alena chose to walk behind him. She was fascinated by the town around her and spent all her time looking at the various structures. Some of the buildings seemed to defy physics. Balconies that seemed to be suspended without the use of supports jutted from buildings.

"Our Temple is unlike anything you'll have ever seen," said Naxis proudly, "I will show you how to get the answers you seek once we get there." He pushed open a pair of enormous metal gates, motioning for Martin and Alena to pass through. After they had done so, he closed the doors behind them.

An enormous ziggurat, carved seamlessly from the rock wall of the chamber they were in, rose several stories above their heads. Martin's mouth fell open involuntarily, and Alena seemed to have lost all sense of thought.

"Amazing, is it not?" asked Naxis as he walked past them, "This temple was built four billion years ago."

Martin shook himself out of his daze, staring at the ziggurat. There were no stairs leading to the top, but there was a door down near the base. Shrugging it off as a difference in Alintean construction, he followed their Alintean guide over to the door.

"When you find a sphere of light," explained Naxis "Do not be afraid to touch it. They will give you the answers you seek." Martin decided to wait and see what he was talking about before analyzing his words. Naxis pushed open the door and Martin crossed the threshold; Alena at his heels.

"Whoa!" The inside of the pyramid was almost solid marble and crystal. Stairs led up to different ledges, and pathways crisscrossed the chamber. It was as if the entire ziggurat was hollow. The internal construction reminded Martin of an M.C. Escher painting.

"I will wait for you out here," called Naxis. Martin made a noncommittal noise before stepping further inside.

Directly in front of him was a sphere of light, just as Naxis had described. It glowed with the seven colors of the rainbow, bright enough to make Martin squint. Cautiously, he reached out and touched it. There was a blinding flash of light, so bright it made the orb in front of him appear dull, and it felt as if he'd gone completely blind.

Through the whiteness, shapes began to appear. He saw desert – endless sand and wind – stretching infinitely in all directions from him. The sky above him was dark, sprinkled with the stars he knew so well. The three stars of Orion's Belt, among others, were all present. Martin knew he was on Earth, at least. Before he could say a word, the image had faded. He found himself standing back in the temple again, Alena at his side.

"Did you..." she asked, looking at him.

"You're going to think I'm crazy," he said, "but I think I just saw a desert."

She stared at him for a moment. "So did I. Is this what Naxis meant? Is this our answer?"

Martin looked around the room and spied another orb of light hovering on one of the ledges. He pointed at it, "Probably only a part of our answer. Let's get to that sphere."

He climbed a flight of stairs and ascended a rope-and-metal ladder to reach the ledge with his quarry. It was Alena this time that touched it. The light grew until Martin saw colors swimming in front of him. When the image appeared again, Martin saw the fundamental difference. There was a meteorite in the sky – a large one at that. It looked like it was going to strike Earth.

Again, the image faded away. Martin blew air through his nose, "I think we're seeing a slideshow. Each image is connected to the last. We saw a desert, and now we're seeing a meteorite preparing to hit the desert."

Alena nodded, "And we're somehow seeing the same images."

"Yes, that too..." Martin trailed off, wondering how that was possible. It was entirely possible that it was Neutral Energy sealed within Light Energy, and that it was carrying a memory of some sort into their minds. He kept this theory to himself for now.

"Let's find the next one."

After a good deal of climbing up and down various ladders and stairs, as well as leaping onto one ledge that had no way of accessing it otherwise, they found their third sphere.

"Ready?" Martin asked, looking over at Alena. She nodded. Again, in almost perfect synchronization, they placed their hands on the sphere.

This time, the image was of the meteorite striking the desert. Dust had been thrown up in a plume several miles high. Down near the base, there was an enormous ridge that was the lip of the crater. The debris that had been ejected were blocking out the stars above.

"What does this–"

The image faded away, leaving Martin and Alena standing in the ziggurat again. Martin shook his head. "So far all we know is that something hit the planet."

"Could it be how the Alinteans got here?" asked Alena, tapping a finger on her chin. Martin nodded, "Quite possibly. Come, the next sphere should provide more answers."

Chapter 42: The Temple

The fourth globe of light was atop a pedestal about a fifth of the way up the slanting wall of one of the rooms. Martin had to boost Alena up on his shoulders so she could reach it. They were both enveloped in light again, and this time the image was not just of the desert.

An island sprawled before them. It seemed to be resting in the only oasis of water in the world. Desert crawled up to the edge of a large lake, and concentric rings of land rose from the still waters, each connected to another by a series of arcing crystal bridges. Standing on the land masses were buildings of every shape and size, their metal walls gleaming in the heat of the desert sun. At the very center of this bizarre ring-city was a large structure that appeared to be a temple; topped with an enormous pinnacle.

"What on earth-" started Martin, but the sensation of being pulled from the vision jerked the words from his mouth. He collapsed, feeling Alena land on top of him as he gave out. He gave a muffled curse and wriggled out from under her.

"A city?" she asked, apparently not taking notice of the fact that she had fallen on him. Martin stood up, rubbing his rear. "Yes, a city. It looked like nothing I've ever seen, though."

Martin looked around, seeing the fifth globe near the top of the room. Sighing, he began ascending the latticework of ladders and ramps. "Let's just get moving."

It took them just shy of an hour (and several wrong turns leading in dead ends) to reach the globe. Martin walked up, placing his hands on either side of the light. The glow came again, enveloping his body in the warm brightness. It didn't seem so bright anymore.

A war was going on. The two factions were recognizable as Humans and Alinteans. Humans were fighting with very primitive weaponry consisting of swords and staves, while Alinteans were doing nothing more than trying to retreat and flee.

"The Purge?" Martin murmured as the image faded. He was back in the temple, shuddering at the image. That wasn't a war: that was *genocide*. The Alinteans weren't even fighting back.

"That was horrible!" cried Alena, kneeling next to him. He looked at her in surprise. Tears were running down her face like rivers. "They... they weren't even fighting! They were just dying!"

Martin placed one of his hands on her shoulder. "It was a vision of the past, Alena," he said quietly. "We cannot dwell on it. It has already come and gone. I admit it is horrible. What can we do, though?"

Alena seemed to compose herself, and Martin sighed in relief. People who cried unnerved him. He was always worried someone would begin crying on him for support and he wouldn't be able to give it.

"Let's find the next globe."

"I don't think I want to," Alena muttered, wiping the traces of her tears from her face. "If it's anything like the last one..."

"It won't be. If these are in successive order, the war will be over." Martin fervently hoped he was right.

A door stood at the top of the room, and Martin pushed it open. Behind it was a large chamber, roughly circular, with a door at the other end. Floating in the center of the room was the sixth orb.

"How many of these are there?" he groused, walking over and jamming his hand into it.

Again, the city was depicted. Its once proud towers were toppled, and flames raced unimpeded through the streets. Humans were running in and out of buildings, searching for the last of the Alintean occupants. There was no more killing, just searching. Martin heaved a sigh of relief – he hadn't wanted Alena to get emotional on him again.

The image faded away. Martin let out the breath he hadn't known he was holding and leaned against a support column. "Let's review what we've seen. I'm feeling a bit tired."

Alena sat down, leaning against the pillar opposite him. "So far, what do we know?"

"Something came down, most likely a ship, and delivered the Alinteans to Earth several billion years ago. It seems humans didn't take kindly to the intrusion and attacked an Alintean settlement. At least, that's what I've gleaned."

Alena nodded thoughtfully, "I got pretty much the same. But why? The Alinteans weren't doing any harm."

"None that *we* saw," corrected Martin, "We just saw the war, not the trigger. They could have attacked first. I'm not going to label any side as innocent until I have more information."

Alena glared at him, "You're cold."

"You're naïve," he countered, "You'd base a decision off of peace-meal information. That isn't a good tactic."

She frowned but said nothing. After resting a few moments, Martin walked over to the door on the far side of the room. It was unlocked, so he pushed it open. "Oh wonderful..."

The room in front of them was identical to the first room they'd been in. The notable difference was that several platforms were suspended by some kind of Air Incantation. Martin shuddered at the thought of jumping across them.

The seventh orb was in the center of the room, thankfully on the ground level, so Martin and Alena walked up. He motioned for her to do the honors. Hesitantly, Alena placed her hands on the sphere.

The ruined city was shown again. This time, the temple was gone. It had crumbled into the watery rings surrounding it. In its place was a large cylindrical building that gleamed in the sun as if new. It looked almost like an upside-down top-hat, with a wide 'brim' around the top. There were several cracks in the structure, and each one was filled with a bluish light.

The image disappeared, and Martin saw the eighth globe appear up on one of the levitating platforms. *What was that building?* Deciding to ponder it after he had all the facts, Martin began to climb some of the stairs in the room. They led to one of the ledges near the spectral orb, and he leapt out to it. Alena landed next to him a moment later, and the platform rocked like a ship at sea.

"Holy-" Martin cursed, "Be careful. We've got to maintain some balance up here."

They maneuvered carefully to opposite sides of the platform, keeping the sphere between them. With a deep breath, Martin and Alena reached out and touched the sphere.

The structure in the city was glowing. A sphere of blue light, several hundred feet in diameter, was hovering above the flattened top of the building. Light was flowing from the top of the cylindrical object into the sphere, increasing its size. Martin had no idea what to make of it. Was it a beacon?

The image faded again, leaving Martin and Alena on the precarious platform in the ziggurat. As carefully as he could, Martin leapt back over to a stable ledge. He motioned for Alena to follow, and she did so flawlessly. Martin's eye cast around for the remaining orb – he was certain there would be a third. So far, the spheres had been in sets of three.

It was up near another door. This one involved crossing a rickety bridge that looked like it wouldn't support a chicken. He gingerly tested it before crossing. The bridge moaned in protest, but it held. He stepped off on the other side, breathing a sigh of relief. He and Alena touched the ninth sphere, and Martin held his breath to see what the building was doing.

The blue sphere of light was still present, but there was a ring of even more blue light emitting from it. It was traveling out at what seemed to be incredible speeds, picking up momentum as it moved. The water around the structure had been lifted up and was forming a vertical wall of liquid – the energy was actually warping it. An explosion had torn the base of the tower apart, and apparently was causing it to malfunction due to the mass amounts of sparks and smaller explosions that were present.

"What the hell-"

The image faded away, and Martin remembered too late not to attempt to speak. His curse was jerked from his mouth as he was transferred back to the ziggurat. He leaned against the wall, his breath coming in gasps.

"A beacon?" asked Alena, mirroring his thoughts. Martin shook his head, "I don't think so." He looked at her, "I think we've just seen something bigger than a beacon."

He regained his breath and pushed open the door, looking inside. Three spheres were visible. One was closest to him, so he reached out his hand for that one first.

The picture they saw was a view from space. It showed a planet coated in dry, brown deserts. At one single pinpoint in the western hemisphere was a single blue dot – a tiny oasis of water. Martin watched the image raptly for a change, but nothing happened. The image faded away without changing.

"What planet was that?" he muttered, looking at the next sphere. It was a few feet above his head on a ledge. He jumped up, catching the edge of the platform with his fingertips and hauling himself up. He held out a hand to Alena, pulling her up wit him. Tenderly, Martin placed a hand on the sphere.

The planet was shown again; only this time the tiny blue dot was emitting an enormous wall of water. The blue liquid was arcing around the planet like a great hand. Martin's jaw fell open. That was the biggest tidal wave he'd ever seen. It looked like it would drown the entire world.

Is this the so-called Biblical Flood?

The image vanished, leaving Martin staring at the wall in front of him. He shook the thought from his head. "What was that?"

Alena shrugged, "You're the genius, not me."

He snorted, casting his orange eye on the twelfth orb. "Let's see if this can give us any answers. He hopped across the tops of a few pillars, watching Alena lest she fall. He allowed her to touch the orb, standing back.

The third and final image in this 'set' was of a familiar planet. The continents weren't very well defined, but he could still see them. They were separated only by about a thousand miles. Apparently this was long in the past; before continental drift had actually formed the recognizable landmasses. On the western side, he watched the ring city sink into the waters like a capsized boat, vanishing without a trace beneath the waves.

The image shimmered for a moment, and Martin found himself back in the pyramid. He shook his head vehemently, clearing the fuzz from it. The last image had left him disoriented.

"Did..." Alena murmured, "Did that wave create the *oceans?*" she asked in disbelief. Martin nodded, "Apparently."

They looked toward the center of the room. A thirteenth orb hung there, but this one was different. It was larger, and the light it emitted was not rainbow. It was pure white. Martin looked at Alena.

"Do we touch it?"

She looked back at him. Martin felt a slight twinge in his stomach.

"Do we have a choice?"

Sighing, the two Tzen made their way back down to the center of the room and stood before the light. It seemed to beckon them, calling them forth. Martin and Alena raised their hands and pressed them into the light.

Chapter 43: The Truth

It wasn't a picture they saw. It was an actual recreation of everything they saw. Martin and Alena stood in the desert, watching the sky as the meteorite streaked toward them. It struck the ground, and a boom echoed through the night air. The low sound seemed to pulse through them as the pillar of dust they had seen was shot high into the air. Bits of debris rained down. Martin was about to tell Alena to move when he saw that the fragmented rock was going *through* them.

The image seemed to fast-forward until it became a blur of colors. Martin saw the crater that had been made by the impact was now filled with water. More importantly, it was also filled with the ringed city they'd seen earlier. Alinteans were present, but it didn't look like they were familiar with the territory.

"How odd..." Martin noticed as one Alintean seemed to stare at the temple in awe. The look on his face (as near as Martin could tell) was of shock. It was as if he'd never seen the building before.

Before Martin could react, humans came pouring out of the city. They raised spears and swords, rushing forward and striking at the Alinteans. There were high-pitched shrieks and buzzes as the strange beings fell to their enemy's blades.

Several of them tried to retreat only to be struck in the back; by *incantations!*

"Tzen!?" yelled Martin, noticing the familiar grasping motion being used by the humans. "What are they *doing*?"

The Alinteans finally got it into their heads to retaliate, using incantations of their own to set fire to the ring city. The flames licked their way across the ground, burning buildings and humans alike. Cries of pain rent the air.

The scene fast-forwarded again to stop at the point when the city was already destroyed. Martin saw several humans creep back in and open the temple. Without warning, the temple seemed to explode, sending bits of shrapnel flying in every direction. The larger chunks splashed into the water as the cylindrical building rose out of the ground.

"What the...?"

Alinteans that were nearby began to make loud sounds at the sight of the structure. Light began to flow out of the water and into the sides of the building through various ports. Martin started as he realized they were Water Threads. The blue sphere appeared at the top of the structure, glowing like a miniature sun.

Without warning, an explosion ripped through the lower levels of the tower, and the entire structure listed to one side. There was a deafening explosion as the ring of energy raced outwards, multiplying the water in the ring city million-fold until the wall of water was high enough to blot out the sky. It then crashed out in all directions away from the structure. The top-hat building seemed to power down at this point; all the lights going out.

The scene changed again. Martin found himself watching from space as the tidal wave raced around the planet until there was naught but a blue sphere of water in the heavens. Slowly, ever so slowly, the water receded into the larger basins, forming the oceans he recognized. The ring city sank, just like he had seen in the images, until it was lost beneath the waves.

The vision ended, and Martin found himself and Alena standing in the ziggurat once again. He was gasping for breath, and Alena was on her knees throwing up. He looked at her for a moment before patting her back and asking if she was alright.

"Martin..." she choked, "...I see it now!"

He stepped away from her, his hands drumming nervously on his hips. "See what?"

She looked up at him, "Martin, they didn't come here!"

An eyebrow arced above Martin's good eye. "Of course they did. We saw it in the vision."

"No!" she coughed and spat up a bit more vomit. "Martin, it was us. *We* came to this world!"

Martin froze. "What?"

"They were here first! You saw it – the Alinteans didn't know about the city or the humans. The city was built *in* the crater formed by the meteor. The humans used the crater as a base to begin their city!"

"But..."

"The Alinteans must have found a way to survive – probably by retreating underground. That's why they're down here!"

It made sense – that was what was frightening. Martin had no argument. It even filled in some of the gaps he'd been wondering about, such as the Alintean who had been in awe of the temple.

"We... we came here?" he choked, sitting down on the floor with a thud.

"Yes!" Alena seemed to have overcome her sickness and was standing up. "We pushed them out! They were here before us! Ask that Balmoch guy, or Naxis. They'll tell you!"

Martin was dumbfounded. His brain had shut down entirely. First he sees the oceans created by mankind, and now he learns that his race is actually aliens. He began to laugh at the irony of it all.

"Alright, let's get out of here. We've got our answers. We shouldn't have been doing this anyway... the Tzen are still fighting on the surface," Alena reminded him. Her statement shook Martin from his laughter. "Right."

They quickly ran from the temple until they met Naxis at the front door. He stared at them for a moment. "Did you find what you sought?"

Alena spoke up first, "Naxis! Were humans here first or Alinteans?"

Naxis tapped his chin, "You saw the spheres. You know the truth. We came here first; we colonized this world. The surface was unlivable, so we came beneath the ground."

"You started beneath the ground?" asked Martin, blinking with his remaining eye.

"Yes. The surface was too dry for anything other than exploration. However, after that abomination of a meteor struck, we sent a party to examine it. Within two days of its collision, we found a city. A *city!*"

Naxis made a derisive sound. "As you probably saw, we were attacked. The humans eventually won by using some terrible device that drowned the world. Everyone on the surface died. Some humans survived; though I'm not sure how. They went on to propagate the world..." he sighed, "While we returned to the tunnels like beaten dogs."

He looked at Martin, and his gaze held all the intensity of a laser. "I know you had nothing to do with past tragedies," he said, "But please understand if others do not immediately trust you. Old wounds tend to reopen with a reminder... and this wound has festered for more than four billion years."

Martin nodded, shooting a sideways glance at Alena. She was smirking at him triumphantly. "How did you know what we saw?" he asked, turning back to Naxis.

"I didn't. I was led to that assumption by your questions. I'm not stupid, you know."

Martin shrugged, "I never said you were. Now, I have a question for you."

"Shoot." Naxis had tilted his head to the left in a birdlike questioning manner.

"The Tzen, like Alena and I, are being attacked about two miles above your heads. We need to help them. Is there any way you can get us back up there? We fell down a shaft to get here."

Naxis thought for a moment. "If you're willing to attempt to fly one of our four-hundred thousand year old craft, I think I can help you."

Martin stared suspiciously at him. "Four billion years old? What's the probability we're going to come out of this alive?"

"Twenty percent."

Martin's face creased into a frown, "Hell no. We've got to get up there in one piece. We're no good to the Tzen in a body bag."

Naxis placed his hands on his hips, "It's the best I can do. If you had two weeks I could prepare a better transport, but this is short notice."

Martin wrestled with the idea. Was it a risk he'd be willing to take? He waged a war back and forth in his mind until finally one side won out. "Show me the craft."

He and Alena were led through a series of passageways until they reached a cylindrical launching chamber. A pill-shaped craft was docked in the middle, nose-cone pointing skyward. Naxis looked up at the ceiling and snorted – apparently this was the Alintean equivalent of a frown.

"That craft will take you directly to a large cavern three miles up. I'm not sure if it connects conveniently to your destination, but I know it connects to the surface."

Martin walked past him, jogging toward the pod. "Naxis, thank you!" He bounded around a corner, stopping at a control panel. It seemed to be a release command for the shuttle. He reached out a tentative hand and pressed an octagon.

There was a low whine as the chamber powered up. Lights flickered on; still bright after two millennia. Naxis came up behind him, "Get in the shuttle – I'll launch you."

Naxis ran his thin fingers across the pad. He pressed a triangle, followed by what looked like an image of Saturn, and then pressed a rectangle. The side of the shuttle opened, revealing a seamless door. Martin poked his head inside. While not very spacious or comfortable, the shuttle was at least equipped with necessary safety measures. It also smelled strongly of formaldehyde.

"Go on, get in," urged Naxis. Martin complied, forcing himself into the oblong chamber and strapping himself into one of the seats. Alena followed shortly after, buckling herself in next to him. Martin noticed she was as white as chalk. Against his nature, he reached out and squeezed her hand.

The pressurized door hissed shut, sealing the two Tzen in the pod. Outside, Martin could barely hear Naxis voice. "Good luck."

The pod shuddered, and for a moment Martin was worried it was going to explode right on the pad. However, it lifted off and roared skyward. Martin felt his insides turn to pulp. The entire capsule was shaking; jarring his bones. He felt like a grain of salt in a salt shaker.

Alena had gone even whiter, and Martin squeezed her hand again. She relaxed a bit, some color returning to her face. She managed a weak smile, which Martin decided was a thank-you.

The pod lurched to a stop, and Martin was jolted against his harness. The material bit against his chest – it would undoubtedly leave a bruise. He winced, unfastening the harness, and stood up. He found another series of Alintean buttons along the inside of the wall and pressed them in the same order as Naxis: triangle, Saturn, rectangle.

The door opened, and Martin caught a whiff of the familiar air of The Hall. They were close. He could also smell blood – he hoped it was that of the Zerolytes.

Bastards.

He reached into the pod, grasping Alena's hand and pulling her through. They stood shakily on solid ground for a moment until the momentary transitional nausea passed before darting down a tunnel. Martin had an instinctive feeling they were heading towards The Hall.

They came skidding to a halt at a large pneumatic door. Martin knocked on it gingerly before coming to the conclusion that it wouldn't open for anything short of dynamite. He was about to give up when the door opened on its own.

He looked at Alena in surprise. She was standing by a pressure plate, and had placed her hand against it. Apparently this was the control mechanism for the door. Martin allowed himself a smile. "Good work."

He turned and faced The Hall. It seemed that the Zerolytes had pushed the Tzen back to Island Nine, but there were still enough Tzen to give the black-robed figures grief. Martin drew out his Tzen rod, checking the position of the nearest Threads.

"Time to go," he said to Alena as he jumped out from the ledge onto a guy wire as thick around as his waist. He ran across the wire like an acrobat, eyes fixed firmly on the enemy. Alena found herself pitying any Zerolyte that

found itself in his path.

Chapter 44: To Win a War...

Martin dashed across the pipes, throwing his own safety to the wind. A fireball streaked past his face, but he managed to pull his head back in time to prevent the loss of such a vital appendage. He leapt from the pipe, Tzen rod momentarily forgotten in the adrenaline-induced rush, and brought both his feet down on a Zerolyte's chest.

The black robed figure was forced backward, and Martin pushed off the body before it fell, tackling a second Zerolyte that was creeping up on him. His head smashed into his opponent's, sending them both reeling momentarily. He took the initiative while his enemy was stunned to give it a well placed kick; it sent the Zerolyte hurtling from the island.

"Martin?" he looked around to see Jason punch a Zerolyte squarely in the nose. "I thought you died."

"Long story," supplied Martin as he elbowed an encroaching enemy in the stomach. "I'll tell you later." His adversary was dispatched by an uppercut to the chin; his neck snapped instantly.

The Zerolytes had conveniently pinned the Tzen in an area with relatively few Threads. Those Threads that *did* exist were running directly through the Zerolyte ranks – not a good thing for the Tzen. Martin mentally swore he was *not* going to let these creatures win.

They were outnumbered four-to-one. Zerolytes, however, were out-skilled by the Tzen. The fight was almost even. Martin could see they had a *chance* of winning. He would have accepted twenty percent at this point – their odds were lower here than in the pod.

Without warning, a sharp metal object nailed a nearby Zerolyte to the floor. He looked up and saw none other than Naxis standing on the guy wire above him. His eyes widened in shock.

The fight seemed to freeze before two voices instantly spoke. The first one was Dais. "Alintean?" The second was one of the Zerolytes. "Demon!"

Fire from the Zerolytes struck the thick cable where Naxis was standing, but the Alintean was gone - he had spread the triangular membranes, pinched the tips between the two 'toes' on the backs of his feet, and taken off like a flying squirrel.

Martin saw him fly in a lazy arc before swooping down ad ramming one of the Zerolytes in the chest. Martin wasted no time in hitting the off-balance creature, knocking it into the waters below.

He nodded at Naxis, and they took up a position back-to-back. Martin's fists were raised; there was no Thread nearby. Naxis was holding a strange weapon that looked like a cross between a rifle and a meat cleaver. The body seemed to be similar to a carbine in construction, but it had a large teardrop shaped blade on the underside.

Naxis swung the weapon, opening a bleeding gouge on the chest of a nearby Zerolyte. Without pausing, he turned around, pointed the weapon at the next enemy, and pulled the trigger. One of the nail-shaped objects shot out, spiking the Zerolyte through the throat. He fell backwards with a gurgle, clutching at his neck.

Martin's eyebrows rose. *Impressive.* Naxis swung the weapon again, stabbing a Zerolyte through the gut hard enough for the weapon's barrel to protrude from his back. Without waiting to draw the weapon out again, the Alintean pulled the trigger, impaling another Zerolyte. After the Zerolyte collapsed, he drew out the weapon and allowed his first victim to drop to the ground.

The Zerolytes began to back away from Naxis, focusing their attention on the less-vicious Tzen. Martin lunged forward, catching one of them by the back of the neck. The skin beneath the hood felt cold and thin; corpse-like. He heaved his body backwards, bracing his arm, and threw the Zerolyte over his head onto the ground. Naxis dispatched it with a stab to the chest.

"Can you use EM?" asked Martin, kicking a bold Zerolyte in the groin. Naxis severed the hunched-over figure's head with a single swipe. "I could, but it wouldn't end well."

Silence suddenly pervaded the cavern. Both Zerolytes and Tzen had stopped. Martin was about to stab a stationary Zerolyte when there was a quake. A small one, but enough of one to get Martin's instincts to fire of like cannons. It came again, this time stronger.

"Footsteps," supplied Naxis as he popped a rectangular clip into his gun and sliding a bolt-action lever into place. Martin looked at the crater where Island Eight had once stood. Something was coming up; something big.

A large leg, spider-like and covered with a thick exoskeleton, rose from the pit to slam onto the edge of the crater. It was followed by another. And another. And another. Four total. These four limbs proceeded to lift the body from the pit, and the mere sight of it made Martin recoil.

The body was as large as a bus, if not larger. Four green eyes were placed in a cross shape on the face, directly above a maw of needle-like teeth. Two jawbones, each separate from each other, hung beneath a third. A thick tongue lolled from the mouth, dripping clear saliva on the ground. A layer of armored scales, each one as big as a dinner plate, covered the body.

"What the hell is THAT?" called Dais, hefting the piece of metal piping he'd been fighting with. Martin stole a glance at the Zerolytes. They seemed as stunned as the Tzen, which quickly convinced Martin it wasn't their ally. Naxis was watching it with an air of caution, rather than fear.

"It's a Zixara," he said, "They're very dangerous, and usually sleep for decades at a time. Our commotion probably woke it up. I'm wondering where it came from – the nearest lair is miles from here."

"There are MORE of those?" asked Alena, eying the abomination with abject terror. It seemed dazed by the blue light in the cavern, but that wouldn't last long. Naxis raised his gun to his red, bulbous eye and took aim. "There's never just one of anything."

There was a bang, and one of Naxis' projectiles embedded itself in the Zixara's body; at the joint where the leg met the body. The creature shrieked; a sound capable of setting Martin's teeth on edge, and listed to the side on its injured leg. Naxis primed the gun again. "Missed."

Martin looked between Naxis and the monster. The Zerolytes were already retreating – this was a good thing. Unfortunately, their motion attracted the attention of the wounded Zixara, which promptly assumed the task of chasing them. This course of action would lead it directly into the Tzen.

"There are three weak points," explained Naxis, "The joints of the legs are weak, as are the eyes. There is also a small spot on the top of the head where the spinal cord joins to the skull. These points can be pierced to kill it. Anything else is worthless."

The Zerolytes could have done with this information. They were firing any Incantation they could at the creature, but the scales reflected them like mirrors. It lowered its head and scooped up a handful of the black robed figures. The great beast threw its head back, swallowing them.

"Oh my god," murmured Alena. "I think I'm gonna hurl."

Martin gave her a disgusted look before drawing his Tzen rod and moving to stand near an Air Thread. "The joints of the legs or the eyes..."

Seeing as the creature had its back to them, the only alternative was the legs. He frowned, clasping the Thread in his hand. The familiar power flowed through him, and he closed his eyes, focusing the power into his Tzen Rod.

"Garahno-Akashik!"

The greenish-white spear of wind roared from Martin's wand, striking the monstrous spider between the jointed armor of the rear left leg. It let out another trilling screech before turning to face its attacker.

Naxis raised his weapon and fired, the bullet piercing the uppermost eye. Black fluid sprayed out, and the creature shrieked again; this time in pure agony. Martin crouched down as it swung a leg in his general direction. Apparently it could even cause damage in its throes of agony. The leg impacted the side of a building, tearing the structure down as if it was a house of cards.

"My lab!" It took Martin a moment to realize that the building the Zixara had crushed was the Medical Lab on this island. He winced. That was going to cause some problems later. He turned his attention back to the creature. If he failed to kill it; there might not be a later.

"Naxis," he moved to stand next to the Alintean, "Can I ask you something?"

Naxis cast a wary eye at the creature before nodding. "Go ahead."

"Can you lift me?"

Naxis stared at him unblinkingly for a moment before the general idea of Martin's plan came to light. "You are NOT going to ride it."

Martin gave him a disgusted glance. "There isn't enough time for this," he cursed, "And the Air Threads down here aren't strong enough to lift me. Please, Naxis, help."

Naxis looked from the creature to Martin before checking a small satchel at his waist. He cringed. "I have only two more clips," he explained, "Your plan might be all we have. Lead me to the highest place in this cavern."

Martin led Naxis onto one of the gondolas – the one that led to the East Caves. By the time they reached the top, the creature had finished its agony-induced rampage and had turned its attention to the Tzen. The Zerolytes that had survived were remaining *very* quiet.

Martin pointed at Naxis' gun. "Does that blade detach?"

Naxis pressed a small button on the side of the gun, and the blade dropped off the barrel into his hand. He passed it to Martin with a look of indecision stamped on his face.

"Just so you know, I'm against this. However, we have no choice."

Martin grasped Naxis around the waist, and the Alintean leapt from the edge, soaring out above the cavern. His flight took a downward angle, and Martin was afraid for a moment they were going to miss the Zixara entirely.

"Let... go..." strained Naxis, pumping his arms in an attempt to gain more height. It barely worked. Martin released, dropping down onto the monster's back. It felt the assault and reared up, trying to throw him off. Martin dug his hands beneath the scales and hung on for dear life.

When the Zixara seemed satisfied its passenger was gone, it bore down on the Tzen with savage intent. Martin scrambled forward, blade in hand, until he reached the neck. Working on the assumption that this thing had similar body structure to a human, he located the point Naxis had referred to.

He closed his eyes, raising the blade above his head. *Whatever Gods still exist, please let me kill it!*

He brought the blade down. Much to his surprise, it sank easily through the flesh on the back of the neck, severing whatever was beneath it. The Zixara let out a howl, thrashing around like an enraged stallion. Martin clenched his hands around the blade as he was whipped back and forth.

Finally, just when it felt like his arms were going to be ripped from their sockets, the struggles began to abate. The creature slowed until it was barely moving, and then stopped altogether. It remained upright for a moment longer before collapsing sideways into the water.

Martin jerked the blade free and leapt off, reaching for the edge of the island. He realized it was about a foot too far. Something jabbed him in the shoulder, and he saw Naxis extending the gun toward him. Without wasting any time, his arms jerked out and caught the barrel of the Alintean weapon. He dangled above the waters of The Hall like a pendulum before Naxis, along with Alena and Dais, was able to pull him up.

He lay on solid ground for a moment before forcing himself to his feet. He tottered for a moment before pointing the blade at the Zerolytes. Without a word, each one faded away. He turned around, presenting the bloodied weapon to Naxis.

"I believe this is yours."

Chapter 45: Flight of the Fallen

A Zerolyte appeared on one of the adjoining islands, followed by another, and then four more. Several hundred of them were popping into the cavern with the Air Gate Incantation, and Martin suddenly realized they were overrun.

"Retreat!" yelled Naxis, "Fall back to the Mainland Shelf!"

The Tzen began to stampede to the gondola, and Martin swore when he realized that even with their depleted ranks they would have to make several trips. It looked as though the Tzen had taken heavy losses – there were only about twenty left.

"I'll hold them off!" Naxis yelled, taking aim and pegging a Zerolyte through the skull. He fell backwards; the movement hindering his allies behind him. Martin grabbed the nearest thing he could reach – a section of metal the size of a baseball bat left over from the Zixara's attack on the Medical Bay, and swung it like a sword. "Not on your own you're not."

Alena stepped forward but Martin froze her with a glare. "Go with the others."

She started to protest, but both Martin and Naxis yelled "GO!" at the same time, which gave her enough of an incentive to go with the other Tzen – an angry Martin was about as desirable as a barbed-wire corset.

Martin swung the metal pipe with all his strength as a Zerolyte made it across the closest bridge. There was a hollow *THUD* and the Zerolyte toppled from the bridge into the waters below. Martin whirled around, driving the end of the metal bar into the stomach of another Zerolyte and then ripping it out again.

"Naxis!"

The Alintean ducked, dodging a fireball that would have taken his head off. He stood up, swinging his bladed gun in an arc and slicing two Zerolytes at once. Martin ducked a knife slash and kicked the blade's wielder away. He jumped out of the way as a large stone was hurled his way, courtesy of an Air Thread that was too far for him to reach.

A bullet whizzed past his ear, thudding into a Zerolyte sneaking up behind him. He nodded at Naxis before turning and swiping a knife from the corpse of the shot enemy. He balanced it between his fingers for a moment before hurling it. The blade sank into the cavity where the face should be on one of the Zerolytes a few feet away. The victim slumped without a sound.

The Tzen were almost halfway done shuttling themselves over to the Mainland Shelf. "Will that really be a safe zone for them?" yelled Martin to Naxis. The Alintean fired another shot, and was rewarded with a yell, "I hope so."

Martin was about to yell something else when a Zerolyte buried a knife in his arm. Hissing in pain, he tore it out and returned it to its owner by ramming it into the Zerolyte's chest.

"The Tzen," said Naxis without breaking his deadly pattern of slashing and shooting, "Are skilled in hand-to-hand combat. These things," he stabbed another Zerolyte, "Aren't."

Martin kicked another one away. "I noticed." He cast a glance back to the Tzen – almost done. There were less than five left. He swung his barbaric cudgel in a circle, belting several Zerolytes senseless.

"Go!" He ducked beneath an attacking Zerolyte and ran for the lift. He jumped onto the metal platform, feeling it sway beneath his feet. Naxis hopped on a moment later, grasping at the lever. As soon as they started moving, the Alintean grabbed his gun and aimed at the lever.

"Naxis-" it was too late. The Alintean had pulled the trigger, and the nail-like projectile had struck the switch near the base, breaking it. The Zerolytes cursed at them, throwing all manner of objects at the gondola. Many of them fell short – a few clattering harmlessly off the edges of the gondola.

Martin knew it was immature, but he couldn't resist making a few faces at the Zerolytes. As the gondola reached the opposite shore, Naxis swung the blade above him, severing the cable in one swipe. The gondola crashed into the water below.

Martin was about to breathe a sigh of relief when he saw something that made his blood run cold. There was one

Zerolyte that stood out from the others. It was at least a head taller than the others, and its black robes were inlaid with not only gold runes but precious stones as well.

"So, you have refused my terms?" asked the figure. The voice was low, carrying an air of malice to it that cut through Martin like a knife. He frowned, but said nothing. The figure stared at him for a moment.

"I give you one final chance," it said at last, "Throw your wands into the waters below and you will be shown mercy."

Martin reached down and grasped a small stone at his feet. He wound up like a baseball player and hurled the rock as hard as he could at the Zerolyte. It missed its target by inches. The Zerolyte watched the rock clatter to the ground behind it before turning back to Martin.

"So be it. You have defied me, Martin Spire, and for that you shall pay – you all shall pay."

The Zerolyte raised its hands to the heavens, "I hereby revoke the Blessings of the Stars!"

It felt as if a vacuum had opened within Martin's chest. All his energy, every drop, was being siphoned out by this inescapable force. He collapsed to his knees in weakness, fighting off the encroaching blackness.

A Fire Thread was winding near the Zerolyte Lord. Martin watched, dumbfounded, as it slowly faded away. The vacuum ceased, and he was able to force his way to his feet again. The Zerolytes had vanished, leaving not a trace behind.

Martin looked for a Thread – any Thread. He would have even welcomed a Solar Thread even though he hated them. Nothing. He cast around inside himself for a trace of the familiar Solar Energy that resided there.

"No..." Martin collapsed to his knees, a look of wild panic on his face. He clawed at his chest frantically, "No!" It was gone. His ability to manipulate energy was gone.

"NO!"

Apparently, every other Tzen had suffered the same fate. They were looking at each other in confusion, trying to decide what to do next. Martin slumped forward, his cheek pressing against the cool stone tiles. "...no..."

Alena walked over to him and knelt down. "Mart-"

She never finished. Martin stood up fast enough to make her let out a small shriek and fall backwards. He turned and faced the group of ex-Tzen. "Get out of my way!" His voice carried a snarl in it that seemed more animal than human.

When they didn't move instantly, he began to push, elbow and force his way through his former comrades until he reached the other side. He took off at a fast sprint, heading for the nearest building he could find – a small residential home. Martin slammed the door behind him hard enough to make small stones fall from the ceiling above it.

Naxis sighed, shaking his head. Alena stood up from where she had landed and walked over to him. "Can't we do something?"

"There is a way, yes," said the Alintean, "But it won't be easy. There will be many trials ahead for young Master Spire..." he turned his unblinking gaze on her, "You see, he's the only one that can survive what we need to do – all because of that little thing wrapped around his heart."

Alena paled. "The parasite."

***

"Martin, please don't do this! I don't care if Naxis says it's a good idea – this is insanity!" Alena had spent the last hour trying to convince Martin not to go along with Naxis' 'insane plan'. This plan involved activating the final gateway to the Alintean home-world of Nihran.

Martin, of course, could have cared less at first. When Naxis mentioned, however, the possibility of returning Martin's power to him, the boy had readily agreed. Alena had heard of this plan and been trying to dissuade Martin since.

"Alena, it's no good," he said as he threw some objects into a bag, "We need that power to defeat the Zerolytes – without it they're going to completely maul us. We're never going to win at this rate."

"That doesn't mean YOU have to go. Why can't Dais go? Or Jason? Or..."

"Because I'm the most powerful Tzen the Earth has had for over four billion years," he snapped, "Or I was..." he touched the spot on his chest above his heart, and Alena knew what he was referring to – the parasite.

Alena fell silent. Naxis had explained all this to her already, but there had to be another way. "And why do you care, anyway?" continued Martin, "I made you into a Tzen – that's what you wanted, isn't it? You got what you wanted, so why are you still here?"

She remained silent. Martin turned to look at her and was surprised to see tears running down her face. "I'm not going to die, if that's what you're worried about."

Alena shook her head, "You don't know that! What if the Alinteans don't take kindly to a human? What if they kill you? What then?"

Martin stared at her for a long time before responding. "Then I die. Everyone dies, Alena."

Alena fell silent again. She opened her mouth to say something but was interrupted by a knock on the door. Martin called for whoever it was to enter, and Naxis poked his face through the door.

"Ready to go?"

Martin slung his bag over his shoulder and walked out to meet Naxis. "Ready."

***

The 'Gate' was enormous. It was shaped like a large ring mounted on a pedestal, and Martin had to fight not to gape at it. Balmoch had personally turned out to see the Final Gate activated. This doorway was created, as he explained, to be a final failsafe. If the Humans ever found them and attacked, this could be used to send a single runner back to Nihran for help.

Now, as he again explained, things were worse. Alinteans, like Tzen, relied on Energy Manipulation for protection. Without it, they were as helpless as an overturned turtle. Help had to be found.

Martin took a deep breath as the age-old portal whirred to life, flooding the center of the ring with a rainbow of energy. Naxis looked at Martin hesitantly. "Are you sure you want to do this?" he asked, "There is no guarantee you'll survive; just a better chance because of the parasite."

Martin looked at him, "I've come this far," he said, "I'm not going to back down now. The Tzen..." he looked away, "I'm going to do this because I have a debt to pay."

He squared his shoulders and walked up to the portal. He eyed it curiously before turning back to Naxis. "Do I just walk into it?"

The Alintean nodded, "When you get to Nihran, good luck."

"Here," Balmoch walked up and pressed something into Martin's palm. "That's the Seal of the Stars; an Alintean icon of Trust. Show it to an Alintean – they'll know you're an ally."

Martin didn't miss the flicker of apprehension in Balmoch's eyes. He took another deep breath, turned to face the swirling myriad of colors, and stepped into the Gate.

Epilogue: Five Months Later

"You think he's ever going to come back?"

Alena was perched on one of the top spires of the Old Palace. Next to her was a friend of less than a year; an Alintean girl named A'aina. A'aina turned her pale blue eyes to face Alena.

"Martin? When he walked through the town most of us felt how strong he was. If anyone can do this, he can."

Alena sighed and looked out toward the islands. The Zerolytes had made everyone pay, alright. They'd slaughtered anyone connected to the Tzen – including Alena's parents. She lived here now – the Zerolytes had burned her home to the ground.

"I just wish he'd hurry up."

A'aina looked back to the light at the top of the cavern, "He'll do it."

The two of them looked down as Jason, now sporting the beginnings of a beard, jogged up. "Good news, ladies," he called, "Martin's alive – we just intercepted a transmission."

Alena quickly descended the tower and practically ripped the printout from Jason's hands. Printed on it in large black letters were some of the best words she'd ever read.

TZEN

REACHED NIHRAN

NOT DEAD

WILL RETURN

MARTIN

Pronunciation Guide:

Note: Columns (left to right) are as follows:

"Name", "Pronunciation", "Translation"* and "Element(s)"

*Translation from Alintean to English

Xidul	Ks-ih-dool	Impact	Air
Ibleuz	Ih-bloo-z	Saber	Lunar
Kuzan	Koo-zahn	Pierce	Ice
Trezin	Treh-zin	Fireball	Fire
Ciduu	Sid-oo	Awaken	Neutral
Kodom-Tzintasa	Koh-dohm Zin-tassa	Burning Ocean	Fire
Sunakare-Dicharis	Soona-car-eh Dih-char-iss	Freezing Blow	Ice
Aburasi-Dokumaray	Aboo-rasee Do-koom-a-ray	Icicle Needles	Ice
Garahno	Gah-rah-no	Hurricane	Air
Akashik	Akah-sheek	Spear	Ice
Abornimaz	Ah-born-ee-maz	Stalagmite	Earth
Lennocma-Oduparon	Lenn-ock-mah Odoo-pah-ron	Heavenly Light	Light
Ahniot	Ah-nee-oht	Shatter	Light
Erhaz-Ahatamz	Err-hah-z Aha-tah-mm-z	Gate Release	Neutral
Nutapriel-Askil	Noo-tah-pree-ell Ass-kill	Self-Armor	Neutral
Unexesael	Unn-ex-ess-ay-eel	Concentration	Neutral
Somesacael	Sow-mess-ah-kyle	Tentacle	Neutral
Lanatoatzen	Lah-nah-tot-zen	Barrage	Dark
Zesrosimiel	Zes-rose-ee-meal	Supernova	Neutral/Solar

Hahiel-Somesacael	Ha-heel Sow-mess-ah-kyle	Double Tentacle	Neutral
Ohdaec	Oh-day-eek	Cancellation	Neutral
Kodom-Akashik	Koh-dohm Akah-sheek	Burning Spear	Fire
Kodom-Dokumaray	Koh-dohm Do-koom-a-ray	Burning Needles	Fire
Kodom-Va'aka	Koh-dohm Vah-ah-kah	Burning Dragon	Fire
Ihrtan-Emonael	Err-than Eemo-nail	Stone Shield	Earth
Sunakare-Garahno	Soona-car-eh Gah-rah-no	Freezing Hurricane	Ice/Air
Nonohaismet	No-no-h-eyes-met	Thunderstorm	Lightning
Onemsatau	Oh-nehm-saht-ow	Crescent	Lunar
Aponracia	Ah-pawn-rass-ee-ah	Volcano	Earth/Fire
Pasroxeir	Pass-row-ks-ear	Spark	Lightning
Asapih	Ass-ah-pee	Flood	Water
Erlcos-Asapih	Earl-cos Ass-ah-pee	Grand Flood	Water
Assnah	Ass-naah	Bolt	Lightning
Lipitel-Xidul	Lip-ih-tell Ks-ih-dool	Prime Impact	Air
Batro-Emonael	Baht-row Eemo-nail	Water Shield	Water
Assnah-Va'aka	Ass-naah Va-ah-kah	Bolt Dragon	Lightning
Tehitot-Ihmeriat	Teh-ih-tot Ih-merry-at	Ground Splitter	Earth
Etlar	Eht-laar	Cage	Light/Dark

Dohar-Osinas	Dough-har O-sin-ass	Wraith's Mist	Dark/Air
Lipitel-Trezin	Lip-ih-tell Treh-zin	Prime Fireball	Fire
Anasapiel	Anna-sahp-ee-ell	Waterspout	Water/Air
Karnain	Car-nayn	Animate	Dark
Oduparon-Lanatoatzen	Odoo-pah-ron Lah-nah-tot-zen	Light Needles	Light
Trehaismet	Treh-eyes-met	Firestorm	Fire
Pasroxeir-Tzintasa	Pass-row-ks-ear Zin-tassa	Spark Ocean	Lightning
Sepab	She-pah-b	Cannon	Dark
Garahno-Akashik	Gah-rah-no Akah-sheek	Hurricane Spear	Air